Adele lifted the weapon's muzzle. "Come out with your hands up!" she shouted through the hatch.

They could use another prisoner, and there didn't seem much risk that the fellow whimpering and blubbering in the vehicle was going to come out shooting, but still good to be careful.

Another roar slapped the harbor. This was more distant than that of the rocket launcher destroying itself, but it was sharper as well. Adele glanced to her left. The Garrison's three antiship missiles rippled in quick succession from their concrete emplacement. They were aimed back toward Brotherhood.

The first missile was already hypersonic when it struck the edge of the plaza and exploded in a bubble of orange—from expended fuel—and black—the powdered basalt.

The second and third missiles punched through the flame. One struck the ground floor of the Gulkander Palace; the other scattered the upper portions of the building, which were already billowing outward as the sidewall collapsed.

Daniel, Woetjans, and most of the *Kiesche*'s crew sprinted up to Adele's vehicle, wheezing and puffing. Spacers didn't spend a great deal of time running, and the would-be rescue party had winded themselves with a short gallop. Adele didn't doubt that they could have fought if there had been anyone left to fight.

Adele released the carbine and shook her right hand. She would have blisters from vents in the barrel shroud. The Medicomp would take care of it; and anyway, it wasn't her usual shooting hand.

THE
SEA WITHOUT A SHORE

DAVID DRAKE

THE SEA WITHOUT A SHORE

A Baen Books Original

Baen Publishing Enterprises
P.O. Box 1403
Riverdale, NY 10471
www.baen.com

ISBN: 978-1-4767-8041-2

Cover art by Stephen Hickman

First Baen paperback printing, February 2015
Second Baen paperback printing, February 2015

Library of Congress Control Number: 2014001467

Distributed by Simon & Schuster
1230 Avenue of the Americas
New York, NY 10020

Pages by Joy Freeman (www.pagesbyjoy.com)
Printed in the United States of America

To Ramsey and Jenny Campbell

ACKNOWLEDGMENTS

How many times have I thanked Dan Breen for being my first reader? This is another time, and believe me, it's heartfelt this time as well.

Dan, Dorothy Day, and my webmaster Karen Zimmerman archive my texts in widely separated locations. That way if the asteroid strikes while I'm still working, my publisher will nevertheless have the most nearly complete version of the manuscript. (Well, I suppose it depends on how big the asteroid is.)

Dorothy, Karen, and Evan Ladouceur provide help with continuity and in their various expertises. For this particular novel, Fred Kiesche and John Lambshead also provided bits of data which I needed. Silly as it may sound, I really will stop work while I search frantically for some point that not one reader in a thousand would notice if I got it wrong. The help I get from my friends is of much more importance than it might seem to a rational person.

Many people provide help for my writing. My wife, Jo, makes my comfortable life possible. I get very focused when I'm working, and I'm working just about all the time. That I'm healthy, well-fed, and live in a clean house is almost entirely due to Jo; we even have an active social life.

My sincere thanks to all those I've mentioned and to the many others who are part of my life and therefore of my work.

—Dave Drake

AUTHOR'S NOTE

I'm going to try an abbreviated version of my usual boilerplate here: I translate the words my characters speak into modern English, and also I translate weights and measures into formats in current use.

It's been a long time since anybody has complained about me using modern English instead of nineteenth-century fustian as though I were a reincarnation of William Morris (heaven forefend!). I do get more or less polite queries about the weights and measures, though.

I generally use historical models in which to find plots for novels in the RCN series. In this case I formed the action on two incidents which occurred in the fifth century BC. One of these was the civil war on the island of Corcyra, a colony founded by Corinth. The other was the Egyptian revolt against Persia (during a period of Persian instability) and the Athenian expedition to support the Egyptians when Persia attempted to reassert control.

Neither of these things sounds very major, does it? Even if you know some classical history, it's unlikely that you'll remember either of them. But between them they led to the Peloponnesian War, which plunged the Greek world into a century of large-scale warfare, followed by Macedonian conquest (the Macedonians weren't Greek by Greek law, any more than the Thracians or the Carians were Greek) and another century of war, and finally by Roman conquest and a peace of tourists and tax gatherers.

It's very hard to predict where a present action is going to lead, but it's a good bet that violent actions are going to lead to violent results; and those results may continue a long way down a very bad road. I suppose it's fitting that the Roman general who completed the conquest of Greece did so by razing Corinth.

I used to think it would be nice if present-day leaders knew more ancient history. The reality is that Messrs Cheney and Rumsfeld didn't seem to know anything about Vietnam. Of course they hadn't served in Nam, as I had.

Finally a note about the dedication. In 1977 Jo and I visited England—my first trip out of the country which didn't involve me wearing a uniform. Friend and writer Ramsey Campbell and his wife Jenny put us up in Liverpool for two days. Jenny cooked us a full English breakfast (with kippers!), which was delicious, and Ramsey gave us a tour of Liverpool that included Liverpool Metropolitan Cathedral (aka Paddy's Wigwam).

The cathedral is a modern structure and has had more than its share of detractors (note the nickname; Liverpool is heavily Irish). That said, the interior gave me a feeling of peace and happiness which I've never felt in another building.

I'm not religious (and was raised to be anti-Catholic), so I didn't expect to have a positive reaction. That's anecdotal evidence, but it was (and remains) my truth. I moved the cathedral into this novel, and I decided this was a good time to thank Ramsey and Jenny for their kindness.

—Dave Drake
david-drake.com

And all around the organ there's a sea without a shore

Of human joys and wonders and regrets

To remember and to recompense the music evermore

For what the cold machinery forgets...

—Alfred Noyes
The Barrel-Organ

CHAPTER 1

Bantry Estate, Cinnabar

Daniel Leary, otherwise Captain Daniel Oliver Leary, Republic of Cinnabar Navy—but here merely "Master Daniel" or "Squire"—stood poised in the bow of the skiff with his arms at his sides. The throwing stick was in his right hand with the line nocked in the cleft and the lure dangling. Hogg knelt in the stern, holding the tiller/throttle of the tiny motor that edged the boat toward the floating weed.

The lure was a streamlined tube about the size of a plump man's middle finger. Its batteries powered the caged contra-rotating props, but control signals came down the line from the handset now resting on the planks in front of Hogg.

When the lure hit the water, it would circle until it picked up the pattern of electrical impulses given off by the nerves of the species it was set for, then home on that source. It was set now for floorfish; two or three sprats would fillet into an excellent dinner for Daniel and Miranda, his fiancée, who was waiting in the manor.

Daniel tensed to make the cast. "Don't get ahead of yourself, boy," Hogg said. "Another ten feet, and *don't* tell me your arm's strong enough to cast into the center from here."

The skiff continued to creep toward the weed. Hogg spoke quietly so as not to disturb the prey, but his voice was as harsh as a rough-cut file. Here off the coast of the Bantry estate their relationship was the same as it had been twenty years earlier when the old poacher took it on himself to teach the young master how to fish and to hunt, and how to be a man.

Teaching Daniel to be a man wasn't part of a plan, but Hogg was a man himself and made assumptions. If he'd been asked, he would have said that Corder Leary wanted a son who would stand up for himself, who would carry out his duties, and who would take responsibility for his own actions.

Overhead, a trio of Barranca birds sailed southward, following the cold current which had bent toward shore during the volcanic eruption hundreds of miles out in the Western Ocean. The birds were so high that even Daniel's sharp eyes couldn't distinguish the two separate pairs of wings on each. The occasional low-frequency grunts of the birds communicating were barely audible, even to ears trained to recognize them.

Looking back on his childhood, Daniel suspected that his father had been too busy chasing money and power to spare any thoughts for the boy who lived with his mother on the Bantry estate. Still, Speaker Leary wouldn't have minded what Daniel was learning, any more than he would have cared about the weather over Bantry while he was comfortable in the Leary townhouse in the capital, Xenos.

Hogg switched off the motor. It was inaudible even while it was running, but Daniel had felt the vibration through the thin soles of his moccasins. The skiff drifted forward on momentum. Daniel swung his right arm up in parallel with the keel. At the height of its arc, his fingers released the line which he'd clamped to the throwing stick till that moment. The lure sailed off in a flat curve that plopped it into the center of the large patch of weed.

"A *nice* cast," said Hogg softly. "You haven't forgotten everything I taught you, I guess."

"I haven't forgotten not to draw to an inside straight, either," Daniel said. He remained upright for a better view, though standing in the small boat would have been dangerous despite the skiff's broad bottom if the water hadn't been still and Daniel's own balance perfect. The skills he'd gained as a boy on Bantry had been sharpened since he'd entered the Naval Academy and begun running along the spars of starships.

Instead of circling as expected, the lure vanished instantly. "It looks like it just sank," Daniel said, squinting. He had a pair of multifunction RCN goggles on his forehead, but they wouldn't help him look through the water. "Do you suppose the motor failed?"

"The motor's running fine, and the props are free," Hogg said testily, looking at the readout on his control unit. "It's just got a bite.

"Unless"—Hogg's delay was too short to have allowed Daniel to speak even if he'd intended to—"that *bloody* weed has caught it. It's the deep-sea weed with thicker hair. But the lure *seems* okay...."

He and Daniel were in the channel between Borden's Cay and the mainland, but recent nor'westers had brought considerable oceanic debris through the inlets, including unfamiliar fish parboiled by the volcano. This patch of weed looked from any distance like the normal inshore variety; but as Hogg had said, it was the open-water species whose clumps were tied together by tendrils sturdy enough to withstand serious storms.

"Want to haul back the lure and try near the creek mouth?" Daniel said, frowning.

He was closer to the weed. He could have noticed before Hogg did that it was slightly darker than it should have been, but Hogg had spent most of his sixty years learning the tricks and whims of nature on the Bantry estate. Missing something that Hogg also had missed wasn't a good reason to kick himself.

"It's still running true," Hogg said, "so don't get in front of yourself. Maybe we're just having fisherman's luck."

Hogg had been concentrating on the holographic readout hovering above the control unit; his fierceness suggested he was planning to take a bite out of the display. A brief smile turned his unshaven face into something remarkably ugly.

Daniel smiled also. Like Hogg, he was used to having luck when he was fishing. Most of it was bad.

The channel wasn't much over a quarter mile wide here. Similar vegetation grew on both the cay and the mainland; but the trees on the mainland shore were taller, and they were much taller farther inland, where storms less often drove salt water over the roots.

Birds shrieked and clucked, but they remained hidden in the foliage. Insect-eaters wouldn't be out in numbers until nightfall, but Daniel was surprised not to see the fish-eaters which were usually snatching meals from the surface of the water or gorging on carrion on the mud. A skiff with two fishermen wasn't reason to frighten them under cover.

"We've got one," Hogg said, adjusting both thumb controls of the handset. "We bloody *have* got one."

The lure was multifunction. When it was attached, the controller sent impulses into the nervous system of the fish. You couldn't actually control the behavior even of a fish, but a disruption equivalent to an unscratchable itch would eventually bring the prey thrashing to the surface as it tried to rid itself of the irritation.

Daniel set the throwing stick down on the floorboards. He touched the trident with hooked barbs of spring steel, then thought again. The pole was only six feet long. That was as much as they wanted to carry in so small a boat, but it wasn't enough to reach the center of the weed from where they now floated.

"I'll go in," he said. He didn't want to foul the lure's prop in heavy weed. Hogg grunted agreement, still concentrating on the controller.

Sitting down, Daniel pulled off his moccasins. He probably ought to take off his baggy trousers also, but sometimes small crustaceans clung to floating weed, and he didn't want to transfer them to his wedding tackle. As he started to his feet again, the skiff rocked violently.

"Bloody hell and damnation!" Hogg said, looking up from the display but not dropping the controller.

Daniel's first thought was that there had been another subsea earthquake, a tremor like those which the volcano had spawned in recent months. The weed lifted in a great swell. Instead of subsiding, it hung in streamers on the dark, twitching mass which floated on the surface of the water.

"On my sainted mother's soul," Hogg said in a tone of reverence. "We've got an adult. What's *it* doing here?"

Daniel had heard enough stories growing up on Bantry—some of them from Hogg himself—to know that if Hogg's mother had been a saint, it was only by comparison with Hogg's father. That aside, there was no doubt that they'd caught an adult floorfish.

If caught was the right word.

"The volcano must have brought it up," Daniel said. Adult floorfish meandered across the bottom at three thousand feet or deeper, though their eggs hatched in marshes and the sprats spent their first two years in coastal waters. "It's sixty feet long if it's an inch."

"And the flesh is no good for anything but feeding pigs," Hogg said with a tone of regret. "Even if we could land it."

He adjusted his controller again.

The floorfish continued to quiver, so Daniel didn't rise from his knees. There wasn't any real risk. When Hogg released the lure, the fish—it was really a blanket with a mouth at one end and a body filled by the gut which processed ooze that the mouth sucked in—would sink back to the bottom.

Daniel grinned. The worst danger that the floorfish posed was that if it didn't find its way back out to sea soon, the warmth and higher oxygen content of the surface waters would probably kill it. In that case, its many tons of rotting flesh and partially digested ooze would make a considerable area uninhabitable until the process was complete. Fortunately, nobody except hunters and sport fishermen spent much time in this swampy portion of Bantry.

The fish continued to wobble like a huge jelly while

Hogg stabbed at his controller. "It won't release!" he snarled. "I don't know if something's corroded or the probes are just too deep in that thick hide."

He stuck his hand into a baggy pocket and brought out a folding knife with a knuckleduster hilt; the blade snicked open. "*I* say we cut the line and chalk it up to experience."

"Do you have another lure?" Daniel said.

Hogg shrugged. "Back to the manor," he said. "We've got three sprats now in the cold chest. That's enough for dinner; and if it's not, well, me and Em—"

That would be the Widow Brice.

"—can find something else. She's not big on fish anyhow."

That was all true, but . . .

"I'll fetch the lure," Daniel said, swinging his right foot into the water carefully. "I was figuring to go in with the trident anyway."

He eased over the side by stages, gripping the gunwale with both hands and lowering himself carefully to reduce the splash. The water was noticeably warm; more sign of the volcanic disruption, he supposed.

Hogg had leaned to his left instinctively to balance Daniel's weight. "I can't turn off the current or the fish'll go right back to the bottom," he said. "That means it's going to keep on shivering like that."

"Right," said Daniel, breast-stroking away from the skiff with his head out of the water. "Well, if it swallows me, you can cut me out with that knife of yours."

The weed wasn't as thick as it looked from even a short distance away. The tendrils which bound palm-sized clumps into mats the size of a soccer pitch parted as easily as gauze between Daniel's hands.

He wouldn't want to swim miles through the weed, but he thought he could if he had to. Twenty yards was no problem.

The line of optical fiber was invisible except that when the sun caught it at the right angle it became a slash of light from the water to the lure on the black/brown skin. Daniel was probably brushing it as he swam/paddled toward the floorfish, but its touch went unnoticed in the weed.

The floorfish had a fringe of fins all along its side. They extended about the length of Daniel's forearm and were stiffened with cartilage, not spines. They appeared to undulate gently, but there was enough power behind the continuous motion to push at Daniel like a strong current when he was close enough to touch the fish.

Daniel paused, then dived and came up like a sprat trying to escape a predator. His outstretched hand gripped the lure, and his weight pulled it free as he slid down the slimy side of the floorfish.

"Master!" Hogg shouted. "Back away! Keep the bloody lure on your bare skin and in the water between you, okay? Don't bloody argue!"

"Between" wasn't a direction, but Hogg must mean the floorfish if he wanted Daniel to back away. The older man's voice wasn't panicked, but there was more stress in it than Daniel remembered since the night Hogg had readied the Bantry tenants against trouble that might sweep in from the darkness. He'd handed the seven-year-old Daniel Leary a shotgun and told him to aim for heads because face-shields weren't as tough as the body-armor which the attackers might be wearing.

No one came to Bantry that night. In the morning, Daniel and the others learned that Speaker Leary had drowned the Three Circles Conspiracy in blood, wiping out the leaders of the Popular Party and their families—save for a few of the proscribed who happened to be off planet at the time the crisis broke.

One of those survivors was Adele Mundy, sixteen-year-old daughter of Lucius Mundy, the leader of the Popular Party. She had just left to study in the Academic Collections on Blythe. At the time, Adele's name wouldn't have meant anything to Daniel, or for that matter to Corder Leary. The girl was a scholar and wholly apolitical.

Daniel, a newly made lieutenant, had met Adele, then Electoral Librarian on Kostroma, five years ago. That meeting had changed their lives. Both of them were better off by orders of magnitude than they would have been without the other's support.

The floorfish submerged like a mass of sludge slipping into the channel. Suction tugged at Daniel, but because the fish's body shaped itself to the water, it was much less of a problem than what a sinking ship of similar size would have caused. The fish left behind an effluvium of ancient mud, cloying and slightly sulfurous.

Something lifted briefly above the undulating weed, then slipped back. Daniel knew what Hogg had seen from the height of the boat.

He knew why Hogg was worried, too.

Daniel splashed, hoping that he was moving toward the boat as Hogg had ordered. It wasn't a very effective way to proceed, but he wasn't about to stretch his legs out behind him to backstroke properly. That

would put his bare, kicking feet very close to the head
of the wolf eel, and the predator's jaws were armed
with six-inch fangs.

Wolf eels attached their sucker tails to floorfish.
They didn't harm or even affect the huge scavenger,
but when the giant maw rooted up some lesser muck-
dweller, the eel snatched it for a meal.

This was an extremely large floorfish, even for an
adult, and the eel was a similarly impressive member
of its species. Because its jaws and belly expanded, it
could easily ingest prey the size of an average-sized man.

"I got the lure set to female eel," Hogg said in
a hoarse whisper. "If it figures you're a female, it
likely won't try to eat you. Just keep coming back. I
don't want to foul the prop in the weed, but I will
if I have to."

"I don't especially want to be buggered by an eel,
either," Daniel said. It wasn't a real concern—like
other fish, the eels sprayed milt onto the eggs the
female had just extruded into the sea—but it made
Hogg chuckle, which is what Daniel had intended.

Hogg would rather die than let anything harm the
Young Master. Daniel didn't want him to leap into
the eel's jaws as the best way of saving his charge.

Daniel continued to splash. He didn't look around.
He couldn't see anything through the agitated water.
Perhaps Hogg could see more.

They were using the lure's field to override the bio-
electrical field of Daniel's own body. Hogg was, at least;
it wouldn't have occurred to Daniel to do that. He'd
certainly think of it should the situation arise again.

"Now, hold the lure in your left hand and hook
your right over the gunnel," Hogg said, speaking from

just above Daniel's head. He was again as calm as he had been years before while teaching his young charge to squeeze rather than jerk his trigger. "When you're ready, you'll swing up and I'll haul you aboard. No problem at all for a strong young lad like you, right?"

"No problem," Daniel whispered. His attendance at temple was sporadic at best, but he really would try to improve in the future.

Daniel's hair brushed the skiff's hull. He fumbled with his right hand, bicycling his legs to keep him up until he could grip a thwart. He took a deep breath and another, consciously trying to slow his heart rate.

He had only had one glimpse of the eel. It had seemed huge. Even allowing for the exaggeration of fear, it was probably ten feet long. Its slender body trailed behind a head the size of a bushel basket.

Hogg gripped Daniel's left arm, just above the elbow. He wasn't putting any pressure on the contact yet.

"On three," Daniel said. "One, two, thr—"

Water exploded as Daniel rolled up and over the gunwale. The eel must have come after him, because Hogg shouted and Daniel heard the *crunch* as Hogg's right arm drove the trident through the bones of the creature's skull.

Daniel rolled into the belly of the skiff. Hogg had gotten out of his way, though Daniel wasn't sure how. He wasn't even sure he still had both legs, and his hands were locked together in mutual reassurance.

Bloody Hell, that was a bad one!

The skiff was rocking violently. Hogg shoved them backward and released the shaft of the harpoon. The little motor was backing with all the power it had available, ignoring the risk of weed clogging its intake.

Daniel raised his head to look over the gunnel. The shaft flailed back and forth, sometimes under the surface, as the fatally injured eel curvetted. The body behind the soot-colored head was so nearly transparent that Daniel could make out the bones of the skeleton.

His guess of ten feet long had been conservative. This eel was probably big enough to have swallowed the skiff itself along with the two men.

"I wonder what the record for a wolf eel is?" Daniel said. "Taken by hand, I mean."

"You want this one as a trophy," Hogg said hoarsely, "then you're going to have to come back by yourself and get it. Me, I'm heading for home; and when I get there, I'm going to get *very* drunk."

"Yes," said Daniel. "I think that's a good plan for both of us."

Xenos on Cinnabar

Lady Adele Mundy—she had been released from the RCN when her ship was paid off, so she could not properly use her naval rank of signals officer—stood before one of the chest-high reading tables in the Long Room of the Navy House Archives. Her personal data unit sat to the left on the table; to the right was the small stack of ships' logs which she was copying; and in the center was a flat conversion device eight inches deep by ten inches across.

The converter was a specialist item and would have cost a great deal to buy, even if she could have found one for sale. This one had been given her as an adjunct to her work for her other employer, Mistress Bernis

Sand—the head of Cinnabar's intelligence service, or at least one branch of it.

Adele didn't think she was flattering herself to believe that she was in her way Mistress Sand's most effective agent. She was fairly certain that the intelligence arms of the Alliance of Free Stars, the Republic's greatest rival and frequent enemy, would have agreed with that assessment.

She put another log in the converter. This was a chip recording, but the format was unique in Adele's experience and may not have been common some seven hundred years ago when, according to the label, the officers of a freighter out of Palafox created it.

The converter whined for a moment, then projected the first entries through the data unit's holographic display for Adele to view while the remainder of the contents was stored. She wasn't trying to absorb all the data on the logs at this moment, but neither was she merely a copyist. She had repeatedly found cases where the labels slapped on quickly by disinterested clerks were seriously in error.

Adele smiled faintly. The clerks probably thought that items which hadn't been incorporated into the general database were of no value. It was true that the logs were valueless except to someone who was very skilled and very obsessive. Even the skilled, obsessive Adele Mundy was unlikely to find any data that she would use during the however many further years of her life.

On the other hand, she had nothing better to do, and she liked gathering data. There was probably nothing she liked more.

Tovera, Adele's servant, stood at the desk to Adele's

left, nearer the entrance. Besides the clerk, a naval rating, they had been the only people present in the Long Room, but an RCN midshipman wearing her 2nd Class uniform—her Grays—had entered and was talking to the clerk.

Tovera moved slightly, facing the doorway. She lifted the lid of the attaché case on her desk, just enough to reach inside.

Adele was by now too familiar with Tovera's ways to be surprised; she didn't even smile. Tovera wasn't precisely paranoid, but she saw no reason why an unfamiliar midshipman might not intend to kill her mistress; therefore she prepared against the possibility.

After all, Tovera had nothing better to do either, and she had never cared about the reasons why she was told to kill someone. She had been trained by the Fifth Bureau, the intelligence service which reported directly to Guarantor Porra, the autocrat of the Alliance. Tovera had changed her allegiance from the Alliance to Adele Mundy personally, but she continued to follow her training.

Tovera did most things by rote. She was a sociopath and far too intelligent to make social decisions for herself. She would have been executed long since if she had done that, because she generally saw the simplest way out of a problem as being to kill the person making the problem.

So long as Tovera did as Adele directed, she would remain within socially acceptable norms. Thus far obeying Adele had given Tovera ample opportunity to kill people, which she liked to do as much as she could be said to like anything.

"Well, Midshipman," the clerk said, raising his

voice enough to be heard where Adele stood, thirty feet away. "I guess despite your exalted rank, you're going to have to check the catalogue just like lesser mortals. And for that you'll have to go back up to the lobby, because the terminal down here's on the blink."

"The catalogue only lists the logs of the *Princess Cecile* while the corvette was on the RCN list," the midshipman said. "I know that she sailed a number of times in private commission, and I've heard that copies of those logs were deposited with Navy House also."

In theory, the midshipman ranked a naval rating. In practice, she was probably on half pay since so many ships had been laid up after the Treaty of Amiens, and nothing was of lower importance to the RCN bureaucracy than a midshipman on the beach.

The clerk shrugged. "Could be, honey," he said. "You're welcome to look to your little heart's content."

"Excuse me, mistress?" Adele called. She had personal experience with poverty, since the Mundy wealth had escheated to the Republic when her parents were executed; besides which, she disliked people who didn't do their jobs. "If you'll come back here, I may be able to help you."

As she had expected, her helpfulness irritated the clerk. He gave Adele a black look and returned to his desk display. He was watching a sporting event, though Adele—who had checked it out of habit—couldn't imagine why a score of men (they were all men) were shoving a stone quoit up and down a grass field.

This basement area of the archives was more a storage room than a library in proper form. Floor-to-ceiling cages of woven-wire fencing marched down both sides of the room. Inside each were file cabinets, but boxes of additional material were stacked on the floors of many cages, particularly those nearer the entrance.

People using the archives could switch on direct lighting to supplement the glow strips in the arched concrete ceiling, but not all the lights worked. Specifically, the cage beside the desk where Adele was working didn't have working internal lights. The unsorted boxes within were lumps in shadow.

The midshipman strode past the clerk's desk without looking back. She was petite and dark-haired, and she was obviously angry.

"It's ridiculous that an RCN officer has to depend on the courtesy of a private scholar to find something in RCN archives!" she said, probably hoping that her voice would carry to where the clerk sat. "Still, if you know where the logs might be stored, mistress, that's the main thing. I'd be very grateful."

Her nametag read HALE. She had probably bought her Grays used, because they had more wear than someone only a few years out of the Academy was likely to have given them.

"I think you'll find them in there," Adele said in a neutral voice, pointing. "In the second box down on the left-hand stack, the metal one. Tovera, help her with your handlight."

Tovera opened the wire gate and gestured the midshipman into the cage. They could be padlocked, but most of them were not.

Hale followed Tovera's narrow beam of light, lifted off the covering box, and took out the clear container within the one indicated.

"Perfect!" Hale said after a glance. "They're on

RCN standard chips, and it looks like they're all of them here. And in order!"

Adele smiled faintly. A stranger like Hale probably wouldn't have recognized the expression if she had even noticed it.

Hale came out, and Tovera closed the cage behind her.

"I suppose you're wondering about these," Hale said as she set the chips on a table across the aisle from Adele. She didn't appear to have noticed Tovera. Adele's servant excelled in being unobtrusive in any normal social setting. "You see, I was in the Academy with two midshipmen who were assigned to Captain Leary, only he wasn't a captain then. You know—the famous one?"

Tovera didn't snicker. Adele nodded expressionlessly. She did indeed know Captain Leary.

"Well, I *knew* them," Hale said. She took an ordinary chip reader out of its belt pouch and set it on her table. "One was pretty sharp, I'll grant, but the other always struck me as being as thick as two short planks. But they've both been promoted to lieutenant with no interest behind them."

She shrugged. "I've got a lot of time on my hands since the peace," she said, "so I thought maybe if I studied the logbooks I could figure out how they did it. Besides being lucky to serve under Captain Leary, I mean."

"You'd be talking about Blantyre and Cory, I presume," Adele said. Hale's age made the identification certain, but she still had to resist her desire to check Naval Academy class lists. "I'll remind you that Blantyre's luck led to her being killed two years ago."

"You knew Blantyre, then?" Hale said in surprise. "I didn't realize . . ."

Adele nodded again. She was wearing a plain civilian

business suit in dark blue. The light here wasn't good enough for anyone but a couturier to realize that the outfit was of top quality. Hale had assumed that she was a private scholar, and Adele hadn't bothered to correct her. Actually, she supposed she was a private scholar at the moment.

"Blantyre struck me as the best kind of RCN officer," Adele said. "Competent in astrogation and other technical subjects, and a fighting officer above all else. But as I said, killed in battle."

"Everybody dies, mistress," Hale said. "Very few die with a record equal to Blantyre's."

She eyed Adele more carefully, but she clearly didn't see anything more than she had at first glance. Tovera wasn't the only one who remained unobtrusive under most circumstances.

"Blantyre and I were friends," Hale said. "I'm not the sort to go put a bouquet on her grave—"

On her cenotaph, Adele corrected silently. Blantyre's body had been vaporized off Cacique, along with those of fifty-odd of her shipmates.

"—but I figure if I can use her record to learn how to be a better RCN officer, that's a better memorial anyway. And—"

Hale straightened slightly, as though she were coming to attention for a reviewing officer.

"—you're right about her. When you beat Blantyre on the Battle Board, you knew you'd done something. But more often than not, she beat me."

Adele smiled very faintly at the pride in the midshipman's voice; albeit probably justifiable pride. She wouldn't have thought anyone could read the expression, but apparently Hale did, because she flushed slightly.

"Please excuse my discourtesy," she said, extending her hand. "I'm Lucinda Hale."

Adele shook her hand with a carefully gauged polite pressure. "I am Lady Mundy," she said, using her civilian rank rather than the one Hale might have noticed in the logs of Daniel's RCN commissions. "I'm pleased to have met you, Mistress Hale."

Her personal data unit flashed a silent signal. Adele glanced at it, reading the oral message which had been converted to text, as she preferred it. "Yes, all right," she replied. "I should be there within the hour."

Tovera was efficiently replacing the set of logs in the file drawer from which they had come. She didn't know anything about the summons, but she knew that her mistress wouldn't leave the archive until she had at least restored it to the condition in which she had found it.

Hale looked as though she might be going to speak further, but in the end she merely nodded. She slipped into her reader the first of the logs of the private yacht *Princess Cecile*, owned and commanded by Captain Daniel Leary. Adele was glad. She didn't want to insult the young woman, but she didn't have time for conversation.

As Adele left the Long Room, she started to put her personal data unit away in the thigh pocket tailored into her trousers. Unexpectedly, the clerk snarled, "You know, it's traditional to leave a little something for the attendant, but I suppose you're too high and mighty to worry about that."

Adele stopped and looked at him, then sat on one of the three chairs in the anteroom. They were standard RCN designs of pressed steel and steel mesh, identical to those of any warship save that these were not bolted to the deck. She brought up the data unit.

"Your name is Dozois?" said Adele. She wasn't in quite as much of a hurry as she had thought. "Yes, Tech Five Dozois."

The data unit's holographic screen was a blur to anyone save the user herself. Adele had a control wand in either hand; she found them the quickest and most accurate form of entry and access. She often used her data unit as a remote-control device for other units. She was doing so now with the clerk's terminal, though he wasn't aware of the fact yet.

"What do you care what my name is?" the clerk said. He got to his feet. "Hey! Whatta you think you're doing?"

"Leaving," Adele said, standing up again and putting the data unit away. She was almost to the stairwell before Tovera turned and followed her.

"I thought he might try to stop us," said Tovera regretfully. "Well, maybe he'll be there the next time we visit."

"I doubt it," Adele said as her boots scuffed briskly up the concrete steps to the outside entrance. "He just sent a message to his immediate superior, copying the Chief of the Navy Board, detailing his failures of performance and adding that he keeps a bottle of gin in his desk."

"I didn't see the gin," Tovera said. She was in front again so that she could step into the street ahead of her mistress.

"Nor did I," said Adele, "but I smelled it on his breath when he was shouting at me."

She gestured toward the tram stop in front of Navy House. "We're going to the Shippers' and Merchants' Treasury to meet Deirdre Leary. I don't know the intended purpose of the meeting."

A tram pulled up at the stop, swaying slightly on its overhead monorail as it disgorged men and women in their best RCN uniforms. Those who had enough rank to have afforded a set wore their Whites, often too tight for them now. They would be uncomfortable waiting in the hall for an assignment clerk to call their name . . . or most likely not to call their name.

Adele and her servant got on when the car had emptied. Tovera punched the address of the bank into the routing computer.

Deirdre Leary was Daniel's older sister and Adele's banker. She was also the representative of Corder Leary and the Leary family interests to both Daniel and Adele. Daniel had broken violently with his father at age sixteen. As for Adele, if she ever came face-to-face with the man who had ordered her family's slaughter, she would shoot him dead.

Adele could imagine many reasons for Deirdre to request a meeting at short notice—no notice, in fact. None of the possibilities were good.

CHAPTER 2

Bantry Estate, Cinnabar

The run back to Bantry village was long and tedious at the best speed the skiff could manage, but Daniel found that he didn't care. He sat, more comatose than relaxed, in the bow while Hogg held the tiller; not that much guidance was required.

"That was too bloody close," Hogg said harshly. He didn't need to detail what he was thinking of.

Even this close to shore on a calm day, the skiff was unsteady when they crossed the inlet through the barrier islands. Bantry's seawall protected the houses, and the commercial fishing fleet needed the inlet to shuttle between the sea and Bantry's processing plant.

"I wasn't afraid at the time," Daniel said, opening his eyes. "Now, every time I think about that eel's fangs, they get another inch longer."

"They were bloody long enough in all truth," Hogg said. "I don't guess you could see him, but *I* bloody could."

"I didn't get a good look till you put a spike through his brain," Daniel agreed. "That was a nice thrust."

"Nice as I ever made," Hogg said, but he sounded desperate and angry rather than deservedly triumphant. "I wasn't bloody sure I could do it."

"I was sure," Daniel said; which was the truth, but he'd have said it anyway. Hogg had been afraid because he had nothing to do but wait while death wriggled toward the young master.

Daniel had been busy trying to splash backward with one hand and to guess where the skiff was *and* where the eel was, while all the time planning how to get himself into the boat while holding the lure in the water with his left hand till the last instant. He hadn't had time to worry about dying, though if asked he would have said it was probable. Wolf eels weren't exactly poisonous, but their fangs were so septic with decaying flesh that the chance of surviving a bite was negligible.

Daniel looked up at the seawall as they puttered toward the Little Harbor, a niche behind a breakwater where small craft could be dragged out of the water. He had thought that Miranda might be waiting up there for him, but the only greeting was a chorus of "Hey, Squire" from Hebney, Colfax, and Riddle, who spent most of their time on the seawall drinking ale. Two of them were crippled and all three were old. They weren't so much idlers as past the ability to work.

Miranda hadn't known when he would be back, after all. And she couldn't have expected an ordinary afternoon's fishing to lead to—well, what it had.

Hogg nosed them into the Little Harbor. "Daniel!" Miranda cried, springing up from the concrete bench cast into the breakwater. She had been on the dock, not up on the seawall. "Oh, darling, I'm so glad to see you!"

"Got it," said Hogg, grabbing a bitt to steady the skiff. He waited to tie up until Daniel had stepped out.

Daniel hugged his fiancée. He was a little embarrassed to have thought that Miranda hadn't come to greet him—and more than a little worried because her greeting was so enthusiastic. Did she know...?

"Daniel," Miranda said, stepping back slightly. "I invited Tom Sand to dinner tonight. If I did wrong, I apologize, but it sounded important, and I didn't know when you would be getting back."

"Of course it's all right," Daniel said heartily as he wondered what was going on. "I'd better get cleaned up. I went swimming to free the lure the last time."

Which was enough to say about the fishing trip, he decided. Miranda knew his work was dangerous, but there was no need to tell her how dangerous bad luck could make his leisure.

He gestured her ahead of him to the cast staircase. The steps were slippery, so that put him in a position to catch her if she fell; a vanishingly improbable event, but a reflexive matter of courtesy.

"That's, ah, the builder, you mean," he added. "Ah, and he's coming for me, not Adele?"

The only Tom Sand Daniel knew was the major contractor who as a favor—though Daniel wasn't sure who the favor had been *to*, exactly—had built the community building which Daniel had given to Bantry. Daniel had gotten on well with Sand the few times they'd met, but they were barely social acquaintances.

Sand was also the husband of Bernis Sand. Daniel knew as little as possible about Adele's intelligence work, but he couldn't help making that connection when heard the name.

"Yes," Miranda said, pausing for Daniel at the top of the seawall. "I told him you were out fishing, so I don't think he could have thought I meant Lady Mundy."

"Another woman would have told me that I was treating her as though she were a moron," Daniel said. "You are far too sweet to say that, even if it's true—for which I apologize."

He grinned and kissed her. A pair of housewives chatting on one's doorway giggled, and a man—one of the trio on the seawall—cackled, "Give her another one, Squire! She's too pretty to stop there!"

Miranda was tall and fair, attractive by any standard. She wasn't beautiful at a glance, but even on first meeting she had projected an *aliveness* that set her apart from the conventionally lovely girls whom Daniel had dated to that moment.

Daniel waved to the idlers but avoided eye contact. He was the Squire whenever he visited Bantry, in fact though not by law. He had the respect of everyone on the estate and their due deference also—but a free citizen's deference didn't mean slavish kowtowing. Though Daniel was first among equals, the folk he'd grown up with *were* his equals as men and women.

"It was a little awkward," Miranda said in a low voice as they walked toward the manor house. "Chloris"—the housekeeper, Widow Greene—"took the call and told me that Master Sand was calling for the Squire. I picked up the phone and said that you were fishing, but that I'd have you call back as soon as you got in. And I called him Tom, because of course we've been introduced."

"Right," said Daniel, nodding. He hadn't seen the problem yet, but he knew there had to be one for Miranda to be agitated.

"He hadn't planned to tell anyone but you that it was him calling," Miranda said. "Chloris recognized his voice, and I didn't realize that he hadn't identified himself. He was surprised when I called him 'Tom.'"

Daniel laughed. "Chloris has an ear for voices," he said. "I doubt she's heard Tom Sand speak more than half a dozen times in all her life, and that just a few words each. *I* certainly wasn't expecting to hear from him."

He looked sharply at Miranda as they reached the veranda. "Did he say what it was about?"

"He asked to come to dinner," Miranda said, entering as Daniel held the door for her. "He said his wife wouldn't be along. I told him that he was welcome, and that if he liked, I'd leave Bantry."

She paused in the front room. The rambling old building was being spruced up now that Daniel was spending time at Bantry again, but the air held a cutting hint of the bleach which was being used on the mold.

"He said he wouldn't think of putting me out, but that yes, he'd appreciate privacy with you during dinner," she continued, holding Daniel's eyes. "I know it wasn't my place to invite him, but he sounded so worried, and I didn't know how to get you."

Daniel took her hands. Miranda was as concerned as he'd ever seen her—afraid that she had interfered in his business. Throughout their relationship, she pointedly had tried at all costs to avoid that.

"Thank you, dear," he said. "You did right. You had to make a decision, and you chose the better of two options. Either was acceptable—and anyway, I wouldn't be upset if you'd guessed wrong."

"So it's three for dinner, Mirandy?" Mistress Greene said, calling across the front room. Daniel and Miranda were still in the entrance hall with old paddles, fishing poles, and yard tools—some of them broken.

"Two, Chloris," Miranda said, looking over her shoulder with a bright smile. "I'm going to check with Gwen Higgenson"—wife of the head of the fish-processing plant—"to see if they've got room at table for me while the men talk business here."

Mistress Greene snorted. "If she didn't, she'd put her husband out in the shed to *make* room," she said, correctly enough.

"Chloris?" Daniel said. "Hogg and I caught some sprats. Tom Sand and I will have those. But I've got to shower! That car of his will make it from Xenos in two hours if he pushes it."

"I've laid clean clothes on the bed," Miranda said. She caught concern in the slight tenseness at the corners of Daniel's mouth.

"No, nothing fancy!" she protested. "Just like what you're wearing"—RCN utilities—"only clean. And a newish pair, one that you haven't split up the seat."

Laughing as though he hadn't momentarily feared that he would find his Dress Whites waiting for him in the bedroom, Daniel walked through the front room on his way to the showers at the back.

Miranda stayed beside him. "I tried to think what Adele would do."

She grinned, but the expression had a wry tinge. "That didn't help much," she said, "because I realized Adele wouldn't be out of contact."

Daniel laughed in real humor as he bent to take off his soft boots. A pair of shower shoes waited just inside the door of the large tile room. He was very lucky to have met Miranda Dorst; sorry though he was that the occasion of meeting had been the death of her brother under Daniel's command.

"Adele isn't a magician, love," he said as he stripped off the utilities he'd worn fishing. The fabric dried quickly, but the many pockets were damp—and probably held weed and mud. "I grant that she seems to be one, sometimes."

Daniel turned on one of the three showerheads. Instead of a drain, the runoff slanted down the floor and through the gap under the outer wall.

One good thing about this Tom Sand business was that Daniel was no longer thinking about the wolf eel and what hadn't—quite—happened. He grinned.

Instead I can worry about what Mistress Sand's husband needs to tell me in secret, and what that means for me and Adele.

Xenos on Cinnabar

The Shippers' and Merchants' Treasury had become Adele's bank shortly after she had returned—returned from exile—to Xenos. It was the first time in her life that she'd had money of her own—a share of the prize money won by Lieutenant Daniel Leary for himself and his crews. Adele, much to her surprise, had been included in the share-out.

As she and Tovera came up the sidewalk, the doorman smiled and opened the bronze-grilled door with a flourish. "Very glad to see you again, Lady Mundy," he said.

Adele hadn't entered the bank in several years; she had no call to. Had the doorman been warned to expect her, or was his visual memory really that good?

She smiled, or at least almost smiled, as she gave the doorman a nod of response. Deirdre Leary was in her different way just as able as her brother, so both were probably true.

Adele stepped into the lobby of dark wood, polished stone, and more bronze. She was sure that the Shippers' and Merchants' handled its affairs with state-of-the-art technology, but it made a point of looking quaintly old-fashioned. *Comfortably* old-fashioned, some people would say.

For those who wanted more modern surroundings, there were other Leary enterprises to accommodate them. Adele noted the significance of the fact that Deirdre, who was the managing partner of most of those enterprises, had chosen the Shippers' and Merchants' as her personal headquarters.

The majority owner in all cases was almost certainly Corder Leary, the man who had wiped out the other members of Adele's branch of the Mundy family. If Adele had looked into the matter and found proof of that ownership, she might feel that she had to do something.

She would never look. She wasn't interested in business.

The tellers' cages were to her right; on her left, across the lobby from them, was the manager's office and a conference room. There was also a door in the back wall, under a painting of two men clasping hands over a table. That door opened and Deirdre Leary came out.

"Lady Mundy, a pleasure as always," she said. "I

appreciate you taking the time to see me on such short notice."

Deirdre had dark red hair and a tightly lacquered expression. Though her features were similar to those of her younger brother, there was nothing of the friendly openness that Daniel projected.

Deirdre stepped back, saying, "Won't you and your servant come into my office?"

"I'll wait in the lobby," said Tovera. Her voice was emotionless. "After all, someone might come in to rob the bank."

"Just as you choose," Deirdre replied, equally deadpan. She closed the door behind herself and Adele.

Adele sat on a carved wooden chair without being directed and took out her personal data unit. Whatever the purpose of this meeting, it was more than simply social.

Adele's relationship with Daniel's sister was equivocal. Deirdre clearly had her brother's best interests at heart, to a greater degree than Daniel probably realized. She had done Adele herself many favors over the years that Adele had served with Daniel. That did not make Deirdre Adele's friend; it just meant that Adele felt a degree of obligation to the other woman, which she would willingly repay if circumstances permitted it.

Deirdre was also her father's representative in matters of business. Adele owed Corder Leary a debt also. Because of her friendship with Daniel, she wasn't actively looking for an opportunity to pay it, but if she ever happened to come face to face with Speaker Leary, she would make every effort to shoot him twice through the eye. Daniel would understand, and Deirdre would certainly understand.

Deirdre settled into the chair behind her desk. The room's furniture was of dark, carved wood with leather seats on the chairs and a leather pad framed by wood for the desktop. "May I ask if you expect to be working on a major project in the next few months?"

"I do not," said Adele. *I'm waiting to die,* she thought. Which of course could be said of every waking moment of her life. In context, all that mattered was that nothing she was doing at present was of the least interest to anyone else—particularly to Mistress Sand.

Because Deirdre waited instead of leaping in with a comment, Adele said, "Daniel is relaxing at Bantry. He invited me to join him, but I wasn't raised to appreciate the delights of rural life."

She smiled slightly.

"Fortunately, Daniel and I know one another well enough that I don't have to pretend interest in his offer to avoid offending him. At some point"—probably very soon, judging from Daniel's past behavior—"he will decide that he wants another command. I will expect to accompany him when he does."

"I see," Deirdre said. She tented her fingers before her on the black leather, then looked up to meet Adele's gaze squarely. She said, "I'm being blackmailed over financial and political matters. I need someone to act for me in the affair. If you are willing to take on the problem, I will give you carte blanche to solve it."

She made a dismissive gesture with her left hand and added, "And of course pay whatever fee you set."

The fee was minor to both of them: to Deirdre because she controlled vast wealth, to Adele because she didn't care very much about money.

"Give me the background to the situation," Adele

said quietly. She had considered the request thoroughly in her several seconds of delay. Her first impulse—as generally—had been to begin searching with her data unit.

She smiled inwardly. It would have been difficult to get the information that way, though it would have been interesting to try.

Deirdre nodded. "A Pantellarian businessman named Arnaud," she said, "has become a member, the leading member, of the Council of Twenty which rules Pantellaria since the planet regained independence following the Treaty of Amiens."

Adele had noticed a minuscule hesitation before Deirdre began laying out the data, but it had been no more than Adele's pause before she decided to pursue the matter instead of walking straight out of the office, the bank, and Deirdre's life. There had been none of the usual maundering: "This must remain secret," or "You'll have to swear not to say anything about this," or other such nonsense.

Deirdre had asked for Adele's help; Adele had asked for information which she would need to provide that help. Nobody who knew Adele would have assumed that she would accept a proposition without learning the details—for anyone except for Daniel Leary.

"At the beginning of the recent war"—between Cinnabar and the Alliance—"Arnaud owned a small repair yard," Deirdre continued. "In the course of the war, and after Pantellaria had been annexed to the Alliance of Free Stars, Arnaud found outside investment to expand his yard and to construct ships of some size. Among the yard's projects were five or six destroyers, which operated as elements of the Alliance Fleet in battle against the RCN."

Deirdre grimaced and stared at her fingers again for a moment, then looked Adele in the face again. "I was the outside investor in Arnaud's yard," Deirdre said. "That is, Bantry Holdings made the investment."

She smiled wryly. "It's been quite profitable for us," she said. "Though peace will require some adjustments."

"I would have expected you," Adele said carefully, "to have worked through a series of cutouts which would make it impossible for the investment to be traced back to Bantry Holdings in a provable fashion."

Then Adele shrugged. "There could be allegations," she said, "but there are always allegations. Your enemies will believe them, your friends will pretend that they don't."

Deirdre made a sour face. "Under ordinary circumstances," she said, "that would be true—though I'll admit that when I looked at the detailed records, I found that the security arrangements weren't as complete as I would have wished them. My primary concern, however, is that Councillor Arnaud is the party threatening me. He probably can prove our close association during the war."

"I see," said Adele, because she suddenly did see. "Please wait a moment."

Deirdre had said that she was the blackmail victim, but in fact the information led to Bantry Holdings, which she now managed. At the time the initial investments were made, Deirdre could not have been more than ten or twelve years old. Corder Leary himself had been in charge.

Adele felt her lips quirk into a smile. She had

allowed herself to pretend that she could associate with the Leary family but not with its patriarch, Speaker Leary, who had murdered her family. Reality had just forced its way to the front, as it had been certain to do unless Adele had died before that happened.

She had two options. On reflection she found herself unwilling to cut herself off from Daniel Leary and through him the RCN, the first real family Adele had known in her life.

"All right," Adele repeated. *In for a soldi, in for a florin.* "What is Arnaud asking from you?"

She brought her data unit live and began searching, starting with the *Sailing Directions for Pantellaria,* published by Navy House. Whatever the specifics of the problem were, the more she knew about Pantellaria, the better off she would be.

"The Treaty of Amiens required that the parties"— the Republic of Cinnabar and the Alliance of Free Stars—"give up all territories captured during the course of the war," Deirdre said. "There were balanced exceptions, but Pantellaria regained the independence it had lost eighteen years earlier."

"Yes," said Adele to show that she was listening. *Of course.* But it was a polite acknowledgment, and she had been raised to be courteous when that was possible.

"Pantellaria had six colony worlds, all of which were controlled by the Alliance during the war and which were returned to Pantellaria under the treaty," Deirdre said. "One of them, Corcyra, declared its independence from the homeworld."

Adele refined her search while she listened. Deirdre continued. "A number of Pantellarians who were closely associated with the Alliance regime fled to

Corcyra. The exiles control a great deal of wealth, even after their assets on Pantellaria have been expropriated. They've been helping to arm the rebels—the independence movement, if you prefer. In addition, the former Alliance garrison of Corcyra was locally recruited and remained on the planet."

Adele continued to read her holographic display. Corcyra held vast quantities of copper. The mining income was sufficient to sustain the rebellion indefinitely, unless Pantellaria was able to sustain a real blockade. That last seemed doubtful when the homeworld itself was disrupted by both the war and its recent change of government.

"Ah," said Adele. She looked past the hologram to Deirdre and quoted, "'The Pantellarian Council has appointed Ermann Arnaud as Commissioner Plenipotentiary of Corcyra, with full authority to return it to the beneficent control of the homeworld.' I would say that Master Arnaud has chosen a difficult task."

"I'm confident that he would agree with you," Deirdre said dryly. "It affects me because whatever Arnaud's original expectation, he is now pinning his hopes on Cinnabar intervention as a signatory of the Treaty of Amiens, returning Corcyra to Pantellaria as part of the status quo ante provisions. Our legal department informs me that Arnaud's interpretation of the treaty language is open to question."

Adele flicked her hand. "It doesn't matter what lawyers say," she snapped. "If we send troops—or ships, more likely—the Alliance will certainly respond by supporting the pro-Alliance exiles. We'll be back in a state of full-scale war in six months, or more likely three."

"Yes," said Deirdre. "My research bureau said within a year, but I accept your assessment. Renewed war would be even worse for my interests than being accused of supporting the Alliance during the recent war, so I have decided not to comply with Arnaud's request. Morality aside, of course."

"Of course," Adele said. She pursed her lips. Partly to give herself more time to analyze the options, she said, "*Could* you have gotten Cinnabar support for the Pantellarians?"

Deirdre spread her fingers before her. She had chunky hands; indeed, she might best be described as a chunky woman. She was no more a raving beauty than her brother was a conventionally handsome man.

Not that Deirdre's looks mattered. From what Daniel had said, she preferred professional companionship to amateurs. Professionals cost only money, which she had in abundance.

"There are a number of hardliners in the Senate who believe we should not have made peace with the Tyrant Porra, as they call him," Deirdre said, smiling faintly. "Senators who feel that Guarantor Porra's behavior toward his citizens is a proper matter of concern for the Senate of the Republic of Cinnabar. And also—"

Deirdre turned her palms up.

"—there are hard-line or personally involved Alliance citizens who certainly are funnelling arms to the rebels. Though of course the galaxy's awash with surplus arms following the general demobilization after the treaty."

Adele nodded agreement. Arms dealers were rarely concerned with the political complexion of potential buyers, so long as they could pay in hard currency.

"A campaign in the streets of Xenos, protesting Alliance aggression, wouldn't be very expensive," Deirdre said. "Combined with discussions with individual senators—"

"Discussions" meant logrolling or simple bribery. Which Speaker Leary would conduct, and very ably, too, based on his past performance.

"—I think it might be possible, yes."

Deirdre didn't bother to repeat that she had already decided against the option. Adele was pleased to deal with someone who assumed that the person she was speaking to could remember a statement made a few seconds earlier.

"If this matter were publicized," Deirdre went on, "it would ruin my chance of getting into the Senate. There's almost no possibility that I would go to jail for treason or even be tried, however. I have always expected to enter the Senate at some point, but I can bear the disappointment."

Adele looked at her. On the face of it, "I can bear the disappointment" was sneeringly ironic. But behind Deirdre's polished deadpan, Adele saw a hint that the disappointment would be real. There had been a Leary in the Senate for almost seven hundred years, and *that*, if not personal ambition, would hurt Deirdre.

Daniel would make a terrible *senator.* But he might feel that family honor compelled him to fill the seat that his father would vacate, upon death if not by retirement.

"How would you like to see the problem solved?" Adele said. A mechanical voice would have held more emotion.

"Any solution which doesn't result in the ruin of

the Leary family is acceptable," Deirdre said. "I'm aware what may be involved in giving an agent of your caliber carte blanche."

You think *you understand*, Adele thought, holding Deirdre's eyes. But perhaps she truly did. The Learys were a notably ruthless family.

"All right," said Adele. She shut down her data unit and got to her feet.

She paused to slip the data unit into her pocket, then said, "My help will be expensive. Do you speak for the Leary family or just for yourself?"

Deirdre cleared her throat. She remained in her chair. "I must ask," she said, "if your price will affect the physical safety of any member of my family?"

"It will not," said Adele with a smile as hard as the muzzle of the pistol she always carried in the left pocket of her tunic.

Deirdre stood and smiled in turn. "In that case," she said, "I accept your proposition. If my personal resources are insufficient to meet your fee, I will commit those of the Leary family."

She walked around the desk and offered her hand.

"On my word as a Leary," she said.

Adele shook Deirdre's hand. "I know what the word of a Leary is worth," she said. She opened the door for herself and followed the waiting Tovera through the lobby.

I have a good deal of planning to do, Adele thought. *But first I need to speak with Daniel.*

CHAPTER 3

The Bantry Estate, Cinnabar

"Here he comes," Hogg said, looking to the northeast. "And he's not half moving."

Daniel rose from his seat on the porch that wrapped around three sides of the manor. Tom Sand's gray aircar was approaching over open country, which allowed much higher speeds than if it had followed the road from Stavingham, the market town for the region. As Hogg had suggested, the car was moving very fast, faster than Daniel would have said was safe, even twenty feet above the ground.

As the driver approached the village proper, he lifted higher still—sunset brushed the bow—and let the angle of attack brake his vehicle smoothly above the houses. The aircar had slowed to a walking pace before it settled to the paved plaza following the curve of Bantry's seawall.

"He's here!" Daniel called into the house as he started toward the car. When he noticed that his servant was coming along, he said, "I don't think I need help to greet a friendly businessman, Hogg."

"I thought I'd chat with his bodyguard," Hogg said blandly, continuing to match Daniel step for step. The driver was opening the limousine's back door for Tom Sand. His uniform perfectly matched the vehicle's finish.

Daniel smiled. He'd noticed that city folk generally thought tenants were louts with no more will than the sheep they tended while not jumping to fulfill the master's whim. That hadn't been his experience. For that matter, sheep had their own opinions also.

"Welcome back to Bantry, Sand," Daniel called. "How hungry are you? Because I thought we could talk and watch the sunset from one of the benches—"

There were a pair of west-facing arbors at the inner edge of the plaza.

"—before we went into the house and had dinner. I've invited the manager of the packing plant and his wife to eat with us; and Miranda, of course."

As usual, life was more complicated than the polite words into which it had to be compressed. Chloris had told Gwen Higgenson that the Squire hadn't caught enough floorfish sprats to feed their surprise guest from the city. Gwen had called the plant, and her husband had rushed home with a dozen sprats. Gwen had filleted them and carried them over to Miranda.

Daniel, when he heard about the confusion, had invited the Higgensons to dinner with the three of them—later in the evening. *It's what I should've done in the first place;* but the whole business had been unexpected.

"I appreciate you seeing me, Leary," said Tom Sand. He was a solid man and not fat, though he obviously carried more weight than he had when he was thirty years younger. At one time, his hair must have been red. "And I'm not going to be able to taste my food till I've talked to you."

He grunted a laugh and added, "We'll see how I feel then."

The arbors had been planted as saplings, then bent and trimmed to shape. They'd been allowed to continue to grow upward; their crowns provided summer shade to the grapes planted around their roots.

Daniel gestured his guest to one end of the bench under the arbor and took the other. Sand settled with a sigh. Meeting Daniel's eyes, he said, "Leary, I'm here to ask you a favor. And I know bloody well that you don't owe me anything."

"I'm not sure that's true," Daniel said mildly, "but friends don't keep that kind of score sheet anyway. Ask away, Tom."

"Ah...?" said Sand, grimacing. "I was glad when your fiancée said that Lady Mundy wasn't here. Now—don't mistake what I'm saying, because I know you'll have to tell her, but this is going to be easier to say as one man to another."

"Go on," Daniel said. *Is Mistress Sand seeing another man?* That seemed unlikely, and it was even less likely that Tom Sand would come here for advice in such a case. Daniel's experience was all on the other leg of such triangles.

"Bernis was a widow when I married her," Sand said. "She was born in Xenos, but Ordos Cleveland, her first husband, came from Oriel County. His family *was* something there." He guffawed. "Sort of like the Learys here, I guess," he said. "But not in Xenos and politics, you see."

Daniel smiled. He was letting his guest tell the story his own way, but he couldn't help wishing that way was a little more direct. The clouds on the horizon were dark in silhouette, but higher in the western sky some cirrus curls were still pink.

"Cleveland came to Xenos and got into finance," Sand said. "Connections helped him there, you know."

Daniel nodded.

"He married Bernis and cut quite a swathe for a few years," Sand said, his voice beginning to rasp. "They had a son, that's Rikard. And then Cleveland went bust in a big way. He went up to the Oriel County property—to think, he said. And he drowned swimming in a lake there."

He spread his hands. "Well, it was ruled an accident, and why not?" he said. "And Bernis went around and took care of what was owing. Cleveland had been borrowing on securities that he was supposed to be holding for clients, I hear; but they were all taken care of. And I married Bernis."

"I believe you made a fortunate marriage," Daniel said. That was true—for Sand. Mistress Sand was a very impressive woman, and she had been a considerable social step upward for a self-made contractor like Tom Sand. Age and—plain—looks aside, Daniel would rather have married the wolf eel.

"The problem is the boy, Rikard," Sand said. Then, bitterly, "He was fifteen and trouble when I met Bernis, he was worse bloody trouble all the time until he ran off three years ago, and now he's back and says he's reformed, damned if I don't think he's the worst trouble of all. *Bloody* kid!"

"I don't get along well with my father," Daniel

said. That was an understatement: he'd entered the RCN Academy at age sixteen after a screaming row with Corder Leary. That the episode hadn't ended in murder showed that both men had better control than their closest associates would have guessed. "I can imagine that a stepson and stepfather have an even harder time."

"It was more than that," Sand said, looking toward the pale horizon. He sounded despairing rather than angry. "He resented me for being an oik—Bernis remarried beneath her, you see. And he resented her for being alive. Cleveland drank a lot. When he took a swing at me with a bottle, I told Bernis to keep him out of my sight or I'd leave."

He looked at his big, scarred hands and grinned ruefully at Daniel. "That's not how I'd have handled the problem with any other man alive," he said.

Daniel grinned back. He'd never doubted that Tom Sand had been raised in a tough school.

"So after boarding school, Bernis got Cleveland jobs with family friends," Sand said. "Hers and her first husband's, not mine. I didn't check up on him, but none of the jobs lasted long. Then about three years ago, he went off somewhere and Bernis didn't hear anything from him. Well, he was twenty-four then, old enough to live his own life. Me, I was just glad he was out of mine."

Spray flashed white several hundred yards out to sea. Moments later came the slap of a fish whose leap had raised the spray. It must have been of some size to be heard over the land breeze.

"So Cleveland's back," Sand said, gravel entering his tone. "He's joined a cult and says he's reformed. He apologized to me like a man, I'll give him that. But he says he's found a treasure on a planet called Corcyra, and he wants Bernis to fund an expedition to dig it up. There's fighting going on, and he wants the treasure to buy arms for his cult, the Transformationists, so they don't get squeezed by one side or the other."

"Corcyra?" Daniel repeated, frowning. "There's fighting there, all right. I can tell you that Admiral Bocale is putting together a squadron right now, just in case the RCN gets involved."

Daniel had been offered command of a cruiser in Bocale's squadron, but he'd decided to remain on half pay a little longer instead. If real war resumed between Cinnabar and the Alliance, Captain Daniel Leary could hope for something more interesting than a cruiser under Bocale. The admiral was known to be so concerned about making the wrong decision that he never made a really right one.

"I guess Bernis knows that, too," Sand said morosely. "She couldn't fund it herself since she paid off the people Ordos bilked, but she's gone to her friends looking for investors."

He turned to meet Daniel's gaze and said, "She didn't ask me, didn't even mention it to me. But I heard."

"What *is* the treasure?" Daniel asked, thinking over what he had learned recently about the Corcyra situation. Whether or not he served under Admiral Bocale, it seemed likely that the RCN would shortly be involved in the region. "It seems to me that you'd have to pay extremely well to get anyone with good sense to go to the middle of a war zone to look for treasure."

Sand nodded. "Bernis believes in the treasure,"

he said. "I don't, but that isn't the main problem. I figure the only crew which'll sign up for the job is one that'll knock Cleveland on the head for his stake. The only question is whether they'll do it as soon as they lift to Cinnabar orbit or hold off till they learn how bad things on Corcyra really are."

He stared at his balled fists as he ground the knuckles together. "Look, Leary," he said, raising his eyes again. "Here's the rub. *I* don't think the universe'd be a worse place without Cleveland in it, but his mother loves him and I love Bernis. It'll break her heart if he's scragged, especially if she found the money to let him go off and do such a bloody fool thing."

Sand took a deep breath. "Leary," he said, "I want you to carry Cleveland on your yacht. I know it won't be cheap, but I've got a good business and I'll mortgage the last paperclip if that's what it takes."

"I think something can be worked out," Daniel said—because his guest needed an answer immediately. There was an almost infinite number of matters to be determined before he lifted from harbor with Rikard Cleveland; to begin with, it probably wouldn't be in the *Princess Cecile*, his yacht.

The details could wait, however. Tom Sand had to know that Daniel was considering the proposition before he would be able to relax.

Daniel stood. "Why don't you stay the night, Sand?" he said. "In the morning I'll ride back to Xenos with you and talk to some people. Ah, and Miranda will come back with us, too, if you've got room in your car."

The limousine would seat at least six passengers, along with Hogg sitting up front with the driver.

Sand rose also, expelling a deep breath. "By *God*,

Leary!" he said. "By *God*! You don't know what that means to me!"

"Let's go in and have some dinner," Daniel said, starting toward the manor house. The episode with the wolf eel had almost slipped from his memory, displaced by the excitement of planning a new project. "I don't know about you, but I worked up an appetite today fishing."

As soon as I get back to Xenos, I'll talk to Adele. But I want to do that in person.

Xenos on Cinnabar

Adele was in her library on the top floor of Chatsworth Minor when she heard Tovera say from the hallway, "I'm sure the mistress will be glad to see you, Captain Leary."

Adele couldn't have heard the words if the door hadn't been open, which meant that before speaking, Tovera had opened it without Adele's notice. Sometimes Adele was bothered by the degree to which she was oblivious of her surroundings when she was working, but she wouldn't accomplish nearly as much if she didn't concentrate. And it wasn't as though she had a choice: she was who she was.

Adele didn't shut down her data unit, but she shrank its display so that when Daniel came to the doorway he wasn't looking at her through a mist of coherent light. It was mid-morning: not early, but much earlier than Adele had expected to see her housemate.

He was on the west coast so far as she knew. He hadn't returned to the townhouse last night.

"I have some business I'd like to discuss with you," Daniel said. "But if this isn't a good time, we can...?"

Adele set down her control wands. She hadn't missed Daniel during the three weeks he had been in Bantry, but she felt a rush of unexpected pleasure at seeing him again.

"I'm going over old logbooks," she said. She was compiling logs of voyages to the Ribbon Stars, the cluster in which Pantellaria and Corcyra lay. "Nothing that can't wait."

Daniel entered the room and closed the door, then looked around. "I don't come up here very often," he said.

"This is the library," Adele said with a deadpan expression. "The suite on the floor below is my living quarters. And no, I don't see much difference in the piles of books and records, either. Is there a chair—there."

She pointed.

"Just put those chip files on the floor. They should have kept dust off the seat, at any rate."

Daniel lifted the stack of frames into which chips—those on top appeared to be transcriptions of local histories—were clipped. Instead of transferring them to the floor, he sat holding them in his lap. He seemed to be ill at ease.

"Tom Sand asked me to transport his stepson to Corcyra to hunt for treasure," Daniel said, packing a remarkable amount of information into a few words. "I've agreed to do so, barring unforeseen factors."

Strictly speaking there wasn't a question in what Daniel had said, but even Adele's doubtful social instincts told her that she had to respond. "I wasn't aware that Mistress Sand had a son," she said, expanding her data unit's display and switching to public records on Bernis Sand. "I know almost nothing about her, except as it directly affects me."

Adele's ignorance of Bernis Sand's private life was a matter of choice. She didn't want to know anything that Bernis didn't choose to tell her. She hadn't delved into Daniel's background, either, though she was pretty sure that she wouldn't have learned anything of significance if she had.

Daniel was politely reticent about the names of women with whom he had been intimate. She couldn't think of any other subject on which a simple question to him would not have brought an equally simple answer. And courtesy aside, Adele wasn't sure Daniel *remembered* many of the names.

She knew quite a lot about Daniel's sister, however. Deirdre would probably be surprised to learn how much information Adele had amassed about someone who was wealthy and notably cautious.

"Mistress Sand has been looking for investors," Daniel said. "She doesn't know her husband has come to me. Tom is afraid that the boy—well, he's twenty-seven, older than I am—will be killed by any captain he can hire to take him to Corcyra in its present condition."

Adele sniffed. "In the present situation," she said, "Rikard Cleveland—"

The name was readily available.

"—and anyone accompanying him will be in a great deal of danger, leaving aside their personal motives."

She checked her data on Corcyra again and raised her eyes to Daniel's. "I would not advise that we take the *Princess Cecile* to Corcyra. Even though she is a private yacht at present, both parties would certainly view her as a Cinnabar warship...as she has been often enough, of course. The Pantellarians have sent six destroyers with their expeditionary force; the independence movement has a single destroyer manned by Pantellarian exiles. A corvette like the *Sissie* would make a significant difference in the power ratio—in either direction."

The *Princess Cecile*, commanded by Captain Daniel Leary, could make a great deal of difference. Adele didn't add that, because it would have been boastful—the *Sissie* was more her home than this family townhouse was—and because Daniel already knew that.

"I'm going to check with Mon," Daniel said. "Bergen and Associates refits a lot of small freighters, and he'll be able to direct me to a solid ship."

Mon had served under Daniel as a lieutenant in the RCN. Adele believed that most people were superstitious, but spacers were more stubbornly convinced of their foolishness than she had seen in most other occupations. When bad luck got Mon a reputation for being a Jonah, Daniel had made him manager of Bergen and Associates, the small shipyard which Daniel's uncle Stacey had willed to him.

The yard had flourished under Mon's direction. Daniel's kindness to a friend and associate had been good business financially.

"I'll need to discuss this with Mistress Sand," Adele said neutrally. She didn't bother to add, "If that's all right with you?" Daniel had come to her with the problem, so he expected her to use her own judgment about how to deal with her end of it—which was primarily information gathering.

Adele assumed that Tom Sand felt the same way, but she didn't care. What he said to his wife Bernis was his own business; what Lady Mundy said to Mistress Sand, who directed Cinnabar's intelligence agents, was Lady Mundy's business alone.

"And of course," Daniel said, "Cleveland himself probably doesn't know about our involvement. I think we should talk to him together, but I'd rather you set up the meeting through his mother?"

He raised an eyebrow in question. Adele nodded crisply. "Yes, I'll take care of that," she said. She didn't foresee a problem with Mistress Sand, but intra-family matters rarely proceeded by logic. She would deal with the situation as it arose; as she did with every other situation.

Daniel grimaced again. Adele realized that he was concerned to be involved with her life outside the RCN. This situation would not have arisen had she not been associated with Mistress Sand.

"Look, Adele," he said, forcing himself to look at her instead of out the window toward the head of the cul-de-sac on which the townhouse stood. He probably couldn't see the tram stop there unless he stood up. "I said I'd do this for Sand because he's a good fellow who needed help, and because I thought it was maybe something that you'd want done. But if you think it's a bad idea, for *any* reason, I'll see Sand and shut the business off to his face."

Adele shrugged. "I do want it done," she said, then smiled. "As much as I want anything done, of course. There are doubtless factors which we don't and can't know at present which could make this a very bad idea."

She smiled more broadly; probably as much of a smile as she ever showed the world. "On the other hand, unpredicted factors can have good results, too. I had many valid reasons for choosing to study at the Academic Collections on Blythe when I was sixteen, but they did not include getting me off Cinnabar ahead of the Proscriptions in which the rest of my family died."

Daniel laughed and rose to his feet. "Well," he said, "I hope we won't learn that we lifted from Cinnabar just before the revolution in which all noble families were massacred, but other than that I'll remain optimistic."

He nodded to her as he opened the door. Hogg and Tovera both waited at the stairhead, good servants waiting for their masters' instructions.

"I'll talk to Mon," Daniel said over his shoulder. "When I've got that nailed down, we can see about Cleveland and what the *bloody* hell he's got in mind."

"Yes," said Adele. Which meant she needed to talk, privately and in person, with Bernis Sand. She keyed in Mistress Sand's private contact address.

CHAPTER 4

Xenos on Cinnabar

The doorman bowed Adele into the lobby, where a cadaverous man in black—probably the club secretary rather than a lower functionary—waited behind a lectern. "I'm to meet Mistress Cleveland for lunch," Adele said, using the name she had been given. "My name is Mundy."

The secretary checked the display built into his lectern, then raised his eyes and smiled falsely. "Why yes, Mistress Mundy," he said, tapping a call button. A boy—if he was older than sixteen, he was badly undernourished—came out of an alcove behind the secretary, buttoning his coat. "Daniel will take you back. The Gray Room, Daniel."

Adele avoided blinking, though the boy's name had been a surprise. "Daniel" wasn't an uncommon name, of course; but that was looking at the matter logically.

The Oriel Club was old, but it wasn't one that members would mention when they wanted to impress other people. It had been founded by residents of Oriel County to have a place to eat and sleep when they had business in the capital. The kitchen was said to be very good on mutton dishes; which made sense, as sheep were the first thing one thought of in the rare instances when someone mentioned Oriel County.

The boy swaggered ahead of her, past a reading room with leather-covered chairs, then through the grill room to the left-hand of the pair of private rooms in back. The three diners in the grill room were decently but not stylishly dressed. They glanced up from their meals—mutton curry in all cases—but Adele was no more interesting to look at than they were.

"The Gray Room!" the boy said, pulling the door open without announcing them to the occupant of the room. He was what you would expect from junior staff in a club whose secretary had to check his files to determine whether a guest was expected.

Bernis Sand sat across the table, facing the door. A decanter of amber liquid—whiskey, unless she had changed her habits since Adele last saw her—and two glasses were already on the table.

"Thank you, Daniel," said Mistress Sand. "We're not to be disturbed unless we call you."

The boy closed the door. Sand smiled grimly and said, "Lock it, if you would, Mundy. Despite my clear direction, it's quite possible that someone will bustle in with a carafe of water or a tablecloth."

Adele snicked the lock and sat down. "I suppose shooting the first few intruders would be overreaction," she said.

"This was my first husband's club," said Mistress Sand. She didn't react to the joke. "I kept the membership after his death. There are times I like to be thought of as Mistress Cleveland, who owns land in Oriel County. Mistress Cleveland and her guests don't attract attention."

Sand was below middle height and solid; it would be accurate though uncharitable to describe her build as cylindrical. Her complexion had been ruddy when she introduced herself to Adele five years before. Now her skin had a gray undertone, and her cheeks sagged.

"I appreciate that," said Adele, "though I wanted to talk with you in a private capacity. My friend Captain Leary plans to visit Corcyra, and I expect to accompany him."

Sand had begun to pour whiskey into Adele's glass unasked. The decanter ticked the rim of the glass hard, but neither broke. She set the decanter down, stared across the table at Adele, and drained the last ounce from her own glass.

"I don't know how you heard about this, Mundy," she said in a rasping voice. "But I'm glad you did. I usually don't know how you learn things, of course."

Not for the first time, Adele realized that people often gave her too much credit. Surely it wasn't unusual for a husband worried about his wife's problems to contact her associates in hope of finding a solution?

Aloud Adele said, "Explain the situation from your viewpoint, if you would."

The way Mistress Sand answered that deliberately neutral request would tell more than the facts of the situation, for which Adele had many objective sources.

"My son Rikard returned from Corcyra two weeks ago," Sand said, showing that she was here a mother, rather than a Cinnabar patriot or an intelligence director. "I hadn't heard from him or of him for almost three years. I . . . well, it was reasonable to assume that he was dead."

She had already refilled her glass; she drank half of the contents. Adele's fingers were busy with her control wands, but she had no desire to try the splash of whiskey in her own glass anyway.

Given the resources Mistress Sand controlled, Rikard's total disappearance did indeed imply that the boy was dead. The deaths of Adele's own family were to her a series of events sealed in a block of crystal. She had no feelings about them: just generalized despair and anger.

Adele recognized that other people had different reactions; and perhaps mothers generally differed. Certainly she felt no empathy with any other aspect of motherhood.

"Rikard explained that he was now a follower of a religion formed on Corcyra, the Transformationists," Sand said. "You can call it a cult if you like."

She grimaced. Nothing Adele had observed of Mistress Sand suggested that the older woman had any religious belief. It must have been painful to learn that her son had embraced religion, and particularly that he'd joined some foreign cult.

"I don't have an opinion on religious matters," Adele said. It was a mild rebuke to anyone who knew her as well as Mistress Sand did. "In any case, the boy has returned unharmed?"

Given the way human beings behaved, Adele suspected that Rikard may have become a Transformationist for no other reason than that it would horrify his mother. Well, that was better than him becoming a traitor to Cinnabar, which might as easily have happened.

"Sorry, Mundy," Sand muttered, taking another drink. "Yes, quite unharmed. Elements on Corcyra have declared the planet independent from its homeworld, Pantellaria, and the Pantellarians have sent a force to regain control. I suppose you know about all that?"

"I have the basics," Adele said. "I'll be learning more; and if you have data that I might not find elsewhere—"

That was extremely unlikely, but it was polite as well as potentially a means of saving time.

"—I'd appreciate seeing it."

"Yes, of course," said Mistress Sand. "I'll have everything sent to you as soon as I leave."

She reached for the decanter. "The Transformationists aren't pacifistic," she said. "They're mostly foreigners like Rikard—though he says there're both Corcyrans and Pantellarians in the, well, faith. They're supporting the independence movement, but they're concerned that whoever wins may decide the Transformationists would make a good scapegoat. They're arming so that they don't look like an easy target."

"Transformationism sounds like an admirably pragmatic faith," Adele said. "Whatever its philosophical tenets."

"Which is some consolation to a mother," Sand said with a brief smile. "Though not a great one."

She set her glass down and said, "Rikard has located what he insists is a treasure buried by the first settlers of Corcyra. I didn't go into the details, but he's not a stupid young man, and he has some experience with subsurface mapping. He held a position with an engineering firm here in Xenos."

Sand grimaced again.

Adele raised her own glass for the first time and

sipped what was indeed whiskey. She didn't doubt that it was a good variety, though that was a taste she had never cultivated. She said deliberately, "I wouldn't thank a friend who told me that I was drinking too much."

Mistress Sand's hand paused halfway to the decanter. She blinked as though she had just awakened to find herself on the Pentacrest, stark naked and singing "The Banner High," the Alliance anthem. She pushed the decanter to the side of the table and said, "Mundy, I have occasionally been concerned that I would be told that you had shot yourself. I don't believe that anyone will ever suggest that you're drinking too much."

"I'll keep that in mind," said Adele, setting her glass down again.

"Look," said Mistress Sand, sitting straighter than she had since Adele entered the room. "I wouldn't have ordered you—well, with you, I mean asked—to get involved, but your involvement is the best news I've had since my son came home."

She smiled wryly and added, "Since he explained *why* he'd come home, that is. I can give you as much official support as you want—and for Captain Leary, as well. If he'd care to take the *Princess Cecile* to the Ribbon Stars under RCN auspices, I can arrange that."

"I will pass on your offer to Captain Leary," Adele said. She felt no need to inform Mistress Sand of what Daniel was thinking. "Does the Republic have a position on the Corcyra situation?"

"Neither we nor the Alliance cares what happens to Corcyra," Sand said. "Oh, there are functionaries on both sides, some of them wearing uniforms, who feel very strongly one way or another. But the position of the Senate and of Guarantor Porra as best we can determine—*I* can determine—is that all the parties involved on Corcyra can go to Hell in their own way, and the more quickly the better."

Sand sighed, touched her glass, and pushed it firmly aside as she had the decanter. "Despite that," she said, "there's a very real possibility that we'll shortly be at war over some silly business involving Corcyra, even though nobody wants it. No sane person wants that."

Adele pursed her lips, looking for the correct phrasing. People in general did not use words as precisely as she did, and she needed to be understood this time.

"If I go to Corcyra as a private citizen," she said, meeting the older woman's eyes, "as I expect at the moment I will do, I cannot guarantee that the actions I take will be to the benefit of the Republic."

Mistress Sand laughed. "Mundy," she said, "I can't guarantee that the sun will rise in the east tomorrow, but I would bet on it with almost as much certainty as I would bet that whatever you do will be in Cinnabar's best interests."

She paused. She was fully herself again: Bernis Sand, whose mind controlled an intelligence apparatus which was more valuable to the safety of the Republic than any battleship in the RCN.

"I can justify all the help my organization provides you, Mundy," she said forcefully. "But in my own mind, I am very clear that you are going to Corcyra as a favor to a colleague."

Adele rose. "I'll get back to preparations, then," she said. "Captain Leary and I will need to talk to your son, probably this afternoon."

"Yes, of course," Sand said, rising also. "I'll tell him to expect your call."

And I'm not doing this for a colleague, Adele thought as she opened the door to the grill room. *I'm doing it for a friend.*

Bergen and Associates Shipyard, Cinnabar

Mon had an office on the top of what was now the Administration Building—it had been Hangar One when Daniel first visited the yard as a boy—but Daniel had asked to amble along the waterside with his manager while they talked. As expected, Mon was delighted to give his co-owner—Daniel had given Mon a ten percent share out of the fifty percent Daniel had inherited—a tour to show how well the yard was doing.

The "Associates" of the yard's name was Uncle Stacey's financial backer—Corder Leary, who had married Stacey's sister and sired Deirdre and Daniel on her. Corder had little or nothing to do with his wife while Daniel was growing up, but he had made financial provision for his brother-in-law on Stacey's retirement from the RCN at the rank of commander.

Deirdre handled all business between the yard and its silent partner. Daniel preferred not to deal with his father, and to the degree that Mon cared—Daniel wasn't sure that Mon even knew the full ownership arrangements—he was probably pleased as well.

"We're replacing all her thrusters," Mon said, gesturing to the *Ezwal*, a small freighter in dry dock. "Three or four might still pass, but the new owner plans to trade in the Nugget Cluster, where his own crew'll have to handle the refits. He wants to put the first major overhaul as far into the future as he can."

Daniel nodded approvingly at the work. Six of the *Ezwal*'s eight thrusters were on a flatcar beside the dock, and the crane was winching up a seventh to join them.

Several of the dockworkers were missing limbs. Mon had continued Stacey Bergen's practice of hiring former RCN spacers, particularly those who were no longer fit for interstellar service. As with Daniel's decision to appoint Mon as manager, it was an act of kindness which had proven to be extremely good business.

"It's always a pleasure to see how well things are going," Daniel said. He beamed at the bustle. The Bergen yard had gotten more than its share of Navy work during the war because employing injured veterans had protected it against the loss of workers to man the fleet. Things didn't seem to have slowed down since the Treaty of Amiens, though. "But I came here primarily to pick your brains about a ship. I'd like to hire—or buy; perhaps purchase would be a better idea—a well-found freighter of a thousand tons or so. You know, a tramp that a crew of six could work but with cabin space for twenty."

Mon looked at Daniel and rubbed his cheek. His black hair was receding, but he had begun wearing fluffy side-whiskers which merged with a magnificent moustache. Mon was much plumper than he had been as a lieutenant, but he looked truly happy—which had never been the case when he wore an RCN uniform.

"Well, I tell you, sir," he said. "I've got three ships myself that'd fit, though only two of them're on Cinnabar right this moment. I own them, I mean—bought them out of my share of the yard's profits and fixed them up. You can have any of them for a florin—buy or rent, I don't care. It'll be a pleasure to turn her over to you."

Daniel frowned. A nearby tramp tested its intake pump by running up to high flow and exhausting the reaction mass back into the pool; the roar gave him time to think.

"I appreciate the offer, Mon," Daniel said as the flow whirred down to a trickle, "but that's scarcely necessary. I realize that the price of shipping has gone up considerably since the treaty, but—well, from the yard alone, my income is very substantial thanks to your good management. Which ships are on Cinnabar now?"

Mon grimaced as he thought. "Well, one is the *Golgotha Dancer*," he said. "She's the one I'd recommend. Twelve hundred tons, two antenna rings, of course, but I just replaced her High Drives. Right now she's in Portola"—on the East Coast—"loading a cargo of fusion bottles for Chateaubriand. But we can land them back on the dock in six hours, that's no problem."

"She's just the sort of ship I have in mind," said Daniel. He'd need to look over any offer before deciding, but he trusted Mon implicitly on the freighter's soundness. "And the other?"

"She's the *Kiesche*, right over here in the end berth," Mon said. He gestured forward and set off down the track around the pool. "Twelve hundred tons, two antenna rings again, but she turns like a cat. I've never seen a ship so handy. In civilian service, of course."

Warships had large crews, which made them handier than merchant ships even with the same rigging, and generally warships mounted more masts than civilian vessels also. A starship's rigging was fully automated, but anyone who expected thousands of valves and pulleys to work perfectly in service was a fool.

Ships lifted and landed on pillars of plasma, and they passed through atmospheres which had their own corrosive possibilities. Without riggers on the hull, a ship would soon become mired in the Matrix and eons away from anywhere her captain wanted to be.

"What *is* her crew?" Daniel asked. What must be the *Kiesche* came in sight at the edge of the inlet channel to Lake Xenos. His first thought was disappointment—the freighter had a rusty, bedraggled look. But that again was a matter of crew size: much of a warship's exterior maintenance was busywork to keep the crew occupied when the vessel wasn't in the midst of a battle.

"I run her with ten," Mon said. "Well, nine most of the time, if I'm honest. You can sling hammocks for twenty easily enough."

They were approaching from the bow, so the nose turret with its single plasma cannon was visible. Daniel nodded toward the gun and said in a neutral tone, "What does she mount?"

"A fifty-millimeter high-intensity piece," Mon said. "From an Alliance pirate chaser originally, I'd guess, but I took her off a freighter out of Trobriand that I was scrapping."

He pursed his lips and looked at Daniel. "Look, sir—I know that's a popgun, but this is a civilian ship, and that's all her frames'll take in real use. You won't find a freighter under five thousand tons which can handle as many as a dozen rounds from a four-inch gun without starting all her seams."

Daniel laughed. "Much as I'd like you to be wrong, Mon," he said, "I know that you're not. And I'm trying to look inconspicuous on this business, so fitting destroyer armament would be a bad idea even if we could."

Now that they were standing on the dock alongside, the *Kiesche* had a sharp, eager appearance. Sure, her hull was streaked with rust, but her rigging was taut and her antennas were straight, with no signs of kinks which would keep the sections from nesting properly within one another.

"Say, there's one more thing," said Mon. "You remember the *Milton*—why sure you do! You captained her in her last fight, so sure you do! Well, she was scrapped right here when she got back to Cinnabar. I put her command console in the *Kiesche* when I was refitting her. A heavy cruiser's console is really too big for a twelve hundred-ton freighter, but the price was right."

Daniel had started down the catwalk to the ship's own boarding ramp. He stopped, put his foot back on the quay, and turned. "You don't bloody say!" he said. "You don't *bloody* say!"

Mon, startled by Daniel's vehemence, said, "Well, the console was first-rate even if I hear that the ship was an abortion, eight-inch cannon on a cruiser hull."

"You didn't hear me say the *Millie* was an abortion!" Daniel said. "Why, she slugged it out with a battleship, and it was the *Millie* who sailed home!"

He caught himself. Sailed home, yes; but under a jury rig and missing her hull aft of Frame 260. She was scrapped when she got home because that was the only option which made economic sense.

"Never mind, Mon," Daniel said. "I'll take the *Kiesche*."

He cleared his throat in embarrassment. "Pardon if I sounded a bit heated. I'm, well...As you say, the *Millie* was my command. And—"

He beamed at the freighter.

"—a cruiser console may cramp the bridge somewhat, but it has full controls and display on the aft side. And *that* will be the perfect location for my communications officer!"

CHAPTER 5

Xenos on Cinnabar

Adele had paused in her transcriptions to sip from her glass of beer. Beer from the Mundy estate—bitters, actually, brewed with germander rather than hops—had been the table beverage at the townhouse while Adele was growing up.

She had never considered the choice as child: what was, was, as with most children in most situations. As an adult, she supposed the beer was to show voters that Lucius Mundy was a Man of the People, despite his rank in society.

The doorman ushered a visitor into the hallway on the ground floor. Adele heard only the murmur of voices through the open door of the library where she was working. She took another sip of beer.

Her mouth was very dry. Forgetting to eat wasn't a real problem, but she shouldn't let herself go so long without drinking, especially with a glass at her hand.

Tovera stood at the stairhead. "It's Miranda Dorst," she said quietly. "She came to see you."

"Send her up," said Adele. What she was doing wasn't important.

Her lips hinted at a frozen smile. *No human activity is important. Everyone dies, everything dies; the Cosmos dies.*

If you are part of a family, however, you have family obligations. Adele had spent her first thirty-one years alone, though until she was sixteen she had lived in Xenos with her parents and sister. When she met Daniel, she had joined a family: she had become a Sissie, a member of the crew of the corvette *Princess Cecile*, and through that fellowship a part of the vastly extended RCN family.

Adele much preferred her current situation, and no one had ever accused the Mundys of avoiding their obligations.

Besides, Adele liked Miranda. She was intelligent and was grounded in the real world: Miranda and her mother had lived in straitened circumstances since the death of her father, an RCN captain. Furthermore, Miranda was extremely tough, though there was nothing in her appearance to suggest that.

Adele's mouth quirked again, perhaps with a hint of regret. Toughness wasn't the first attribute strangers thought of on meeting Adele Mundy, either.

Miranda came up the three flights of stairs ahead of Tovera. It was an unusual display of Tovera's favor that she did not interpose herself between her mistress and an approaching visitor.

"Good afternoon, Miranda," Adele said. "Put those chip files on the floor—"

Or she could hold them in her lap as Daniel had. It was all one to Adele.

"—and sit down."

Miranda entered, looking about with her usual bright interest. She wore a pantsuit of brown tweed under a short cape which was either tan or gold, depending on the angle of the light. She wore her perfectly tailored garments with grace, as she had done all things of which Adele was aware.

Adele knew that Miranda and her mother, Madeline, continued to make their own clothing. She had never asked whether that was whim or a philosophy on the Dorsts' part. It certainly wasn't a matter of necessity anymore. Daniel was a notably openhanded man, and he wasn't stinting his fiancée and her mother.

"Thank you for receiving me, Adele," Miranda said. She placed the files on the floor and sat without touching the chair with her hands. "I realize that you're always busy."

Adele shrugged. "I'm transcribing logbooks," she said. "I will often find useful information in primary sources which isn't carried over into compilations. I need to skim the contents as I copy the logs, however, so that I have an idea of what is in each one. In a crisis, the real index is in my mind."

She smiled faintly. She saw no reason to pretend to Miranda that she wasn't good at her job.

Then she said, "What do you want from me?"

Miranda looked blank for a moment, then clapped her hands in delight. She began to laugh.

Adele's lips stiffened. *I was too abrupt.* Well, people who knew her didn't visit for small talk.

"Oh, I'm sorry," Miranda gasped through her gust of laughter. "Please, please—"

The laughter got the better of her again. She stood

and unexpectedly took Adele's hands. Her firm grip was a reminder of Miranda's comment that she played field hockey at school.

Miranda straightened and released Adele's hand. "I apologize," she said. "I realize that was very impolite, but I've..."

She backed into her chair again without taking her eyes from Adele's. "Adele," she said, "that's the first time I've laughed in, well, since Master Sand came to Bantry in a flurry. I've been trying to pretend everything was all right so that Daniel wouldn't worry about me and I'd make it worse."

She swallowed, then gave Adele a transfiguring smile. "And then I came here," Miranda said, "and you were *you*, and I didn't have to pretend anymore. About anything. It was such a relief."

Adele supposed she'd just been complimented. Others might not feel it was a compliment, but—she smiled as broadly as she ever did—that was rather the point of the statement, wasn't it?

"I can generally be expected to be me," Adele said. "But since that wasn't what you came expecting to learn, my question still stands."

"Is there anything I can do that will help Daniel with whatever he's preparing to do?" Miranda said primly. "I'm not asking where he's going or what he's doing or, or—" She was losing her careful calm. She paused, swallowed, and resumed, "Or anything I shouldn't know about. And I came to you, because you'll tell me the truth."

"Yes," said Adele as she considered the situation. "You have to remember that most of Daniel's previous experience with women—"

All his previous experience, so far as Adele had seen.

"—has been with the type who struggle every day in deciding which color earrings to wear. He knows that you're different, but when he's busy he is probably operating by rote rather than thinking."

Miranda smiled toward her clasped hands, then looked up at Adele. "At parties I've met some of Daniel's previous acquaintances," she said. Her voice was soft with good humor. "They're lovely, very lovely. Which explains how their genetic material survives in the human species."

"I've had similar thoughts," Adele said. Miranda was a *remarkably* levelheaded person. "As for your question, I don't know anything you can do for Daniel. Beyond what you're doubtless doing already, of course. However—"

There had been a hint of disappointment in Miranda's expression. It vanished at the qualifying "However—"

"—since you're here, there's something you can do for me. I'd like to analyze a situation I'm involved in in front of an intelligent neutral party. I don't care about your opinion."

"All right," said Miranda. Her expression was alert; but then, it usually was. "If it's all right for you to speak to me. Security, I mean."

"In my experience," Adele said, "'security' is a word people use to conceal information. I'm a librarian. I was trained to make information available to others."

She felt her lips quirk toward a smile. "If my superior decides she cannot accept the way I handle information," Adele said, "she can discharge me. Or call me out, I suppose. I've seen no indication to date that she feels any concern about my behavior."

Miranda smiled very broadly, but she did not speak.

"I expect to visit the Ribbon Stars in the near future," Adele said. She had emptied her glass. She reached for the pitcher, then thought of her guest and said, "Would you like some beer? Or, well, anything—I'm sure the pantry is well stocked."

The Shippers' and Merchants' Treasury rented the use of the second floor of Chatsworth Minor for meetings in a private setting. They stored various entertainment paraphernalia—like wine and liquor—in the cellar against need. While Captain Leary was on Cinnabar, he had the use of the Treasury's space, which he thought he was renting from Adele directly.

"Beer would be fine," Miranda said, "if there's—oh!"

Tovera stepped through the open doorway and handed Miranda a tall glass like Adele's.

Adele poured. "Ah," she said.

Adele had no reason to be embarrassed—her visitor was unexpected and would take what she was offered. Still. "I should warn you that this is bitter beer from Owsley County. From Chatsworth Major, in fact, though the estate is no longer in the Mundy family."

"Thank you," Miranda said. She sipped, then drank deeply. She didn't say how delightful the taste was, or how she had always liked bitter, or any one of a dozen other brightly false statements that Adele expected. She just drank.

"Don't blame Daniel too much, Miranda," Adele said, speaking what she had just thought. "You're easy to underestimate."

She refilled her own glass and said, "The oldest human settlement in the Ribbon Stars is Pantellaria, a First Tier colony. After the Hiatus—"

The thousand-year break in interstellar travel which resulted from the war fought with diverted asteroids by Earth against her original colonies. The wonder was not that the war had ended human star travel but rather that it hadn't ended the human species.

"—Pantellaria planted colonies of her own in the cluster. One of them, Corcyra, was found to have rich veins of copper."

Miranda nodded, but she didn't speak. She was carrying Adele's statement that her opinion wasn't desired to the point of not saying anything.

I've overreacted again, Adele thought. *I'm not a monster that people have to be afraid of!*

And as Adele thought that, she realized that it wasn't true, that she had killed scores, probably hundreds of people, mostly with head shots. She *was* a monster by the standards of most people.

"Pantellaria was forcibly annexed to the Alliance eighteen years ago," Adele said. "That set off the most recent period of war between ourselves and the Alliance, the one which just ended with the Treaty of Amiens. Pantellaria regained its independence with the treaty, but there were quite a few citizens, including most of those who had become leaders during Alliance rule, who weren't happy with the independent government."

Adele let her eyes travel around the room. She almost never *looked* at the library's familiar disorder, though she spent at least half her waking hours in the room. Because Miranda Dorst faced her expectantly, Adele noted that the grain of the bookcases matched that of the moldings of the walls; the wood for both came from Chatsworth Major, and the work had probably been done by the same woodwrights when the townhouse was first built.

The glass fronts were dusty. Everything in the room was dusty. The cleaning staff had been directed not to touch Adele's books and files, but something had to be done.

"Would you like me to clean while you're gone?" Miranda said.

She's reading my mind! But of course she wasn't doing anything of the sort. Miranda was following Adele's eyes and probably reading her expression, then coming to the logical conclusion from the evidence.

"I don't mean 'straighten up,' which would be horrible," Miranda said, "but to remove dust with a very small vacuum. A static broom would be worse than straightening, wouldn't it?"

"Yes," said Adele. "Careful cleaning would be helpful."

She remembered the cleaner—he had been male; after the fact Adele realized that he probably *never* listened to anything a female employer said—who had carefully interfiled chips from two separate files to bring them into order by date. It hadn't occurred to him that Adele was moving chips from one pile to the other after she had processed them.

"Adele, is something wrong?" Miranda said.

What must my face have looked like? Adele thought. She said, "Not now, thank you. I was talking about Pantellaria. A number of Pantellarians on the losing side politically fled to Corcyra, taking as much movable wealth as they could. There was unrest on Corcyra anyway—the colonists thought far more of the planetary income was going to the homeworld than was justified."

"Were they correct?" Miranda said. The discussion of cleaning seemed to have put them back on the more equal basis that Adele preferred. So long as the younger woman didn't decide that her own opinion should matter to Adele.

"Taxation—levies generally—were high while Corcyra was part of the Alliance," Adele said. "The newly independent Pantellarian government wasn't showing any sign of reducing them. On the other hand—"

She shrugged.

"—Corcyra might well have gained a reduction by measures short of war. And I don't know of a historical example of a colony or client state which didn't think it paid more than a fair proportion of its wealth in taxes or tribute."

Miranda nodded agreement but didn't speak aloud.

"With the exiles supporting independence, Corcyra revolted from Pantellaria last year," Adele said. As she had hoped, the situation on Corcyra was coming into clearer relief in her mind, just as the library had to her eyes. "And three months ago a Pantellarian expeditionary force landed to recover the planet."

"I've always understood that it's difficult to transport an army from one planet to another," Miranda said. She sat upright, her hands crossed in her lap, like an obedient student. "How many soldiers did Pantellaria send?"

Adele nodded crisply, a stern teacher acknowledging a student's intelligent question. She said, "The expeditionary force is of two thousand troops with light armor. They're accompanied by a naval force of six destroyers, whose crews could provide another thousand personnel if used as ground troops. And an uncertain number of Corcyrans are supporting the Pantellarians as a sort of militia."

Adele paused to smile thinly, then realized it would be a good time to take a drink. She half filled her glass—all that remained in the pitcher. Before she could put down the empty pitcher, Tovera took it and replaced it with a full one.

Two house servants hovered nervously down the hall, holding trays with more beer and glassware. When Adele glanced toward them, they snatched their eyes away.

"The more difficult question is the strength of the defenders," she said. "All settlement is along the River Cephisis. The mining region, the Southern Highlands, appears to be entirely hostile to Pantellarian control, though that doesn't mean all miners are ready to pick up a weapon and march down the river to attack the expeditionary force, which landed near the mouth. Still, there are about thirty thousand miners. Based on similar historical situations—"

Adele smiled grimly. If more politicians knew anything about history, there would be fewer wars. *And if wishes were horses, then beggars would ride.*

"—most of the miners would shoot at the expeditionary force if it attacked the Highlands. They're not trained, though, and they don't have a real leader."

She cleared her throat, then remembered to drink. "The Pantellarians landed at Harbinger in the Delta," she said. "The planetary capital was at Brotherhood at the base of the Highlands, the port of the mining region."

"But the exiles?" Miranda said, leaning forward slightly.

Adele nodded again. A *very* clever student. "Yes," she said. "The exiles include some former military officers, and they've brought with them enough professionals to provide a training cadre for the Corcyrans whom they've hired. They have money. One of the two factions calls itself the Corcyran Navy and defected with a Pantellarian destroyer. The exile factions make up only a few hundred troops each, but such evidence as I have suggests that those are likely to be the equal of a similar number of Pantellarian regulars."

"Are Pantellarian regulars any good?" Miranda asked.

"I'm sure some of them must be," Adele said. "I have no record of any, however."

Miranda's smile indicated that she understood not only what Adele had said, but also what she meant. *Daniel has a real prize here.*

"The largest body of trained troops on the rebel side," Adele said, "is the former Alliance garrison—about a battalion, five or six hundred men. It wasn't repatriated when Pantellaria became independent, because most of them were recruited on Corcyra. There's no data about their quality as troops, but they're trained and equipped. When Corcyra rebelled, they took the name the Corcyran Army. Records from other sources on Corcyra—"

Everything that Adele had gleaned from Mistress Sand's files.

"—continue to refer to them as the Garrison. They were the instrument of Alliance control until independence, and they're not well liked by anyone else on Corcyra. They're nonetheless the strongest single element of the forces opposing the Pantellarians."

Adele considered whether or not to explain what

she would be doing. *Why not?* she decided. What had held her back was what she considered decent reticence; others seemed to think she was secretive. *I don't hide my personal life; I just don't see a need to broadcast it to the world.*

"My particular interest is in a religious group, the Transformationists," Adele said. "There are about five hundred of them settled in the valley of a tributary of the Cephisis, fifty miles south of Brotherhood. This is deep into the mining region, but their community is devoted to harmony and mutual support. They don't appear to have a philosophy or ritual beyond that. I'm not one to come to for explanation of spiritual enlightenment."

"Do they have soldiers?" said Miranda, filling her glass again.

There's enough dust here to make anybody thirsty, Adele thought. She'd let things go too long because she didn't care.

"The Transformationists have a hundred personnel in the siege lines around Harbinger," Adele said, "but they appear to rotate their troops back and forth from the Pearl Valley frequently. I would judge they must have three hundred people capable of serving, though they may not be able to arm more than half that number."

She paused and considered. "The Transformationist troops don't show gender distinctions," she said. "The Garrison and the local volunteers—the miners, basically—have almost no women."

Miranda frowned. Though she hadn't asked, Adele explained. "That sort of prejudice is common on less advanced worlds and among the less educated classes of advanced ones. The classes which provide most miners and professional soldiers, that is."

Adele smiled faintly. "Tovera and I have not infrequently found it an advantage," she said. "But of course, I never expected to like reality."

"Yes," said Miranda. "I understand that." Her expression softened and she added, "Though reality for me has improved a great deal since I met Daniel."

Adele nodded. She decided not to say that this would change very quickly if Daniel should die violently, which was a probable result of the way he lived his life.

And then she smiled: *Miranda knows that.* Her brother had been vaporized in a space battle which could as easily have claimed Daniel instead—or Daniel also. Miranda was focused on her present life, which was very good.

As is mine, but somehow I can't accept that.

"Yes," Adele said aloud. "I should learn from you."

She cleared her throat and said, "I will be involved with the Transformationists. Helping them, I suppose, because my principal has business in Pearl Valley, and they'll expect him to sing for his supper, so to speak. There's nothing more of importance which I can think to tell you, though I should know more this afternoon, after I speak with a man who just arrived from Corcyra. If anything changes, I will tell you."

Miranda rose to her feet in a single, smooth motion. "Thank you, Adele," she said. "I feel better now."

Adele grimaced. "I can't imagine why," she said. "I don't even know what help I'll be providing to the cultists—"

She hadn't meant to use the word, but it was adequately descriptive for the present purpose.

"—since they probably don't know themselves. People rarely do, I've found, though they believe they do."

Adele realized that she was describing the situation as though she would be assisting Daniel to help Rikard Cleveland. A simple way to carry out her own mission for Deirdre would be to arrange that Arnaud captured Corcyra without Cinnabar assistance.

Would that be treason? And to whom?

Adele smiled sadly. For the first time, she understood the way her parents had made the decisions which had led to their heads being displayed on Speaker's Rock.

"Adele?" Miranda said. "If Daniel were fishing with no communicator along, how would you contact him in an emergency?"

Adele pursed her lips. It wasn't a question she had expected, but she didn't really care what information people wanted from her. It was her job to provide information, period.

"Fishing on the Bantry estate?" she clarified. Miranda nodded agreement.

"I would use satellite imagery to track his boat," Adele said. "If I were at Bantry myself, I would borrow an aircar to reach him. Tovera can drive, well enough."

"I learned to drive an aircar," Miranda said. "But I'd have to call you to access the satellites. If the situation arose again, that is."

"Yes," Adele said. "Of course."

Tovera led the girl downstairs again to the front door. Adele went back to her logbooks.

I hope Daniel knows what he has there, Adele thought. *I certainly do.*

✧   ✧   ✧

Daniel had never thought about the appearance of the Sands' townhouse: it wasn't the sort of question that interested him. If someone had asked him what he expected Cleveland House would look like, he would have guessed it was something like Chatsworth Minor or The Almoner, the Leary townhouse in Xenos.

"This is," he murmured to Adele as they waited for a servant to take them to Rikard Cleveland, "unexpected."

"Yes," said Adele. From her curt tone, her opinion was as negative as Daniel's own.

"It looks like a bloody whorehouse," Hogg said, voicing much the same thought, though without the disapproval. "A bloody *fancy* whorehouse."

The Sand residence stood in a row of houses much like Chatsworth Minor in age though of relatively modest construction. Two had been knocked together to create Cleveland House, as it now was called. The new common facade lighted the three-story entrance hall with a large, east-facing circular window.

Adele glanced up at the window and said, "That's called an oriel window. Master Cleveland had a sense of humor."

She looked around at the twisted pillars of colored marble and panels with gold designs inlaid on panels of polished red stone. The frieze just below the coffered ceiling was made of iridescent tiles in primary colors and gold.

"A pity," Adele added in a voice dry enough to suck moisture from desert air, "that he didn't have a sense of taste as well."

"Master Rikard will see you now in the main hall, sir and lady," said the servant who had gone into the interior of the house. The doorman remained with them in the hall. "Will your servants...?"

"They'll wait here," Daniel decided. The stone benches built against the front wall didn't look particularly comfortable, but Hogg was used to sitting in a hunting blind during winter storms. Daniel understood very little of Tovera, but he was confident that personal comfort wasn't one of her priorities, either.

"A glass of cider wouldn't come amiss," said Hogg. He was deliberately prodding the pansy servants of this knocking shop.

Which meant he hadn't taken a good look at these servants: fit young men who spoke with cultured accents. They weren't the sort of staff you would expect in a house like this, but they *were* the sort that people like Mistress Sand had around them. Hogg's rural upbringing had played him false.

Before Daniel decided how to respond, Tovera said in a tone of amused disdain, "Take a look at them, Hogg."

Hogg did. He then spread his hands on top of his thighs, palms down. "Sorry, buddy," he said to the nearer servant, the doorman.

"I'm sure there's cider in the cellar, Captain Leary," said the other man.

"I guess I've drunk enough this morning already," Hogg said, "and I haven't had a drop." He looked at Daniel and said, "Sorry, master. Won't happen again."

The guide bowed Daniel and Adele into a large hall. He was smiling. Daniel paused, looked at the man more closely, and said, "If your name is Hutton, I was in the Academy with your brother."

"That would be my cousin Julius, Captain Leary,"

the servant said. "When he's next in Xenos, I'll tell him I've met you. He'll be envious."

A slender man stood in front of a vast green fireplace. He walked forward to meet them, extending his right hand. If the entrance hall had been gaudy, this room was that in spades. It too was a full three stories high.

The whole ceiling was a skylight of stained glass. The pilasters which supported it were topped by gargoyles rather than capitals, and the fluted shafts had been gilded. Paintings of men in armor and women in gauzy dresses marched around the walls' upper range, while mural tiles of a hunting scene set in a forest covered the band at floor level.

The floor level was mirrored. Daniel found the effect disconcerting because it multiplied every movement.

"Captain Leary," said the young man, shaking Daniel's hand. He bowed to Adele and said, "Lady Mundy. I'm Rikard Cleveland, and I'm honored to speak with you."

Cleveland nodded toward the huge fireplace. "I'm told," he said, "that you could roast a whole ox on that hearth."

If this whelp thinks he's going to impress a Leary with that . . . Aloud Daniel said, "On Bantry we were more given to fish fries. But each to his own taste, of course."

"I understand perfectly," Cleveland said. "This hearth, and the way he rebuilt Mother's family home generally, sums up an aspect of my father's character. I aped his flamboyance, his self-importance, and his need to be seen to be important by other people. Whatever you've heard about my behavior before I left for Corcyra is quite true, or at any rate the truth is just as bad."

"I see," Daniel said. His opinion of Cleveland's character had just risen—and also his opinion of Cleveland's intelligence. *If he's chosen this absurd room to demonstrate his present self-awareness, then there may be more to the Corcyra business than I've assumed*.

"I was spared Father's taste for malachite and gilt," Cleveland added, smiling broadly. He nodded again toward the fireplace of dark green stone with black markings. "Which is a small blessing, I realize, in comparison with the rest."

Daniel laughed. "Not so very small, *I* think," he said. He gestured the nearest of the room's several square tables; they were of a size for cards.

"Are the chairs around those tables comfortable?" he asked. "If they are, I'll pick one that doesn't require me to look at the fireplace."

Cleveland smiled again and waved them to the table. When his visitors took places on opposite sides, he settled into the chair between them with his back to the door.

"I felt alone my whole life," Cleveland said. "My father had no use for me. I mean literally: I was of no use in advancing his ambitions, so he ignored my existence. Mother tried. I think she would have tried harder if I hadn't determinedly driven her away because I wanted to be a great *man* like my father. And because I was such a nasty little prick, I didn't have any friends—which I didn't realize, because I was surrounded by spongers."

Adele had taken out her data unit. Cleveland glanced

at her, but he didn't comment or show concern. He probably knew something of Adele, but even so, her behavior often disconcerted people who expected her to pay obvious attention to them while they were speaking.

"Now, I'm not offering this as an excuse for my behavior," Cleveland said. "Which of course it isn't. But I want you both to understand why the fellowship I found within the Transformationist community had such a powerful effect on me. I won't be surprised if you continue to think of me as daft, but do accept that I'm quite sincere in my daftness."

Daniel glanced at Adele. Her control wands moved in subtle fashions, adjusting the information which danced above her personal data unit like dustmotes in colored sunlight. The holograms coalesced only at the angle of the user's eyes.

She was letting Daniel take the lead in the discussion, though if Cleveland thought Adele wasn't listening to him, he was badly mistaken. It was quite possible that she was reading the conversation as a text crawl on her display, of course. Daniel knew his friend preferred to observe reality through an interface.

"Master Cleveland," Daniel said, leaning forward, "I don't have any problem with what other people believe, so long as they don't expect their beliefs to affect my behavior. I gather you believe there's a treasure on Corcyra. My colleague and I have come here to learn why you believe that."

"The Upper Cephisis River Valley is a mining region," said Cleveland. He didn't appear to be put out by Daniel pressing him. "At the time Pantellaria and its colonies joined the Alliance—"

He paused and smiled. Daniel smiled back.

"—the Transformationist Assembly, which is legally a corporation, refiled its land claim under Alliance law. This was simply a precaution."

And a very wise one, Daniel thought. The Transformationists might be religious loonies, but they were neither stupid nor politically naive.

"Among the information deposited along with the claim was a certified assay of Pearl Valley showing that neither copper nor any other ore is present in significant amounts. This isn't required for a claim, of course, but I presume it was done to turn away Alliance bureaucrats who might assume that we—that the Assembly of the day—was sitting on vast mineral wealth."

"That sort of thing has been known to happen," Daniel said. *And not only when the new overlords came from Pleasaunce.* Greedy administrators were a reality of imperial rule, and the Republic of Cinnabar was as surely an empire as the Alliance was.

"I looked at the file," Cleveland said. "As well as the assays, it contained a microwave scan of the subsurface rocks. While I was still on Cinnabar, I'd been employed by an engineering firm owned by a friend of my mother."

He smiled ruefully. "Not employed very long, of course," he said, "but I picked up some rudiments. There was an object thirty feet down in the rock, small—no larger than a man's head—but of a very irregular shape. The scan proceeded down the full length of the valley, which allowed the computer to create three-dimensional models. The software couldn't model this, however."

Adele didn't look up, but her wands had paused. Knowing her habits, Daniel suspected she had a real-time image of Cleveland's face inset on her holographic display, just as she did while talking with others on the bridge of a starship.

"All right," said Daniel. "You've found an anomaly in the ground. Why do you believe it's a treasure?"

Cleveland nodded, smiling again. He'd gained his first point.

"Do you know anything about the settlement of Corcyra?" he asked.

"I know a little," Daniel said. And by now Adele probably knew quite a lot, but he didn't say that aloud. "It was settled from Pantellaria about five hundred years ago, initially as a farming colony. The copper deposits were discovered shortly thereafter. Corcyra became a major mining center—as it remains today."

"That's the official story," Cleveland said, nodding.

"It's the true story," Daniel said, frowning. "The records of the discovery, the minutes of the Council of Pantellaria approving the colony, the names of all thirty-seven hundred colonists in the initial migration—they all exist. I've seen them, and I believe my colleague can show them to you right now if you're in doubt."

"I could," said Adele without looking up. "But I suspect Master Cleveland is referring to the legend that there was a Pre-Hiatus settlement on Corcyra before the Pantellarians arrived."

"Yes, Lady Mundy," Cleveland said, turning his eyes toward Adele for the first time. "Though not Pre-Hiatus—I don't know of any evidence supporting that belief. But I believe I've found evidence that Corcyra was settled from Bay about eight hundred years ago, long before Pantellaria discovered the planet and sent its colony."

Adele's wands danced like the surface of a pond in a rainstorm. She said, "Bay settled Ischia in the Ribbon Stars eight hundred years ago. That was the only colony ship which Bay sent out. Before end of the century, Bay had collapsed into civil war from which its civilization never recovered. The factions were using fusion bombs, and they stopped fighting simply because the infrastructure could no longer support weapons more advanced than spear throwers."

"The colony ship from Bay, the *Coalsack 5747*, was under Captain Pearl," Cleveland said. "That's correct, isn't it?"

"Yes," Adele said. "The only further data I have on the venture is that there were some thirteen thousand settlers."

"Cleveland," said Daniel. He hoped he kept the sudden concern out of his voice. "Did you get this idea of a treasure because the captain's name is the same as that of the valley your church is set up in?"

If the boy had done something so silly, the whole business was absurd—and he was probably too deluded to listen to reason. Much as Daniel would like to help the Sands—

"No, Captain Leary," Cleveland said with a smile of calm amusement. He was, after all, Daniel's senior by a year or two. "The coincidence of names caused me to look into Ischian history, however. There was a surprising amount of information available on Corcyra, since the planets are neighbors and Ischia was a major trading partner of Corcyra and of Pantellaria as well."

"You have the advantage of me there," Daniel said.

He felt embarrassed, even though he hadn't actually said anything insulting about Cleveland's intelligence or common sense. "I know nothing of the other stars in the Ribbon Cluster, save Pantellaria."

"Captain Pearl landed on Ischia as planned and disembarked the colonists," Cleveland said. "He and the crew were to be colonists also, in the normal fashion of colony ships. Ordinarily the ship, the *Coalsack 5747*, would have been cannibalized for the colony's use, but there were two factions within the colonists. Not long after landing on Ischia, Captain Pearl lifted off again with most of the crew and about a thousand of the original colonists. The *Coalsack 5747* was never heard of again."

"Bloody hell," said Daniel. He shook his head, feeling a little queasy at the implications of what Cleveland had said. "I'm not surprised the ship disappeared. It may not have made it into orbit after liftoff. Colony ships are huge, and they're not built for repeated liftoffs and landings."

"Was the division among the colonists due to the religious arguments which led to the civil war that broke out on Bay a generation later?" Adele said. For politeness' sake, she looked at Cleveland this time as she spoke.

"I don't know, Lady Mundy," Cleveland said. "My source here is an Ischian history which I suspect was intended as a school text. What it says is that Captain Pearl and his confederates stole a great treasure."

"Could that not have been the ship itself?" Adele said. "The cargo had largely been landed when Pearl lifted off again, but the loss of the ship must have been a great handicap to the new colony."

"The *Coalsack* may have been the treasure, certainly," Cleveland agreed. "Nothing else appearing, I might assume that it was. But there's the buried anomaly in the Pearl Valley."

"The fact that the ship lifted from Ischia doesn't prove that it landed on Corcyra," Daniel said, but his tone was mild. He was becoming intrigued, more or less despite himself. "As I say, it may well have broken up on Ischia."

"Not in sight of the ground," Cleveland said. "I'm sure from the tone of the history that it would have been recorded as the just retribution of Providence on the traitors."

Daniel nodded in understanding. Adele raised her eyes again and said, "I would like to see this history, if I may."

"The original is waiting at the door with Gillfin," Cleveland said. He was gaining assurance as the interview went on. "Your reputation preceded you, Lady Mundy. I made a copy, but you may be able to learn things from the original which have escaped me."

It struck Daniel that the boy must have inherited his mother's intelligence as well as her strong jaw and broad forehead. His willowy height, however, owed nothing to Mistress Sand's short, blocky frame.

"What decided me to return to Cinnabar and attempt to mount an expedition," Cleveland said, "was the port computer at the capital, Brotherhood. It's the main starport, where the river broadens and forms a pool at the base of the foothills."

"Yes," said Daniel, nodding cautiously.

"The computer comes from a starship," Cleveland said. "I know, that's common: a computer which can calculate navigation in the Matrix has more capacity than any use in normal space requires."

"Yes," said Daniel. "No matter how old it is."

"This computer—it's in the Manor, Brotherhood's government building," Cleveland went on. "This computer was manufactured on Bay. And nothing so sophisticated has been manufactured on Bay for the past seven hundred years."

Adele's wands were in quivering motion. "I'll want to see the computer," she said to her display. "Will that be possible?"

"I don't think it would be difficult if you were in Brotherhood," Cleveland said. "It certainly wasn't for me."

He cleared his throat and added, sounding diffident again, "May I ask a question, please? Does your question mean that you're thinking of investing in the expedition?"

"You've convinced me to provide the ship and crew for the expedition at my own expense," Daniel said. He assumed that was what Adele intended, but it didn't matter. She had made him lead, so she would back him whatever her personal opinion. "I'll talk to Mistress Sand. I expect that she can outfit the vessel from her own resources, so there's no need of outside investors. We'll need a cargo, you see, and she's well-placed to provide it."

He smiled at Cleveland and rose to his feet. "You've found the, well—the treasure, we'll call it for now. For that you'll keep a third. Your mother will get a third. And I will get the remaining third. Can we shake on a partnership on those terms?"

He offered his hand.

Cleveland stood, looking stunned. "Captain Leary," he said. "This is very fair, more than fair. But I've already discussed arrangements with Captain Sorley of the freighter *Madison Merchant.* He has been willing to carry me if I indemnified him against loss in a war zone. That's why I asked Mother for financial help."

"I don't know Captain Sorley," Daniel said, his mind racing through possibilities. "Have you signed a contract yet?"

"Based on his record," Adele said, still seated and scrolling through data, "Captain Sorley has never kept a contract in his life. Of course I have only a few of his aliases. It could be that under other names he's more honest."

"What?" said Cleveland. He slowly extended his arm, though he continued to stare at Adele.

Daniel grasped his hand and shook it firmly. "There, partner," he said. "I'll keep you informed of developments. I don't think it will be long before we can lift from here and get to work."

Adele rose to her feet and slipped her data unit into its pocket.

"Yes," she said. "And Master Cleveland? I strongly advise you not to discuss the matter further with Captain Sorley. He is a liar, and a thief, and very probably a murderer. You would soil yourself by spitting in his face. Do I make myself clear?"

"Ah," Cleveland said, "Lady Mundy, we Transformationists attempt to find good in every human being."

Adele stepped briskly toward the door. "I told you that Sorley was *probably* a murderer," she said over her shoulder. "That benefit of the doubt was all the good I could find regarding the man."

Daniel, still smiling, nodded to Cleveland. He followed Adele out.

CHAPTER 6

Bergen and Associates Shipyard, Cinnabar

A shipyard crew was replacing the *Kiesche*'s High Drive nacelles under Mon's direction. A wrench made the hull ring with a burst of impacts. Adele supposed she should think of Mon as manager instead of lieutenant as she continued to do.

She smiled mentally. For all that Mon's present was one of plump success, she suspected that he still considered an RCN officer to be of higher rank than a wealthy businessman.

Another team from the yard was replacing the original purging system of the *Kiesche*'s plasma cannon with a much higher capacity unit salvaged from a four-inch gun. Sun, Daniel's longtime gunner, was on the bridge to oversee the work. The workmen didn't appear to need much oversight, and Sun, to his credit, wasn't interfering.

The third group of workmen wore coveralls without markings and were upgrading the *Kiesche*'s sensor and commo suites. There were two women on the bridge and three men out on the hull. They came from

Mistress Sand's organization; Adele hadn't bothered
asking what their cover identities were.

As expected, they didn't need any more help than
those working on the plasma cannon did. Adele was,
nonetheless, present. Like Sun, she was keeping her
mouth shut.

Because the bridge was crowded by men who had
removed an access plate to repipe the purging system—it
squirted liquid nitrogen into the cannon between shots,
cooling the bore—and by the women who were working on the command console, Adele was at one of the
workstations at the rear bulkhead.

Sun stood at the other, but he wasn't watching the
flat-plate display. He turned to Adele and said, "Do
you know what they're doing to your rig on the hull,
mistress?"

"Not really," said Adele, looking up to the man
standing beside her. "As much as they can without it
being externally obvious, I suppose. I'm not a hardware
expert, as you know."

She didn't suggest that he talk to the crew doing
the work, because she knew they wouldn't tell him
anything. She wasn't sure they would tell *her* anything
beyond "I'm afraid you'll have to ask Mistress Sand,
your ladyship."

Sun, a close-cropped man in his early thirties, had
the skill and experience to be gunner on a battleship.
His formal rank on the *Princess Cecile* was gunner's
mate because corvettes like the *Sissie* had no slot for
the exalted rank of gunner. As for tramp freighters
like the *Kiesche*, in the rare instance when they had
to fight it out with a pirate, the captain would probably control the gun.

"Did Six ask you to look over this installation, Sun?" Adele asked.

"No, ma'am, he didn't," Sun said with an unexpected look of concern. "I heard from a buddy here in yard that Six, well, 'Captain Leary,' he said, was fitting out a ship and they was fitting a bigger gun."

He gestured to the bow. "Which they're not, you know, but for lots of things a fifty-millimeter is better than a four-inch if it cycles fast enough. Which it does with this rig. Nobody's going to be shooting missiles at a tramp like this, right?"

"I don't imagine they will," Adele said, answering out of politeness. She had no more knowledge—or concern—about the question than she did on what the must-have fashion accessory for the season's debutantes was.

If a missile, tons of metal moving at a measurable fraction of light speed, squarely struck the *Kiesche* or even a battleship, everybody aboard would be vaporized. There was nothing a signals officer could do to prevent that from happening, so Adele didn't think about the possibility. If it happened, she would be beyond all care.

"Well, anyway, I dropped by the yard to watch," Sun said. He frowned and then blurted, "Ma'am, you don't think Six plans to leave me behind, do you? Because, well, he didn't call me before he started this."

He gestured again.

"I don't know what Six intends for crew," Adele said carefully, because she really didn't know. "This business—"

She turned up her right hand.

"—the antennas and the rest of it, they were decided

less than twenty-four hours ago. That I can tell you of my own knowledge."

Sun sighed with obvious relief. "Well, maybe he just didn't have time," he said. "Though, ma'am? When you see him, you'll put in a good word for me, won't you? I won't let you down, I swear it!"

"You never have in the past, Sun," Adele said truthfully. She didn't answer the precise question, however. She would no more interfere with Daniel's decisions on personnel than she would try to plot a course through the Matrix.

"Ah, Sun?" she said, since the gunner clearly wanted to talk. "A ship like this doesn't carry a dedicated gunner, of course. I would think that even in peacetime you could find a place with much higher status."

"Higher than sailing with Six, ma'am?" Sun said. "That's a joke! Why, I'll bet there's not a gunner on a battleship, senior warrant officer or not, who's earned a quarter as much as I've made from prize money sailing on the *Sissie*!"

He grinned ruefully and said, "Mind, it didn't stick to my fingers very well, but that'd be true of battleship pay, too, for me at least. And status, that's not something you buy with florins anyway. Ma'am, I'm a Sissie, and there's not an RCN bar on Cinnabar where that won't buy me free drinks for as long as I can lift my arm to pour them down."

One of the workmen installing the purging system turned. He was a grizzled, heavy-set man with an artificial left foot.

"Amen to that, spacer!" he said, then went back to tightening a clamp.

Adele remembered that the fellow's name was

Hodson, a Tech 2 who'd lost his foot when a broken line swung a Stellite thruster nozzle wide as it was being replaced. That was on Sexburga, years before.

I wasn't thinking of them as people, Adele realized. She had been talking to Sun as though the others on the bridge were images on a display.

Sun cleared his throat. Very possibly to turn the subject away from a disturbing one to which only Daniel could give an answer, he said, "What's that you're looking at, ma'am? She's not the *Kiesche*, is she?"

Adele glanced at the flat-plate display. She'd been accessing the main console through her personal data unit, but the bulkhead display was echoing the data she had called up. "No," she said. She switched to an external viewpoint—a harbor-control camera. "This is the *Madison Merchant* in Portinga Harbor. An acquaintance of mine was thinking of sailing on it. I decided to see what sort of ship it was while I'm waiting here."

"You can read the diagnostics board of a ship in Portinga Harbor?" Sun said in amazement.

"Yes," said Adele. She didn't add, "You're seeing the data, so obviously I can do that." Sun was a good man and a shipmate, and he was quite skilled in his own specialty.

Sun frowned at the realtime image of the ship. "Ma'am, could you flip back to the diagnostics?" he said.

"Yes," said Adele, doing so with a minute twitch of the wand in her left hand. "Is something wrong?"

"Ma'am, with a tramp freighter it'd be a miracle if there wasn't something wrong," said the gunner. "Right here, though..."

He looked at Adele with an expression of great

concern. "Ma'am," he said, "I don't know how good a friend this guy is. But if you care about him, I'd say you ought to tell him not to ship aboard this *Madison Merchant*. There's a lot of things about a ship that you've got to eyeball. Computers won't tell you how much metal's left on the thruster nozzles or the wear on the High Drive motors. But look at the pumps here!"

Adele followed Sun's pointing finger. "It appears to say fifteen percent flow," she said. "But the ship is sitting in harbor, so it's just keeping the reaction mass tanks topped off, isn't it? Doesn't most of the water go straight back into the harbor?"

"Right, right," said Sun, "that's the flow. But you're not looking at the pump output up here, see?"

"A moment, please," Adele said crisply. Even with Sun pointing again, it took her a moment; the data captions weren't meaningful to her. "This one?" She highlighted a line. "Eighty-three percent?"

"That's it," said Sun. "Anything over eighty percent is in the red zone, and they're only managing fifteen percent flow from that output. Ma'am, it's not just that it's crap performance. It means that the pump's failing. Pretty quick it's going to quit dead, and where are you then if you're landing the sorts of places that a ship like this one lands?"

The little gunner drew himself up with a look of moral outrage, like a priest objecting to the sinfulness of the times. "That was my specialty before I struck for gunner, you know, ma'am?" he said. "Tech 2, Fluid Systems Specialty."

"I did not know," Adele said, switching back to the external view of the freighter. "I assure you, I will inform my friend in the strongest possible terms that he should not travel aboard the *Madison Merchant*."

As indeed I have already done, Adele thought as she closed the connection.

Woetjans tilted one of the bank of windows on the outer wall of the fifth-floor office so that she could see the shipyard's pool without looking through glass. Grimy glass, Daniel noticed. He suspected that Mon spent as little time as possible in this office even when he hadn't lent it to Daniel and his bosun to put together a crew list.

"For riggers, I'll just see who hasn't shipped out since the *Sissie* landed," Woetjans said, rubbing her big knuckles together. She was six feet six inches tall, rangy, and stronger than any man of her size whom Daniel had met. "We'll have our pick."

Woetjans was also as ugly as a weathered fencepost. She and the riggers which she as bosun commanded worked in suits stiffened with fiberglass armor—hard suits—to protect them from the punctures otherwise certain when they were moving quickly among the raw edges and broken wires of a starship's rigging.

Rigging suits were a better alternative than watching your air supply vanish into the Matrix, but on the inside they pinched and rubbed the wearer's every projecting body part from the forehead to the toes. Woetjans' skin was worn into calluses on cheeks, knuckles and doubtless many of the places which her clothes covered. While that didn't greatly detract from the bosun's appearance, it certainly didn't help.

"I'm only offering standard wages, you know," Daniel said doubtfully. Spacers weren't in desperately short supply as they had been for decades while the fleets of Cinnabar and the Alliance battled across the length and breadth of the human universe. Still, every member of the *Sissie's* crew was exceptionally skilled. They wouldn't have any difficulty finding berths.

"And I don't want you telling them that they'll have shares in a treasure," he added. Though they would, of course, *if* there were a treasure. "Cleveland believes the treasure exists and maybe his mother does, mothers being as they are, but *I* don't. I'm going to babysit the boy as a favor to a friend. And a friend of Adele's. Lady Mundy's."

"I guess any of those things'd be reason enough," Woetjans said, returning to the console where Daniel sat. "A friend of yours or the mistress, I mean. And I don't care what you say—if the people who've sailed with you in the past hear that you're going to look for a treasure, they'll be sure they're going to find one. No matter *how* you warn them."

Daniel sucked in his lips and nodded agreement. "I know," he said, "but they're wrong. Well, they're all adults."

He grinned. "As much as I am, anyway. And I guess telling the Sissies that we're going into a war zone and it'll be dangerous wouldn't put any of them off, either."

He felt his muscles tighten. "By Hell and all its demons, we've been through some hard places together," he said. "I'll tell the *world* we have!"

And that was the key: been through. The surviving Sissies believed that because of what they'd survived in the past, they didn't need to fear anything that might happen in the future. That was nonsense; logically they knew how many of their former shipmates had been killed or maimed during the years they had sailed under Daniel Leary—under Six, his communications identifier.

But superstition has a bigger part than logic in the way spacers view their world; and Daniel, a spacer to the marrow of his bones, felt the same childish confidence.

"That leaves us the ship side," Daniel said. He brought up that portion of the crew list of the *Princess Cecile* at the moment she landed on Cinnabar after the recent operations in the Macotta Region.

Daniel had wondered whether the Bergen and Associates office would have a decent computer. In fact it had a console salvaged from the *Milton*, similar to the one on the *Kiesche's* bridge. As he rode up the elevator to this top floor, he had noticed the bracing Mon had added to the building. When he saw the massive console, he understood why.

The bosun as chief of rig was responsible for all the personnel whose duties were on the exterior of the hull during operations. Woetjans knew the riggers personally, their strengths and weaknesses.

The ship's internal workings were the province of technicians under the chief engineer, the chief of ship. The captain and bosun knew the technicians by sight, but they didn't have the intimate knowledge of them that Pasternak had. He had been chief engineer on the *Milton* and since then on the *Princess Cecile*, though a corvette was far smaller than the normal berth of so senior an engineer.

"Can Pasternak help us?" Woetjans said. "I figure we only need two, three techs on a ship this size, right?"

"I intend to sign on four," Daniel said firmly. Every

spacer on the ship side was one fewer under Woetjans. "And any Academy graduate will be able to turn a hand to the fusion bottle. We'll have several officers besides me."

He stretched at the console. "I'm hoping to get a response from Pasternak today with his recommendations," he said. "To tell the truth, I was hoping to hear something yesterday, but I don't know how well Pasternak keeps up with message traffic when he's relaxing at home. I gather he's something of a celebrity in Wassail County, where he comes from."

"Master?" somebody bawled in the yard outside.

Daniel and Woetjans both went to the windows and looked out, moving faster than a civilian would have believed possible. Hogg stood on the drive which circled the pool. He hadn't bothered to look for a loud hailer, let alone a wired link to the office console, but he'd cupped his hands into a megaphone.

"Pasternak's here," Hogg bellowed. "I sent him up to you."

"Right!" Daniel said. He waved in case Hogg couldn't understand the reply, since he wasn't sure his lungs were as good as those of his servant.

To Woetjans he added, "Well, I guess that explains why I haven't heard from the Chief sooner."

She laughed. "In Wassail County, he probably had to take an ox cart to the nearest tram station," she said.

Daniel smiled as the elevator out in the hallway whined to a halt. That was an exaggeration, but Wassail County certainly wasn't known as a technological hub.

"Good to see you, Chief," Daniel called to the spare, slightly stooped man of sixty who got off the elevator. His hairline was moving back. "But you didn't have to come here, you know. I just needed recommendations for the Power Room crew of a tramp."

"Your message came, and I got here as quick as I could make it," Pasternak said. The engineer looked more agitated than Daniel had seen him since the time they were outside the ship and under small-arms fire. "I left my duffel bag down with Shorty Graves at the gate. I knew him since he was a wiper. Before his lost his legs, I mean."

"Chief," said Daniel, "all I expect from you is recommendations. This isn't the *Sissie*, it's a tramp that'll be crammed to the gills with a crew of twenty. And, ah—we're heading for a mining world where there's a war going on. On the ground, I mean, where we'll be."

"Well, I've got a recommendation," Pasternak said, suddenly forceful. "Me. And don't tell me it's just a small plant. They can be trickier than a battleship installation. I've run both and I know!"

He paused to lick his lips. While Daniel was still deciding how to reply, Pasternak resumed, "If you're short of crew, I can run the plant myself. That's all a tramp usually has, and there's nobody you'll find who'll do as good a job as me."

"I know that, Chief," Daniel said. "I plan to assign four to the Power Room."

"Right, that's plenty," Pasternak said, nodding. He looked at the bosun and said, "And Woetjans? I'll make sure that a couple of them have rigging experience so they can double in brass if they have to. You're signing Sun, right? I'd want him even if you didn't need a gunner."

"I've talked to Sun, yes," Daniel said. "Ah—Chief? I'm surprised that you're so determined to ship on a voyage which I expect to be both unpleasant and unprofitable."

"Then you'll have me?" Pasternak said with a sigh of relief. "Thank the blessed heavens!"

Daniel smoothed what would otherwise have become a frown. He most certainly had *not* given the Chief a slot...though he knew he was going to.

"Sir, you don't know what it's like at home," Pasternak said. "My wife, she figures she's the Squire's wife now, so she wants me to stay home and play the Squire, you know? And I'm not the bloody Squire, I'm the third son of the mechanic on the Squire's estate. And Emily can't see that. She thinks it's enough to own the estate myself now, which I do, and have more money than anybody else in Wassail County. Which I do, too, not that that's saying much."

He took a deep breath and then another. Daniel had seen Pasternak running repair operations on ships that had been battered by plasma bolts or, in the case of the *Milton*, had lost fifty feet of hull to a missile. The Chief had been fiercely decisive, and he hadn't shown either worry or relief.

"I can't say, 'I want to ship out,' not and not have Emily and the boys shouting so loud you could hear them in Xenos," Pasternak said. "But I tell them, 'Six needs me,' and there's not a word from any of them. The Squire is off to do his duty, you see. That's what a gentleman does."

He smiled raggedly. "Well, that's what Ivan Pasternak does, too," he said. "Only I'm no bloody gentleman."

Daniel stepped forward and clasped hands with the engineer. "You'll do for me, Chief," he said. "Round up the rest of your team and report back here soonest.

I'll want your report on the plant, not that I don't trust Mon's people."

Pasternak strode back to the elevator. The smile on his face could have lighted a stadium. The door closed behind him, and the cage started down.

Daniel grimaced. He turned to Woetjans and said, "Look, I know that for a job like this, you'd expect a younger engineer who didn't mind mixing it up if things got rough. But demons take me if I could turn down the Chief when he begged me!"

Woetjans shrugged. "It'll be a cold day in hell that you hear me say that my riggers need help from the ship side in a dustup," she said. "And so far as that goes, I figure Pasternak'll bring Evans, and he's worth two in a fight anyway."

She grinned. It made her look even uglier than usual. "That's mainly because you can't hurt Evans by hitting him in the head," Woetjans said. "But with you and Mistress Mundy aboard, nobody else needs to think, right?"

Daniel seated himself again. "I don't know that I'd go that far," he said, "but so long as you're satisfied I suppose it's all right."

"Six," said Woetjans. "I've never served with a better engineer than the Chief there. But as for what makes me satisfied—you making the decisions satisfies me. It's sure worked so far."

CHAPTER 7

Bergen and Associates Shipyard, Cinnabar

"Hey, Six," called Sun from the hallway. "This one says Cory sent her. I've never seen her before, though."

Daniel had been vaguely aware of the elevator stopping on the other side of the closed office door, but he was lost in details of the Pantellarian navy since independence on the command console. Adele had supplied up-to-date information. Daniel didn't know whether the data came from Navy House files or somewhere else, and he wasn't going to ask.

"Send her in," Daniel called as he rose from the console's seat. It was time for a break and a stretch anyway. Cory was negotiating for rations for the voyage, but that shouldn't have required Daniel's input until there was a contract to sign.

The young woman who entered wore RCN utilities without insignia. She was as much a stranger to Daniel as she had been to Sun, who was acting as doorman because he had both the rank and the intelligence for the job.

She braced to attention and saluted. "Sir!" she

104

said. "I'm Lucinda Hale! And Lieutenant Cory didn't direct me to apply, he just said that there might be a crew slot open!"

Hale's salute was clumsy, although she had obviously tried hard. Perversely, that made a better impression on Daniel than drill-team execution would have. He'd always been terrible at Drill and Ceremony himself.

"Close the door and sit down, Hale," he said. Moments before, he'd expected that the visitor would be leaving as quickly as she had arrived, but he was intrigued with her comment about Cory; and Daniel needed a break; and anyway, she was an attractive young woman. "Now, explain what you mean about Cory."

"Sir, Lieutenant Cory told me that the *Kiesche* was already oversupplied with officers, but that you might have a crew position open," Hale said. She reached forward, holding a data chip. "This is my file, sir. Cory and I were in the same class at the Academy, but I don't mean we were close. We knew one another."

Daniel took the chip, but he was frowning and didn't insert it into the console yet. "You heard the *Kiesche* was fitting out and contacted Cory?" he asked.

"No, *sir*," she said. "Cory called me out of the blue. I'd never heard of the *Kiesche*, and I don't think I've seen Cory twice since we graduated."

"I see," said Daniel, which he certainly did not. Well, he could check with Cory later, if he needed to. He called up the chip's data and added, "You've passed your lieutenant's boards."

"Yes, sir," Hale said, "but there isn't a chance in Hell of me ever being promoted so long as we're at peace. I don't have any interest. And not much money, though enough that I'm not starving, strictly speaking, while I'm on half pay."

"I noticed your utilities were new," Daniel said without emphasis as he continued to scan the data. This console appeared to have access to all the records in Navy House. Mon might not know that, but Daniel was sure that Adele did.

"Yes, sir," Hale said. She screwed her face up over a thought, then blurted, "Sir, I didn't know what to wear. There wasn't time to get a set of Whites tailored, and anyway, that'd have been wrong. You want spacers, not a clotheshorse. I want to make the RCN a career, and I'd rather be a common space under you than third mate on the freighter *Mare's Nest*."

Daniel laughed. "The sort of ship you're talking about doesn't have a third mate," he said, "or a second mate, generally. But if you went far enough out in the sticks you could get a master's papers on the basis of your record here."

The chip Hale had given him was a direct copy of the Navy House original, with no embellishments or omissions. That was a mark in the woman's favor, regardless of whether it meant she was honest or that she was too smart to risk getting caught while improving what was already a respectable record.

"Sir, I've been hanging on, hoping that a midshipman's slot will open up," Hale said. "I had good marks at the Academy, and my service record is good, too. There's nothing to boast about in two years as midshipman on a destroyer that never saw action, but there's no black marks, either. I thought I might have a leg up on a new graduate when they were making up the roster on a battleship coming out of ordinary."

Daniel looked at her and pursed his lips. "We *are* going out to the back of beyond," he said. "It won't be a pleasure cruise, though the crew will probably eat better than anybody on an ordinary tramp out there does. Even the captain."

He grinned, then sobered again. "Did Cory say why he called you?"

"Sir, I couldn't have been more surprised to hear from my mother," Hale said, shaking her head in puzzlement. "And she's been dead three years. I thought of calling him back, but I didn't have much time as it was if I was going to buy a set of utilities—"

She pinched the loose fabric of her sleeve.

"—and get up to speed on a Lewiston Mark 17, which is what the Sailing Registry says the *Kiesche* has for a fusion bottle."

"Good judgment," Daniel said mildly. He highlighted an item on Hale's service record. "You were on the small-bore team?" he said.

"Yes, *sir*," Hale said, visibly brightening. "I was Academy Champion my last three years. And I was runner-up to Cadet Dorst when I was first-year, but I won't pretend I'd ever have beaten him if he hadn't graduated."

She frowned. "You don't suppose that was why Cory called me, do you?" she said. "He was second-team football, I think, but I wouldn't have bet he even knew I shot small-bore."

Daniel was thinking. As often, the silence drew Hale to speak further, saying, "I wasn't interested in football—and I certainly wasn't any good. But I'll venture to shoot with anybody you want to name."

"Will you indeed?" Daniel said mildly. He wondered

what Sun would say to that. Probably something more polite than Hogg's response to the same statement.

He looked Hale over again. "Footer is good training for the rigging," he said, "but I've found myself in places where having people who knew how to use stocked impellers has been handy."

There was a booklet of notepaper in the console's top tray. Daniel pulled off a sheet and wrote on it with his stylus.

"Take this to Woetjans," he said, handing the note to Hale. "She's on the *Kiesche* down there in the pool. Tell her to run you up and down the rigging enough to make up her mind. If she's satisfied, she'll assign you to a watch."

Hale hopped to her feet. "Thank you, sir!" she said, attempting to salute again. She forgot that she had the note in her right hand and made an even worse hash of it than she had before. The midshipman, soon to be common spacer if she was as fit as she seemed, bent to pick up the note she'd dropped.

"We don't salute much on ships I command," Daniel said. "Which is as much for my benefit as it is for the sort of spacer I like to be with in hard places."

Hale went out laughing. She was in so much of a hurry that she went down the stairs instead of waiting for the elevator to return.

Daniel shook his head in wonder. It was remarkable that he was finding so many people who were enthusiastic about crewing a scruffy tramp freighter into a war on a mudball planet.

Of course, Captain Daniel Leary was pretty enthusiastic himself.

Xenos on Cinnabar

"There's somebody waiting at the stop," said Tovera as the monorail rocked, slowing. She opened her attaché case.

"That's scarcely surprising at a tram stop," Adele said, but she slid her data unit away and stood beside Tovera at the car's front window. Tovera's instincts were very good, in a manner of speaking. Adele supposed she read body language—and the more accurately because she had no emotions herself.

The plastic windshield had been clear when installed, but it now was covered with scratches, road film, and bug spatters: the trams rarely got to speeds which would crush an exoskeleton, but they were even more rarely cleaned. All Adele could see through it was a blurred figure getting up from the bench; probably a man of middle height, wearing loose garments.

Tovera closed the attaché case which held her submachine gun. "It's Cory," she said.

How can she tell?

What is Cory doing here?

Has something happened to Daniel?

The car opened. Adele stepped out behind Tovera and said, "Cory, why are you here?"

Adele thought, *I shouldn't snap at him because I'm worried about Daniel.*

If her abrupt greeting bothered Cory, he gave no sign of it. "Ma'am, I was just waiting for you," he said. "I thought I'd sit here because it's a nice afternoon. And we didn't have houses like this on Florentine, where I come from, you know."

He gestured with his open left hand, palm up. The

tram stop was at the head of the narrow cul-de-sac. At the bottom was Chatsworth Minor, four stories of brick above a stone basement, with stone tie courses and wrought-iron balcony railings. The three houses on either side of the cul-de-sac were of similar age and style.

"After four hundred years there aren't many left in Xenos either, I suppose," Adele said. Whatever Cory had to tell her can't have involved a serious danger or he wouldn't be so relaxed. "The neighborhood didn't become run down, and the families here aren't the sort which prefer change over stability."

Cory had a quiet smile and rarely seemed to be disturbed by anything. He was so easygoing that Adele had initially thought that he was simpleminded, but the young midshipman had taken to the commo suite like no one Adele had met before or since. Everything else, from astrogation to ship-handling, had proceeded from the confidence Cory gained from that first success under Signals Officer Adele Mundy.

Adele glanced at the sky. The sun was below the tall houses, though it was still half an hour short of true sunset.

"Would you care to come in for dinner, Cory?" Adele said.

She didn't imagine the cook would have difficulty feeding a guest. Indeed, the fellow would probably appreciate a healthy appetite: Adele ate very little, and Daniel, when he ate at the townhouse, wasn't particularly interested in food, either.

"Oh, no, ma'am," Cory said in surprise. "I just thought I'd tell you that I dropped a word to Lucinda Hale like you wanted. I'm pretty sure she'll be applying as common spacer. She seemed pretty excited at the chance, in fact."

Adele looked at him without expression. She thought, *I didn't tell you to do anything of the sort!* Which was technically true, but it was what Adele had hoped would happen when she asked Cory about his classmate.

"I didn't know how much of a secret it was," Cory said, smiling cheerfully, "so I thought I'd come by instead of calling, you know? And I didn't use your name to Hale. She may figure it out on her own, but it won't have come through me."

"Your caution does you credit, Cory," Adele said. "Though it was probably unnecessary in this case. Thank you."

"My pleasure, ma'am," Cory said. "I'll let you get off to your evening now."

He pressed the tram call plate, then turned to face Adele again. "Hale was always nice to me, you know? At the Academy, I mean. She'd smile or say hi, and it doesn't sound like much, but there were days that it really helped."

"I imagine it did," Adele said, but she spoke so quietly that Cory probably didn't hear the words over the squeal of a tram car braking to stop.

She walked toward the house with Tovera behind her. She remembered the cul-de-sac filled with Popular Party supporters and her father addressing them from the third-story balcony the night he had been elected tribune. The cheers were still loud in Adele's memory.

And Midshipman Lucinda Hale's smile was bright in Cory's memory. The past wasn't dead so long as there was someone who remembered it.

The same could be said of the scores of men and

women whom Adele had glimpsed only briefly over her gunsight as her finger took up the pressure on her trigger. For they visited her in the dark hours before dawn, and she knew they would be with her until she, too, died.

CHAPTER 8

Xenos on Cinnabar

Adele stepped back and looked critically at the row of clothing arranged neatly on her bed in Chatsworth Minor. The two bulkiest items were a 2nd Class uniform—her Grays—and a civilian suit of the highest quality in case she had to appear as Lady Mundy.

She did not expect to wear either garment when visiting a mining world as a civilian. She certainly hoped that she did not wear either.

Adele was used to living with very little in the way of personal possessions. She could have gotten along quite comfortably with a set of clothing sufficient to satisfy local propriety, the pistol she normally carried in her left tunic pocket, and her personal data unit.

She didn't really need the pistol. She felt more comfortable armed, and the pistol had saved her life and the lives of her colleagues on a number of occasions, but comfort wasn't something Adele Mundy expected from life.

Adele could even do without the data unit. On

balance, though, she would rather die than to live without the data unit. Well, neither should be necessary.

The data unit projected an attention signal as a fist-sized ball of red light thirty inches in front of Adele's nose. She took the unit out and saw that Bernis Sand was calling. Rather than hold the discussion as a text conversion as she normally would, Adele said, "Adele Mundy speaking."

As best as Adele could remember, Mistress Sand had never before called her directly. Their meetings had always been arranged discretely by third parties. Adele supposed that the use of cut-outs had been chosen for security's sake. That meant either that this call wasn't anything to do with the Republic's business—or that it was a sudden crisis.

Or both, of course.

"Mundy," said Mistress Sand, "my son went out two hours ago. I learned from the attendant of his quarters that he had said that as a matter of ethics he needed to inform Captain Sorley that his ship would no longer be required. Rikard wasn't a prisoner here, of course."

She's probably regretting that now, Adele thought. Which was silly, of course: mother or not, Mistress Sand was not the sort to imprison her son because he had become ethical.

Adele's own parents would not have had any hesitation about imprisoning their children, if their own principles required it. Her mother would have sacrificed things she held of more importance than her daughters if it would bring about the victory of the Common People. The Common People under the enlightened leadership of Esme Rolfe Mundy and her associates in the Popular Party, of course.

Lucius Mundy's guiding principle was as starkly simple as the barrel of a gun: he would become speaker by whatever means were available. He wouldn't have regarded imprisoning his bookish elder daughter as a sacrifice if it advanced his agenda.

"Just before I called you," Sand continued, "a pair of porters arrived with a handcart and a note from Rikard saying that he was moving out. I was to give his luggage to the porters. There was only the little he'd brought from Corcyra and a few suits that I'd bought him to make him presentable while he was here in Xenos."

"The note was in your son's writing?" Adele said. Tovera had appeared in the doorway, silent and emotionless. She had listening devices all over Chatsworth Minor.

"Yes," said Sand. "When asked in the correct fashion, the porters said that they were to take the luggage to the Dancing Girl, which I gather is a tavern. Money was a sufficient inducement. I sent them off with the luggage."

"All right," said Adele. She was looking at the address of the Dancing Girl, an establishment near Portinga Harbor. There was no imagery available, which irritated her but wouldn't really matter. "I'll discuss this with my colleagues and we'll deal with it."

She thought for a further eyeblink, too swiftly for the hesitation to register with the other party. "Mistress Sand," she said. "Keep your people clear of the area. They would complicate matters. Good day."

"Six and Hogg are packing in his suite," Tovera said quietly. "Miranda is there, because they're going out tonight."

As Adele passed her on the way out the door, Tovera smiled and said, "I suppose we're going out, too."

Adele shrugged. Dockside taverns were out of her range of experience. Daniel would make the decisions this time.

His door opened off the next landing down. She rapped on the panel and said, "Daniel? A word."

The door whipped open. "Come in," said Daniel, wearing his Grays. Both couches in the sitting room were covered with clothing. "Can you convince Hogg that I won't need my Dress Whites on a voyage to Corcyra?"

Miranda, wearing an attractive suit of pink and gray, sat on a chair. In her lap was a cape, gray on the outside with a pink lining. She was dressed for any gathering short of a dress ball, and her vivacity would probably carry her through even that. She smiled pleasantly at Adele.

Whereas Daniel's servant had a truculent look. He stood arms akimbo with his fists clenched on his hips.

"No," said Adele, "I can't. Though of course you're right."

As she spoke, she realized that the question had been meant rhetorically. When Adele's mind was on other things, she had a tendency to deal with statements at face value. Her mind was usually on other things.

"Cleveland went to see Captain Sorley in the Dancing Girl at Portinga Harbor," Adele said. She realized that Daniel had held his tongue for her, waiting for her to explain her visit now that he'd seen her expression. "He's just sent for his luggage. A handwritten note."

"Everything in that part of town is a dive," Hogg said, his expression changing subtly.

"I think I may have been there..." Daniel said,

his eyes focused on things beyond the present room. "In my second year, with Fessenden, because his brother-in-law was a ship's captain and we hoped to touch him for a loan."

The lines of his face sharpened. "Which we did, enough to get extremely drunk on, at least," he said. "Adele, how recently did this happen?"

"Cleveland has been gone for over two hours," she said. "The porters to take the luggage just left Cleveland House."

"Right, what I hoped," said Daniel, nodding. "Hogg, you and I will fetch the boy immediately. I'll wear these—"

He pinched the seam of his Grays. They were a new set, a proper male counterpart to Miranda's suit.

"—to show Sorley that he's dealing with gentlemen, not dockside trash who can be shanghaied without repercussions. The sooner the better, I think; before they settle down."

"I'll come along," said Adele. She patted the closure over the data unit in her pocket. "It will be a new experience."

Hogg and Daniel traded looks. "Ah, Adele?" Daniel said. "I'd really rather you not. I don't expect trouble—Hogg and I will go in and come back with the boy before Sorley knows what's happening. And I know that the Xenos docksides can be rough, but people *aren't* shot here the way that can happen on some places we've landed. That isn't something that I want to change, frankly."

Adele looked at Daniel, then at Hogg, and back to Daniel. *They know the environment and think that I'd be in the way.*

"All right," she said.

"Thank you!" Daniel said in relief. "Come along, Hogg. Darling—"

This to Miranda over his shoulder as he started down the stairs.

"—I'll be back for dinner, I swear I will!"

The front door banged. *Boys off on an adventure,* Adele thought. *Without me.*

She took out her personal data unit. She planned to inform Mistress Sand about the situation, but that would wait.

Aloud, but without looking up from her work to the girl standing transfixed with her cape in her hands, Adele said, "Miranda, do you have a more pedestrian change of clothing here?"

The nearest tram stop was half a block from the Dancing Girl. Daniel had plenty of time to size the place up as he walked toward it. Daniel was striding briskly; Hogg was a half step behind him and to the side, shambling rather than properly walking. Hogg covered the ground, and though it didn't matter here, he was just as quiet as he would have been in the Bantry woodlands.

"We better not stay long inside," said Hogg. "It looks like it's going to fall down the next time somebody inside farts."

"It's quite an interesting building, Hogg," Daniel said. They walked in the center of the street, which was reasonably clean because a thunderstorm the previous evening had washed the garbage down the storm drains and into the nearby harbor. "It may be as much as a thousand years old. In another part of

Xenos, it would be on the historic register and protected from demolition."

"I said what I said," grunted Hogg.

The Dancing Girl was in the middle of the block. All the buildings here had originally been freestanding, but with the years they had sagged outward in the middle so that they now touched one another and could only bulge farther toward the street.

The Dancing Girl's sign was a wooden silhouette hanging by two rings above the sidewalk. The right leg above the knee had split off along the grain in past years, and it had been decades if not centuries since the paint had been renewed.

The sashes of the bay window covering one side of the front—the door and its jambs filled the left side—had small panes. They were protected by chain-link fencing in a steel frame rather than fancier grillwork.

The ancient timber posts had bowed but showed no signs of breaking, and the fabric of the walls must have been mesh covered with something either flexible or easily renewed. Originally that would have been mud under plaster; mud probably remained the choice, because nothing was cheaper.

Men and a few prostitutes loitered on the street in small groups. Most of them were standing, but boxes and an overturned bucket provided seats for a few. Two men leaned against the Dancing Girl's window grate.

All the onlookers followed Daniel and Hogg with their eyes, but no one spoke. Daniel nodded to the pair in front of the tavern, much the way he would have acknowledged Bantry tenants who caught his eye from a distance.

Hogg stepped past him and pushed open the door,

scanning the tavern's interior with his right hand balled in the pocket of his loose jacket. Daniel entered, but until the door swung closed behind him he watched the pair on the sidewalk out of the corner of his eye.

The barman looked at him without emotion. Four male spacers sat dicing on a circular table, while a woman standing beside them watched. Two more spacers, one wearing a saucer hat with a circle of gold braid, sat in a corner banquette.

A staircase with a central landing angled upward between the banquette and the end of the bar. Removed from this place and refurbished, the stairs would probably be worth a great deal to a recently wealthy merchant who wanted to buy antiquity for his new townhouse.

"Captain Sorley?" Daniel said pleasantly to the man with the saucer hat.

There were two public houses in Bantry: laborers' taverns, neither of them fancy. One still had a floor of rammed earth, covered with rushes from the banks of Hoppy Creek. The rushes weren't replaced as often as they might have been, and the clientele of both houses included farmers just in from the fields and wearing lugged boots. Daniel didn't expect ferns and soft music in a tavern.

That said, there wasn't a pig run in Bantry as foul as the floor of the Dancing Girl. There seemed to be a layer of brick beneath the slime. Unlike the street outside it wasn't sluiced clean by rainstorms, nor was it cleaned in any other fashion. The stink suggested there was excrement as old as the building itself.

"Who the bloody hell are you?" Sorley said. He was middle-aged, short, and could have looked trim if he'd made any effort; as it was, he was scruffy.

Though Sorley remained seated, the man with him in the banquette stood up.

"I'm Captain Daniel Leary," Daniel said, walking toward the stairs. "I've come to fetch Master Rikard Cleveland to a business meeting."

"Well, he's not here!" Sorley said. The men at the circular table were getting to their feet. "Look, buddy, get your ass out of here now while you can still walk!"

Daniel nodded acknowledgment and started up the stairs. The treads were as solid as bedrock, whatever the condition of the rest of the tavern.

"Hey!" Sorley shouted. "Schmidt, he's coming up! Get 'em, boys!"

A large man holding an iron pipe the length of his forearm appeared at the top of the stairs. He was wearing an undershirt with a scoop neck; his beard merged indistinguishably with the black hair curling up from his chest. He grinned at Daniel and started down.

The bartender had moved to the far corner of the bar. He held the mallet he used to set the bung in barrels of beer, but he obviously didn't intend to get involved in the customers' affairs.

"It's too late to leave now, smart-ass!" Sorley said. "I've got two of my boys posted in the back alley, too!"

Daniel leaned over the stair railing and gripped the neck of a stoneware bottle from the rack behind the bar. The bartender shouted and stepped forward. Daniel swung the bottle as though the bottom were a stamp and Schmidt's right instep was the document he was sealing.

Schmidt was wearing spacer's boots, soft and flexible so that they could be worn inside a rigging suit. The bottle didn't break. The bones of the big man's foot did. He screamed and pulled his foot up.

Daniel gripped Schmidt's left ankle with his free hand and jerked his leg out from under him. Schmidt crashed down on the base of his spine and bounced to the landing. Daniel broke the bottle over Schmidt's head, bathing both of them with gin. He shoved the unconscious man down the remainder of the staircase.

Hogg was at the base of the stairs, facing the rest of Sorley's crewmen with a chair held out in his left hand and his knuckleduster—he hadn't clicked open the knife—in his right. As though he really did have eyes in the back of his head, he dodged the slumping Schmidt.

Daniel didn't see anybody following Schmidt, so he glanced back at the tap room. The bay window shattered, spraying glass onto the floor. The woven-wire screen held for the first blow, but a second bowed it inward. This time the frame and wire together flew into the room ahead of one of the spacers who had been loitering outside. His companion had probably been the first object to hit the window.

The door burst open ahead of Woetjans. The spacers who had hesitated to rush Hogg on the staircase turned at the new commotion. Woetjans swung a length of pressure tubing forehand and backhand, smashing two of them down.

More spacers—and former spacers; there was Hovenmeyer, who'd lost an eye when ice broke from the *Sissie*'s rigging on an unnamed world when he happened to be looking upward—crowded into the tavern. They were carrying clubs of one sort or another, generally heavy wrenches.

Two or three of Sorley's men tried to fight and were knocked down immediately. They'd be safe enough on the floor, because most of the Sissies arriving wore spacer's boots just as Schmidt had. Despite the enthusiastic kicks from the rescue party, the fallen crewmen were unlikely to sustain cracked ribs or ruptured spleens.

Powerful lift engines howled in the street. Through the splintered frame of the window, Daniel could see the stilt-legged tender which Mon had begun using as a mobile crane in the shipyard. It would transport people only if the passengers were willing to cling to struts with no protection against weather, windblast, and buildings that the tender happened to brush.

The Militia might have complained if they had noticed it—vehicles in the Xenos airspace were *very* tightly controlled—but that would have been a problem for another time, involving a judge rather than a coroner. A moment ago, having a squad of Militia burst into the tavern would have struck Daniel as a pleasant surprise.

One of Sorley's men stumbled backward. Instead of fending him off with the chair, Hogg slugged him behind the ear with the knuckleduster. Daniel grimaced, but the man had brought it on himself when he decided to join a gang of his fellows to beat a couple strangers.

The tap room was already crowded. Mon joined his men inside. He didn't carry a club, but he'd pulled on the gauntlets from a rigger's suit. The smear on the knuckles of the right glove looked like blood.

Adele and Tovera followed Mon. Daniel smiled. *I thought she agreed too easily,* he thought.

It was just as well that Adele had second-guessed him, because he'd misjudged Sorley. This business had been a deliberate trap: not just the abduction of Rikard Cleveland, who knew where a treasure might be, but also an attempt to cripple or kill Captain Daniel Leary, whom Sorley had decided was his main rival in the treasure hunt.

Daniel smiled wryly. This hadn't been one of the times when his reputation had been an advantage.

Miranda entered the Dancing Girl. She was in a dark blue suit, probably the one she wore when she visited Bergen and Associates with him, and she carried a hockey stick.

Miranda looked around the confusion. She wasn't looking for *him*, as Daniel first thought, but rather seeing whether there were any proper targets for her stick. Only when she was sure that opposition had been downed did she relax and smile at Daniel.

"Pipe down!" Daniel said, using his command voice. Those present were spacers used to obeying orders, at least when they trusted the person giving them; they quieted immediately. The wheezing breaths of Schmidt at the bottom of the stairs—the stoneware bottle had given him a concussion if not a fractured skull—were the loudest remaining sounds.

"Woetjans," Daniel said in the relative hush. "Sorley's got two more in the alley behind here."

"Right," said Sun from beneath the landing where Daniel couldn't see him. He must have come in by a back door. "They're going to stay there a while, too."

Speaking of Sorley... The merchant captain had apparently ducked under the banquette table. Now that the fighting was over, he was inching upward.

He'd lost his hat, and he was bald from his eyebrows to mid-skull.

"Captain Sorley," Daniel said, "I very much hope that we find Master Cleveland unharmed."

"I'm quite all right, Captain Leary," Cleveland said from the top of the stairs. "I . . . I'm very glad to see you, but I haven't been harmed. Lady Mundy?"

"Yes," said Adele. Her left hand was still in her tunic pocket.

"I ignored your advice," Cleveland said. He bowed. "I apologize for the trouble I caused you and others by my decision."

"This is the most bloody fun I've had since the *Sissie* lifted from Madison!" boomed Evans as he straightened. He'd been wiping the head of his eighteen-inch adjustable wrench on the dungarees of the spacer he'd knocked down with it.

That's probably the opinion of most of the rescue party, Daniel thought. *And maybe mine as well.*

Aloud he said, "We'll escort you to your family home, Cleveland. We'll talk on the way, but I think the *Kiesche* will be lifting rather sooner than we had discussed."

Adele said something in Woetjans' ear. "Evans and Crick!" the bosun ordered. "Go up and get his gear. Take it to the *Kiesche* on the tram, not the bloody tender like we came."

"Right," said Daniel. "Captain Sorley? Would you come out here, please?"

"Look, I got a *right* . . ." Sorley began. He didn't move from his corner behind the round table.

Barnes and Dasi grabbed opposite sides of the table. They were bosun's mates and used to working together without signals that anybody else could have seen. They ripped the table from the floor and hurled it into the rack of bottles behind the bar.

The bartender ducked with a yelp, saving himself. Wood, bottles, and various liquors sprayed over the taproom. Spacers shouted and laughed.

The riggers turned toward Sorley. He threw his hands up and cried, "I'm coming! Look, I don't have any fight with you!"

That much was certainly true.

"Thank you, Barnes and Dasi," Daniel said, "but you can step back now. Captain Sorley, I'm asking you in the presence of these witnesses—"

Including Adele, who was certainly recording the whole affair.

"—if you renounce any right or interest in Rikard Cleveland and any matters he may have discussed with you?"

"Yes, yes!" Sorley said. "Go on, rob me like you're going to do anyway. *I* don't care!"

"Then I think we're done here," Daniel said pleasantly. "Master Cleveland, we'll take you home now."

"Tovera and I will escort Master Cleveland," Adele said crisply. "You have a dinner date with your fiancée, I believe."

"Yes," Daniel said. "I do."

He looked at his uniform. He'd split several seams, in particular the crotch. And something had splashed—gin diluting Schmidt's blood, probably—to cover most of his right side. "Ah . . ."

Miranda stepped close and hugged him. Daniel realized for the first time that she was trembling. "We'll eat in," she said. "I told the cook before Adele and I left the townhouse that we probably would."

"Right," Daniel repeated, licking his dry lips. Reaction was beginning to hit him, too. "We're done here, then."

"Not quite, master," said Hogg. "This shitworm—" He thumbed toward Sorley.

"—tried to kill us both or the next thing to it."

"I'm not going to dirty my hands on a man who's too cowardly to fight," Daniel said. He was trying to control his breathing. He wanted to gulp air through his mouth and nostrils both. "We'll leave now."

"I never minded getting my hands dirty," Hogg said.

He punched Sorley in the stomach with the knuckleduster. Sorley crumpled to the floor with only a wheeze.

Hogg kicked him in the ribs. "Or my boots," he said. "I'm a peasant, you know."

Hogg grinned. "Now we're ready," he said, sauntering toward the gaping doorway.

CHAPTER 9

Bergen and Associates Shipyard, Cinnabar

"There'll be some who say she looks dumpy," Daniel said in the interval while the first load of cargo was stowed in the *Kiesche*'s hold and the second lowboy waited on the quay. Adele sat on the bed of the emptied vehicle. "Mon says she's handy, but he means handy for a tramp freighter, of course."

In fact the *Kiesche* looked dumpy to Daniel also, just as she would to anyone used to the slender lines of warships. Warships didn't carry cargo, and short, fat cylinders provided much greater interior volume than long, thin ones.

"Given your record of success," Adele said. She was working on something with her personal data unit; she didn't look up. "I can't imagine anyone objecting to your choice of a ship. *I* don't object."

Daniel wondered what Adele's personal opinion of the *Kiesche*—or of the *Princess Cecile*—was, or if she even had one. Most people thought of familiar machines in human terms, as though they had will or even personalities. Adele didn't appear to do that.

"Are your quarters satisfactory?" Daniel said. "I'm asking because you wouldn't complain if there was something wrong."

"Quite satisfactory," Adele said. Her control wands moved and paused, adjusting the data on the holographic screen before her. "I have a bed, which converts rather neatly into a chair and desk. Further, I think it is very unlikely that it will rain aboard the Kiesche, as it did a number of times during the period when I often slept in culverts."

"The reaction-mass piping doesn't pass near the bridge quarters," Daniel said. "I suppose it's possible that the bunks I've added in the cargo hold might be flooded, but your rank hath its privileges. Cramped though those privileges might be."

There were four curtained bunk alcoves—calling them cabins would have been silly—in the bridge compartment. Daniel had allotted them to himself; Vesey, the first mate; Cory, the second mate; and Adele. Cory had offered his alcove to Pasternak, who had accepted it gladly.

The off-duty crew was intended to bunk in the triple stacks against the port and starboard outer bulkhead at the rear of the compartment. Because the Kiesche was heavily overcrewed on this voyage, Daniel had added additional accommodation in the hold. Their cargo of carbines and automatic impellers would probably be valuable to the Transformationists, but it was primarily aboard to conceal the real purpose of the voyage. The crates didn't begin to fill the available volume.

Daniel wondered what Adele was working on. It might not directly bear on the voyage, but he had come to accept her belief that there was no useless information. At least not if you had a librarian as skilled as Adele Mundy to sift the data when need arose.

"Send the next load!" Pasternak shouted from the main hatch.

"Last load!" the straw boss from the shipyard bellowed back. He and his team of three began shifting crates of weapons from the second lowboy to the conveyor, which in turn rumbled the cases toward the *Kiesche*'s hatch.

Pasternak, as chief of ship, was responsible for striking the cargo away in the hold, though most of the involved personnel were riggers, Woetjans herself among them. Vesey was at the command console for the present, though Daniel planned to take the *Kiesche* up to get the feel of his new vessel.

"Loading should be complete in three hours," Daniel said, his eyes on the ship. "If Cleveland is aboard by then, I intend to lift off as soon thereafter as I can."

The Dorsal A antenna was extended as usual in harbor to provide a vantage point, but it should take only minutes to lower it and lock it into its cradle. There was a panoramic camera at the masthead, courtesy of Adele's other employers. The installation probably made the *Kiesche* unique among tramp freighters, but no one would examine the ship carefully enough to notice unless they were already very suspicious.

"He and Lieutenant Cory have left Cleveland House," Adele said. "The tram system estimates they should arrive—"

Her wands twitched the air.

"—within two minutes."

"You're in touch with Cory?" Daniel said, hoping

that he kept irritation out of his tone. He had sent Cory and Hale to meet their passenger and accompany him back to the shipyard.

He had sent Hogg as well, rather than a husky spacer or two. Hogg wasn't polished, but he was used to operating in urbane society. Generally that involved keeping his mouth shut and being ignored; a large countryman who happened to be travelling in the same tramcar as two young gentlemen and a lady of the same class.

"No," said Adele. She must have heard something in his voice, because she turned to face him for the first time since she had sat down on the lowboy. "Tovera asked if she might go with Cory and Hale. Ordinarily she wouldn't have left me alone, but she seemed to think I would be safe enough so long as I didn't leave the shipyard."

"I see," said Daniel. "Ah, I apologize for, well, for being surprised."

He thought Adele smiled as she returned to her display, but he wasn't sure. Even if she were smiling, he might have read the expression in her eyes rather than on her tight lips.

"I didn't specifically thank you for disobeying me last night," Daniel said, though that was overstating his request to Adele before he went to snatch Cleveland back. "Ah, and Tovera was very well behaved, which I noticed."

"I've never known Tovera to disobey any direction I gave her," Adele said in the direction of her display. "She doesn't expect to understand all of them—and of course, she often doesn't. She simply accepts my decisions and carries them out to the best of her ability."

"That's quite a...responsibility," Daniel said. He had to raise his voice. The crates holding the automatic impellers were moving up the conveyor; their steel straps clacked like gunfire on the rollers.

Adele looked toward him again. For an instant, there was nothing at all in her face, but he had the impression that her eyes were on things in the distant past.

"Daniel," she said, "it's exactly the same responsibility as I carry for the pistol in my pocket. Neither one in their association with me has ever killed anyone without my direction."

"Right," Daniel said, looking away. He was watching his crew slide the cargo aboard and stow it in the stern hold, but that was simply an excuse.

Missiles launched at Daniel's command had almost certainly killed more people than his friend had with her pistol, but Daniel hadn't been watching his victim's faces when they died. Scores of times, hundreds of times; sometimes so close that their blood splashed back in a red shower.

"Daniel?" Adele said to his profile. He turned back toward her in surprise. "How do you plan to take your leave from Miranda?"

"We, ah, did that last night," he said awkwardly. "Well, this morning at the townhouse. I think it's easier on her if she doesn't come to the harbor, you see."

Adele nodded. "Miranda asked me to tell you at a suitable time that she disagrees with you there," she said. "The decision is yours, of course. But you have nothing really to do for the next two hours, and your fiancée is waiting in Mon's office."

"What?" Daniel said, looking up at the bank of windows.

Adele went back to her data unit. She didn't respond, because there was nothing really to respond to.

"Right," said Daniel. "*I* am captain of the *Kiesche*, and *I* make the decisions on anything to do with the ship and its crew."

He rose to his feet. "If you will, Officer Mundy," Daniel said, "inform Lieutenant Vesey that I'll be back in two hours. Until then she is to do whatever she feels is necessary to prepare the *Kiesche* for immediate departure."

Daniel strode toward the main building. Rikard Cleveland had just entered the shipyard with his escort. Daniel waved, but that was nothing the *Kiesche*'s captain need concern himself with, either.

Not for two hours, at least.

The roar of ions quenching in the water of the slip seemed louder than Adele, on the bunk in her alcove, was used to. She supposed that was because the freighter's hull and frames were much thinner than those of the *Princess Cecile*.

The *Kiesche*'s four thrusters were arranged in a diamond pattern instead of side-by-side pairs like those of most starships. Pasternak was running up the bow and stern units together, checking flow and seeing that the Stellite petals of the nozzles moved smoothly when bathed in plasma.

Adele wondered what the advantage of the arrangement was. The answer was probably "none," given that it was so uncommon.

She wore an RCN commo helmet for its sound-cancelling effect. Rather than view data on the face-shield as most spacers did, though, she linked her personal data unit to the console as she would have done on the *Sissie*. On a warship she would have been at a console with its own sound-cancelling system.

Checking the ship's internal networks by habit, Adele noticed that Cleveland was netted in. Someone had given him a commo helmet, though he probably didn't know how to use it.

Cleveland lay on a bunk in the bridge compartment by his own choice. Daniel had offered him an alcove, but the youth had said that he didn't want to be given any mark of honor. Being treated as a common spacer would be part of his penance for his past behavior.

Adele's smile would have been visible if anyone had been looking at her, which of course they weren't as the *Kiesche* prepared for liftoff. People who spoke of penance and divine retribution believed in an ordered universe.

Adele's sister, Agatha, was eight years old when she was killed and her head displayed on Speaker's Rock. The sergeants who stabbed the little girl to death believed they were acting according to the terms of the Proscriptions which followed the Three Circles Conspiracy.

They weren't: the Proscriptions applied only to adult members of the families involved, the Mundys included, but it wasn't a time when legal details were getting much attention.

The killers *certainly* didn't think they were instruments of divine balance. They were emblems of the universe in which Adele lived.

Still, if Rikard Cleveland wanted to believe that by punishing himself he approached oneness with his universe, so be it. He wasn't hurting anyone else; and he certainly wasn't hurting innocent eight-year-old girls.

Adele had been going over the *Fleet Handbook for the Ribbon Stars*, the Alliance equivalent of the *Sailing Directions* issued for each region by Navy House. Because Alliance influence in the Ribbon Stars had been great even before Pantellaria's temporary annexation, the *Handbook* was generally more detailed than corresponding Cinnabar information. Comparison of the two was therefore worthwhile—to the degree that any human activity was worthwhile.

Most people wouldn't have added the final proviso. Adele did.

On the other hand, she wasn't going to learn anything from the *Handbook* which would cause her to interrupt Daniel and the *Kiesche*'s crew in their liftoff preparations. For no better reason than her paired thoughts—that Cleveland looked lost, and that he would not have killed a young girl—Adele opened a two-way link to his helmet.

Those were good reasons, after all. "Master Cleveland?" she said. "If the equipment is in proper order, we will probably lift off within the next half hour."

"*Who?*" said Cleveland. He sat up so abruptly that he bumped his helmet on the bunk above his.

Adele had an inset of the boy's face in a corner of her screen, using imagery from the recording unit in the compartment ceiling. She thought of cutting her image onto his display, but there didn't seem to her to be any advantage in that. Instead she said, "I'm Adele Mundy. I don't have any duties at present, and I thought I would offer you, well, companionship. I'm not a spacer, but I have a good deal of experience by now on vessels as small as this."

The *Kiesche* was close to the same displacement

as the *Princess Cecile*, though the latter—though any warship—was more sophisticated. Besides, Adele knew Daniel's routines.

"*I see,*" said Cleveland, lying back again. He was frowning over a thought.

The thrusters idled down to a hiss. The port and starboard pair lighted in their place, their roar and vibration sharpened as Pasternak sphinctered the nozzles. Even at low output, the *Kiesche* rocked fore and aft as though balanced on a teeter-totter.

"*Lady Mundy,*" Cleveland said. "*On the ship which brought me from Karst to Cinnabar, I asked if I might go out on the hull while the ship was in the Matrix. Have you ever done that?*"

"Yes," said Adele. She didn't amplify the bare statement. The only privacy she and Daniel had for discussions out of the crew's hearing was on the hull. "If you wish, you'll be able to do that on this voyage as well."

"*I don't,*" Cleveland said. "*I thought that being in the Matrix, and seeing the whole cosmos arrayed about me, would be similar to the feeling I get in the Chapel in Pearl Valley. There I know that God is real and that all humanity, not just me and fellow Transformationists, are one with Him. It's a wonderful realization. It's transforming, in fact.*"

Adele heard the smile in his voice. Her initial information about Cleveland had come from his mother and stepfather. The boy himself had said that he was a different person than the one his parents had known ... and Adele was beginning to believe that he might have been telling the truth.

"*Was* it the same experience?" she asked. Cleveland seemed to have drifted into a reverie.

"Unfortunately, it was not," Cleveland said. *"God was there, certainly. But I felt utterly alone—lost to life and to my fellows. I entered the airlock and hid there until one of the crewmen noticed me, because I didn't know how to work the mechanism. The crewman took me back within the ship's hull, where it was a little better. I haven't completely recovered yet. I'm not sure I ever will."*

Adele considered how to reply. "Captain Leary describes his feeling in the Matrix in religious terms," she said at last. "He speaks of the cosmos as having existence rather than anything to do with humanity. It will be interesting to see how he feels in your chapel."

"Lady Mundy?" Cleveland said. *"How did the Matrix affect you, if you don't mind my asking?"*

Adele shrugged, which of course the boy couldn't see. "I'm not religious," she said. "I see colored lights, but nothing more. It reminded me of the holographic display of a computer on standby."

She sniffed. The sound would have been laughter in another person.

"The difference is that I could have tuned the computer display," Adele said. "I think that decoding the cosmos is beyond me."

"Six to ship!" Daniel's voice boomed in the helmets and compartment loudspeakers. *"Prepare for liftoff in thirty, that's three-zero, seconds! Six out."*

The thrusters built to full power, roaring like hungry monsters. Adele leaned back on her bunk and waited for the by-now-familiar acceleration.

CHAPTER 10

Corcyra System

The *Kiesche* hung three light-minutes from Corcyra. The tramp's upgraded sensor suite gave Daniel an excellent view of the planet, but Pantellarian vessels on patrol would be very unlikely to observe the newcomer.

Daniel had the highest regard for Pantellarian optics, which were as good as or better than anything produced on Cinnabar. He had less regard for the crews of Pantellarian destroyers like those sent to Corcyra. Even first-rate personnel would have difficulty scanning a three-light-minute sphere without specialized equipment like that which Adele's other employers had provided the *Kiesche*.

"Officer Mundy...?" Daniel said on the general push. On a vessel with a larger or less select crew, he might have used the command channel or even a two-way link, but whenever possible he liked to give his people as much information as there was. "I'm not seeing anything in orbit over the planet. Are you, over?"

"No," said Adele. *"And we have enough data that*

138

a ship hidden in the planet's shadow would have emerged by now, regardless of its orbital period."

She forgot to say "over" when she ended her reply. Daniel smiled: Adele normally forgot.

"Cleveland?," Daniel said. "Did you hear any discussion about Pantellarian patrolling practices before you lifted from Corcyra? I assume you were aboard a blockade runner, over."

"Well, there wasn't really a blockade, Captain Leary," Cleveland said. *"Ships land at Brotherhood daily or thereabouts to load copper ingots. I bought passage on one that was bound for Karst, the Evelyn. The captain said the Pantellarians—actually, he said the Spigotties—don't patrol because they're afraid that an Alliance squadron will sweep up anything in orbit. While they're in port, they're protected by antiship missiles."*

Daniel smiled, though no one looking at him would have seen any humor in it. As much as Daniel hated anything, it was lazy incompetence, even in an enemy.

The *Kiesche* was in free fall. High Drive emissions could have been detected much more easily than the ship itself. Under the circumstances, Daniel thought about bringing them up to 1g with the High Drives and thumbing his nose at the enemy . . . but that would be pointless.

"I'm sure that was what the Pantellarian commodore told Governor Arnaud," he said.

"The admiral," Adele said, correcting him. *"Admiral Stanzi."*

"The admiral told Arnaud, then," Daniel said. "I don't think he really believes the Alliance would break the present truce with the Republic in order to help a motley crowd of miners on a piss-pot colony. I *do* think that Stanzi and his crews, particularly his officers, aren't up to the drudgery of a blockade. Pantellarians aren't cowards, by and large, but they do tend to be lazy scuts, over."

"Sir," said Cory. "*Not to take the enemy's side, but it would be very difficult to run down blockade runners with destroyers. Unless you were going to shoot on sighting, maybe, but there's regular trade with Corcyra, with Hablinger, I mean. Over.*"

"*Five to ship,*" Vesey said. She was opposite Daniel on the command console at present as the senior fighting officer under the captain. When the *Kiesche* had reached Corcyra orbit and Daniel was sure that they weren't going to be fighting or fleeing in the next few minutes, Adele would trade places with Vesey. "*Chasing blockade runners would improve the skills of the crews. Which drinking in dockside taverns, as I presume they're doing while in port at Hablinger, will not do. Over.*"

"Six to ship," Daniel said. "The Pantellarian navy has a culture different from ours in the RCN. For which I suppose we should be glad, over."

In the general pause, Cleveland said, "*Sir? I believe the Pantellarians escort their own transports down. They send up two destroyers, the captain told me, but they don't bother copper traders even when they're both in orbit at the same time. Ah, over?*"

He's really trying, Daniel thought. If Cleveland had grown up under Tom Sand instead of a flash nobleman who'd never grown up himself, things might have been different.

Or not, of course. Daniel Leary certainly wasn't a copy of his father, the Speaker.

"Six to ship," Daniel said, sitting as straight as he could during free fall. "I'll take us in now. Don't expect the kind of precise astrogation that you've gotten used to on the *Sissie*. We're going to be an hour and a half on High Drive before we reach Corcyra orbit, and the computer is going to land us just like the *Kiesche*'s captain is a cack-handed drunk like every other tramp captain out this way."

Daniel took a deep breath. Though he kept his tone measured, he was feeling the excitement rise as it always did when he went into action. There wouldn't be any shooting immediately, and perhaps never in the course of the voyage, but this was action nonetheless.

"They aren't going to learn that we're RCN until we're ready to tell them, Sissies," Daniel said. "But they'll learn then, by heaven!"

He took another breath. "Ship," he said, and how often had he used these words? "Prepare to insert in thirty, that is three-zero, seconds."

Corcyra Orbit

"Thank you, Vesey," Adele said as she took the lieutenant's place at the back of the command console. The *Kiesche* was in free fall, so the exchange was simplified by Vesey hooking a boot around an armrest, pulling Adele to the console, and finally pushing her down onto the couch.

When Adele first joined the RCN—or at any rate, became a member of the company of RCS *Princess Cecile*, a corvette in the service of the Republic of Cinnabar—it disturbed her that she was so clumsy, aboard ship generally and particularly when the ship was in free fall. She had come to accept if not approve of the situation.

Adele was better at certain things than anyone else in the crew—and very possibly better than anyone else in the RCN. And she was hopelessly incompetent at other things which even the wipers in the Power Room did with reasonable skill. There were other people to do or to help Adele do the things she was bad at, but there was nobody you would prefer to have with you if you needed to open an enemy's database.

Or to stand beside you in a gunfight. Tovera had the same skills, but not even Tovera could equal her mistress in planning a complex action which might involve slaughter at each stage.

Adele strapped herself onto the couch after she started to drift off again. Vesey, who had expected that to happen, had waited to catch Adele by the ankle and to hold her until the harness clicked.

"Thank you, Vesey," Adele repeated, coldly furious with herself. *If Vesey and probably everybody else in the crew knows that I'll forget to strap myself in, why can't I remember it!*

The console was already displaying feeds from the planet below. The sites had been chosen by algorithms tailored to Adele's specifications by specialists in Mistress Sand's organization, or possibly by specialists working for Navy House, whose services had been loaned to Mistress Sand for this purpose.

Occasionally Adele heard or saw a comment which made her wonder how important she was considered by the highest levels of the Republic's bureaucracy. The thought shocked and disturbed her, because Adele's self-image was that of a librarian of considerable skill, whom nobody ever thought about.

Except when she got angry, of course, and then Mundy of Chatsworth was apt to come out. But arrogant nobles were a soldi a dozen in Cinnabar society.

"Freighter Kiesche *out of Xenos to Brotherhood Control,"* said Vesey, using the 20-meter band. Corcyra did not have a working satellite communications system since the Pantellarian invasion, so shortwave was the first choice to raise somebody on the ground. *"Request landing instructions, over."*

Vesey, now in Adele's alcove, was handling the commo. She was adequately competent at every aspect of what might be required of an RCN officer, including communications duties, but Cory and Cazelet were far more skilled at them.

They were acting as Adele's aides in sorting the information pouring in from databases below, however, so Vesey was on the boards. She was hugely overqualified for a job which on a tramp freighter was ordinarily carried out by a technician who moved his lips when he read.

Adele focused on the information displayed in greater resolution than it had been by her personal data unit. She almost-smiled when a thought at the back of her mind drifted to the surface before receding: the fact that Adele had been concentrating on the data before and during her move to the command console probably had something to do with the fact that she had forgotten to strap herself in.

As usual, for both items.

Adele sank into information, a world in which it didn't matter that a spacer was detailed to watch her whenever she was on the hull—even though a safety line anchored her to the ship. First things first: Brotherhood Harbor was a half-loop west of the present channel, formed when the Cephisis River changed its course a millennium ago. A canal with locks now reconnected the upper end of the cutoff to the main channel to keep the harbor level high. Ships drank large volumes of water to refill their reaction-mass tanks, and they vaporized even more with their thruster plumes as they landed and lifted.

Two antiship missile batteries protected Brotherhood. They were not interconnected by a single targeting apparatus and were not even operated by the same organization. The battery in a concrete emplacement was crewed and controlled by the Garrison.

The other unit was equipped with more recent, higher velocity missiles, but its triple launcher was protected by only a cursory sandbag revetment. The leaders of the Corcyran Self-Defense Regiment had brought the battery with them from Pantellaria, along with a great deal of money, which permitted them to recruit locally. Very few of the exiles themselves were in uniform, but the Regiment appeared at close inspection to be a respectable fighting force—just as Mistress Sand's files had suggested it would be.

"Ma'am, I've put together data on the Freccia," said Cory on a net he'd created for himself, Adele, and Cazelet. *"That's the destroyer in harbor, the Corcyran navy as they call it. I thought it might save you some time before you send a report to Six, over."*

"Captain," Adele said, forwarding the file unopened. If Cory was going to be so punctilious, she would do the same. "Lieutenant Cory compiled this data on the

Corcyran destroyer. I don't have the knowledge base to assess it, so I'm passing it directly to you. Over!"

"*Thank you, Mundy,*" Daniel said. His inset image was smiling from the corner of her screen. "*Cory, please brief us, over.*"

"*Sorry,*" Cory muttered. The problem with an organization like the crew of the *Princess Cecile*—and the still greater problem when the corvette's personnel had been winnowed from a hundred and twenty to twenty—was to know whether to behave like family or like members of a hierarchical military organization.

Adele was certainly poor at following procedure, because in her heart she *wasn't* part of a military organization. That didn't cause her difficulties, because nobody else aboard thought of her as a junior warrant officer of the RCN, either.

It didn't matter to ordinary spacers, because they understood the bounds of familiarity in the same fashion that tenants on the Bantry estate did. They might joke with Six before going on liberty, but if they met him out of uniform, he was still Six—just as he was still the Squire to a tenant in Xenos. They didn't need the trappings of authority to understand their relationship to their betters.

Adele smiled in sad memory of her mother. Esme Rolfe Mundy believed that all human beings could rise to the ideal which the Rolfes and Mundys already embodied. She would never have used the term "betters" in that fashion, and she would have been horrified if she had heard her daughter do so.

In fact, Adele didn't believe in the distinction between the lower orders and their betters, either; though having lived many years on the bottom of society, she was unable to romanticize its residents as her mother had. That said, most of the members of the so-called lower orders whom Adele had met *did* believe in the distinction.

A few of them resented it; more of them would have said that the separation was ordained by heaven. Most simply accepted the division as they accepted sunrise and got on with important matters like sex and putting food on the table.

Cory and Cazelet, the younger commissioned officers, were the ones most affected. They operated informally under Adele in collecting and sorting the data which poured into Adele's console at every landfall. Their skill at these tasks was part of the reason that Captain Leary's missions had been uniformly successful, but the tasks were no part of their RCN duties—and they still *had* RCN duties.

Cory, the *Kiesche*'s second lieutenant and therefore senior to the freighter's signals officer, didn't know whether to give important information to his formal superior officer, the captain, or to Adele, the informal superior at whose direction he had gathered the information. The real answer was "give it to either one," but that wasn't a response which RCN regulations could accept.

"*Sir, the* Freccia's *got all her thrusters and High Drive motors, and her fusion bottle was replaced just last year,*" Cory said. "*She's got a full crew according to the books, but they're thirty percent landsmen hired here on Corcyra. And I don't trust the books.*"

"*Nor should you,*" said Daniel. "*I never knew a Pantellarian ship where the captain didn't collect the*

*pay of at least ten spacers in a hundred, slots that
were never going to be filled, over."*

"They only keep an anchor watch on board," Cory
said. "I doubt they could get under way in less than
six hours, and that's if the stores are loaded. Which
again the books say they are, but I doubt it. The
Freccia's no danger to us, sir, over."

"*Freighter* Kiesche *out of Xenos to Brotherhood
Control,*" Vesey repeated, since she hadn't gotten a
response the first time. "*Request permission to land,
over."*

Adele guessed from the available data that the
crews of the missile batteries were asleep or even that
the batteries were unmanned at present. That sort
of sloppiness at a port which might be attacked at
any instant would horrify her, but she had too much
experience of fringe worlds—and of human nature
more generally—to doubt that it was possible.

*If everyone were like me, it would be a very dif-
ferent universe. A very polite one. And probably very
dangerous.*

A starship landing nearby would awaken the sound-
est sleeper, and someone startled out of a sound sleep
might very well roll to the firing switch and press it.
Fortunately, the batteries' electronics took a minute
or more to calibrate after they were turned on, and
both were cold at present. Adele would be watching
that status readout carefully.

"Daniel?" Adele said. "Captain Leary, I mean.
Although there's been no fighting around Brotherhood, and so far as I can tell no Pantellarian threat
to it, all three of the main rebel military organizations have at least a third of their strength in and

near the city. Based on ration returns for troops in
Brotherhood against those in the siege lines around
Hablinger. Over."

Adele wouldn't have had to give her source to this
group, but she had too often made a statement to
strangers and gotten the reply, "You can't know that!
You're guessing!"

Fewer people would have responded in that fashion
if they knew what went through Adele's mind when
someone did, or if they noticed her left hand dipping
toward her pistol. Much of what Adele had learned
over the years involved ways to avoid putting herself
in situations which would make her angry.

Angrier would be a better description. Anger—at
life, at the universe, and especially at herself—was
the bedrock of Adele's personality, as she well knew.

"*Freighter* Kiesche *out of Xenos to Brotherhood
Control,*" said Vesey yet again. "*Request landing
instructions, over.*"

"*They're worried about each other, then,*" Daniel
said. There was a touch of humor, or at least speculation, in his tone. "*Or they individually are each
planning a coup. Not so?*"

"I don't believe either the Regiment or the Navy
thinks that it's strong enough to launch a coup with
any chance of success," Adele said. "I find recent
plans in the Garrison's database which suggest that
its leaders may believe they could succeed."

She would review at leisure the data her systems
were pulling in, but experience had given her an eye
for relevant detail in a quick scan. She added, "I very
much doubt they're correct, given the loathing with
which every other organization on the planet appears

to regard them, but arrogant stupidity isn't uncommon among leaders. Even nonmilitary leaders."

"*Point taken,*" said Daniel with a chuckle. "*Some of us military leaders are smart enough to listen to advisers who don't have a military background, however. But what about the Transformationists we're involved with?*"

He and his friend Adele were chatting now; neither of them was thinking about the others on the net. Adele was therefore startled when Rikard Cleveland said, "*Sir! We have no troops in Brotherhood, just the company of a hundred at the siege of Hablinger. We have no interest in ruling Brotherhood or Corcyra; we just want to worship without interference. That is, over.*"

Well, perhaps he has a right to be offended, Adele thought. Aloud she said, "Cleveland's statement is correct, Captain. As far as I can tell."

"*Officer Mundy, do you have any doubt on that point, over?*" Daniel asked more sharply than Adele expected. He had a right also: he was Six, and he could ask any question he pleased aboard his own ship.

"My only doubt, Daniel," Adele said, deliberately defusing the situation by using his given name, "comes from the fact that I have not yet managed to enter the Transformationist database in Pearl Valley. Alone of systems on the rebel side, that is. In theory, it might be filled with plans for galactic conquest, but I very much doubt it. I think these religious dreamers simply have someone very good in charge of computer security."

"*Freighter Kiesche, you are cleared to land,*" said a voice, responding on the 15-meter band. "*Pick any available slip; but be warned: if you're not on the seawall, your cargo will have to be lightered to and from your holds because the floating gantries aren't working at present, over."*

The Regiment's antiship missile battery had gone live. Adele sent its control module the lockout command which she had prepared as soon as the *Kiesche* reached orbit and she learned the model of the unit.

Accidents happen; but if they were accidents for which Adele could have prepared, then she felt that she deserved to die. She would regret that she had failed her shipmates in her last instant, though.

"Roger, Brotherhood Control," Vesey said. *"Kiesche out."*

"Officer Mundy?" Daniel said. His inset image was smiling.

"Go ahead, Six," Adele said. "Any further information I need will be easier to gather on the ground. Out!"

She smiled also, pleased to have remembered the correct protocol. For a change.

"Ship, prepare for landing," Daniel said and hit the EXECUTE button on his virtual keyboard. The thrusters roared as the *Kiesche* braked toward Brotherhood Harbor under the control of the ship's computer.

CHAPTER 11

Brotherhood on Corcyra

Adele stood beside Daniel while the main hatch began to squeal open. Most of the *Kiesche*'s crew was in front of them in the hold, which was fine with her; she felt no need to be the first of the freighter's personnel to set foot on Corcyra. Steam and a nose-wrinkling whiff of ozone swirled in through the crack.

There was a shriek and clang: the hatch had jammed. Only a hand's breadth of air was visible between the upper edge and the coaming.

"Hold one!" called Cory over the hatch speakers. "I'll back it—"

"Keep clear!" said Woetjans as her arm swept one of the riggers a step sideways. Evans swung a bronze mallet with an ease that belied its twenty-pound weight, striking not the jammed piston but rather the plating to which the unit was bolted. The deck jumped under Adele's soft-soled boots.

"Try it now!" Woetjans shouted through the open bridge hatch. The piston shuddered, then resumed pushing the hatch downward—but more smoothly than before it had jammed.

The bosun had clearly moved the rigger aside because she knew that Evans wouldn't think to be sure no one was behind him when he brought the mallet around in a roundhouse swing. The squat technician was impressively strong, but Adele knew from previous voyages that he had the intellectual capacity of an eggplant.

Daniel, his lips close to Adele's ear, said, "How do you think Hale is working out?"

Adele pursed her lips. She let her eyes shift beyond Daniel to where Vesey and Hale stood beside the cargo: stacks of crated carbines.

"She hasn't called herself to my attention," Adele said. "I suppose that's a recommendation: she's behaved as a member of the *Sissie*'s crew is expected to behave, doing her job well and not requiring unusual notice. Though it's the *Kiesche*'s crew now, I suppose."

Adele pursed her lips again. "I met Hale in the Navy House Archives before you and I discussed this mission," she said. "I'm not sure she connects me with the scholar she chanced into in Xenos."

"Umm," said Daniel, nodding. His eyes were on the hatch as it tilted downward, pulled by the hydraulic piston.

Adele felt cold with embarrassment. A different person would have blushed.

"Daniel," she said. "Hale implied that she and Blantyre had been rivals at the Academy. She was looking for the logs of the *Princess Cecile* as a private vessel for lessons as to how Blantyre's career had progressed so much faster than her own. Through Cory

I suggested that she might wish to apply for a crew position on the *Kiesche*. I apologize for interfering with the crewing of the ship. I should have told you."

"It doesn't appear to me that you interfered," Daniel said. He grinned at her. "And Hale seems to be working out very well. She's intelligent and not afraid to work."

He coughed into his hand and added, "I'm not sure Hale *did* recognize you in different clothing and circumstances, but she certainly recognized Tovera, which was a sufficient clue. She's quite intelligent, as I said."

The hatch, now boarding ramp, clanged onto the outrigger. Some ports had extendable walkways which could be connected to the boarding bridge, but here at Brotherhood there was only the concrete levee surrounding the harbor. Iron ladders reached from the top of the wall down below the surface to accommodate changes in the water level.

"Let's go!" Woetjans said. She and four riggers trotted down the ramp, carrying the freighter's own extender. At the bottom they began expanding the first ten-foot section by attaching the air pump and turning a valve.

Steam, ozone, and stench entered the compartment. Ships in port ordinarily voided their wastes into the slip in which they floated. Their thrusters incinerated anything organic, including native algae or its equivalent.

Spacers got used to the smell. Human beings had an amazing ability to get used to things, as Adele had learned in slums even before she joined the RCN.

The swatch of Brotherhood which Adele could see through the hatchway was as familiar to her as the smell. They were on the city side, but warehouses and shops catering to spacers were built all around the pool.

A concrete roadway circled the top of the levee, though that was above eye level from the hold. What Adele *could* see was the heavy-duty crane trundling slowly around the pool on double overhead tracks, hauling behind it a flatcar with three heavy pieces of equipment; she thought they were generators.

The top and bottom plates of the extender had swelled open. The riggers didn't wait for it to fill completely before shoving it into the water attached to the second section, which they began to inflate in turn. They had brought four sections, but two sufficed to reach the nearest ladder up the levee wall. The team locked the second firmly to the ramp while the pump charged it.

"I knew the town was on a hill," Daniel said, nodding toward the view. "I didn't expect the peak to be so high, though. The top must be a hundred feet above the river."

"One hundred and twenty-one feet at average river stage," Adele said. Her data unit was in her hand, but she didn't need to check it. "Brotherhood is built on a volcanic intrusion, not a mud bank. The river changed course from the east side to the west side of the plug, but it remained in the same channel farther downstream."

Woetjans strode across the extender, riding the springy surface with the ease of experience, and lashed the far end to the ladder. "We're set, Six!" she called, waving the wrench in her right hand.

"The liberty party is released!" Daniel said. "Remember, spacers, it's daylight only!"

The crew shouted a variety of things—including,

Adele noted, "Up Cinnabar!" That wasn't a problem since no one, official or otherwise, was waiting on the levee to greet the *Kiesche*'s arrival. Eight of the waiting spacers trotted down the ramp and extender.

"Half of each watch," Daniel said to Adele. "It would look odd if a tramp captain didn't give the crew liberty on landing. Of course, most tramps would have been much longer on the voyage than we were."

"They're not wearing liberty suits," Adele noted. The spacers were wearing ordinary slops—though cleaner and newer than normal duty garb on board. She had expected them to be in RCN utilities decorated with patches and ribbons to make them stand out among those they met on the ground.

"While we're not exactly trying to keep our identity secret here," Daniel said dryly, "I didn't think that RCN battle ribbons and patches for RCN warships were really required as a way to introduce ourselves."

Woetjans and her team were walking up the ramp; Barnes looked back over his shoulder as if regretful that he was still on duty. Remaining in the hold with Adele were Rikard Cleveland and Tovera; Vesey and Hale, who were in charge of replenishing the *Kiesche*'s supplies; and Hogg and Daniel.

Hogg opened the arms locker welded to the bulkhead beside the bridge hatch. He took out a submachine gun and a pair of holstered service pistols, much heavier than the little weapon in Adele's pocket.

"Master?" he said, looking at Daniel. "You want something?"

"Umm," said Daniel. "The wrong image for talking to the port authorities, I think. I'll trust to your protection, Hogg."

"That's what I figured," Hogg said. "Vesey? And you, Hale. Take these. Unarmed women are chum in the water in a place like this. Right, Master Cleveland?"

"It should be all right in daylight," Cleveland said. "Ah . . . I have my pin."

He touched the pearly white trefoil he'd attached to his collar.

"Militia members don't have trouble," he added. "Lady Mundy and her servant will be with me."

"I appreciate your concern, Master Cleveland," Tovera said. Someone who didn't know her might think she meant it. "I'll feel safe knowing that you'll protect me."

"Well, it's not me," Cleveland said, taking the thanks at face value. "It's the pin. We Transformationists aren't the largest faction on Corcyra, but we're respected."

Vesey took a pistol and cinched the belt around her waist. As if feeling the question in Adele's gaze, she looked up and said, "I've been practicing, ma'am. I'm not very good. I don't think I'll ever be good. But I know how to shoot it."

"I doubt it will be necessary," Adele said in a neutral tone.

In fact Adele suspected that Vesey's intellectual coolness would make her extremely effective in a gunfight, where most participants closed their eyes and jerked off shots as quickly as they could. Her only doubt was whether Vesey could bring herself to pull the trigger, even if it were a choice between that and certain death.

"If you don't mind," Hale said, "I can't hit anything with a handgun—"

"Take it anyway," Hogg growled, bouncing the remaining pistol in his palm to call attention to it.

"—so I'll carry one of the carbines from our cargo,"

Hale continued as she walked over to the weapon cases. "I've cleaned the top case and checked them for functioning when I was off-watch."

Hale must already have thrown the pair of levers locking the stack to the deck. She lifted down the top case—a hundred pounds or so between the weight of packaging and the ten carbines, Adele noted—and raised the lid.

Hogg frowned, but he looked more startled than angry. Hale rose with the carbine in her left hand. "Master Hogg," she said. "I would appreciate it if you'd hand me a charger of ammunition for this. I put a carton in the arms locker."

"Yeah, sure," said Hogg in a mild voice. He put the extra pistol back in its drawer in the locker and, bending, fished two chargers from the box on the floor of the locker.

"The arms locker is normally locked, Hale," Daniel said.

She stiffened to attention instead of taking the tubular magazines Hogg was holding out. "Sir!" she said, eyes front. "I was armory officer aboard the *Kipling*! Apparently I failed to turn over my key! I'll give it to you at once!"

"Belay that, Hale," Daniel said. He wasn't laughing, but the crinkling at the corners of his eyes suggested that he wasn't far from doing so. "I think the key is in good hands."

"If you're ready, Hale," Vesey said, "We'll be off to Beardsley and Owens."

She glanced at Daniel and said, "I'm starting with them. If I'm not satisfied with the quality, I'll work down my list of provisioning merchants."

"Carry on, Vesey," Daniel said. "Hogg, you and I will hike up to the Manor, which is what passes for Government House here, while Officer Mundy and our principal make contact with the Transformationist representative."

Vesey and Hale, the latter with her carbine ported across her chest, had started across the floating extender. Daniel grinned to Adele and said, "Hale is working out *quite* well, I would say."

He and Hogg set off. Adele looked at her companions. Her data unit had plotted a route to Master Graves' office—Brother Graves, as he went by here—but there would be psychological advantages to putting Cleveland in charge here on familiar ground.

"Guide us, please, Master Cleveland," Adele said, sliding her data unit away.

Tovera lifted the lid of her attaché case slightly, and the familiar weight rode in the left pocket of Adele's tunic. Just in case the pin on Cleveland's collar wasn't enough.

Hogg waited for Daniel at the top of the levee, eyeing the town. The ground beneath the tramway pylons was generally clear. Beyond that, instead of a broad esplanade for pedestrians and vehicles, there was an alley into which displays and seated loungers edged. Now that the crane had passed, some people were spilling into the tramway also.

That was probably safe enough if you were sober—the crane couldn't move faster than a walk, even without a load—but Daniel didn't imagine the driver would bother to slow for someone sprawled between the pylons. The crane's clearance had looked to be about a foot, but the car it pulled moved on full-width rollers to spread the load. Anyone under them would become a smear on the cracked concrete.

"We've been worse places," said Hogg, looking to right and left. "They aren't short of bars and knocking shops, anyway."

"Rather than find our way between the buildings," Daniel said, "we'll walk to our right till we get to the avenue up to the government buildings." He wore dark-blue utilities without markings, but his battered blue saucer hat had gold braid.

"Fine by me," Hogg said, adjusting the sling of his submachine gun so that it hung across his chest with the muzzle to the left. The barrel was horizontal, and he kept his right hand on the grip.

Daniel smiled as they walked along the harborfront. He kept to the tramway, but Hogg walked on his left and shifted his weapon to point at anyone who might be blocking his way. Hogg had the countryman's view of cities as dangerous places inhabited solely by crooks who would rob him or worse if they got a chance.

That was an overstatement everywhere Daniel had been, even here in Brotherhood—a port and a mining town; both places which collected people who did brutal work which not infrequently brutalized them. Hogg and his submachine gun weren't so far out of the norm that they aroused comment, though.

The buildings were low—mostly two-story along the harbor and one or two as you moved back from the water. The roofs were universally of corrugated plastic: fire orange when installed but easing through beige to cream after a few years of exposure.

Most structures were walled with stabilized earth

sandwiched between sheets of tough white plastic; where the sheathing had cracked, the black core showed like splotches of shadow. Frontages along the harbor had often been painted, but sunlight had faded primary colors into pastels and pastels into shimmers on the plastic.

A man shambled toward Daniel from the alley between two taverns. Hogg snarled a curse and angled the muzzle of his weapon.

"Please," the beggar said. His hair was a knotted gray cascade, and his features looked as though they had been dipped in acid. He retained all four limbs, but the muscles were shrunken over the bones.

"Bugger off!" Hogg snarled.

The beggar dropped to his knees in the street, not quite in their path. Daniel stepped deeper into the tramway and drew Hogg with him by touching his shoulder.

"Please," the beggar whispered as they passed. They didn't look back.

"We didn't make him that way!" Hogg said. Daniel did not reply.

At the base of the central avenue was a flagpole. The banner drooped in the still air; all Daniel could see was that it included blue and white stripes. Parked there was a wheeled armored car which looked like a civilian panel truck with a new body of steel-ceramic sandwich and an ungraded suspension. The automatic impeller on a ring mount accessed through the cab did not have a gunshield.

The vehicle had been painted dark gray, but the original legend on the sides was now covered with a white rectangle and the words ARMY OF CORCYRA.

Whoever held the stencil had let it slip midway in the spraying process.

A platoon of troops in gray battledress lounged around the car and on the harborfront. Their original patches had been removed. Most but not all now bore in their place lengths of white ribbon embroidered with *Army of Corcyra* in black. They paid no more attention to Daniel and Hogg than the civilians had.

"That truck wouldn't stop a slug," Hogg muttered as they started up the slope. "Wouldn't even slow it down. Well, maybe this popgun—"

He patted the submachine gun's receiver.

"—but not a real impeller."

"I'm surprised they bother with vehicles here," Daniel said. "It'll brush buildings even on the waterfront, and it certainly can't maneuver in the city proper."

The central avenue was thirty feet wide and paved with crushed rock in a plastic matrix. The result was ugly, but even worn it would provide secure footing in the rain.

Narrow streets led off to either side and meandered up the slope. They ranged from what Daniel would call alleys to mere walkways which separated the backs of houses. Most dwellings had gardens walled either with fieldstone or with panels of structural sandwich like the sides of the houses. The dark green foliage of bushes or small trees overhung the walls, and occasionally Daniel could glimpse bright flowers through the slats of latticed gates.

"They grow things here," Hogg said. There was a hint of approval in his tone, though nothing a stranger would have heard. "You don't often see that in a city."

"There's money in Brotherhood," Daniel said. "For

the people who supply the mines and the miners who've made their piles, at least. They ship a lot of copper."

From orbit he had noted a dozen freighters of roughly the *Kiesche*'s size in harbor. The war might have reduced trade to Corcyra, but there was enough profit to be made to justify the risk in the mind of many captains.

They had reached a flight of twelve full-width steps midway to the top of the avenue. Daniel turned to look back the way they'd come. He could see the *Kiesche*; Cory had raised the base section of the Dorsal A antenna. A spacer, probably Sun, sat in the crosstrees with a sailcloth bundle the length of a stocked impeller.

At the east end of the harborfront was the Garrison's antiship missile battery. The launcher was lowered beneath the revetment, but two gray-uniformed personnel sat on chairs in the offset opening.

Daniel looked left. He couldn't see the Regiment's battery past the building roofs, but the destroyer *Freccia* floated midway down. She looked slender to Daniel; Pantellarian ships had a reputation in the RCN for being flimsy, though nobody denied they were fast. She mounted seven ten-centimeter plasma cannon in three turrets. The two dorsal twin units were raised to provide more internal space in harbor, and the triple ventral turret would be underwater.

Daniel scowled. Mounting plasma cannon in threes was the sort of flashy nonsense you expected from Pantellarians. It slowed aiming, reduced reliability, and made it much more difficult to clear stoppages.

"Eh?" said Hogg, noting Daniel's expression. "What's wrong?"

"Nothing, Hogg," Daniel said, grinning broadly. "But if I were in charge of the Pantellarian navy, heads would be rolling in the Design Bureau."

They continued up the avenue. Hogg seemed to relax as they rose farther from the coarse congestion of the harborfront. The shops and restaurants facing the avenue or the streets immediately off it catered to a less brutal clientele.

Daniel continued to smile. Hogg fit in better with the dives near the water, but it would take him a few days to become acclimated to the Corcyran environment the way he had to the Strip outside Harbor Three on Cinnabar.

Daniel glanced back from a higher level. A pair of warehouses had been converted to barracks across the tramway from where the *Freccia* was docked. A watchtower had been erected at the back of one.

Daniel didn't see heavy weapons there, but they could have been hidden by the roof. Two men in light blue Pantellarian naval utilities leaned against the railing, occasionally viewing the town and harbor through optical devices. On their showing, the navy was somewhat more alert than the platoon of the Garrison at the base of the avenue.

At the top of the avenue was the three-hundred-foot plaza fronting the Manor. A retaining wall supported the near end, but the fill must have shifted over time. The flagstones there lay irregularly and now sloped toward the harbor.

There were thirty or forty people on the plaza, including a juggler, several prostitutes, and a drunk facedown in his vomit. Hogg barely scanned them before he raised his head to take in the Manor itself.

"Where the bloody *hell* did that drop from?" he said. He sounded delighted.

The four-story Manor had brick walls and projecting towers of light gray stone. The corner towers were round with conical roofs, while the two attached to the frontage were half-octagonal and battlemented on top.

It looked like no other building Daniel had seen in Brotherhood—or anywhere else, for that matter. Because of the distance the Manor was set back from the edge of the ridge, only its gambrel roof had been visible from the harbor.

"Adele says it's the oldest building here," Daniel said. "It's been both government headquarters and a working hotel for several hundred years, but it's been here longer than that. There's no record of who built it originally or why they built it."

They started toward the arched entrance. "This is like being back in the woods," Daniel said as he hopped from one tilted block to another.

"They're not covered with wet leaves, though," said Hogg.

Two prostitutes moved to intercept them. They weren't impressive at a distance, and a closer approach didn't improve their appearance. Daniel slanted slightly to his right. That would take him past the women, who seemed barely able to hobble.

Hogg waved and called, "Maybe later, girls."

"Really?" Daniel said, frowning.

"Maybe if it's dark enough," Hogg muttered. "And I'm drunk enough. Which has happened a time or two, young master."

He grimaced and added without meeting Daniel's

eyes, "Look, I feel sorry for 'em, okay? Some of 'em wasn't half-bad girls in their day."

"Right," said Daniel. He thought about the beggar on the harborfront, but he said nothing further aloud.

In front of the Manor was an oval ornamental pool, thirty feet long and ten feet across at the center. A pair of prisoners, leg-shackled together, shuffled toward the pool with a hand barrow. Daniel skirted the other end, wondering if it had at one time been planted with water flowers.

To his amazement, the prisoners tipped their barrow's contents of kitchen waste into the water. Potato peelings, grease, and unidentifiable bits swirled on the surface.

"What did you just do, you scuts!" Daniel shouted. The nearer prisoner was a hulking brute who outweighed him by a hundred pounds, but Daniel was so angry at the sudden vandalism that he would have done the same even without Hogg standing close by with the submachine gun.

"Bugger off," said the smaller man at the back of the barrow. He was hunched. His pointy face had the features of an unhealthy rat.

"I'm working off my sentence," the big man said. He smiled shyly. "They says I kilt a man."

Daniel blinked, as much at the pleasant expression as at the words. "Did you?" he said. "Kill him?"

"Dunno," said the big man. "I was drunk. I guess maybe I did."

"But why dump garbage *here*?" Daniel said, disarmed by the prisoner's obvious good nature.

"Bugger off," the other prisoner repeated. "Kelsey, we gotta get back."

"Higgens, you learn some manners or I pull your head off," Kelsey said. He didn't sound exactly angry, but there was a burr in his voice that hadn't been there before. "All they gonna do when we get back is lock us back to that anchor chain in the basement. I druther talk to this gentleman."

Higgens turned his head away. Kelsey watched him sternly for a moment, then smiled again to Daniel and said, "The sponge here eats the food, you see. There it goes!"

Daniel looked down. The water had been still: now the surface was in trembling motion as a current drew the scraps along one curved side of the pool.

Somebody turned the filter on, he thought. Then he saw a tentacle the thickness of his arm, covered with writhing cilia which were drawing the water toward them.

Daniel shaded his eyes to look below the surface. Directly beneath him was a grating which normally would have covered a filter and pump. Something pinkish-gray and as big as a steer's torso grew on it, concealing most of the grate. There were four tentacles like the one he had seen, all shimmering with cilia.

"You say it's a sponge?" he said, kneeling to get closer.

Over the striped body crawled flat bronze creatures the size of a man's thumb. They could have been blotches of color on the hide had Daniel not seen that they were moving slowly.

"Don't you fall in, sir!" Kelsey warned. "It'll eat you quick as it'll eat a rat!"

He knuckled his bearded chin. "And I allus heard it was a sponge, but I don't know. I'm not, well, I ain't got much schooling, you know."

"I saw it eat a drunk last year," Higgens said. "He screamed like you wouldn't believe. Wouldn't have done no good to pull him out, because once it stings you it's all over. So I been told, anyhow."

"Thank you, Kelsey," Daniel said, straightening. He fished a florin out of his purse, then thought a moment and found a second coin. "And you too, Higgens."

He flipped the coins to the prisoners, one and then the other.

"Come, Hogg," Daniel said. "We have business with the port authorities."

But as soon as we get back to the Kiesche, he thought, *I'll have Adele learn more about this sponge.* It was the most interesting thing Daniel had seen on Corcyra yet.

CHAPTER 12

Brotherhood on Corcyra

When Cleveland reached the top of the ladder, Adele gave him the jute rag on which she and Tovera had already wiped their hands. The harbor level had dropped several feet in the recent past, and the bottom four rungs were slimy with a mixture of lubricant, algae, and the organic waste which nourished the algae.

"Ah, thank you, your ladyship," Cleveland said. He turned his head, obviously looking for a place to deposit the rag.

Adele took it between her right thumb and forefinger. "I prefer to be called Mundy, Cleveland," she said. "In Xenos, and certainly here."

She dropped the rag into the slip. "Returning like to like," she explained with a cold smile. "I can no more clean up this harbor than I could remove all negative and discourteous people from the human race."

"I . . ." Cleveland said. He suddenly smiled. "I understand, Mundy. I'm trying to do the latter, starting with myself; but until I have become perfect, I won't bother the rest of humanity."

He cocked his head slightly. "From what I've seen," he said, "you have less need of correction than anyone I've previously met."

"It depends on what you mean by 'negative,'" Tovera said. Her grin reminded Adele of a skull's. Perhaps skulls also had a sense of humor.

"Rather than go up Central Street," Cleveland said, gesturing to the sloping boulevard leading straight up toward the Manor, "I suggest we go through the town. It may be a little longer, but this end of the plaza is an obstacle course that I'd prefer to avoid."

Adele shrugged. "You know the town," she said.

Cleveland led them briskly across Water Street—or whatever it was called here. Adele reached for her data unit, then caught herself with a grim smile.

"Cleveland?" she said. *If Tovera can learn to mimic a sense of humor, I can give the impression of being a socialized human being.* "What is the name of the street that circles the harbor? I'm just curious."

"That's just Harborside, your . . . that is, Mundy," he said. He gestured ahead of them, moving his left hand from side to side. "Now we're on Sweeney's Alley at this end, but it'll be Crescent Alley at the top when we reach Ridge Road."

The passage they'd turned up seemed to meander between the structures rather than them being built to either side. It was generally about ten feet wide, though occasionally the corner of a building narrowed by it.

"Are all the streets here this way?" Adele asked. The alley had no sharp angles, but she couldn't see more than thirty feet ahead or behind because of twists in the course.

"This is the widest street after Central," Cleveland

said. "Generally, at least. People built where the slope allowed them to. Every ten years or so the harbor district gets flooded, from what I've been told."

Adele followed him under a balcony enclosed in carved wood screens. The lower half of the screen on the downhill side had cracked away and was replaced by a sheet of plastic.

Tovera waited two steps back until they were clear. Her right hand was fully inside the case which held her submachine gun.

Cleveland didn't appear to notice; Adele suppressed a frown. She could not object to Tovera's extreme professional care, and in theory it shouldn't have affected Adele. Tovera wasn't directing *her* to scan rooftops or to be ready if a gunman leaned over the gate across the way. Irrationally it *did* induce paranoia in Adele, though her intellectual control prevented that from being visible to anyone outside her mind.

The gate Adele had been considering darkened as a middle-aged woman stepped to it. The vertical stripes of her loose dress did little to reduce her bulk; she held a trowel in her right hand.

"Madame," Cleveland said, smiling as he passed. To Adele's surprise, the woman's stony expression dissolved into a smile which took ten years off her apparent age.

Adele nodded to the woman but didn't attempt a smile. She had found in the past that her smiles rarely struck strangers as friendly. Which was fair, as Adele rarely felt friendly toward strangers.

The flower beds she glimpsed past the gardener were gorgeously colorful. They looked unplanned, but Adele understood patterns well enough to realize that what she saw was as carefully structured as one of her own databases.

"Brotherhood appears to be," Adele said, then paused to word the rest of the statement correctly, "a more ordinary community than I was expecting in the midst of war."

Cleveland turned his head and smiled. "Some members of my faith believe that the presence of our fellowship only fifty miles south in Pearl Valley helps make Brotherhood such a pleasant community," he said. "Despite the port and the miners which are the basis of the economy. I prefer to think that people are generally decent when given an opportunity to be."

Adele felt a wry smile tug at the corners of her lips. *Whereas I myself consider it a good day when I don't feel a desire to shoot one of the people with whom I have to deal.* She supposed that both reactions were within the acceptable norms of civilized society.

"This is Ridge Road," Cleveland said as they rounded a curving house wall. "We'll turn to the right here."

On the ten-foot-wide street was the first motorized traffic Adele had seen since they started up the hillside. Two men were guiding a cart with hub-center motors from left to right; on the bed rode what looked like a refrigeration unit.

Coming the other way was a chain-driven vehicle on four high, flimsy looking wheels. It looked like something built locally from spare parts; on the front axle was a triangular metal pennon stencilled with a light-blue trefoil.

The woman driving from a saddle was beautiful and well dressed. She was alone on the vehicle, but it ambled at the pace of the squad of soldiers on foot escorting her. The troops' battledress was striped black on dark green; they carried stocked impellers comparable to the carbines in the *Kiesche*'s hold.

"Ah, that's Caleira driving the buggy," Cleveland said. "She was working as an entertainer—she may be local, but I wouldn't know. She's now the companion of Mistress Tibbs, the chief administrator of the Self-Defense Regiment. Their headquarters is on the other side of the Square, so I guess that's where she's going. And the navy headquarters is in the building alongside theirs, but they've both got their barracks by the harbor."

"I see," said Adele, noting the information mentally. She would transfer it to digital form as soon as she got an opportunity. The troops were well-turned-out, and they hadn't given her the impression of being bravos looking for a fight, the way many uniformed gangs did here on the fringes. "And Brother Graves?"

"Across the street and two doors up," Cleveland said and started across. Another vehicle of some sort was visible to the right, but it seemed to be parked. Men were carrying pipes from it; the only moving traffic was pedestrian.

Adele could see the plaza to the left; the paving blocks nearer the slope rippled like the sea, just as Cleveland had warned. The building which faced the plaza was a palace built of either stone or stone-clad concrete. Farther from the plaza were two-story shops and offices, some with apartments above, on both sides of the street.

Between a clothier's shop and a tavern—not a dive— was a door painted a pearl white. Cleveland swung it open to a flight of steps upward. The panel moved with the weight of steel, but it hadn't been locked.

Tovera touched the edge of the door. "I'll close it," she said courteously to Cleveland. "So that you can lead."

"Right!" said Cleveland, skipping up the stairs two at a time. The door thumped shut. If he realized that Tovera didn't trust him behind them, his pleasant smile gave no sign of it.

Adele followed. She found these wooden treads relaxing. She was more used to metal stairs.

Adele heard minute hesitations in Tovera's steps as the servant glanced over her shoulder. She wondered if Tovera's need for constant vigilance made her unhappy. Perhaps she no more regarded it than she did breathing.

Cleveland opened the door at the head of the stairs. "Brother Graves?" he called. "I'm here with, ah, Mistress Mundy. Captain Leary is dealing with the port authorities, but Mundy is a partner in the expedition."

"Please come in, mistress," said a small, middle-aged man wearing a tan business suit with a thin brown stripe. He was balding from forehead to mid-scalp, but his voice was lively and the hand with which he shook Adele's was firm. "I'm Graves—and don't worry about 'brother,' since you have no reason to regard me or Cleveland as your brothers. We appreciate your help all the more for that reason."

The office was a single room, though there was a door in the back wall which probably led to living quarters. There were couches along two walls, and a pair of chairs flanked the entrance.

The other item of furnishing was a commercial console which Adele realized was as powerful as a starship unit. She smiled at the thought. *It's probably configured differently.*

"I don't know how much help we can be," she said aloud, suppressing the reflex to explain that she wasn't Daniel's partner. In fact she was his partner, in every respect except the legal ones which didn't matter to either Daniel or herself. "It seems to me that digging up the treasure is more a matter for a mining engineer than"—*how to describe the* Kiesche's *crew?*—"generalists like ourselves."

"Mining engineers are twenty a dandiprat on Corcyra," Graves said. He gestured to the couch, then seated himself on one end of it. "I'm one myself, as a matter of fact. The political situation on Corcyra, however—"

His wry smile seemed warm, but there was sadness behind it.

"—is such that bringing mining equipment openly to Pearl Valley would arouse suspicion. And almost certainly violence by one of the competing parties, if any inkling of the purpose got out."

Adele made another mental note, this time to check the meaning of "dandiprat." From context, it could be anything from a coin to a vegetable . . . but that wasn't the matter at hand.

"The cargo we brought is weapons," Adele said, sitting on the other end of the couch. Cleveland took a chair, while Tovera continued to stand near the hinge side of the door. "We thought we would blend in that way and explain our presence in an acceptable fashion. When we've examined the situation, we'll acquire such machinery as we need here."

Graves grimaced. "Yes," he said, "yes, you're right, of course. But that brings its own problems. I cringed when I saw the manifest you transmitted from orbit, because I'm sure it will cause others, the Garrison at least, to attempt to get the arms for themselves."

"Do you mean, to hijack our cargo?" Adele said, trying to keep her tone neutral. Tovera smiled slightly.

"Oh, they wouldn't do anything that raw!" Cleveland said, looking from Adele to Graves. "Why, neither the Regiment nor the navy would allow that to happen even if Mursiello were willing."

Graves spread his hands palms up and looked down at them. "I'm an engineer, Brother Cleveland," he said. "I think such an action would show very bad judgment on Colonel Mursiello's part, but—"

He raised his eyes. His expression was the same sad smile as before.

"—I don't have a high opinion of the colonel's judgment even now. Still, what I'm expecting is pressure to sell the cargo to another of the parties instead of delivering it to the consignees."

Graves clenched his fists again. "I ought to be at the port office, too," he said, "but I told myself I wouldn't be much support in that sort of unpleasant hectoring. I still should have gone."

He looked up. Adele shrugged. "I don't think Captain Leary will be unduly swayed by someone shouting at him," she said. "How will you get the cargo to Pearl Valley? Doing that will reduce the risk of trouble, I presume."

"Yes, of course," Graves agreed. He rose and went to the console. "That much I can take care of. There's a barge under contract to us. I'm alerting the crew so that they'll be ready to perform at any schedule that you, that Captain Leary, sets."

He used a virtual keyboard to make entries. The holographic display was unreadable from this side, but Adele's personal data unit was absorbing that input and all others within the office.

Graves looked toward Adele through the holographic blurring. He said, "I'm not a very good representative under these conditions, I'm afraid. I'll only say in my defense that none of our community has the right personality for cutthroat beggar-your-neighbor dealings such as have become the only way business is transacted in Brotherhood. Some of us *did* have that personality. I did myself, I'm sorry to admit."

He gave Adele a smile of warm fellowship.

"But that was before I felt the kinship in Pearl Valley and became a Transformationist myself. There doesn't seem to be any way to go back, thank goodness. Though sometimes I feel that the old me would be useful to the faith."

"Will the weapons be of any use to you?" Adele said. She was mostly successful in hiding her frown.

"We'll fight to save ourselves and our faith," Cleveland said. "Brother Graves shouldn't denigrate himself. He's been a very effective advocate for our community in the Independence Council. I know, having just come back from a separation of many light-years—"

Cleveland forced a smile. His expression was that of someone just released from torture, trying to put a brave face on what he had undergone.

"—what it means for him to remain here and deal with people who are boiling with hatred and hostility every hour of every day."

Adele said, "Given the problems within your coalition"—it stretched a point to call the Independence Council a coalition, but this wasn't a time to debate word choice—"I'm surprised that the rebellion has been as successful as it has."

The current status of the war had the Pantellarians besieged on the Delta, whose agricultural output was of no importance to Pantellaria or concern to the rebels in the south. Adele presumed that the miners were paying more for food, which now had to be smuggled from the Delta—not difficult, from what Daniel had said about the situation around Hablinger—or brought in from a greater distance. People in Brotherhood weren't going hungry, however.

"It wasn't always like this," Cleveland said, shaking his head. "It wasn't like this even when I took ship for Cinnabar. And at the beginning, well—"

He circled his right hand.

"—it was a war, which is—"

He waggled his hand again, looking for a word.

"Antisocial," Graves said, smiling. He returned to the couch from which he'd risen to alert the barge crew.

"Right, antisocial by definition," Cleveland said. He smiled, too, but his eyes were focused on the base of the console. "But within the independence movement, the rebels if you wish, there was great enthusiasm and, well, brotherhood. Like nothing I'd seen anywhere beyond the Transformationist community."

"The sort of spirit that gets nations into wars," Adele said, "rarely lasts long. Usually it doesn't last beyond the first set of casualty returns. I'm sorry if that sounds cynical."

"As I said," Graves replied, "I'm an engineer. Whether or not I like a situation has nothing to do with whether your description of it is accurate. In this case, however, there's more to the matter than there would have been in similar cases."

Cleveland nodded. "The assault on Hablinger," he said. To Adele he added, "Twelve of our community were killed, and the other organizations lost many more."

Graves nodded also, but he said, "It wasn't just the losses. The Pantellarians underestimated us, the independence movement, but in turn we underestimated them. We'd driven them back into Hablinger by sheer numbers and enthusiasm."

He grimaced at the final word.

"The Council believed that we should use our momentum and sweep the Pantellarians off the planet—or into the sea, if they didn't board their ships quickly enough."

Graves spread his hands and looked at Adele. "There were probably ten thousand Corcyrans under arms at that time," he said. "Most of them weren't in any real organization, and they were armed with odds and ends or not even armed, but ten *thousand*. I'm a member of the Council. While I don't know that anyone would have taken notice if I'd opposed the assault, I was strongly in favor also. The war itself was evil, and this was the quickest and therefore best means of ending it."

"I wasn't there," Cleveland said. "I was to be part of the third Transformationist contingent. The survivors were withdrawn at once and replaced early by the second contingent. The Pantellarians had used their ships."

This information was part of the files which Mistress Sand's office had sent to Adele. She listened now without comment. The impression she got from those who had spoken to the victims at the time had a vividness which third-party reports could not provide.

"We'd assumed the destroyers were merely escorts for the transports," Graves said. "Instead it was a trap. They were hoping to wipe out resistance in one stroke, and they very nearly managed to do so. The ships came over at low level, using their plasma cannon. They slaughtered over a thousand of us—there was no cover. We were attacking over the rice paddies."

"I didn't think you could fire ships' guns in an atmosphere," Cleveland said, shaking his head. "I thought the guns blew up if you tried."

"It erodes the bores of plasma cannon badly," Adele said. "And the range is short. But they don't blow up, no."

Daniel frequently used his plasma cannon against ground targets, and he'd taught his crews to do so as well. That meant the certain replacement of the thick, stubby iridium cannon barrels after every use, but in a battle everything—certainly including the cost of hardware—was second to winning.

"For some reason, the Pantellarians didn't counter-attack then," Graves said. "We were able to regroup."

"Independence troops couldn't run away through the paddies any more easily than the Pantellarians could attack," Cleveland said, smiling faintly. "Otherwise I'm sure no one would have stayed in the lines around Hablinger. Certainly I wouldn't have stayed if I'd been there and had the choice."

"Yes," Graves said. "The only proper highways in the Delta are the two on top of the levees to either side of the river. Near Hablinger, the bed of the Cephisis is nearly thirty feet above the paddies. Getting onto the roads quickly would be impossible, and it would have been suicide with the destroyers strafing. But I'm still surprised they didn't counterattack."

"I doubt Governor Arnaud deliberately drew you into a trap," Adele said. She was reporting Daniel's analysis of the file data, but she could have come to the same conclusion herself. She had gained experience of wars and with irregular troops in the years since she had met Daniel. "I suspect the expeditionary force reacted in desperation. Using warships in that fashion is very dangerous, even if the captain is skilled in atmosphere maneuvers. Few of them are."

She smiled with the cold pride of a Sissie—a member of the crew of the *Princess Cecile*—whose captain was an exceptional ship-handler and whose example had drawn his officers to emulation. There might be Pantellarian officers whose skills rose to the level of an average RCN officer, but Adele would not believe without proof that any of them could equal what Daniel and Vesey had accomplished more than once in her experience.

"The naval officers might have been willing to abandon the troops," Adele continued aloud. They certainly *would* have been willing to leave the infantry in the mud, in her opinion. "But the destroyers wouldn't have been able to actually make space voyages without several days of preparation. Or more. They probably attacked you half-crewed as it was. Nothing less than a crisis would have forced the commanders to risk their ships as they did."

Graves looked as though she had just dumped ice water over him. "You mean that if we'd given them a chance to escape," he said, speaking with great care, "they wouldn't have slaughtered us?"

Adele grimaced. "I don't know what would have happened," she said. "There are too many variables.

I'm reasonably sure that without the spur of necessity, Pantellarian naval officers wouldn't have been willing to risk their ships in a low-level attack of that nature. A lucky impeller slug could have shattered several thruster nozzles. A clumsy ship-handler would have crashed when his thrust was suddenly unbalanced."

She was uncomfortable with the discussion. The past was information; that was her life, or would be her life in a perfect universe. The future was prediction; that was part of her present duty as an RCN officer, guiding the actions of her fellows, her family.

Speculation on what would have happened if some factor had been different was a third thing, a pointless and *foolish* thing so far as Adele was concerned. Changing one aspect of a past complex situation could not change the present—nothing could change the present—and the side-effects of that single change were beyond what Adele's intelligence could determine with any degree of certainty.

She smiled coldly at Graves. *There may be humans better able to calculate those side-effects than I am, but I haven't met them yet.*

Aloud Adele said, consciously changing the subject, "Then the disaster at Hablinger caused the coalition to fracture?"

Graves nodded, looking relieved to leave the subject. Adele wasn't sure what happened to her face when she was angry. She had thought that her expression simply went blank, but the reactions of other people suggested that there was more going on than that.

"The casualties were stressful, certainly," Graves said, "but all the parties had agreed on the attack, and the casualties were fairly evenly spread also."

"Most of the dead were miners," Cleveland said. "Men—mostly men—who weren't members of any of the groups. They'd been treating the whole business as a big bar fight until the destroyers swept over. After that most of the survivors went home as quickly as they could, though we still outnumber the Pantellarians around Hablinger."

"It was clear that we couldn't simply assault the Pantellarian lines again," Graves said. "We couldn't have gotten any of the troops to obey that order. Someone suggested in the Council meeting—I think it was Mistress Tibbs—that we buy antiship missiles and place them in the front lines. Both she and Captain Samona hoped to be able to acquire missiles from Alliance sources, but they weren't able to do so."

Adele nodded crisply. If the Alliance, or even one well-placed Alliance bureaucrat, decided to risk breaking the Treaty of Amiens either out of pique at Pantellaria or simply to earn some under-the-table cash, there was a good chance of rekindling a war that would destroy civilization.

"We found the Republic of Karst was willing to deal with us," Graves said. "Karst isn't allied with either Cinnabar or the Alliance, so its only concern is with the reaction of Pantellaria itself. It didn't seem terribly worried about that, but it wanted considerable trade concessions from Corcyra for its help."

"I see," said Adele. She concealed her frown behind a bland face.

Adele and Daniel had personal experience of Karst, an independent regional power of considerable significance. When the old headman—dictator—had died, his nephew and successor had taken Karst from being a strong Cinnabar ally into the Alliance camp ... for a matter of weeks, until RCN forces under Captain Daniel Leary had destroyed the Alliance fleet in the region.

The young headman had been assassinated almost immediately, and Karst had retreated to neutrality under her new leaders. The Treaty of Amiens had followed quickly, leaving Karst a pariah—trusted by neither superpower, but too strong to be punished without more effort than either Cinnabar or the Alliance wanted to expend.

Karst had lost much of its trade in the aftermath of the war. Gaining a monopoly on Corcyran copper would cause—not quite force—other powers to resume dealing with Karst and thus to pave a road out of the diplomatic wilderness for her.

"The problem was deciding who would go to Karst to negotiate," Graves said. "The three major independence factions all suspected the others would use the negotiations to gain supreme power for themselves after the Pantellarians were driven out."

He smiled faintly. "I suspected that, too," he said, "but I believed that the rival parties would keep one another honest without my personal involvement."

Adele nodded without looking up. Graves was showing himself intelligent and pragmatic.

"In any case," Graves said, "the Council sent a three-person delegation to Karst with full authority to negotiate the deal. The exile factions sent their seconds in command, but Colonel Bourbon of the Garrison went himself. Bourbon had been commanding all Council field forces at the Hablinger front while his deputy, Major Mursiello, forwarded supplies and dealt with Council matters."

Graves shrugged. "I didn't have a high opinion of Mursiello," he said, "but he had handled his duties well enough, as best I could tell. The delegation hired a transport and lifted for Karst four months ago. Two months ago, a messenger from Colonel Bourbon said there was an agreement in principle and that the delegation would be returning shortly."

"That was just before I left for Cinnabar," Cleveland said. "I thought—well, I hoped. That the fighting would be over before I returned."

"Many of us had our hopes up," Graves said with a sigh. "A week after the messenger's arrival, a ship from Ischia arrived with a message for the Council, signed by all three delegates, saying that they had been captured by Ischian pirates who were holding them for ransom. And that is where the business rests at present."

"How much is the ransom?" Adele said. None of this information had been in the files from Mistress Sand.

Graves opened his hands. "It's trade concessions," he said. "Much like the demands by Karst. Though of course Ischia can't offer missiles, and simply getting the delegates back wouldn't end the war. I admit I agree with Colonel, as he now calls himself, Mursiello, who takes that position very strongly."

"Did Mursiello engineer the kidnapping?" Adele asked. She had her data unit on the desk. Her wands quivered as she made a further search of the main Garrison database, looking for hidden or closed files which might have escaped the initial cull that her equipment had made from orbit.

"I don't think that Mursiello has the intelligence or the imagination to plan such a coup," Graves said.

"The Ischians have had their own problems since the Treaty of Amiens, and this is very much the sort of thing they might have come up with themselves."

He frowned and pursed his lips before continuing, "I very much doubt that Mursiello wants his predecessor back, however, and I'm not sure that he wants the war to end until he's consolidated power on Corcyra in his own hands. He's moved his headquarters into the Gulkander Palace on the plaza, and it's rumored that he's gathering troops in the neighborhood of Brotherhood, though he's not moving additional forces into the city."

I can check on troop movements, Adele thought. In fact she probably had the information already. The locations hadn't meant anything to her without context, however.

"The palace?" Cleveland said in surprise. "What did they do with the collections?"

Graves shook his head. "I hope they're being stored," he said, "but Mursiello has the culture and spiritual enlightenment of a barroom swamper. I suppose we have more immediate concerns than what happens to books and antiques."

"What collections are these?" Adele said. Worrying about objects in the midst of a war in which human beings were being killed in large numbers would seem perverse to most people. However, if one believed as Adele did that nothing *whatever* mattered in the long term—then all things mattered equally.

She smiled in her mind, but her face remained still.

"Arn Gulkander, a Pantellarian governor of the past century," Graves said, "was a great collector of books, art, furniture. He built a real palace on the plaza—perhaps you noticed it as you came here? It's just a few doors down."

"Yes," said Adele. She reminded herself to keep her eyes on Graves. She was being polite, because he was answering a question for her personally.

"Gulkander loved Brotherhood and retired here with his family," Graves said. "His descendants have lived here ever since, though they weren't of any political significance. They fled to Pantellaria at the declaration of independence, because that's where their investments are. Mursiello would have ousted them as quickly as he did their caretaker, I'm sure."

"I see," said Adele, standing. "Thank you, Brother Graves. I have a much better understanding of the situation than documents alone had given me."

The two men rose also. "It's been a pleasure, mistress," Graves said, offering his hand.

Cleveland said, "We're trying to preserve our community in difficult circumstances. By helping us, I truly believe that you're helping humanity in at least a small degree."

Clearing his throat he added, "I'll remain with Brother Graves for a moment, if you don't mind."

Adele turned; Tovera had already opened the door.

"Tovera and I can find our way back to the ship," Adele said.

But before we do that, I'm going to visit the Gulkander Palace.

A dozen men and two or three women relaxed in chairs on the Manor's wide veranda as Daniel mounted the three broad steps up from the plaza. Several men and one of the women wore uniforms, but the only person to acknowledge Daniel was an older man in a rumpled jacket and a saucer hat which had seen better days.

He nodded, and Daniel nodded back: a merchant skipper greeting a fellow. Like was calling to like. Naval officers weren't the only collegial group, although Daniel had come to feel that way during his years in the RCN.

Daniel smiled. Groups were not only inclusive, they were exclusive if you let them be. *I'll make an effort not to let that happen to me in the future.*

The double doors were open, so he walked through into the lobby. There were chairs of several different styles: mostly wood, but a number of plastic extrusions and at least one steel unit that had come from a starship and was bolted to the floor as if it were still on a ship. There were spacers who weren't comfortable sitting on something that wasn't really solid.

"Right," called the man standing behind a long waist-high table. A computer sat on one end of the table, but he was sorting through a tray of hard copy beside it. "Need a room?"

"I'm looking for the harbormaster," Daniel said. "I haven't decided about a room yet."

"Suit yourself," the clerk said equably. He pointed through the archway to his left and said, "Turn to starboard and go down to the end of the corridor. All the town offices are on that end of this floor."

He grinned and added, "Don't be surprised if nobody's in the office. Sometimes David's chatting with Tommy in the Customs office, though."

The lobby ceiling was over twenty feet high. The round windows in the top range allowed enough light to read by at this time of day. The lobby was pleasantly cooler than the air outside had been, though the doors were open. Area lights hung in clusters from the ceiling, but the cans into which they'd been installed were brass and appeared to have been hand-pierced in the distant past.

"It looks like a nice enough place," Hogg said as they started down the hall beyond the archway. "To tell the truth, I'm feeling overdressed."

He patted the barrel of his submachine gun with the fingers of his left hand. He was the only openly armed person that they'd seen in the building.

"Nobody's complaining, Hogg," Daniel said. "And *I'm* certainly not."

The last door on the right-hand side was open, but the office was empty. Daniel turned, wondering which office was Customs and whether it was even on this corridor. A man was hurrying toward them from one of the rooms they had passed, making an effort to button his blue jacket.

"You're the guys with the arms shipment?" the fellow said. "I'm Kalet, the harbormaster. Go on into the office, will you? And tell me—"

He followed Daniel and Hogg into the office and slipped between them to the workstation on the desk.

"—who's your sponsor? I didn't get that from your transmission."

"Sponsor?" Daniel said. Polarizing blinds turned the room's two windows a startling red, but the light passing through them was neutral. "I'm the *Kiesche's* owner, if that's what you mean."

"No, no," Kalet said. He typed with his index fingers alone, scowling in determination. "I mean, which party are you delivering to?"

"Oh," said Daniel. He hadn't sat on either of the rickety chairs facing the desk; he wasn't sure they would hold him. "The Transformationists."

Kalet stopped typing and stared at Daniel. "Them?" he said. "Why, you got enough guns for a division aboard! What're those dreamers going to do with a load like that?"

Daniel shrugged. "That's not my problem," he said. "They were loaded Free On Board on Cinnabar, and I'm delivering them to the consignee here. My purser's talking with the local agent now."

The *Kiesche* carried a thousand carbines and ten automatic impellers: enough small arms to equip an understrength regiment, perhaps, but not a division on any civilized planet. Daniel smiled at the thought.

"Look, I'm not sure I can clear this," Kalet said. He grubbed a bandanna from the side-pocket of his jacket and wiped the sudden sweat from his forehead. "There's going to be trouble, I know it—"

Daniel rested his knuckles on the desk and leaned onto them. "There won't be trouble with *me* if you do your job," he said, hearing his voice roughen.

"I—" Kalet said.

"Master!" Hogg said, moving slightly to put his back against the sidewall. A group of people crowded into the doorway, blocking one another's passage and snarling.

First to enter was the woman wearing a gray business suit that wasn't quite a uniform. The two men—who did wear uniforms—had shoved one another apart, and she slipped through. The men followed instantly. More armed men crowded the hall, but they halted at the doorway.

"Hochner!" the woman said. She was tall and wore her hair as a tight sheath for her skull. She'd been a brunette but had let her hair go mostly gray instead of dyeing it. "You know the rules: no thugs in the Manor. Do *you* want to be the moron who made the Garrison outlaws to everybody on the planet? Do *you* want to explain to Mursiello what you've done?"

The bulky man with red hair and a shaggy beard wore what seemed to be Garrison utilities with a great deal of gold braid added. Though he clenched a fist at his side, he turned to the doorway and said, "Bili! Take the company outside. I don't need you here."

"I'm Eugenia Tibbs, Administrator of the Self-Defense Regiment," the woman said briskly to Daniel. "I'm here to purchase your cargo."

"The Corcyran navy will better any other offer you get here," said the other man: tall and very dapper, with thin, curling moustaches and a pointed goatee. "I'm Captain Samona, and I can transfer the credits to you before we leave this room."

"I have precedence, Samona!" Tibbs said. Turning quickly back to Daniel she said in an attempt to be jolly, "I assure you that the Regiment is by far the best-funded and most trustworthy organization on Corcyra."

"Now look here—" Samona said.

"Now both of you pissants shut up!" Hochner said. His shoulder boards bore the two solid squares of a captain in the Alliance Army; the Garrison had been enrolled in Alliance service and probably used the same insignia.

"In fact," Hochner said, backing to put himself between Daniel and the faction leaders whom he was facing, "why don't you both get your asses out of here? The Garrison's the only real power here on Corcyra, however much you lots swank around with your Pantellarian accents!"

"Excuse me, sir," Daniel said. He tapped Hochner's right shoulder. "You're crowding me."

Hochner slapped at Daniel's hand without turning around. "Then move back!" he said while both exile leaders gabbled at him in rising voices.

The harbormaster, Kalet, had moved into the corner behind his desk. He watched the verbal brawl with a miserable expression.

Daniel grabbed Hochner's right wrist with his left hand and bent it up behind his back. Hochner roared and spun to his right. Daniel punched the bigger man in the pit of the stomach.

Hochner gasped. Because he was already off-balance, he fell forward onto his knees. With difficulty he managed to stretch out his right hand so that he didn't sprawl on his face.

"Want me to put the boot in, master?" Hogg said hopefully.

"I don't think that will be necessary, Hogg," said Daniel. He stepped forward and put his back to the harbormaster's desk so that all three faction representatives were in his range of vision. Kalet was certainly not a threat.

"I appreciate that you all find this matter to be important," Daniel said calmly, "but you're dealing with the wrong party. My cargo belongs to the consignee, the Transformationist community. You need to deal with them."

"What's he doing?" said Mistress Tibbs, glancing to Daniel's side. His eyes followed hers.

Hogg snicked open the blade of his knife and bent over Hochner. Daniel frowned, though he didn't object aloud. He didn't remember Hogg exceeding what he thought his master would consider reasonable . . . or at least would consider on the edge of reasonable.

Hogg used his right little finger to jerk slack in Hochner's gunbelt, then sliced through the leather. He pulled up the portion containing the holstered pistol, then straightened, closed the knife, and dropped it into a baggy pocket.

"I'm just looking ahead, lady," Hogg said. "Like a peasant learns to do, you know? And—"

His tone hadn't been friendly before. Now it rasped like a cross-cut saw.

"—I'm a freeborn citizen of Cinnabar, *not* a thug, and I'm good enough for this Manor or any bloody place on Corcyra. Got it?"

"Forgive my question, citizen," Tibbs said. There was laughter in her eyes if not quite in her words. "I assure you, I didn't believe that your master needed thugs to protect him from such as Captain Hochner."

"We'll go now, I think," Daniel said. He turned his head toward the harbormaster. "Master Kalet, I will take it that I've fulfilled my obligations to the port authorities. If there's some additional form to sign or the like, please bring it to the *Kiesche* and I'll see that it's taken care of."

He nodded to Tibbs, then Samona. "Mistress," he said. "Captain. I don't believe we have any business to transact, but you can find me on my ship if there is."

Hogg dropped the holster on the floor and thrust the pistol under his belt. It was a standard Alliance service weapon, much like the RCN equivalent which

Daniel wore when formality required him to. Daniel was quite a good shot with longarms, but he didn't like handguns.

"I'll call on you shortly, Captain," Samona said brightly as Daniel walked past.

"And I," said Administrator Tibbs.

Daniel and Hogg walked through the lobby at the same businesslike pace as when they had entered. The desk clerk called, "Decided on a room?"

"I'm going to look up an old girlfriend first," Daniel said. "I may be back."

He'd thought of taking a room to camouflage his intentions—he certainly wasn't going to sleep away from his command after that meeting—but he'd decided he wanted to get back to the ship as quickly as possible. Under other circumstances, the Manor might have been a pleasant change from the cramped quarters of a tramp freighter, but the center of Brotherhood was a bomb ready for a spark. The civilians had no choice but to stay; but Daniel did, and he was exercising it.

Thirty or forty Garrison soldiers stood or sat on the veranda; they looked ill at ease but not hostile, rather like a pack of dogs milling in an unfamiliar environment. Daniel nodded bare acknowledgment to the squat fellow with sergeant-major bars, but he stepped past briskly to avoid a chance of conversation. The civilians had moved on.

Hogg had kept his face front to avoid eye contact, which in his case might have meant a challenge. Hogg could look like a simple rustic, but he didn't have Daniel's skill at projecting friendly confidence when he was expecting everything to blow up in an instant.

"Think we're going to have to shoot our way out

of this?" Hogg said as they crossed the plaza at a quicker pace than they'd kept when they approached.

"I don't think so, no," Daniel said. "But I'll admit that I've been wishing I'd spent more time on pistol practice when I had the leisure."

"I'll give you this," Hogg said, patting the submachine gun's barrel with his left hand—the hand that wasn't on the grip. "Hochner's piece ought to do all right for me."

They started down the slope toward the harbor. The *Kiesche*'s plasma cannon seemed to be locked—it probably wasn't—straight ahead, because anything else would arouse comment.

In the crosstrees of the raised mast was a crewman with a long canvas-wrapped bundle, almost certainly a stocked impeller. Without using his goggles' magnification, Daniel couldn't identify the spacer, but from his size he was probably Barnes—which meant Sun was at the controls of the plasma cannon.

"I hope we're being unreasonably concerned," Daniel said. "If we're not, though, I couldn't ask for better people around us than we've got."

Hogg grunted. After a moment he said, "*I* hope the mistress is aboard when we get there. I figure we're going to need some magic on this one, and I don't know a better magician than her!"

CHAPTER 13

Brotherhood on Corcyra

"There'll be guards at the front entrance," Tovera said, eyeing the side of the building as they walked along Ridge Road toward the plaza. "It wouldn't be any trick to get in through one of those windows, and there's a door in the alley that looks like it's into the basement. There may not have been anybody down there in fifty years."

"There's no reason they shouldn't allow access by an off-planet scholar, Tovera," Adele said. "I want real access to the collections, not a peek and escaping in a hail of gunfire. If simply asking doesn't get us in, I'll consider other methods."

The five ground-floor windows along this side were grated. Though the wrought-iron bars looked sturdy, over the centuries the bolts fastening them to the wall had wept long trails of rust down the pale limestone. A prybar would pop the gratings off, likely enough, and the two upper ranges of windows didn't have even that much protection.

A squad of Garrison soldiers had built a shelter by stretching a tarpaulin between the palace front and two of the trees protected by ancient stone curbs along this edge of the plaza. The troops had moved chairs and couches into the shade and were cooking on a grill which generated power from a fuel cell. It was enameled field-gray and was probably military issue. None of the soldiers was female, but half a dozen civilian women ate and drank with the guards.

Another soldier sat in the recessed doorway. He was either asleep or so close to it that Adele could have stepped around his legs and entered unchallenged if she had wished to.

"Excuse me, my good man," she said primly. The doorway was arched. The wooden panel which was still closed was carved with half a complex coat of arms. "I'm here to view the Gulkander Library. Will you direct me, please?"

"Whazzat?" said the soldier, jerking alert. He straightened, banging his head against the stone. The carbine slipped off his lap, and the steel buttplate clattered on the pavement. He grabbed for his weapon.

Adele flinched internally, though if the carbine had gone off, the slug would have taken the soldier in the belly without endangering her or Tovera. The indicator on the weapon's receiver showed that there was a loaded magazine in place, which wasn't always a certainty with troops of this quality.

"How do I go about viewing the Gulkander Library, please?" Adele repeated calmly. So far as she could tell, the other guards were ignoring what was going on in the doorway. Tovera kept an eye on them, however, while smiling in bland innocence.

"Ma'am?" the soldier repeated, blinking at her. "Ma'am, you better ask the El-Tee. Lieutenant Pastis, I mean."

He put a palm on the threshold as though he were about to stand up. He held that pose with his mouth open, however, until Adele and Tovera had gone through the door.

A broad corridor ran down the center of the interior. The coffered ceilings on the ground floor were fifteen feet high. They reminded Adele of those of Chatsworth Minor when she was a child.

As an adult and titular owner of the townhouse now, she spent no more time on the ground floor than it took her to climb the stairs to her own apartments on the third and fourth floors, but when she was a child she had wandered throughout the house. Her parents had used the rooms on the ground floor to entertain their more common—vulgar—political guests: the ward heelers and, Adele was now sure, the men whose gangs protected Popular Party rallies from hecklers and who broke up opposition rallies.

It was garishly romantic when Adele was a child. *I really* was *a child,* she realized. *Or I could have been.*

Adele did not regret her childhood, any more than she regretted the weather: it simply was. She had been quiet and bookish from the first. Her father was always on the public stage, whether or not there was another human being present, and her mother was too immersed in ideas to notice facts. Neither had been concerned that their older daughter lived in a world of information and arrangements of information instead of playing with other children.

And why should they have cared? Adele had access

to everything she wanted. She had used that access to hone her skills to an exceptional, perhaps a unique, degree. She was a productive member of society, to the degree that mattered. It hadn't mattered to Adele herself until she met Daniel Leary and became a member of his society, his family: the RCN.

The space to the left of the entrance was open; it had probably been a waiting room for those attending the governor. Now it was railed off into an orderly room containing two clerks at consoles and a desk behind which a lieutenant sat comparing the flimsy in his right hand with the flimsy in his left. From his scowl, the comparison wasn't going well.

"Excuse me," Adele said, sharply enough to get somebody's attention. "I'm here to view the Gulkander Library. I'm Lady Mundy, on Corcyra as a Cinnabar envoy—"

That wasn't quite a lie, but it was close enough to make Adele uncomfortable.

"—but I wish to see the library as a private citizen."

"Bloody hell," the lieutenant muttered. The hand-lettered card on his desk read ADJUTANT. "Look, if you need your hand held, you're out of luck. The books were moved to storage in the basement, and I don't have any bloody idea of what you'll find."

"I'll be all right, I think," Adele said, no more dryly than she said most things. She looked down the corridor. "How do I get to the storage area?"

The room which balanced the orderly room on the right side of the front had brass-mounted double doors. The valves were closed, showing holes where the original decoration—probably a brass coat of arms—had been removed. In its place now was the legend COMMANDER IN CHIEF. The letters had been cut freehand with a great deal of skill from white-enameled sheet metal.

Ranged on both sides of the hallway were plush chairs which matched the couches outside with the guards. They would serve for people waiting, but they appeared simply to have been moved out of the way when the rooms were converted to Garrison use.

Farther back were three doors on either side, mostly open. Between the first and second on the right side was a staircase leading upward.

"You see the stairs?" the lieutenant said, pointing. "Well, the door beside it, that's the way down. And good luck to you."

"Thank you," Adele said, more polite than the fellow's behavior required. She strode toward the indicated doorway. She might have to come back for a key; and besides, she preferred to be polite.

Tovera, ahead of her, had opened the door with no difficulty and peered in. "The only light is glowstrips in the ceiling," she said when Adele joined her. "Not many, and they're dusty."

"It will serve," Adele said. The basement appeared to be as deep as the ground-floor ceilings were high. She started down the metal stairs.

"I'll wait here in the hall, mistress," Tovera said, being more formal than usual because others might overhear the conversation. "I don't think you'll need my expertise in this venue."

"I agree," Adele said as the door closed above her. Tovera meant that her mistress wouldn't need a bodyguard in this dim, barren expanse of concrete pillars and accumulated trash.

Unless a pack of dust mites attacked, perhaps. No doubt Tovera would rush down when she heard Adele begin shooting at mites. Otherwise, Tovera sitting in the hall outside the door was in a better position to defend her mistress than she would have been down here in the gloom.

The stacks of books were at some distance from the bottom of the staircase, and they were in much better order than Adele had expected to find them. Broken furniture and odds and ends of other trash—sports equipment, a perambulator with three wheels; similar items—had accumulated around the staircase over the years, but book movers had cleared a path through it so that they could place their loads near a wall and even cover them with plastic sheeting.

Adele wondered whether the job had been done by the Gulkander family's librarian rather than the Garrison soldiers. She had braced herself to find ancient volumes tossed down the stairs to fall any which way on the clutter.

She squatted. This wasn't ideal, either, but Adele had learned a long time ago that the only ideal she could expect to find was the silence of death.

She smiled wryly. And if the many religious believers were correct, she might not have even that to look forward to.

Adele removed a layer of sheeting from a stack at random and began a preliminary assessment of the books. Her personal data unit had an external light, but rather than use it, she let the unit scan and record the spines through various sensors and project the result on its holographic display.

Adele watched and was dumbfounded. "Antique

books" could have meant anything. Brother Graves was an educated man, but he wasn't a bibliophile, and he had probably not seen the collection personally. This could have been a gathering of genealogical records from Yerevan or wherever the Gulkander family came from originally.

These books were pre-Hiatus.

At least some of these books were printed on Earth before starflight.

These books were sitting in a dusty cellar among trash. The Gulkander descendants couldn't have known what they were worth—let alone appreciate what they were—or they would have sold them generations ago, and certainly no other person on Corcyra understood now.

That was unfair: the librarian must have had an inkling to have taken as much care as he had, while doubtless under pressure from Philistines with guns to move faster. Perhaps Adele would be able to find the fellow after things had settled down here.

Adele wasn't sure how long she had remained, lost in a wonderful garden, before Tovera had moved her hand through the holographic screen and said, "Mistress, we have to move. Mursiello's bodyguard is going to capture the *Kiesche*. There's been no electronic signals, so whoever's on communications watch wasn't able to warn Six."

Adele came out of her brief visit to paradise. "Explain," she said. She set down her data unit and carefully closed the book on top of the stack: a volume of Chaucer published by the Kelmscott Press.

She wondered if she would think first of the book if someone appeared in the doorway and began shooting down at them. *I probably would. Tovera could deal with the attacker.*

"Captain Hochner, commander of Mursiello's body-guard company, came in shouting," Tovera said. "He'd tried to push Six around and hadn't been pleased—"

Her tone was as dry as a salt desert, but nonetheless Adele could feel the amusement—and pride—underlying the words.

"—with the result. He told Mursiello they had to seize the cargo. He'd take his company and pick up the company already at the harbor before anybody had time to react. The adjutant started arguing with him, and Mursiello couldn't understand what the fuss was."

Adele put the volume back on top of the stack where she had found it, then dragged the plastic film back over the books. Perhaps she could come back and properly curate this splendid collection, but that would require that she survive the next few minutes.

"They were all shouting at the top of their lungs," Tovera said, "so I could follow what was going on. I was afraid that I'd call attention to myself if I got up to warn you before Hochner and his troops went out. I want to say that the gunfire would've warned you, but as focused as you get, I'm not sure that would have worked."

"Yes," said Adele. "We won't be able to reach the ship ahead of the troops ourselves, so I'll send a warning and we'll attempt to conceal ourselves until matters sort themselves out."

"Hide here in the basement?" Tovera said. Her tone was neutral, but she was certainly intelligent enough to doubt that it was a good idea.

"No," said Adele. "Find the alley door that we saw coming past and open it while I warn the others."

"Opening the door" might be a matter of turning the latch, or alternatively it might mean blowing the panel off with beads of plastic explosive. Tovera would choose the method which seemed best to her, and Adele would live with that choice. She was quite sure the door would be opened.

"Signals to ship," Adele said. Her data unit was coupled to one of the consoles in the orderly room above. From there the heavy flex she had seen running into a hole hacked in the molded ceiling would carry it to the transmitter and to the antenna on the roof. "Emergency. Garrison troops, two companies at the start, are about to seize the ship and her cargo. The other factions aren't involved at this time."

She took a deep breath. She must next explain her own plans, which meant she had to formulate them.

"Tovera and I will make our way to the harbor, but we won't attempt to board the ship at this time," she said. "We will proceed as circumstances dictate. Oh—and in two minutes, the Garrison transmitter will begin jamming all short- and medium-wave frequencies. Signals out."

Adele gave the Garrison console a further set of instructions with quick movements of her wands. She stood, slipping the data unit into its pocket.

"The door's open," Tovera said. She gripped her small submachine gun openly in her right hand; the attaché case in which she normally concealed it was in her left, still holding equipment of occasional use.

The submachine gun was of frequent use.

Adele drew her own pistol. "We'll head for the harbor, quietly," she said.

"Not to Graves' office?" Tovera said as she led

Adele between concrete pillars to where she'd located the door.

"I don't want to involve Brother Graves in this business," Adele said.

And apart from that courtesy, she thought Graves would be a hindrance in the firefight which seemed likely to break out at any moment.

"I won't say I feel safe now," Daniel said to Hogg as they reached the base of the boulevard and the soldiers relaxing around the flagpole. Ignoring them, Daniel turned toward the *Kiesche*'s berth. "But at least we're out of pistol range for Hochner and his crew."

Hogg looked up the hill. Because the slope bulged midway, where the steps were, you couldn't actually see the harbor road from the plaza, even the south edge of the plaza.

"Yeah, I guess," Hogg said. "I'll be glad when we get to a nice clean battlefield where I know who the sides are."

"Captain Leary?" a voice called from behind them. They turned, both more quickly than a friendly greeting would have required in other circumstances. Rikard Cleveland jogged to catch up with them. He was alone.

"Where's Officer Mundy?" Daniel said. He'd tried to keep concern—and anger—out of his tone. Judging from the civilian's reaction, he hadn't succeeded very well.

"Sir?" said Cleveland, his friendly grin going blank. "I think Lady Mundy and her secretary may have stopped at the Gulkander Library. I . . . the building is right on the plaza, and there didn't seem to be any reason that they shouldn't. I came straight back."

"Sorry, Cleveland," Daniel said. He turned, and they walked together down the cluttered roadway. "I had a, umm, difficult time clearing the harbormaster's office, and I was just concerned that there'd been problems at your end, too."

"Oh, no," said Cleveland. They passed on opposite sides of a barrow loaded with fruit—Terran apples and other sorts which didn't look like anything Daniel had seen before. "Brother Graves has arranged for a barge to load the cargo tomorrow at whatever time you choose. He and I talked about community business, and Lady Mundy went off on her own. The Gulkander is a library, as I say. It's supposed to be a remarkable collection."

"Her *secretary*," Hogg repeated with emphasis. His chuckle meant that he had relaxed also.

The *Kiesche* was in sight, and a welcome sight she was. Daniel hadn't carried a communicator, because that would be out of place for a merchant captain. He had started to second-guess himself even before he ran into Captain Hochner, but intellectually he knew he'd made the right decision.

Lieutenant Cory had taken charge in tight spots in the past and had shown himself clear-sighted and competent. Brave went almost without saying in an RCN officer (though bone stupid was not disabling or even uncommon). Cory on the ground would make better decisions than Daniel at a distance.

"I had expected to leave an anchor watch on the *Kiesche* and go upriver with the guns," Daniel said. "I'm now thinking that I may want to stay aboard for a little while. I expect the parties to lose interest in the ship and crew as soon as the cargo's been off-loaded, but Hochner's the sort who might take it into his head to...well, I don't trust what he might do the next time he gets drunk."

"I wouldn't mind sticking around for that to happen myself," Hogg said in a deceptively mild tone.

The *Kiesche*'s slip was a hundred feet away. A load of copper ingots was crawling slowly down the tramline behind the gantry, but Daniel and his companions would be aboard five minutes before the crane passed in front of the ship.

Woetjans appeared in the entry hatch. She cupped her hands into a megaphone and bellowed, *"Six! Here! Soonest!"*

Daniel broke into a run. Hogg followed, cursing, but he quickly fell behind. Cleveland gave a yelp from farther back yet, since he hadn't reacted instantly to the summons.

Daniel had never liked running. Though he was fit from regularly climbing the rigging on the voyage out, those muscles were quite different from the ones which took him lumbering across the floating extension—he timed the bridge's rippling rise and fall reflexively—and up the freighter's boarding ramp. He was panting, but that didn't matter.

"The mistress called from town," Woetjans said as Daniel panted past her on the way to the bridge. "The Garrison's sending a couple companies to grab the ship. All's aboard now but her and Tovera, and Vesey and Hale. The mistress says she can't get back before the trouble gets here."

"Right," said Daniel as he threw himself onto the command console. Cory was on the facing seat. "Cory, light the thrusters and close the hatch. Do we have a link to Adele, over?"

Daniel was speaking as though he were on intercom, though he wasn't until that instant. He knew by the way the *Kiesche* trembled that Pasternak was already cycling reaction mass through the thruster installations.

All four nozzles lit at Daniel's command, though starboard was a half-step behind the others and caused the ship to lurch. The hatch began to rise, groaning unhappily. Daniel hoped it wouldn't stick, but that wasn't a critical problem.

We'll have to leave the extender. Well, if we get out of this with nothing worse happening, it'll be a win.

"*Daniel,*" said Adele's voice, "*tell Vesey to wait for me at Beardsley and Owens. I don't have a link to her. There won't be any radio communications in thirty seconds, over.*"

The signal was strong despite the roar of the thrusters across the RF spectrum. *She must be sending through the Garrison's own communications system.*

"Adele, stay low and take care of Vesey," Daniel said. "I'm going to deliver the guns to the Transformationists and come back as quick as I can. I hope I'll have company—"

From what Cleveland had said, there should be three or more hundreds of his fellow cultists back in Pearl Valley. They ought to be willing to help the people who had just dropped an arsenal in their laps.

"—but regardless, I'm coming back."

A telltale on the display went from green with a touch of turquoise to a fierce, saturated red. The change caught Daniel's eye, but he didn't know for an instant what it meant—besides not being good.

"*Six,*" said Cory over the intercom, "*that's the mistress jamming Garrison commo—all radio-frequency commo, that means. I'd linked Vesey, so she's got the word, over."*

Daniel had been right not to worry about Cory in a crisis. "Ship, prepare to lift. We're going upriver so bloody low that we're going to be a cloud of steam for at least the first ten miles, so be ready for a rough ride."

Cory had run the thrusters up to full power with the nozzles open to dissipate the searing, sparkling exhaust. Even so the *Kiesche* bucked on thrust and on steam boiling from the slip in gulps and surges.

"Six, Dorsal A is up and Barnes is out there!" Cory said. *"Do you want me to fold it down, over?"*

"Negative!" said Daniel. "We may want the height, and we'll deal with the antenna carrying away if we have to. Does Barnes have commo, over?"

"Master Cazelet give me his helmet, sir," croaked the big rigger over the intercom. Unquenched ions must be flaying his bare skin, his throat included when he talked. *"I can still shoot, and Master Hogg's out here with me."*

"Roger that," said Daniel. "Don't shoot unless I give you the word, though. Break."

He took a deep breath, then began to close the petals of the thruster nozzles. "Lifting! Six out!"

Daniel brought the *Kiesche* into a hover, perhaps the most difficult piece of shiphandling he'd ever been called on to manage. It would've been bad enough in a warship, even the *Princess Cecile,* which he knew so well. He had to balance the ship on a tight cluster of four poorly harmonized thrusters instead of the eight that were spread the greater length of the *Sissie's* hull.

Further, he had to keep her within ten feet of the

surface in the buffeting of steam and reflected thrust, because if she rose higher she became a potential target for the Garrison's antiship missiles. As it was, the raised foremast was bobbing well above the horizon line of the missiles in full depression. Daniel doubted the Garrison crew would launch on the mast—or that they would hit it if they tried—but the shock of a hit would tip the *Kiesche* off her column of thrust and probably drop her into the harbor on her side.

"Ship, hang on!" Daniel repeated. He didn't trust the thrusters' gimballing mechanism, so he cut flow by a minuscule amount to the front unit. It was fed by a separate line, so the other three remained at their previous output.

The *Kiesche* began to tilt forward. Daniel brought up thrust by the same slight amount on all four nozzles. The freighter moved—fell—out of her slip in a nose-down attitude and skidded into the harbor at a pace increasing to a fast walk.

They curved around a barge load of ingots that might have sunk the *Kiesche* if they'd collided. Only then did Daniel see the water taxi which had been hidden by the bulk of the barge. He widened his curve by dialing down the starboard thruster, then brought up power again before the *Kiesche* wobbled into a crash.

Surge from the freighter's thrust swamped the little flatboat, but the boatman and his two passengers would be all right if they clung to the hull. At least they hadn't been seared to skeletons in the exhaust plume.

The gate between the flume and the main channel of the Cephisis was closed. There was a blockhouse as well as the wicketkeeper's shelter, but the occupants of both had abandoned their posts and were legging it along Harborside. They were already at a safe distance.

The *Kiesche* mushed over the dyke, jolding slightly. Reflection from the steel girder was sharper than from the bodies of water it divided. Daniel could probably lift higher now because they had Brotherhood and the intrusion on which it sat between them and the Garrison battery, but for the moment he saw no reason not to continue as they were doing.

"Ship, this is Six," Daniel said. "Next stop, Pearl Valley!"

And then back to pick up—to rescue, if necessary—Adele and the others. And to pay out Captain Hochner, if that seemed appropriate.

CHAPTER 14

Brotherhood on Corcyra

Adele and Tovera were walking briskly along Harborside when the roar of a ship running up its thrusters echoed about the pool. That was a common event in any harbor, but this time the sound wasn't quite right, even to Adele's ears. Spacers were turning or even coming out of shops to look, so Adele turned also.

The *Kiesche* was skidding across the pool, under full power but holding scarcely above the surface instead of rising at an accelerating pace. The ship seemed headed for the shore—

No. It bumped into the flume which fed water to the pool. Moments later it disappeared around the island.

Spectators babbled in amazement to one another. Most of the opinions appeared to include the words "drunk" or "bloody fool," but a number of them were complimentary in tone. Adele walked on.

The only thing Adele had known about how Daniel would react to her warning was that he would react in the best available fashion. She didn't need to concern herself with him or the *Kiesche* generally until she had more data.

"It's next after the tavern," Tovera said conversationally as she followed Adele. "Want me to lead?"

Adele sniffed. "No, thank you," she said. Her left hand was already in her tunic pocket, though neither she nor Tovera had carried a weapon in plain sight after they found the alley behind the Gulkander Palace empty.

They proceeded in single file. The streets of Brotherhood were rarely crowded. Quite a few of them were narrow, however. Adele and her servant had guessed their way along byways instead of proceeding to Central and marching down it. When they had reached Harborside after a few dead ends, they turned to the right and sauntered as though they weren't in any kind of hurry.

Adele smiled minusculy. They *weren't* in a hurry. Vesey and Hale were as safe in the outfitters' as they would be anywhere, and they would wait for Adele to arrive however long it took.

The *Kiesche*'s unusual behavior had drawn everyone—including the apron-wearing bartender, though he had gone inside again—out of the tavern. Half a dozen of them, all well on the way to being drunk, continued to stand in the road. Adele started around them, stepping into the tramway.

A short, stocky man saw the movement and caught her right shoulder. His arms were long, as though to make up for his bandy legs.

"Give us a kiss, sweetheart," he said, drawing Adele toward him.

There was a *clunk*; the drunk's eyes rolled upward. Tovera had hit the back of his skull with the corner of her attaché case. Adele skipped out of the way as the fellow toppled forward. His friends didn't seem to notice.

The front of Beardsley and Owens was windowed, though there was a sturdy steel grating outside the casement and the expanse was glazed with eight-inch by twelve-inch panes instead of two or three rolled plates. The window display was of coiled cable, pipe fittings, and tools—but the items had been dusted recently. It really looked like advertising rather than an assortment of junk.

"Do you want me—" Tovera said.

"No," said Adele. She pushed the door open with her right hand.

The big store was dimmer than outdoors, but Vesey was directly in front of the door. She stood with her back to a pallet of eight-liter paint cans and her hands crossed in front of her. There were half a dozen other customers in the store and at least two attendants, but Adele didn't see Hale for a moment.

Motion drew her glance to the right; she saw the muzzle of Hale's carbine lifting toward the ceiling. The weapon must have been lying across a low counter, covering the doorway by seeming accident.

"Good to see you, Vesey," Adele said, since the lieutenant hadn't addressed her until she was sure that Adele wanted to be recognized. "There was some excitement in the harbor. The freighter *Kiesche* proceeded upriver in surface effect."

"No doubt her captain had his reasons," Vesey said in a neutral voice. No one in the store was paying obvious attention to the newcomers.

Tovera had paused in the open doorway. She came all the way in and looked around. Hale walked over to join them also.

"Will they hide us here in their warehouse or the like?" Adele said quietly. "There hasn't been an alarm, but there may be one momentarily."

She smiled wryly. "Or however long it takes for the Garrison technicians to realize that the jamming is coming from their own equipment, which might be longer than I expect. We've given these people a good order, so they should be predisposed to help us."

Vesey looked about rather nervously. The paint display hid her completely from the back of the store, so her jumpiness wouldn't be noticed. Tovera stood at a cross aisle, seemingly relaxed, which was sufficient for any concerns Adele had.

"Mistress, you're in command, of course," Vesey said. "But I suggest we go immediately to the *Freccia*. I'm sure—well, I *think*—that the navy will be pleased to help us. I've been talking with the proprietors here—"

She nodded toward the counter in back, though it and she were mutually out of sight, thanks to the paint.

"—and from what they say, the three militias are just short of being in open warfare. Both the others hate the Garrison, and apparently the civilians in Brotherhood all do also."

"Yes, we'll do that," Adele said, turning. "Thank you, Vesey."

"We'll be back with loading instructions," Vesey called. She waved toward the counter, then followed Adele out of the store.

The destroyer and the buildings which had become the naval barracks weren't much farther along Harborside. Adele and Vesey walked shoulder to shoulder, ahead of their companions.

Adele smiled without letting her lips move. Vesey

had become a very useful naval officer under the tute-lage of Captain Leary. And it wouldn't be completely unreasonable to suggest that association with Lady Mundy had demonstrated to Vesey that a woman didn't have to become a man to function in a man's world.

As they approached the *Freccia*, an officer whom Adele recognized from imagery as Captain Samona was crossing the boarding ramp. Instead of being aluminum or plastic, the Corcyran navy had built a sturdy wooden ramp. It was braced against the dock on one end and the destroyer's entry hatch on the other; a double hinge in the middle adjusted for the depth of water in the pool.

"How can they lift off with all that lumber?" said Hale, her first words since Adele met her in Beardsley and Owen. "It'd take hours to disengage it!"

"Well, in an emergency they could just ignore it," Vesey said. "It doesn't seem to be attached to the deck of the entry hold, so if they raise the hatch, the bridge would fall away."

She frowned. "The wood would probably burn in the thruster exhaust," she added. "But in an emergency..."

"I don't think Captain Samona wants to lift," Adele said, considering her data and the assessments she had heard Daniel make. "Any more than Admiral Stazi in Hablinger wants to make orbital patrols; or lift, I suppose. This isn't the RCN, and the *Freccia* more particularly isn't a warship under the command of Captain Leary."

It's all data. Looked at properly, everything in life is a datum.

Two spacers, a man and a woman, were on guard at the base of the boarding bridge. They were probably more alert than they might have been if their commanding officer hadn't just passed, but Adele noticed that their uniforms were clean and they handled their submachine guns as though they'd had some training.

Adele strode up to the guards; Vesey halted a step back. The male spacer had two anchors on his sleeve rather than the female's one, so it was to him that Adele said, "I'm Lady Mundy of Cinnabar. The Garrison has attempted to steal the cargo of arms which the freighter *Kiesche*—"

She pointed across the harbor without breaking eye contact.

"—brought to Brotherhood. I need to speak with Captain Samona at once."

"Yes, *ma'am!*" the spacer said. "He just got back. I'll tell him you're coming!"

He pulled the communicator from his belt sheath and broke squelch as Adele and her companions marched past. The female guard stared in amazement; the male spacer prodded at his communicator. It might be a while before he realized that the Garrison's powerful transmitter was jamming the airwaves.

"A pity," said Tovera. "I thought we might have to kill them to gain access."

"What?" said Hale. "I . . . *What* did you say?"

Vesey turned her head slightly and said, "Tovera was joking, Hale. She has a dry sense of humor."

Tovera has no sense of humor at all, nor any emotions. She's become very good at pretending that she does, however.

By now, Tovera was often better at pretending to be a normal human being than her mistress was. But then, Adele had never seen the point of the exercise.

The wooden bridge might be impractical, but Adele noted that its solidity underfoot was a pleasant change from the queasy uncertainty of most boarding bridges. She was in a mood to find something positive in any situation which would meet her half way. Her smile was grim, but the thought did make her smile.

There were several spacers in the entry hold, but none of them seemed to be on duty—let alone on guard. Adele picked one at random and said, "I need to speak with Captain Samona at once. I'm an envoy from Cinnabar."

"Well—" said the spacer, glancing toward the hatch forward.

"Is someone calling for me?" Samona said, reentering the compartment suddenly. Adele had assumed he'd gone up the companionway to the bridge. "I heard my name."

"I'm Lady Mundy," Adele said. Living as a member of society seemed to require a great deal of repetition, though she supposed she shouldn't complain so long as saying something once to each individual was sufficient. It wasn't always enough. "Colonel Mursiello has attempted to seize the Cinnabar vessel *Kiesche* with its cargo of arms. We've come here to warn you."

Living outside human society was cold, damp, and provided less food than satisfied even one of Adele's limited needs. In other circumstances one might describe it as dangerous, but the slums compared favorably with Adele's present life in the RCN under Daniel Leary. Danger didn't concern her one way or the other.

"Come up to the bridge, if you will, your ladyship," Samona said, bowing Adele toward the up companionway. She couldn't judge his capacity as a naval officer, but he was certainly a gentleman.

She climbed the steel stairs at the brisk pace which she had learned in the closed stacks of major libraries. It hadn't occurred to her at the time that it was good training for an RCN career.

"The Garrison is jamming the RF spectrum to prevent you and the Regiment from communicating," said Vesey, her voice echoing up the armored tube of the companionway. "Captain Leary sent us to warn you in person."

That's not right. Vesey's lying!

Adele forced her lips into a smile as she stepped through the hatch at the top of the companionway and turned right toward the *Freccia*'s bridge. She wasn't a spacer by any stretch of the imagination, but she had enough experience by now to know that a warship's bridge would be in the bow, on the top level.

Vesey is intelligently lying, to encourage Captain Samona to believe the truth more quickly than would otherwise have been the case.

The truth was that the Garrison had resorted to force in a fashion which might lead and perhaps had already led to a full-scale coup attempt. Vesey had seen her duty and had done it, with less hesitation than Signals Officer Mundy might have shown.

A junior officer started out through the bridge hatch, then stopped and backed in again when he saw Samona following Adele. "Sir!" he called. "Something's going on! One of the freighters seems to have gone crazy, and the Garrison's started jamming everything!"

"Right!" said Samona, striding past Adele to sit at the command console. "Castiglione, sound General Recall and Action Stations. Engineering, light the thrusters!"

A klaxon in the outer hall began to hoot. It was

unpleasantly loud on the bridge because all the ship's hatches were open. The PA system was squealing in every compartment, adding to the din.

Bending close to Samona's ear, Adele said, "Captain? The Regiment has a microwave tower on top of its headquarters building on the plaza. You could warn Administrator Tibbs of what's going on."

"Right!" Samona shouted back. "Castiglione, connect me to the Regiment by microwave soonest! Over."

"And if I can borrow a console with a satellite link," Adele said, "I believe I can warn both Captain Leary and the Transformationists."

Samona waved generally to the empty consoles on both sides of the bridge, then went back to his microwave conversation. He was showing himself to be thoroughly competent, which was a pleasant surprise to Adele.

The *Freccia* shuddered as her pumps began circulating reaction mass. They were some while short of lighting thrusters, but the Corcyran navy was doing quite well so far. Whether or not it was performing well enough was a matter for a later time.

Adele sat at what was probably the astrogation console and got to work.

Pearl Valley on Corcyra

The *Kiesche* rested on the sports field beyond the Transformationist chapel and the rest of the community. Daniel's eyes were closed. He had nothing useful to do until the ground cooled enough to open the ship for unloading.

He wasn't exactly asleep, but he was relaxing. He needed rest more than he'd understood until he handed the conn to Cory and rose from the console.

Three sharp taps snapped Daniel's eyes open. He hadn't bothered to draw the curtain of his alcove when he flopped onto the bunk, but Cazelet was standing outside the "hatchway" and knocking on the stanchion with his knuckles.

"Sir?" Able Spacer—and half-pay RCN lieutenant—Cazelet said. "Master Cory says the locals believe the ground is cool enough to begin unloading and ask us to open up. Do you wish to take command?"

"Thank you, Cazelet," Daniel said, swinging his feet over the side of the bunk and standing up. "Tell Master Cory to carry on, though I'll probably be talking to the local leadership about matters not concerned with the ship or her cargo."

Matters like retrieving his personnel from Brotherhood.

Cazelet stepped back and reported to Cory. The interchange had been perfectly formal and proper. The fact that Cory was within ten feet of Daniel and listening to the exchange made it a little silly. Daniel realized that his behavior—collapsing on his bunk—had surprised and probably concerned his veteran shipmates.

Aloud he said, to Cazelet but therefore to everyone on the bridge, "I've handled ships at low altitude before, Cazelet, but I hadn't previously tried these particular games with a tramp freighter. Heaven willing, I'll never do it again. It would be easier to balance an egg on my nose—and an egg wouldn't kill us all if it toppled over."

Cory turned in his seat as the main hatch began to shudder open. He said, "We knew you could do it, sir."

Daniel could have given a number of different responses. The one he chose was the one that came most naturally. He smiled and said, "I hope your confidence in me is never misplaced, Cory."

He glanced over Cory's shoulder at the main display's real-time imagery. The upper band was the quadrant of their immediate surroundings centered on the main hatch; the band below it showed a reduced panorama of the remaining 270 degrees.

Figures in gloves and work clothes were laying sheets of perforated steel planking across a stretch of sod seared dead by the freighter's plasma exhaust. In the background was the forklift whose prongs held the remaining sheets of PSP. To the side, out of the work crew's way, stood an older man and woman, each holding a briefcase. They weren't dressed much differently from the laborers.

Nor was Daniel. He tugged at the utilities he'd been dozing in—the left trouser leg had ridden up to his knee—and donned the worn saucer hat which had been lying around the Bergen and Associates' office.

The whine and vibration of machinery ended with a shudder and a heavy thump. The hatch was now a boarding ramp, its edge bedded firmly in the ground. The work crew placed the final section of PSP so that it mated with the ramp's lip.

"Time to greet the local authorities, I think, Cory," Daniel said. He followed his acting captain into the entry hold and walked beside him down the ramp. The air was still sharp with ozone and thick with burned sod, but the usual steam bath of a water landing wasn't present.

"That's Brother Altgeld, who's still the community coordinator, I guess," Cleveland said quietly. "And beside him is Sister Rennie, who was a colonel. She's acting as the community's military adviser."

"And doing a good job, from what I can see of the defenses," Daniel said, smiling as though he were discussing the bright sunlight. There were two racks of eight-inch bombardment rockets on gimballed mountings positioned to cover the field from either long side. In the center of the far end was an automatic impeller, dug in with overhead cover and camouflage.

The field was the only clearing for several miles in any direction in the forested expanse. Apart from Pearl Creek itself—twenty feet wide at this point—there was no other landing zone for anyone arriving by air.

"Sir, are you ready for us to begin off-loading?" called a workman in a cultured Pleasaunce accent.

"I've got it, Six," Cory said, walking toward them. The *Kiesche*'s crew waited aboard for orders as to how they would best help.

Daniel slanted left and joined the older couple. "I'm Daniel Leary, captain of the *Kiesche*," he said. "We have your cargo safe—"

All but the single carbine with Hale, he suddenly remembered.

"—but I had to leave four of my shipmates in Brotherhood to prevent Garrison troops from seizing the guns. I hope I can depend on your help to get my people back."

"They've been in touch with us, and they're all safe," said Altgeld. "You will have our help, though I hope you're not planning a head-on assault."

Rennie gave her colleague a hard smile. "Captain Leary's reputation isn't founded on head-on assaults, Robert," she said. She turned to Daniel, still smiling, and added, "But I think we could manage even that if it were necessary. These guns mean that none of the parties will attack us without a great deal of thought."

"Sorry," said the man, offering his hand. "I'm Brother Altgeld, and I used to be a ship's captain—in the merchant service, which I gather is not your normal field, Captain Leary. I've been chosen community coordinator, and I tend to worry about everything which could go wrong. Much of which *has* gone wrong in the past two years, I'm afraid."

"I'm Rennie," said the woman, also shaking hands. "Sister Rennie at present, but Colonel Rennie of the Alliance forces in the not too distant past."

She raised an eyebrow as she stepped back. "I hope that's not a problem?"

"It isn't," said Daniel. "I was just commenting to my colleagues that your heavy weapons are very well placed for defense against a sudden assault."

"Thank you, Captain," Rennie said. She was short and roughly tubular in build; fit, short-haired, and probably deeper into middle age than she seemed at first glance. "It's not the sort of thinking which I would prefer to be doing, but I haven't forgotten how."

"I suggest we all go into the office annex," Altgeld said. "I wouldn't have cared to make a dirt landing the way you did, Captain Leary. Quite apart from the danger of it, the sod holds heat and reradiates it in a fashion that I find quite unpleasant."

"I wouldn't mind getting something cooler under these thin-soled boots myself," Daniel said. "Lead on, Brother Altgeld."

The Chapel was a circular building, an hourglass in section rather than a triangle, though the inverted upper cone was much smaller than the lower portion.

Opaque struts provided strength with the spaces between them filled by colored glass. The windows looked muddy from outside, but the building's interior would be gay with the light behind them.

"I see only barracks," Daniel said, gesturing toward the community. He couldn't be sure how many long, two-story buildings there were, but he could see at least a dozen spaced farther back among the trees. "Don't you have private dwellings?"

"We actually prefer to live in groups," Rennie said, "though people are free to live apart if they want to. We have two single-family cottages, though you can't see them from here. Generally newcomers start out in a cottage, but they always move to the group homes before long."

"Ah, Brother?" Cleveland said. They'd reached the nearest of three single-story buildings near the Chapel. Altgeld was turning the door latch. "Would you like me to help with the unloading?"

Everyone, Daniel included, turned to look back toward the *Kiesche*. The forklift was backing onto the PSP trackway with six cases of carbines on its prongs. Inside the hold, members of the ship's crew were readying the next stack for transfer.

At the end of the track, among the trees where the ground was firmer, waited a sizable portion of the community, grouped six or eight apiece around high-wheeled handtrucks. Daniel judged there were at least a hundred people and more than a dozen trucks.

"I think things are well taken care of, Brother Cleveland," Altgeld said. "Come and join us. This bounty is entirely your doing."

He looked at Daniel and added in embarrassment,

"And your and your companions' doing, Captain. Forgive me."

"Cleveland's parents provided the cargo," Daniel said, following Altgeld into what turned out to be a single office filling the building's interior. "I'd say you were right the first time."

"How do you figure to store the guns?" Hogg said as he walked in after the others. He wasn't carrying a shoulder weapon, but heaven only knew what was in his baggy pockets. A short-barrelled pistol and his folding knife were as much a part of his routine wear as his boots were, and not infrequently he had produced a grenade when the need arose.

"We're dividing them among the dwellings," Rennie said. "There is at least one person in each block who has firearms training, and usually several. We're not expecting a sudden raid by Pantellarian forces—and frankly, I don't believe the Garrison has transport for such a thing, let alone the training. Nevertheless, we're prepared."

"Now that we have sufficient arms," Altgeld added, "everyone will be trained. Even me."

He smiled. "I don't know how much Brother Cleveland has told you about our company," he said, "but while we truly believe in the fellowship of all people, we cut our philosophy to the times."

"I've never seen the point in discussing religion," Daniel said. He shrugged. "That aside, there's nothing in what you say that I'd take exception to."

"I rather thought that might be the case," said Altgeld. His smile made him look even more tired than he had when Daniel had first seen him out the *Kiesche*'s hatchway. He settled himself onto a chair of wicker on a wooden frame and said, "Sit down, please. Or stand, of course—"

He grinned at Hogg, looking like a pile of wrinkled clothing beside the door.

"—and tell us—tell Rennie, primarily—what help you want."

Daniel sat on the edge of a similar chair and leaned forward. "I'm glad that Lady Mundy has been in contact with you," he said. "My second officer informed me that she and her companions were taking refuge with the navy, but I've been fully occupied with bringing the ship here. I was able to broach a possibility with her, however, and in a moment I hope you'll let me talk to her to confirm the plan from her end."

He nodded toward the console at one end of the room, salvaged from a starship like many of those in service at a distance from major centers of civilization. When the starship's thrusters and High Drives were burned out and her hull was good for nothing but scrap metal, its astrogation computer was still more powerful than necessary for any ground-based requirements.

That certainly included secure satellite communications, if the operator knew his business. The Transformationists might be mystics, but they included mystics with very impressive real-world skill sets—as Sister Rennie proved.

"Yes, of course," Altgeld said, rising to his feet. "Olga and I will leave you alone with the console."

"No, no, please sit down," Daniel said, smiling. "I could contact Lady Mundy through the *Kiesche*'s equipment if I wanted privacy. I'd like you to be present, since this is going to require your agreement and support."

Altgeld settled back; Rennie hadn't moved. She

had certainly realized that Daniel didn't need their console to speak with Adele.

"As I understand it," Daniel said, "the problems within the independence movement started when Colonel Bourbon was taken prisoner. Is that correct?"

Altgeld looked at Rennie, who shrugged. "Yes," she said. "The serious problems."

Daniel nodded crisply. "The present situation isn't sustainable," he said. "Before long the other three factions will begin open warfare within Brotherhood. The fighting may draw you in also, but whether or not that happens, the Pantellarians will seize the planet. Ordinary people will support Pantellaria because it will be the only body which can reimpose law and order. Which is what most people want more than they want ideology."

Rennie looked at the frowning Altgeld and said, "Independence is an ideology, Robert." Turning to Daniel she said, "I agree with your assessment, Captain."

"I suspect that the leaders of the Regiment and the navy agree also," Daniel said. He had served under officers *much* less quick on the uptake than Rennie was showing herself. "I've asked Adele—Lady Mundy, that is—to propose to the other factions a meeting of all parties here—"

He gestured with his right hand toward the wall behind him and the community beyond.

"—in Pearl Valley, because even the Garrison leaders will trust your community to keep your collective word. Which they wouldn't the other parties in the coalition."

"*I* wouldn't trust the other parties," said Altgeld. "And in former days, I wouldn't have trusted myself."

He shrugged. "Merchant service is a hard school," he said. "But now, yes."

"And we have enough strength here to enforce a truce," Rennie said, nodding. "Whereas for us to assault Brotherhood successfully would be more problematic."

Rennie grinned. Her expression reminded Daniel of Tovera's on occasion.

"At this meeting," Daniel said, "I'm going to propose that my crew and I travel to Ischia and there arrange the release of the imprisoned envoys at my own expense."

"Is that possible?" said Altgeld.

"Will the factions in Brotherhood agree?" said Rennie simultaneously, leaning forward.

"I believe it's possible, yes," Daniel said, feeling himself relax. The questions were practical ones. They meant that the Transformationists were already in agreement. "And as for the other factions..."

He turned his hands palms-up before him.

"I won't know for sure until I speak to Lady Mundy again, but she said that Captain Samona is on board and that Administrator Tibbs, though less enthusiastic, has given her tentative approval. Mundy won't contact Colonel Mursiello until I tell her matters are arranged at this end, but neither she nor I think Mursiello will be able to object. His own troops, at least some of them, would turn on him if he blocked the rescue of Colonel Bourbon."

Altgeld stood. "Make your call, Captain," he said. "Matters are arranged at this end."

"And I," said Sister Rennie, also rising, "will make arrangements to receive our visitors in mutual safety and convenience."

She looks like Tovera again, Daniel thought as he walked to the console.

CHAPTER 15

Pearl Valley on Corcyra

Adele could have ridden in the truck's cab between Captain Samona and his navy driver, but she had decided that the cross-bench in the box was probably a better choice. The canvas sides were rolled up to the roof so the visibility was just as good in every direction except forward, and it would be easier to get out if they were ambushed. Spray which the four lift fans kicked up from the Cephisis River clung like a heavy mist to those in back, but she was used to that sort of thing.

The air-cushion truck was large enough to hold a platoon, but there were only four navy personnel in the back with Adele and the other three Cinnabar nationals. The Transformationists—which in this case meant Brother Altgeld relaying Daniel's decision—had directed the other three factions to come with only six people each.

Samona was holding rigidly to the limit. He probably felt that he couldn't bring enough gunmen with him to make a real difference if everything went wrong, so he was gaining good will by obeying the rules. In front of

Adele, he had ordered the *Freccia's* sailing master—the destroyer's highest ranking space officer with Samona gone and his lieutenant hostage on Ischia—to come in at low level in an emergency. After the Pantellarian ships' attack at Hablinger, that was a credible threat.

Adele wasn't expecting an ambush. Tovera, to her left on the bench, and Hale, on her right to the other side of Vesey, seemed to feel otherwise. Hale might not have been so nervous on her own, but Tovera's alertness seemed to have infected her.

Adele's lips quirked. Tovera was always alert and always expected an attack, but Tovera was a sociopath and not really human. An ordinary human being who acted the way she did would be insane. Hale would have to learn that.

Or go insane, of course. There were always options.

The truck slowed, then turned hard left with the S-bend skidding which was the inevitable province of air-cushion vehicles. Vesey half rose and bent over Hale to look forward, clinging to one of the hoops which supported the roof and sides.

"We're on the creek now," she called over the fan howl. "The settlement should be less than a mile—"

Vesey jerked back and shouted, "Whoa!"

She's been shot! Adele brought the pistol out of her pocket without thinking of what she was doing. The small weapon wouldn't be effective at any distance, but it was what she had.

Branches banged against the cab and then along the hoops as the truck lurched onward. They would have slapped Vesey in the face, possibly blinding her, if she hadn't dodged quickly.

The truck was pushing through foliage on both

sides now, and repeatedly the skirts bumped over rocks above the surface of the stream. There was less spray, but leaves and occasionally living creatures were scraped into the truck box.

A bronze-colored creature no longer than an index finger flopped from a branch and immediately struck at the nearest object: Tovera's left boot. Hale raised her carbine to use the butt as a pestle. "I'll get it!" she said.

"No!" said Tovera, bending over.

Hale hesitated. Vesey put her hand over Hale's, though her eyes were fixed on the creature. Adele thought it had tiny legs around the margin of its body, but she might have been seeing a flap of translucent skin. It was almost certainly poisonous.

"It'll *bite* you," Hale said, amazed that her companions didn't appear to see the obvious.

Tovera's hand moved; her fingers pinched the creature just behind the head. With the same motion, she flipped it over the side of the vehicle. It was still writhing and apparently unharmed.

There was a tiny splotch of yellow where the creature had been attached to the gray boot. Tovera looked at Hale and said, "Thank you. But I felt that professional courtesy was called for."

Vesey chortled; Adele smiled. Hale, nonplussed, lowered her carbine.

"Six kept the ship on the surface all the way up the river," Vesey said, looking sideways but seated firmly in the center of the bench with Adele. "It's a pity he lifted here instead of clearing it for us."

"There might have been people here in the creek that he couldn't have seen until he was on them," Adele said, following Vesey's eyes.

And the foliage was alive and full of lesser life. Daniel was certainly ruthless enough to let his thrusters sear a lethal path across a forest, but it was the sort of thing he preferred to avoid. This far up the river, the *Kiesche* was beyond the slant range of antiship missiles from Brotherhood.

There wasn't a great deal that Adele cared about; certainly not other living things, with the exception of a few human beings who had taken her into their friendship and protection. She appreciated people who did care, though. People *should* choose to behave well to their surroundings, human or otherwise.

"Surely Captain Leary didn't come this far in surface effect?" Hale said. "Really, I don't think that would be possible. Flying fifty miles in the atmosphere would be an amazing job in a tramp freighter, even at five hundred feet or so."

Tovera leaned forward. "It's possible," she said. "From what I've seen, Lieutenant Vesey could do it. Not so, Lieutenant?"

Vesey looked embarrassed. "Not so well as Six, certainly," she said. "But if I were forced to try, I believe I would have managed the business, yes."

She gestured toward the open back of the truck to change the subject from herself. "As for what Six did, though, there's no question, Hale," she said. "The mud bar at the mouth of this creek had been baked to shale. You could see it broken into plates after we'd driven over it."

Tovera grinned, still looking at Hale. "Stay with Vesey," she said. "There's no end of things you can learn. If you survive."

Tovera returned to surveying the forest they were

bucking through. Adele thought about the interaction she had just witnessed. Vesey was quiet and easily overlooked. Hale, a much more forceful officer, had probably been taking her as a cipher to be ignored or even elbowed aside despite her rank. Thanks to Tovera, that wouldn't happen now.

An ordinary human being, Cory for example, wouldn't have thought of correcting Hale's mistake until it had flashed up as an open problem. *I wonder if a smart sociopath who works at it isn't better at being human than most human beings are?*

Another aspect of the business occurred to Adele, though she kept the frown of doubt from reaching her face. Tovera worked at displaying herself as an intelligent, caring member of Adele's circle—the intelligence was real—because she had attached herself to Adele. Tovera's natural behavior was more similar to that of a weasel than to that of the caring pedagogue she had just mimicked.

Adele let herself smile broadly enough that a stranger would have recognized the expression. *I've found a reason for living: to encourage Tovera to be a kinder, gentler person when kind, gentle behavior is appropriate.* The universe being what it was, the natural Tovera had many opportunities to display herself—or itself—nonetheless.

Captain Samona slid open the window between the cab and the truck box. "I see it ahead!" he called.

A woman in coveralls stood by the riverbank. She waggled one of her orange paddles in the air, then pointed both paddles in parallel past herself.

"That's the *Kiesche!*" Hale said, leaning out to look forward. Adele could see a starship through the windshield, but she couldn't have sworn that it was the *Kiesche*. In any case, that was Daniel waving from the base of the ship's ramp.

The truck slowed, hopped, and then stopped thirty feet from the *Kiesche*. The navy personnel—at least two of the four were simply gunmen, not spacers—used the skirt for a step as they exited by the back of the truck. They jogged around on both sides to flank Captain Samona as he got out of the cab.

Vesey hopped to the ground and reached upward to take Adele's hand and brace her as she followed. Hale watched with a slight frown. She hadn't been a member of the crew for long enough to automatically offer the mistress help with any physical test.

Vesey smiled at Adele and said, "It's good to be back."

"Yes," said Adele, walking toward Daniel. He had now been joined by a pair of middle-aged strangers.

She heard Hale saying, "I didn't realize you'd been here before, Lieutenant."

Adele smiled. It must be difficult for an outsider like Hale to work into an existing family, but she was trying.

Hogg stood by the ramp with his hands in his pockets, looking toward the ground car which was pulling into the clearing. Following it was a six-wheeled truck with a pintle-mounted automatic weapon. Hogg's stocked impeller leaned against the outrigger beside him. It threatened no one and was easy to overlook—unless something unpleasant started to happen.

The ground car settled as the driver released the pressure in the hydraulic suspension which had given it an extra thirty centimeters of clearance. Administrator Tibbs got out.

Brother Graves had said that the road from Brotherhood to the Transformationist settlement was circuitous and occasionally rough. The Regiment didn't have a full-sized air-cushion vehicle, so their envoys to the conference had decided to travel this way instead of coming upriver in a pair of air-cushion jeeps.

"Lady Mundy," said Daniel, "allow me to present you to Coordinator Altgeld and the community's military adviser, Sister Rennie."

"Lady Mundy," said Rennie, offering her hand after Adele had shaken with the coordinator, "I'd appreciate a moment to chat with you and your servant before the general conference gets under way. If that's agreeable to you, Captain Leary?"

"Lady Mundy doesn't need my approval to speak with anyone she pleases," said Daniel, his tone minusculy guarded.

Adele understood Daniel's concern. The unexpected is rarely a spacer's friend. Or a spy's, come to that.

Tovera stepped between Adele and Rennie. "Where were you planning to take us?" she said harshly to the Transformationist.

"I thought we'd step to the edge of the field there," Rennie said in a mild tone. She nodded to the belt of waist-high grass between the mowed field and the natural forest. "That way we remain in sight of everyone, but we're out of the line of fire of the impeller in the hummock we'll be standing next to."

Tovera barked a laugh. Adele had heard her servant laugh before, but the timbre of this sound was like nothing in the past.

"Sure," Tovera said. "Let's get out of the way."

Adele followed Rennie and Tovera. When she got

close enough she saw that what she'd taken for a natural swell in the ground was actually covered with chameleon fabric which mimicked the surrounding grass. She didn't doubt that there was an automatic impeller concealed within.

Rennie nodded minusculy toward the hillock. "The man there is a former Land Forces sergeant," she said, "and the best gunner I've ever met. I can't imagine why the Pantellarians would want to attack us, but I'm not privy to their internal counsels. Colonel Mursiello and his cronies don't need a reason to attack someone— just an opportunity. I want them to regret it if they decide they have an opportunity here."

Rennie breathed deeply. "Lady Mundy," she said. "I've told my colleagues, and your colleagues after the *Kiesche* landed, that I was an Alliance colonel in my life before I joined the community here. This is true, but I think I should add to you—"

"Because she'll learn it herself!" Tovera said.

"Of *course* Lady Mundy would learn it—and would learn even if you didn't know already, mistress," Rennie said, her voice suddenly hard. Her eyes locked with Tovera's for a moment, then flicked back to Adele. "That I was not a colonel in the Army of the Alliance but rather in the Fifth Bureau."

"I'll keep that in mind," said Adele. "I was a librarian before I joined the RCN, and those habits of thought still color my perceptions."

Rennie nodded. "Yes, they do," she said. In a voice that might have been wistful she said, "I was sent to Pearl Valley fifteen years ago, investigating. I pretended to be a convert, of course. To my surprise I found real kinship, a wonderful thing. Nobody cared what I had been or why I had come here, even after I confessed. It's an amazing feeling."

She smiled, her eyes on the past. "It transformed me," she said. She laughed to make a joke out of what she had said, if anyone chose to believe that it was a joke.

It wasn't a joke, of course. Adele said, "I understand what it means to become a member of a family after a lifetime of being alone."

The thrum of powerful fans sounded, approaching from the north. "That will be the Garrison's two armored personnel carriers," Rennie said. "If they've been able to get both of them airborne, that is. Let's head for the Chapel."

Tovera said, "Let's not get too close till the Garrison has landed, though."

"Umm?" said Adele, looking from Tovera to Rennie.

"There are meter-high steel spikes in the bushes near the Chapel," Rennie said. "We've asked our visitors to stay at least fifty meters out, so it shouldn't matter; but if someone did try to land an aircar too close to the building . . . well, you can't tell how far a fan blade will fly."

They walked toward the Chapel as two APCs came in low over the treetops, one of them laboring. Adele joined the laughter as the Garrison vehicles suddenly jerked away as they started to land beside the Chapel's porch.

Daniel followed Hogg through the wedge-shaped doorway of the Chapel and stutter-stepped before he regained his stride. He really disliked the habit of some people to stop in doorways with others—with Daniel himself—behind them, but the sudden wash of peace that came over him had almost made him do the same thing himself.

The room was not a rotunda though the interior floor plan was round. Daniel looked at the ceiling as he walked down the aisle toward the table at the far end. The roof sloped upward to a central tower covered with a frosted skylight. The sides glowed blue, and the metal tracery which strengthened the translucent panels flowed in curves which were themselves soothing.

The tall windows between the wall buttresses were of colored glass. Most of them gave the interior a feeling of the blue depths of the sea, though there were swirls and blotches from the whole spectrum visible when Daniel looked directly at the panels. The wall opposite the entrance was red in emphasis, but the light through it was nonetheless peaceful.

"This is the most lovely building I've ever been in," Daniel said to Brother Altgeld.

Altgeld smiled. "It was a very peaceful spot from the beginning," the coordinator said. "Our records say that was the reason the Chapel was built here."

The table at the base of the central aisle was rectangular. Mursiello was presumably the man in an Alliance dress uniform with the hollow stars of a colonel on his shoulder-boards. He had appropriated one end of the table, and Captain Hochner sat to his right on the long side nearer the entrance.

Samona and Tibbs, each with an aide—the Regimental aide wore a Pantellarian major's service uniform—were both on the opposite long side. Adele was seated on the right end of the near side, and Sister Rennie was beside Hochner.

Daniel started toward the seat between Rennie and Adele. "Please take the end spot, Captain Leary," Altgeld said in a clear voice. "We're gathered to hear your proposals. That place will allow you to address all the principals without turning your head."

"*I'm* not here to listen to somebody telling us to make nice-nice with the Pantellarian oppressors because they're friends of Cinnabar," Mursiello said. He glared in challenge at Daniel. The room's acoustics were excellent.

Daniel chuckled as he took the place offered to him, but he put his hands on the back of the chair instead of sitting down. "As best I know," he said cheerfully, "my government doesn't have a position on whoever's in charge on Pantellaria—or Corcyra, more to the point. Certainly *I* don't. I'm here as an entrepreneur, I suppose you'd say."

Nobody at the table spoke. Beyond them, the ranks of curving benches would seat about six hundred people; most of the spaces were filled. Apart from the normal creaks and shuffling of a large gathering, the spectators might have been miles away.

"Now, I've got a military background, as I'm sure you know," Daniel said, "but it doesn't take an expert to see that the present stalemate is ruining Corcyra. You're shipping about half the copper that you were before the Pantellarians landed, and your prices are lower as well because of the perceived risk in case Pantellaria tries to enforce a real blockade."

"They won't," said Captain Samona.

"*Perceived* risk, Captain," Daniel said. "The reduced prices are a matter of record, as you can check as easily as I—"

As Adele.

"—did."

Mursiello muttered something under his breath, but no one interrupted again.

"The quickest way to break the stalemate in a good way—good for independent Corcyra, that is—is to get antiship missiles from Karst," Daniel said. "And the best way to do *that* is to get your envoys back from the jackleg pirates holding them and execute the deal which those envoys have already negotiated."

He grinned at his listeners. "You won't do better the next time," he said, "and the folks ruling Karst may well be having second thoughts already. I've dealt with them, remember."

"We *can't* get the envoys back," Mursiello said. "Those idiots on Ischia want us to gut the country, give away the next twenty years—"

"It's not that bad!" said Tibbs, glaring at Mursiello like a bright-eyed bird. "They want the carrying trade, but their prices—"

"They want the trade, Karst wants the trade, everybody wants a piece of us!" Mursiello said. He slammed his fist on the table. "Well, they're not going to get it!"

"Colleagues," Daniel said. "I think—"

"Mursiello, you were a police sergeant on Pantellaria before you decided to take Alliance money to beat up miners here," said Captain Samona. "Prospering as a thug doesn't make you a statesman!"

"You can shut your gob now, you stuck-up prick!" Mursiello said, lurching to his feet.

Hochner was standing also. He'd found a replacement for the pistol Hogg had taken away. Now he unbuckled his holster flap with his left hand and put his right on the butt.

A Transformationist from the nearest benches gripped the back of Hochner's neck with one hand. He twisted his wrist up with the other.

The pistol clanked to the floor. Hochner tried to turn but couldn't. His face was turning purple, a combination of strain and fury. The man holding him was easily in his fifties and didn't look particularly strong, but Hochner wasn't going anywhere.

The Transformationist's face was calm and expressionless. *I wonder what* he *did before he found god?* Daniel thought.

Altgeld touched the point of Hochner's hip. "Please sit down, Captain," he said. "We take seriously our promise to keep all our guests safe."

You certainly saved Hochner's *life,* Daniel thought. If Hogg—or Tovera!—had stopped the Garrison officer, it would have been messier and quite permanent.

"Siddown, Hochner," Mursiello said, dropping back into his chair. He was angry, but he kept his eyes on the table in front of him. He must have realized that there were hundreds of people in the room with him, and scarcely a soul would mind if he were strapped to the conference table and flayed alive.

Hochner sat down beside Brother Altgeld. The man holding him moved back to the bench; he was so nondescript that Daniel wasn't sure he could tell the fellow from those seated to either side of him.

Tovera is pretty colorless also, come to think.

"I understand your qualms about paying extortion to Ischia," Daniel said. "Apart from anything else, you *can't* give both Ischia and Karst the same thing, and getting your envoys back won't help unless you have the missiles also."

Everyone was looking at him. They looked like fish coming to the surface of a pond when they expect to be fed.

"Therefore," Daniel said, "I propose to gain the release of the envoys by my own efforts. I don't require any financial contribution from Corcyra, before or after the fact, but I want your agreement to ratify my actions if that becomes necessary. I want it clear that *I'm* not a pirate."

He wasn't lying, but he was allowing his listeners to believe things that he hadn't said. For most of the parties it didn't matter—though as a matter of course, Daniel didn't like to discuss his plans with people who had no reason to know except their curiosity.

Mursiello and Hochner were another matter. It was important that *they* believe Daniel was going to attempt the impossible.

"Just how do you plan to do this?" Mursiello said. "I don't think you can!"

"You may be correct, of course, Colonel," Daniel said, "but in that case you haven't lost anything. I mean you personally and the independence movement also. As for my plans—"

He looked around the table again, still smiling.

"—I'll say just that I hope to release the hostages without violence, but I will use any means which the usage of the civilized galaxy deems to be proper for dealing with pirates. As the Ischians have shown themselves to be."

There was silence. Mursiello still glowered, but there was a cunning look beneath his hostility.

"It appears to me that an attempt to free the prisoners by violence," said Altgeld, "may cause the Ischians to execute them. Or indeed, that the prisoners may be killed in the attempt?"

Daniel nodded. "Yes," he said, "those are certainly

possibilities. War has risks, life has risks. But I point out—"

He deliberately shaped his expression and tone on the stern models his father had used when urging the Senate to take a difficult course because the alternatives were worse.

"—that if you don't achieve the return of the prisoners, the Ischians will offer them to Pantellaria. In fact, I'm surprised that this hasn't happened already. And the Pantellarians will certainly execute them as traitors."

"Leary's right," said Administrator Tibbs. "We have nothing to lose."

Captain Samona nodded and said, "Yes, Leary's offering the best chance we've had to get our people back and maybe to win this war. Go ahead, *I* say."

Altgeld looked at the Garrison commander. "Colonel Mursiello?" he said. "Are you willing for Captain Leary to make the attempt under the auspices of the Independence Council?"

Mursiello's face worked with suppressed anger. "All right, waste your time, Leary," he said. "But it *is* a waste of time, you know!"

"Then I believe we're done here," Altgeld said. He and Rennie got to their feet. "All of you are welcome to stay with us as long as you like. No one will try to convert you, though I'll warn you that our community here is a very pleasant place to remain."

Adele was putting away her data unit. "Thank you," said Daniel. "I need to prepare the ship for liftoff. The sooner we start, the sooner we'll be able to return."

Assuming we're not all dead. But Daniel always assumed that he would succeed, and that had generally turned out to be true.

CHAPTER 16

Platt's Compound on Dace

The six submachine guns fired more or less together, though the first burst came before Hogg shouted "Fire!" and the two last followed him shouting "Cease fire!" There might have been yet another burst at the end if Hale hadn't grabbed Furstein by the right wrist and twisted his hand and weapon skyward.

Daniel was philosophical about the shooting. He hadn't been under any illusions about how his spacers measured up as marksmen. That was one of the reasons he'd set the crew to weapons practice here on the shore of the island.

"I've got them aiming at holographic projections right now, Master Platt," Daniel said to the soft-looking bald man facing him beside the wall of Barracks #1. The shooters were a hundred yards away, so the gunfire was only an unpleasant crackling against the strong breeze. "Not a one of 'em would have a problem if I told them to blast you to cats' meat instead. So tell me about the Corcyran envoys again, only this time make it the truth."

Platt closed his eyes, but he couldn't keep tears from leaking out under them. "Don't," he blubbered. "Don't don't don't..."

"Bloody hell, Evans!" Hale said. "You've got to take out the empty magazine before you can put in a fresh tube!"

Hogg and Hale were doing the training, but Daniel suspected that Hale was learning as much as the spacers under her charge. Her experience on a marksmanship team at the Academy would have given her a very false impression of what "shooting" meant to the average spacer. She had to understand the reality before she found herself commanding spacers in a firefight.

"Just tell me how the envoys were captured," Daniel said soothingly. "Or arrested, if you want put it that way. You're not in any trouble if you just tell me the truth."

He'd figured the gunfire would make Platt uneasy, but he hadn't expected the fellow to be such an abject coward that the implied threat made him incoherent. Daniel tried to hide his disgust when he realized that Platt had soiled himself in fear. Well, they wouldn't be staying on Dace for long.

Platt's Compound was one of eight settlements on the planet, all more or less the same. Dace was a low-lying world. Shallow seas covered ninety percent of the surface, and when a storm really got going, it could circle the planet several times before subsiding.

Large-scale colonization and normal agriculture were impossible, but it was a good place to take on reaction mass, and it provided seafood protein in simple factories which sucked in water and compressed the creatures which they filtered out. There was nothing in the seas more complex than a rotifer.

Platt's had two barracks, a processing plant, and a residence which was only half the size of normal barracks. All the buildings were formed from slabs of edge-welded structural plastic. In good condition they were watertight. They would have floated off in storms if they hadn't been anchored deep into the rock.

The permanent staff was four women and eight men, all members of one family. The women doubled as prostitutes; probably the men did also. Daniel hadn't always been fastidious, but he found it hard to imagine that even the randiest spacer, no matter how much he had drunk, would have found the Platts enticing. No doubt he was wrong.

"It was nothing to do with us," Platt said. He didn't open his eyes. "We just made the call, you see. This ship from Ischia landed at Riddle's Place—"

Near the south pole.

"—and said there was five hundred thalers for anybody who told them that a ship bound for Corcyra had landed at their compound. Just told them, you see? And five hundred thalers, that's real money!"

Gunfire ripped along the shoreline. Platt whimpered and hunched forward, screwing his eyes closed again. Hale shouted at Evans; she was getting hoarse.

"You're fine, Platt," Daniel said, patting the fellow's shoulder. "Just tell us the whole truth and we'll be gone like we were never here."

Butler, the engineer of the *Cordelia*, the ship which had been returning the envoys from Karst, was still on Corcyra when Daniel was looking for information on the capture. Butler said that they'd landed at Platt's on Dace, the usual layover between Karst and Corcyra. They normally spent three days on the ground, mostly to rest the crew: the *Cordelia*'s fore-rigging was in bad condition, and the splices required clearing constantly.

A ship from Ischia had landed after the *Cordelia* did, but that wasn't a matter for comment or concern. That night the crew of the Ischian ship had abducted the envoys from Barracks #1 at gunpoint, leaving a ransom demand for the *Cordelia*'s captain to deliver to the Independence Council on Brotherhood. Butler had been in Barracks #1 at the time, but he'd been drunk and knew nothing about the business until well after the Ischians had lifted. From what the captain said, there hadn't been much to know.

"We called Riddle when the Corcyrans arrived, that's all we did," said Platt when he regained enough composure to speak. "The Ischians landed that night and paid us, just like they said. And then they took off again, and it wasn't till next morning I knew that the Corcyrans had gone off with them. That's *all*."

"The envoys were taken prisoner at gunpoint," Daniel said. "Which you *knew*."

"Not so," Platt whimpered to his hands, knotted together before him. "There wasn't a shot, not one shot. My daughter Hyacinth, she was entertaining some of the Corcyrans, and she maybe said something about a gun the next morning, but I didn't think nothing about it."

Daniel considered the situation. Platt hadn't told him much that he and Adele hadn't deduced before they lifted from Corcyra, but hearing it firsthand was good practice whenever possible.

The kidnapping had been well planned and executed, not a spur-of-the-moment thing by individuals who might now feel they were in over their heads. Daniel had been ready to deal with matters either way, so the datum wasn't simply good or bad. It was crucial that he—and Adele—knew which it was, however.

"All right," Daniel said. "We'll be lifting before nightfall, but I'll pay you the normal landing fee. You can be gone, now."

"Ah, captain-sir?" Platt said. "Will you be, well... the shooting, I mean. It gets on the nerves of me wife and daughters, you see?"

Daniel gave Platt a hard smile. "I think the weapons training will end after the next sequence," he said, trying to suppress his contempt for the man. "We'll use your shore for a briefing to the crew since there isn't a building here large enough to hold us."

He made a quick chopping motion with his hand when Platt seemed to be about to speak further. "And before you ask," Daniel said, "we won't be paying anything additional for the opportunity to raise a marquee on the shore for the purpose."

Daniel turned on his heel and walked back toward the *Kiesche* and Adele. The reason besides information that he'd chosen to land on Dace was that it was a good place to inform his crew about his plans.

The Kiesches were brave and loyal beyond question, but they were spacers. A captain who expected his crew to remain sober and discreet on the ground was either very inexperienced or out of his mind.

Daniel was neither of those things. Waiting till they landed on Dace to explain the situation meant that nobody on Corcyra would learn about his plans until the *Kiesche* returned—or some other ship arrived with news of the disaster on Ischia. Daniel hoped and expected the first option, but he wouldn't survive to care if matters worked out the other way.

Adele looked at the assembled faces, feeling uncomfortable. Normally her briefings would be aboard ship. Even if the whole crew of the *Princess Cecile* was listening, most of the personnel would be in separate compartments.

The *Kiesche*'s only quality imaging equipment was on the bridge, which wouldn't hold the whole crew. Though the freighter carried only a fraction of the *Sissie*'s complement of over a hundred, the twenty staring faces kept Adele from pretending that she was alone with data on a display.

"Ischia has been settled in over a hundred valleys," she said, displaying the planet with its populated continent toward her audience. "There is a federal government, but for the most part the valley clans are independent. We have to do with the Monfiore clan."

She highlighted a section in the southeastern quadrant. Pasternak had rigged a speaker from the ship's PA system to amplify the signal from Adele's personal data system, but she had to use the system's own projector for imagery. A sailcloth marquee was necessary so that the greenish sunlight wouldn't overwhelm the little unit's holographic capability.

"The valleys provide enough food for the inhabitants," Adele said, "but there's nothing agricultural of such quantity or quality that it's worth exporting. Ischia builds sturdy ships of moderate size, and much of the population is working or has worked as spacers. Ships and ships' crews, along with small quantities of forest products, bring in all the foreign exchange."

The breeze off the water was freshening, making the marquee rattle. Woetjans had decided it would be safe, so Adele knew her concern about it blowing away was unjustified. Still, the quicker this was over and she was back on the bridge, the better.

"Ischia is an Associated World of the Alliance," Adele said. "Her spacers served on Alliance warships, but much of the Fleet has gone into ordinary since the Treaty of Amiens, just as the RCN has."

Her audience murmured agreement. These spacers were the cream of the cream; all of them could have found berths in the merchant service and probably in the RCN even in its current reduced state. Spacers they knew, spacers whose families lived in the same apartment blocks as their families did, were out of work, though. It would be a while before the merchant service expanded to prewar levels.

Adele showed imagery of several Ischian-built starships. Daniel and Cazelet—whose family had owned a shipping firm before they fell afoul of Guarantor Porra and were executed—had assured her that the vessels were typical Ischian construction.

There was no need for the images, but they provided something for spacers to focus on during the lecture. Adele had learned in childhood that most people didn't have the passion for data which so consumed her.

"Ischia has a particular problem," she said. "During the eighteen years while Pantellaria was annexed to the Alliance, Ischian ships were given a monopoly on the carrying trade between Pantellaria and the five core worlds of the Alliance. Guarantor Porra was rewarding a court favorite whose brother was the Alliance

Advisor on Ischia. Despite the large fee the advisor was taking, Ischia did very well out of the trade."

Vesey and Cazelet were listening to the briefing on the console on the *Kiesche*'s bridge, ready to start liftoff procedure instantly. Pasternak was in the Power Room, cycling reaction mass. The chief engineer wouldn't light the thrusters until the crew was aboard, but it wouldn't take this group long to board in a crisis.

"Since Pantellaria regained its independence," Adele said, "the new government—the Council of Twenty—has refused landing rights to any ship with Alliance registration, including ships from worlds which are Associates of the Alliance. This is being described to the Pantellarian people as a rebuke to their former Alliance overlords."

Adele paused, forcing herself to look around the semicircle of her audience: her shipmates, her family members. Daniel was grinning; others smiled to meet her eyes or frowned in their determination to understand, somehow, what the Mistress was telling them. *I have to remember that it isn't just me against the universe anymore.*

Adele was still alone in the dark hours of the morning, when she was visited by the faces of those she had killed, of the many she had killed. *But I'm not alone now!*

"Some of you may be thinking that the Council is taking reasonable retribution on Pantellaria's oppressors," Adele said. As she spoke the words, she realized that the only people in *this* audience likely to think in those terms were the commissioned officers. Ordinary spacers were only concerned with political decisions as they were affected by them, and *nothing* that happened on Pantellaria affected the *Kiesche*'s crew.

"The Pantellarian councillors are oligarchs," she said, grimacing at having used a word that would mean nothing, *nothing*, to the spacers. "Rich folk, rich folk from rich families, running things for themselves and not for the people."

She spoke harshly because she was angry with her own inability to communicate. Her audience read her tone as righteous indignation and responded with nods and grunts of approval. Evans even slapped one big fist into the other palm and muttered, "That's how it always bloody is, ain't it?"

Adele paused. Yes, it generally was; on Cinnabar as surely as on Pantellaria and on the worlds of the Alliance. The spacers were unsophisticated, but they weren't all stupid; and even a stupid man—which Evans was by any reasonable standard—could see straight through to a point which a highly educated noblewoman was ignoring because it wasn't in the compartment she was examining at present.

"Quite right, Evans," Adele said aloud. "Three of the twenty members of the Council have shipping interests and expect to make a great deal of money out of the embargo on Alliance hulls."

She cleared her throat. "One Ischian clan, the Monfiores, decided to reverse the disastrous loss of trade by kidnapping the envoys of the Corcyran independence movement. They've demanded a ransom of three million Alliance thalers or the carrying trade from Corcyra on the same terms as under the Alliance. The Monfiores specialized in the Corcyran copper trade, and that's probably how they got good enough information on the envoys' route to carry out the very sophisticated operation which took place here on Dace."

Forgetting her audience, Adele added, "I hope to get more details when we reach Ischia."

That was true, but it had nothing whatever to do with what Adele was supposed to be explaining to the crew. Before she could get angry with herself again, she noticed that the spacers were nodding in approval again. *The Mistress is on the job. She'll know where the Ischian buggers bought their socks before she's done.*

Adele smiled visibly at her audience. She had learned from observation over the past few years to interpret people's reactions even when she could not in a lifetime imagine why they thought the things they did. There are many kinds of information.

"The Corcyran council did not agree to the terms," Adele said. "They have allowed us, allowed Captain Leary, to use his own efforts to free the prisoners, however. Remember that though we're dealing with a single clan rather than all Ischia, it seems probable that the Monfiores' attitude is shared generally across the planet. Certainly the depression is planetwide."

Adele cleared her throat and forced herself to look around her audience again. She had become a good—an exceptional—pistol shot through constant practice at the range in the basement of Chatsworth Minor. She doubted that she would ever become a good public speaker, but she had a better appreciation for the value of practice than most people did.

"Are there questions before I move aside for Six?" she said, not really expecting a response.

"Ma'am?" said Cory. "Why haven't these Monfiores

sold their prisoners to Pantellaria, because by now it must be pretty obvious that Corcyra isn't going to pay the ransom they're asking."

"I apologize," Adele said. "I should have covered that without being reminded. I'm speculating because my information isn't recent enough to have an answer directly from Pantellarian files, but the background suggests a familiar pattern. Commissioner Arnaud is a member of the Council and probably the most important single member of it."

She paused to order her presentation. *If my father had come to me, I could have predicted that his coup would fail,* Adele realized. Though at age fifteen, the skills she had since developed working with Daniel Leary might not have been sufficient to the task.

And it wouldn't have mattered anyway, because Lucius Mundy would not have believed her, believed *anyone,* saying something which he didn't want to be true. That common human trait was something else that Adele had learned in the years since the failure of the Three Circles Conspiracy.

"Arnaud has nineteen colleagues, however," she continued. "While none of them have openly declared themselves Arnaud's enemy, many"—and perhaps all—"have privately indicated disquiet about Arnaud's intentions if he should return to Pantellaria after a great military victory. One may reasonably speculate that they would rather that Arnaud fail, though they could not be seen to actively work against him and become traitors in the eyes of the general populace."

"Ah, Mundy?" Daniel said. They hadn't discussed the background in detail, because until recently the Pantellarian invasion itself hadn't been part of their own mission. "Why did Arnaud take the risk of commanding the expedition? Because he must have known that it would be risky simply to be off-planet when his colleagues were unfriendly. Or frightened of him, which is even worse."

Adele nodded, closing her eyes for a moment. "Again, this is something I hope to learn more about when we're back on Corcyra," she said. Her voice was being amplified; Daniel's had not been, but she and the audience heard him easily over the breeze. "Arnaud owned three copper mines on Corcyra, which the Independence Council nationalized; that probably affected his planning. The factor I cannot determine without access to Commissioner Arnaud's mind, however..."

The smile she gave her audience was thin and as hard as chipped flint, but it was a smile.

"Which is still beyond my capabilities. The factor is whether Arnaud really is aiming at autocracy—tyranny, dictatorship, whichever term you prefer—as his fellow Board members believe. My information makes me doubt that he could have succeeded in seizing power before he took command of the expedition. If he should manage to recover Corcyra, however, his chances of a successful coup would be much better."

"But ma'am?" Cory said. The eyes of the audience swivelled toward him like those of spectators at a tennis match. *Cory has developed a very respectable voice of command during the time he served under Captain Leary.* "Arnaud *can't* succeed, can he? Not now. Even without the Corcyrans getting missiles from Karst, the best the Pantellarians can hope for is a stalemate."

"Information suggests..." Adele said. The information was from Deirdre Leary, not Mistress Sand, but her only concern with data was its accuracy. "That Commissioner Arnaud hopes that Cinnabar will support his attempt to recover the planet. I do not believe that his hopes have much chance of being fulfilled."

In the larger scheme of things, it didn't matter if human civilization collapsed into a renewed death struggle between Cinnabar and the Alliance. In terms of human beings, though, it would be a very bad thing.

I don't really feel that I'm human; but my friends certainly are. The spacers watching Adele didn't understand her smile, but it was a real smile.

Adele took a deep breath. She was wrung out, much as she would have felt after a gunfight.

"Captain Leary," she said. She didn't make it a question, because she very badly wanted to get out from under the gaze of her shipmates. "Please take charge."

Adele's first thought had been to go back to the *Kiesche* and sit at the console. She caught herself and instead took Daniel's seat on the bench, between Cory and Woetjans.

"Fellow spacers," Daniel said, grinning. "I want you to know that I plan to ransom the captives, not stage an armed prison break. I think we'd be a little outclassed taking on a whole planet, even if we were back in the *Sissie*."

The spacers cheered. Adele suddenly realized that without thinking she had slid her data unit away in its pocket, but Daniel didn't need amplification.

"But I'll tell you this also," he said, roughening his tone a little. "I plan to get the people we came for, and I'll do whatever it takes to do that. Are you with me?"

The bellowed response sounded as though it came from caged animals rather than human beings. Adele listened in amazement and delight. *They'd react the same if Daniel announced that they were going to climb up the throats of plasma thrusters at full output. And I'd be with them.*

"Then get squared away, spacers," Daniel said. "We'll lift in four hours."

They cheered again. *All of us are cheering.*

CHAPTER 17

Above Ischia

Daniel opened his eyes as the *Kiesche* finished shuddering back into the sidereal universe. He'd found extraction from the Matrix this time to be startlingly nasty: he felt as if all the nerves on his left side were being ripped out of the skin.

But extraction was never pleasant, and the process was over for now. He rubbed his left forearm with his palm and scanned the plot-position indicator to which his display was set.

"*Freighter* Kiesche *to Ischian patrol vessels* B113 *and* B117," Cazelet said. "*We request landing clearance for Jezreel.*" The central town of the Monfiore clan. "*Over.*"

Cazelet must have had an unusually easy extraction. He certainly sounded brighter than Daniel could have managed.

"Ship, prepare for High Drive," Daniel said. He gimballed the three High Drive motors as closely as possible to the freighter's axis of motion and switched them on. They vibrated badly; Motor Two cut out several times in the first twenty seconds.

Daniel waited until the motors had steadied, then brought the total impulse up to one g. This took the *Kiesche* out of free fall and began to brake the momentum she had brought with her from the Matrix.

A ship could only change her speed in normal space, but the constants of velocity and distance varied from one bubble of the cosmos to the next. Ships moved between universes, each time multiplying their rate of motion relative to the sidereal universe. When they finally extracted from the Matrix, they were many light-years from where they had inserted.

Astrogation computers could provide solutions for anyone who knew enough to program a destination. A moderately skilled astrogator with current data could cut transit times by as much as half over those of a console's solution. Skilled astrogators viewed the cosmos from outside the hull and refined their courses according to the momentary energy levels which they read in the apparent colors of the bubble universes they observed.

Commander Stacy Bergen, the brother of Daniel's mother, was renowned as the best astrogator ever to wear the uniform of the RCN. If he had a rival, it was Daniel Leary, the nephew whom Bergen had trained from infancy.

"*Patrol vessels* B113 *and* B117," Cazelet repeated. He had been using tight-beam microwave with separate sending units aimed at the widely separated Ischian ships. This time he added a short-wave hailing frequency, 15.5 mH in the 20-meter band. "*This is freighter* Kiesche *out of Corcyra, seeking permission to land at Jezreel, over.*"

The *Kiesche* had extracted 29,000 miles above Ischia,

performance that most captains—and most crews—
would have considered miraculous. Even Daniel had to
admit that there had been a good deal of luck in the
result, though an experienced RCN officer was expected
to come within 50,000 miles more often than not.

The patrol ships were in powered orbits at 100,000
miles, where tramp freighters were most likely to
extract. Images captured by the *Kiesche*'s newly fitted
optics showed that *B113* and *B117* were small freighters coupled to huge tanks which allowed them to hold
station at 1g acceleration for months instead of weeks.

Tugs could replace the water buffalos when necessary and probably rotate the crews. The duty was as
boring as that of a lighthouse keeper on the ground,
but Daniel knew there were people whose personalities were a perfect fit.

If Daniel simply concentrated on his display, he
could pretend that he was back in the *Princess Cecile*:
the consoles were effectively identical. The freighter's
limited sail plan had prevented Daniel from taking
advantage of subtleties with which the corvette would
have saved a few minutes here, a few hours there, on
the way to Ischia. All in all, however, the *Kiesche*
was a sound little vessel which had amply justified
Sun's praise of her.

"Kiesche, *this is One-three*," a male voice responded
from *B113*. The vessel was slightly more distant than
its sister, but she and the *Kiesche* were in approaching
orbits. "*What is your cargo, over?*"

"*Sir?*" said Cory, using a jumpseat and a flat-plate
display. He was using a two-way link rather than the
general push, though any communications aboard a
ship where Adele had set up the net included her.

"The Monfiores have issued a general alert, and some of their neighbors are doing the same thing. They're not planning an ambush, but everybody's supposed to grab his gun and be ready, over."

During the rebuild, four flat-plate displays had been added to the freighter's bridge. Daniel realized that he didn't know whether Mon had done the work on his own hook, or if was a gift from Adele's other employer. They didn't add computing power, but they used only an insignificant fraction of the command console's capacity unless they were attempting astrogation.

"Understood, Cory," Daniel said. That was what he had expected. The people who had planned and executed the envoys' kidnapping would certainly be ready to respond to a smash-and-grab rescue attempt.

"B113," Cazelet said. According to Daniel's display, he was on microwave only, but he was continuing to copy the other patrol vessel. *"We're not carrying any cargo. We've come to discuss the release of Corcyran envoys with the Monfiore clan. Kiesche over."*

Sun had a gunnery array up on the third flat-plate display. Daniel didn't imagine that the *Kiesche* would need her 50-mm popgun, but neither was there any better present use for the unit. Knowing that the gunner was ready to respond probably calmed some of the spacers; and Daniel rather liked knowing it also.

"*Kiesche,*" the patrol vessel said, *"this is your first landing here. Be aware that customs officials will be on the ground by the time you're ready to open your hatches. There is a one-percent tariff on everything imported to Ischia, and we're bloody serious about it. Your ship will be confiscated if you try to evade the tariff, over."*

"*Understood, B113,*" Cazelet said calmly. "*We have no cargo on this voyage, over.*"

"*Sir,*" volunteered Cory, "*they run their whole planetary government off the tariff. There isn't much government, but they're still being pinched by the way trade's shut down to the planet, over.*"

"Thank you, Cory," Daniel said. "That could be important, over."

Daniel hadn't bothered to learn about the planetary government since his dealings would be with the Monfiores alone. It was comforting to know that there was no chance of an Ischian destroyer appearing if things went wrong, though.

"*They don't search ships in orbit,*" Cory said, "*but they ask where you're landing and send an aircar from the nearest customs station on the ground. If anybody gets gay with the inspectors, the clan's neighbors come in and take care of things. That hasn't happened in thirty years though, over.*"

There had been a period at the beginning of the Hiatus when Cinnabar had a similar government—or lack of government. The Xenos region expanded, either by conquest or the voluntary association of families in other regions. The Learys of Bantry had joined Xenos—and had used that alliance to bludgeon other families on the southwest coast into submission to them as well as to the central government.

Corder Leary was a proper descendent of those ancestors, and perhaps his son was, too. The ability to see the way a situation was developing and to get on the right side of those developments was as useful to an RCN officer as it was to a politician.

The fragmented nature of Ischia's settled terrain

had allowed the clans to remain largely independent. Ischia wasn't a place where you would look for great art or—Daniel smiled—great libraries; but as with isolated patrol vessels, there would be people that the life suited.

"*All right*, Kiesche," the orbiting controller said. "*You're cleared to Jezreel. One-one-three out.*"

Daniel paused a moment, then said, "Ship, this is Six. We're going to start hard braking in . . . one minute. When we disembark in Jezreel, we will not be carrying side-arms, repeat *not*. This is going to go fine unless somebody screws up, and I am not going to make it easy for these boneheads on the ground to screw up. Six out."

He pressed EXECUTE with both thumbs together, the way he had learned to do as a cadet on a training ship which was older than his grandfather. That seemed a lifetime ago, but it was only ten years.

The High Drive motors switched to maximum impulse, and the plasma thrusters added their roar to the high-frequency buzz of matter recombining with antimatter. Daniel leaned back into his couch, since there was no need to fight the braking thrust. When they dropped a little deeper into the atmosphere, he would have to shut off the High Drive to prevent the exhaust from eroding the throats, but that wouldn't happen for some minutes.

The harbor at Jezreel filled one quadrant of Daniel's display. It was a pool of modest size formed by damming the river which had carved the valley. There were six ships floating idle there, probably a sign of the collapse of planetary trade. They didn't fill the harbor, but Daniel wouldn't have wanted to land a vessel larger than the *Kiesche* on the surface area remaining.

Daniel had inset a realtime image of Adele, facing him on the other side of the console. Her expression was her usual one of unemotional focus. Daniel had no idea of what she was working on; he rarely did.

But he was sure that when the time came, she would provide something that he suddenly realized that he needed. *Whatever* he suddenly realized that he needed.

He grinned.

Jezreel on Ischia

The main hatch began to grind downward. It hadn't jammed again, but it still vibrated badly every time it opened. Steam and ozone swirled through the rear compartment and onto the bridge, but they had no effect save for occasional sneezes.

Adele got up stiffly. Vesey quickly took her place on the couch. She would command the *Kiesche* while Daniel was heading the negotiations with the Monfiores.

Daniel arched his shoulders backward to stretch his torso. "Time to meet our hosts, I think," he said.

Hogg grunted, his hands thrust deep into his pockets. Tovera said nothing, but her eyes flicked to Adele and away.

The last member of the negotiating team was Cazelet, who stood stiffly by the hatch to the stern compartment. He wore new utilities which, for a spacer on a tramp, were dress clothes. He had the business expertise which the task required, though he had admitted that he was uncomfortable bargaining for lives.

Adele wasn't sure how long she had been sitting at the console. That was the beauty of losing herself in work, of course: it took her from a world of human realities to one of information, which was much more to her liking. Aches and stiffness were far down the list of aspects of the real world which she found uncomfortable.

"Six!" said Cory. He could now move to the command console, but he apparently didn't want to leave whatever he was doing at the flat-plate display. "There's a four-inch plasma cannon aimed at the harbor from the hillside to port. It isn't new—it must've been there for decades. And it isn't netted into the defense computer, so I can't switch it off."

"Officer Mundy?" said Daniel. He grinned. *Does he know or is he just guessing?*

"There is an icon on our displays beside the gunnery lockout," Adele said. "If it is activated—and I don't expect that to happen unless I do it—the power goes out in the Jezreel community. The cannon has a backup generator, but that will not switch on."

"Thank you, Officer Mundy," Daniel said. "Hmm... Lady Mundy, I think, for this purpose. Please walk beside me down the ramp."

Adele nodded and followed him through the hatch. The rest of team fell in behind.

The spacers in the rear compartment held submachine guns and stocked impellers. Apparently the order that the crew shouldn't carry guns outside had convinced them to be armed while still on the freighter. *Heaven help us if Evans starts shooting!*

Daniel stepped close to Woetjans and whispered something, then strode toward the entry hatch without the pause Adele had expected. She hopped after him to catch up so that they stepped onto the ramp together. Behind them she heard the bosun bellow, "All right, Sissies! Hand your guns to Hale right bloody now and she'll unload them. Then slide them back into the arms locker, got it? Now!"

"Some risks," Daniel said, "are unavoidable. Being shot in the back by your own people shouldn't be one of them."

The sunlight was pleasant. Adele didn't usually have an opinion about landscapes, but Jezreel seemed, well, *nice*. Most harbors were cesspools, literally; ships emptied waste into the water, and often the city's sewers drained into it. The plasma exhaust from ships landing and lifting incinerated the floating organic materials and mixed the smoke with steam to form a thick miasma.

"The flow from upstream must flush the pool constantly," said Daniel with approval. He must have been thinking the same thing that Adele was. "And of course, there hasn't been much movement through Jezreel because of the slowdown in trade."

A delegation of four locals waited at the head of the floating pier which they had extended to the *Kiesche*'s starboard pontoon. They looked grim-faced, but they weren't obviously armed.

The fifty or more men whom Adele could see among the houses up the slope from the harbor, and about half the similar number of women, *did* carry guns openly. The buildings themselves had walls of cast concrete and roofs of structural plastic, but gardens and window boxes softened their appearance.

"Rather a pleasant little community," Daniel remarked cheerfully as they walked down the ramp. "I'm sure that you and I can work matters out with them."

"You always think that," said Adele.

"And I've always been right," said Daniel. "Well, I've usually been right."

In a louder voice he said, "Gentlemen, I'm Captain Leary, and this is Lady Mundy, both of Cinnabar. We're here to talk about the Corcyran envoys whom you're holding."

"I'm the Elder Paul," replied the man of fifty, one of the pair in the center. "These are three of my councillors. We know your reputation, Leary. If—"

Paul's voice, never friendly, became as harsh as a war cry.

"—you think you're going to waltz in here and steal our prisoners away, you'd better think again!"

Adele imagined that she was watching on a display. She absorbed information better that way than she did if she had to think about interacting directly with other human beings. She hadn't told anyone else about her trick, but all people needed to know about her methods was that they worked.

"I'm sorry that I have the reputation of being a fool," Daniel said mildly. "I volunteered to come here because it appeared to me that your demands could be accommodated without difficulty. And of course I'm neutral as to the political situation on Corcyra. There are parties in Brotherhood who would just as soon that the envoys *didn't* return."

He smiled knowingly at Paul. "As you have probably guessed by now yourselves," he added. "But is there a place we could sit down while we discuss? I'd offer my ship, but I'm afraid the only space large enough on the *Kiesche* is the hold, and the amenities there are rather spartan."

"We'll go up to my house," Paul said. "The meeting room's there."

He turned and started up the path toward the buildings. He was scowling, but that might have been in embarrassment at the way he had greeted Daniel. His voice had lost its harsh rasp.

"Do they meet our terms or don't they?" said one of the councillors, a man of seventy with a long face and eyebrows bushy enough to make up for his baldness. He glared at Paul. "I don't see there's much bloody discussion to have."

"I believe we can accommodate your requirements, yes," Daniel said as though the question had been directed to him—as it should have been, Adele thought. "But Commissioner? Matters must be much simpler here than they are back on my family estate if you believe that a negotiation like this has a yes or no answer."

"Louis," snapped the Elder Paul. "If you think this meeting's a waste of your time, why don't you go mind your corn and the rest of us will talk to these parties from Cinnabar."

The old man looked aside. In a low voice he said, "My corn's doing just fine. Same as it's done since before you was born, Paul Monfiore."

The path led past a group of men, one of whom was missing his left leg below the knee. Most were tattooed. The name Schliemann on a biceps, between a pair of nymphs, was probably the RCN heavy cruiser of that name.

"Good morning, spacers," Daniel said, nodding pleasantly.

A few muttered "Sir," and one even attempted a

salute. They shifted their bodies so that the carbines they carried were less obvious.

A pair of women sat on the front stoop of the house nearest the harbor. One was knitting while her younger companion suckled a baby. The older woman tugged her ball of pale blue yarn a little to cover the butt of the service pistol in her knitting basket.

Adele supposed she might have followed Daniel's lead and said something friendly to the women, but she had no more experience with that sort of small talk than she did with knitting. She prepared to nod crisply and pass on.

On New Year's Day Adele's mother had distributed gift baskets to the wives of Popular Party workers. When Adele turned twelve, Esme Rolfe Mundy had decided that they would hand out the baskets together. Adele had been a quiet if not precisely dutiful daughter, but her refusal to undergo *that* experience had finally convinced even her mother.

Perhaps I should have viewed it as a learning experience which would aid me in my RCN career, Adele thought. She smiled, and the two women smiled back.

The Elder Paul turned toward a house halfway along the road into which the path expanded. Its frontage was about the same as those to either side, but it had been dug farther back into the hillside. A young man with Paul's features pulled the door open and held it as the elder and councillors, then the Cinnabar contingent, entered.

There was a cloakroom to either side of the front door. Past the door in the partition wall was a meeting room with chairs for fifty people to sit. The seats were full, and there seemed to be nearly as many others standing. Even so it was only a fraction of Jezreel's adult population.

Paul led the way down the central aisle toward the dais. There were six folding chairs, identical to those on the floor of the hall. Paul and his councillors took the four in the middle.

Adele hesitated. Daniel stood by the chair on the left end of the row and bowed Adele toward the other empty, making a courtly sweep with his right arm. Hogg and Tovera seated themselves on the edge of the dais, facing the audience with smiles on their faces.

Adele sat down. Hogg looked crazed, and Tovera's expression was that of a demon. At least the audience was being given fair warning.

I suppose it's up to me to kill the four on the dais, Adele thought. *Though Daniel will certainly be knocking heads together if the Monfiores decide to attack.*

The idea made her smile. That in turn made her wonder whether she more resembled Hogg or Tovera. She smiled still wider.

If the audience was a fair sample, people in Jezreel were tall and lanky, with a tendency toward red hair and long jaws. Adele took out her data unit but restrained herself from checking on inbreeding within Ischia's separate clans.

Paul rose to his feet. "All right!" he said. "We've been waiting for the Corcyran representatives. Here they are, only they're from Cinnabar. It doesn't seem to me that there's anything for us to talk about till we hear what they've got to say."

He turned to look down at Daniel. "Captain Leary, you claim you're going 'to accommodate our requirements.' Those were the words you used. Tell us how."

Paul didn't use or need an amplifier; the hall had good acoustics, and Paul had apparently trained his lungs by bellowing across the valley or similar rural pursuits. Adele had nothing in common with the audience in this hall, but she suspected Daniel—or Hogg, or any other Bantry resident—did.

When Paul sat down, Daniel rose and reversed his chair. He put his right foot on the seat. With his hand on the chair back, he said, "Thank you, Elder and Councillors—"

He nodded toward them, then faced the audience again.

"—and thank you, citizens, for the chance to speak with you. I told the Corcyran council that I was sure that you and I could work matters out. Your elder—"

Daniel gestured toward Paul, though he didn't take his eyes and his smile from the audience.

"—told me that he knew my reputation. Well, I hope I understand you better than he understood me, because I think that you Monfiores are traders and honest spacers, some of the best there are. I'm pretty sure I recognized some of my old RCN shipmates as I walked up from the harbor."

I wonder if that's true? It was possible, certainly; and the underlying implication of the statement was true; that Ischia and Cinnabar had no quarrel with one another.

"What the Monfiores *aren't*," Daniel said, raising his voice slightly, "is pirates. Until now. And I believe that if you're offered an honest deal, you'll stop being pirates."

The uproar in the hall was to be expected. The anger in it surprised Adele, though; enough that she held her left hand above her tunic pocket.

They really don't think of themselves as pirates,

she realized. *And they certainly don't like to be reminded that what they did on Dace was piracy, by their standards as well as by Daniel's.*

"Everybody sit down!" Paul said, rising to his feet. Daniel remained where he was. "Sit down and shut up! This is a business meeting, not a lynching!"

The room settled with the scrape of chair legs on the floor and the whisper of angry breathing. Paul turned to Daniel and said, "You're here to negotiate. Let's hear more of that and fewer insults!"

Daniel nodded pleasantly. "Ischia has been treated very badly in the past two years," he said. "By fate certainly, but especially by the new government of Pantellaria. Among the things which *haven't* screwed you over, however, are the independent Corcyrans."

"We offered them a fair deal," said the councillor to Paul's right. Adele scrambled through data, but without images she couldn't tell whether the speaker was Councillor Maurice or Councillor Patric. It was something to concentrate on.

"Yes, sir, you did," Daniel said, glancing over his shoulder and giving Patric or Maurice a friendly nod. "But it's a deal that they couldn't accept and still get the weapons they need to fight the Pantellarians. The same bastards who're screwing Ischia, and in particular screwing you Monfiores! You used to be able to trade with Corcyra at fair rates for both sides. Not so?"

The councillors—including Louis—nodded. There were murmurs of agreement from the audience.

"We need *trade*," Paul said. His voice was harsh, but he remained seated. "Fairness is fine and justice is fine, but we have to feed our children!"

Agreement rolled across the room like surf rushing

to the shore. Instead of waiting for it to subside, Daniel raised both arms, palms outward. "I agree!" he said. Even more loudly he repeated, "I agree! I'm offering you trade with Dunbar's World!"

The noise in the hall broke into chaos, rising and falling. Daniel waited where he stood, both hands on the chair back.

The Elder Paul rose and tried to speak into Daniel's ear. Adele doubted that Daniel could understand the words, but the sight of the two leaders trying to talk made the babble of the audience subside.

Paul turned to face his people again. "Quiet!" he said with his hands raised. "Quiet so that I can ask Leary a question!"

In the relative silence he turned to Daniel and said, "I know about Dunbar's World. All the trade's held by Cinnabar. Are you committing the government of Cinnabar in this deal?"

"Off-planet trade with Dunbar's World is held by a cartel of Cinnabar companies, not by the government of the Republic itself," Daniel said. "There are five trading companies involved. Two of them are owned by Corder Leary, my father."

He spoke toward the audience. If he had boomed the answer directly at Paul, the elder would have reacted subconsciously to a threat even though he knew intellectually that it was not hostile.

"Now..." Daniel continued over the excited babble. The audience had understood that Daniel had said that Corder Leary would do what his son requested. That most certainly was *not* true. "I've got some clout on Dunbar's World myself. I was able to help the current government with a problem—"

A war. A war they were losing until Daniel intervened.

"—they were having a few years ago. That will help you on Dunbar's World. As for the Cinnabar cartel, my colleague Lady Mundy has come here with full authority to negotiate on behalf of all Leary enterprises."

"That's correct," said Adele. She raised her data unit. "I have this authority."

Nobody can hear me.

Hogg stood and made a megaphone of his hands. "She's got it!" he boomed. "Any bloody thing the mistress says is true! But she's a *lady*, see, and she's not going to scream her lungs out for yobs like me and you!"

There was no logical reason that Hogg's statement should be taken as authoritative, but it was. There was a gush of laughter; then the audience quieted again.

"Now," Daniel resumed, "I'm telling you that the existing cartel and the government of Dunbar's World are going to back the deal. I'm not telling you that you won't have trouble on the ground with shipowners and dock gangs who liked things the way they were before."

"I guess we can handle that," said the Elder Paul.

"I guess we bloody well can!" replied a burly, tattooed man in the audience.

Adele's lips quirked upward. *"Come on, Sunshine, if you think you're hard enough."* How often have I run into that attitude since I became a Sissie?

Daniel crooked his finger toward Adele. She put the data unit away and joined him and Paul—and the three councillors, by the time she got there. Cazelet waited at the edge of the dais, and the two servants stood with their backs to their principals, beaming at the milling audience.

"Elder Paul?" Daniel said. "Lady Mundy will present her credentials, but her aide Lieutenant Cazelet will be handling the detailed negotiations. For myself—I wonder if you'd mind if I took a look at your community? It reminds me of Bantry, where I grew up."

"I'll have my son Giorgi take you wherever you want to go, Leary," Paul said. "Louis? The rest of us will adjourn to your sitting room. The mob here isn't going to break up any time soon, and I want to get this agreement down as quick as we can!"

CHAPTER 18

Jezreel on Ischia

"I'm Giorgi," said the man who'd held the door of the Elder's house when the delegation entered. "My father said you wanted to see Jezreel?"

Daniel clasped hands with him. They were much of an age, but Monfiore was taller by a head and probably didn't weigh—Daniel thought ruefully—any more than Daniel did.

"I'd like to get out of *here*," Daniel said, making a minute gesture, his hand close to his body, toward the locals clumping to chatter in the street outside the Elder's house. "And frankly, I'd prefer to see some of the countryside rather than houses. Even very nice houses don't interest me very much."

A number of the locals were watching them intently. A woman looked as though she were about to join them, but Giorgi's glare thrust her back.

She wore a floral bonnet and sashes of red and green crossed over a dull yellow dress. The cut of the garments was closer than those Daniel had grown up with, but the color sense of Jezreel residents was identical to that of Bantry peasants dressed in their "best" clothes.

Daniel glanced at Hogg, who shrugged and said, "Guess I'll look around some on my own. There might be a poker game somewheres."

"Shall I get the aircar?" Giorgi said. "It's around the back."

"I don't think we should go any distance," Daniel said, "but if we could wander down to the riverbank, that would be relaxing. From here it looks remarkably unspoiled."

Giorgi laughed. "Above the town, yes," he said as he took them toward the head of the street. "The shipyard is three kilos downstream, and that isn't so pristine. Though there hasn't been much construction recently, so even that isn't a waste pond."

He walked at a swinging pace which did as much to fend off would-be companions as the hard look he gave those they passed. Daniel kept up without difficulty. There wasn't much room for walking on the *Kiesche*, but he and Hogg had been tramping the whole of the Bantry estate since he was six years old. Climbing the rigging to view the Matrix kept him more fit on shipboard than he was after staying in Xenos.

They left the road for a path slanting down toward the river. Short logs or in one case a squared stone block reduced the slope in a few places, but it was still meant for pedestrians moving in file.

"I noticed that you weren't carrying a gun when we arrived," Daniel said as they neared the river. A similar path bordered the water in both directions. "I gather Hogg noticed also, which is why he didn't stick with me."

Giorgi grunted. "Because he didn't think that I could kill you with my bare hands?" he asked without looking over his shoulder.

"Because he thought you weren't stupid," Daniel said. They'd reached the riverbank. "I suppose he meant it as a compliment."

"Sorry," Giorgi said. He stopped and met Daniel's eyes. "It wasn't Father's idea, but he went along with it. Schweitzer said that we needed to put the fear of heaven into you right at the start or you'd run roughshod over us."

"Let's walk upstream," Daniel said, gesturing. The current was slow, in part because the dam and pool had raised the level above it as well. "But you didn't agree with Master Schweitzer?"

"I captain the freighter *Bird Girl*," Giorgi said. "She's there in the pool."

He gestured. The six Ischian ships were indistinguishable from this angle, but that itself was sufficient identification.

"I was on Tumbler when the *Heimdall* landed in the naval harbor on her way to join Admiral Peterson's fleet," Giorgi continued. "I guess if you're not afraid of a battleship, we're not going to scare you with small arms."

Daniel laughed. "I bloody well *was* afraid of the *Heimdall*!" he said. "I was in the cruiser *Milton* at Cacique, and I don't know any cruiser captain who wouldn't be ready to foul himself trading salvoes with a battleship."

He cleared his throat and said, "But no, a group of armed civilians weren't going to affect my negotiations."

"Well, I'm sorry," Giorgi said, his eyes lowered. "I told Father we'd be making fools of ourselves, but he hasn't been off-planet since before I was born. He's not stupid, but he thinks in terms of—"

He spread his arms in a double gesture.

"—this valley and maybe Ischia. He doesn't...well, he's seen your record, but he *didn't* see the *Heimdall*, and he doesn't know what the record means. I'm glad things worked out like they have."

Daniel squatted. Bright green plants rose out of the water and grew on the boggy margin of the path. The stems were five-sided, and the oval leaves sprang from each side in turn as they spiraled upward.

Attached to an outcrop thrusting into the river was what looked like a small version of the "sponge" he had seen in the pond in front of the Manor in Brotherhood. Daniel set his left palm on the rock and leaned his weight onto it.

"Careful there!" Giorgi said. "That pinkie-gray fire-pot there will give you Hell's own bite. Your whole arm'll be swelled up for a week, and you'll feel it in your joints every time the weather changes for the rest of your life."

"They're local here?" Daniel said. He lowered his face—carefully—toward the water to peer closer. He thought he could see bronze specks the size of wheat grains, junior versions of the parasites on the sponge on Corcyra.

"Anywhere there's fresh water," Giorgi said. "They're a nuisance if you're going to be swimming or watering your stock, but other than that they're not a problem. The shellbacks keep them down."

Standing behind Daniel, he leaned over also. "There's one, you see?" he said, pointing to the upstream side of the rock.

A darkly iridescent oval the size of a man's palm rubbed close to what was here a firepot. Daniel had taken it for the top of another rock until Giorgi called it to his attention. Scores of legs—Daniel saw mostly the motion through a foot of flowing water—rippled along the edges of the creature. The shellback wasn't doing anything immediately obvious, but the adjacent patch of the sponge's body was bare of cilia.

Daniel stood up in two stages, making sure that Giorgi had enough warning to move back. "I sometimes think of becoming a naturalist when I retire," he said, smiling broadly to his guide. "But that's a long time to come, I hope. And I'm not really organized enough to do a proper job of that."

Though if Adele should retire at the same time, there'd be a chance for some rigorously reported, first-rate fieldwork on planets which nobody else had given more than a glance at!

"Captain," said Giorgi, turning to face Daniel. For a moment he seemed on the verge of saluting. "I want you to know that I opposed the whole idea. Like you said, we Monfiores are spacers, traders. We're not *pirates*."

He balled his fists. Daniel listened with a friendly smile, ready to react if Monfiore got carried away and swung at whatever happened to be closest.

"My father said that sometimes an elder has to make hard decisions to save his people," Giorgi said. "*I* say that if being elder means being a criminal, then somebody else can have the job! I'll go to Pleasaunce and sign on as wiper on one of their ships."

Daniel thought of the decisions he made regularly, as an RCN officer and as a man. Many people had died because of those decisions. Some of the dead were his own personnel, and some were innocent of anything except being in the wrong place when Daniel Leary had a task to accomplish.

Daniel continued to smile. "It's over," he said. "At least I trust that it's over. I think that the deal offered is fair, and I'm sure that your fellow citizens will see that it is."

"I wouldn't bet," Giorgi said, smiling also, "that a general meeting of my fellow citizens would be able to agree on what day of the month it was. But I'll swear to you that I'll do whatever *I* can to end our descent into piracy."

A siren began to wind from the tower on the roof of the Elder's house. Giorgi glanced up and said, "Speaking of general meetings, that's the call. Most people will be taking part by computer, but I need to get back to the hall. By heaven, we're going to accept your offer or I'll know the reason why!"

"I certainly hope you do," Daniel said, following Giorgi up the path as quickly as they had come down it, regardless of the slope.

And if you don't, I'm confident that the same offer made to a consortium of three or four neighboring clans will convince them to attack you, and I'll get the prisoners back that way. It was what Corder Leary and his distant Leary ancestors would have done if it were necessary to accomplish a mission.

Adele shut down her data unit and rose from the table in Councillor Louis Holper's kitchen. Cazelet and the four Ischian officials remained seated. Tovera smiled sardonically; she stood against the concrete

outer wall between the door and the window, a casement with six panes.

Through the door to the sitting room—it didn't have
a table for the locals to place their large data units,
so the negotiators were in the kitchen—Holper's wife,
Mitzi, nervously pretended to dust knickknacks on egg-
crate display shelving. It was a pleasant little home for
the two of them, and surprisingly neat given that the
decision to adjourn here had been spur of the moment.

"Do any of you see a reason that I should remain with
you?" Adele said. Her tone and the fact she was standing made her own opinion clear, though she was quite
willing to make it more clear if someone pressed her.

"I can't imagine that we will, Lady Mundy," Cazelet
said before the locals could offer an opinion. "The
rest of the business should be quite straightforward.
Shall I call you at the ship if something comes up?"

The only thing Adele could do that Cazelet couldn't
was to kill everyone in the house. That shouldn't be
necessary, though if Adele had to endure more drivel
about freight rates, it was a possible result. All the
more reason for her to leave.

In other circumstances Adele might have worried
about leaving her agent unsupported in a room with
four opponents, but Cazelet's background made him far
more sophisticated than the Ischians. Nor were they
going to browbeat one of Captain Leary's officers....

"No, I think I'll visit the prisoners," she said aloud.
"Master Holper, could your wife guide me, please?"

"What?" said the councillor. "What? Mitzi! The lady
here wants you to take her up to the lodge. Can you
do that or should I get—"

"Get *who*, Louis Holper?" his wife snapped, stepping

into the kitchen. She was already untying the strings of her apron. "I guess I'm not crippled up yet, and I'll thank you not to tell her ladyship that I am!"

She turned to Adele and half-curtsied, half-bowed. Stepping to the outside door, she said, "If you'll come this way. It's just up to the top of the ridge."

They went out in file, Mistress Holper in the lead and Tovera closing the door behind them. A score of locals, men and women both, waited in the street talking nervously. When they saw Holper and her companions, one called, "Mitzi? What's going on?"

"That's for the people whose business it is, Susey Lainz," Mistress Holper said. "Which isn't you nor me either one. You ought all to go home. I'm taking our visitors up to the lodge. And we don't need help doing that!"

Adele wondered how much political say women had on Ischia. That the elder and councillors were all men might be chance—four was a small sample. Still, she'd noticed in the past that the farther you got from the centers of civilization, the less likely you were to find gender equality.

That didn't bother Adele particularly; it was simply data. In addition to taking a detached attitude about most things, she was always aware that the pistol in her pocket gave her the power of life or death over anyone who came within fifty yards or so of her.

She smiled. There had been times where that was a surprisingly comforting thought.

Stone steps at the back of the house led up to a track as substantial as the one from the harbor. It was wide enough for two, so Adele chose to walk beside their guide.

"We use the lodge for gatherings, you know," Mistress Holper said as she trudged briskly upward. "Weddings and the like, parties. It's a nice place. We treated your friends just as good as if they was our own."

She breathed deeply and looked at Adele. "Your ladyship?" she said. "Is it going to be all right? I know it's not my place to ask, but we've all been so frightened when we heard that Cinnabar was coming down on us! We should never have done it, we know that, but it looked like the only way, and that know-it-all Schweitzer, he kept saying it'd be fine, it'll be fine."

She spat. "And where is our Darrell now?" she said. "Hiding in his own root cellar, I hear!"

"Captain Leary's offer is very fair," Adele said. "So long as your community wants peaceful trade, that's what you'll have."

She wondered if she should have explained that she and Daniel didn't represent Cinnabar. Quite apart from the fact that the mistaken assumption was to the benefit of Daniel's position, Adele herself had the authority of the Leary enterprises. That wasn't precisely "the Republic of Cinnabar," but Adele suspected that Corder Leary could move the Senate in any direction he chose in dealing with worms like the Monfiore clan of Ischia.

"Oh, that'll be a blessing," Holper said. "You can't know what a blessing that will be."

Because of the steep slope near the top of the ridge, they had been unable to see the lodge for some minutes. The paved track ended in a stone staircase to the right. When Adele started up the steps beside Mistress Holper, the lodge rose into view ahead of them.

A husky man got up from a wicker chair as they

approached. "Hey, Mitzi," he said. A long baton leaned against the side of the building, but he didn't have a gun. "Are you spelling me?"

"These are the envoys, Phil," Holper said. "Heavens be praised, I think we're shut of this filthy business."

"I'm Lady Mundy," Adele said, since it didn't appear that their guide would think to introduce her. "With my aide. We're here to see the prisoners."

The lodge had waist-high stone walls and louvered windows—closed at the moment—above them to the roof of structural plastic. It would be simple enough to break a couple windows and crawl out, but it couldn't be done without enough noise to alert the guard with the riot stick.

"We treat them nice as you please," Holper said as Phil opened the padlock closing the chain which bound the handles of the double doors. "You'll see if they don't say that!"

"There isn't much reason for them to break out, is there?" said Tovera, eyeing the situation with her usual amused detachment. "Do they even know what planet they're on?"

"Look, this was none of my idea," the guard said. "I'm just up here because I'm a citizen, you see?"

He threw the door open and stepped aside, turning his face away so that he didn't have to meet his visitors' eyes. Mistress Holper said, "I'll wait here with Phil. Take all the time you want."

"I'll wait out here," Tovera said to Adele as she entered the building. Her smile might have been described as pitying, though pity was as difficult to associate with Tovera as love would be.

"I'm Lady Mundy from Cinnabar," Adele said,

addressing the hostages. They must have gotten to their feet when they heard the door rattle. "My colleague Captain Leary and I are here to secure your release. The details are being worked out now."

The Monfiores must by now realize how badly they had miscalculated. Nonetheless, they were going to benefit from their piracy, their kidnapping.

Adele had never been concerned about fairness: she had been born to privilege, then had spent a comparable length of time in abject poverty through no fault of her own. Both those states were facts. Fairness and justice were matters for philosophers to discuss. Not for librarians, and certainly not for politicians.

"Well, we've waited long enough!" said the rather pretty young man who must be Penning Almer, aide to Mistress Tibbs of the Regiment. The woman in a Pantellarian naval dress uniform, rather the worse for wear now, would be Lieutenant Angelotti of the *Freccia*, while the heavyset man of fifty was Colonel Bourbon, despite his civilian clothes.

Bourbon was the only one who mattered, so it was to him that Adele said, "I'm afraid, Colonel, that the delay in our arrival is less surprising than the fact that we've arrived at all. Colonel Mursiello, as he now calls himself, was something less than enthusiastic about getting you back."

"That *bastard*," Bourbon said, but he sounded more bitter than angry. He ground his right fist into his left hand as though he were pulverizing something in a mortar rather than smashing it with a hammer. "I didn't trust him, not a bit, but I thought it was safer to leave him in charge on Corcyra for a couple

weeks than it would have been to put him together
with the junta ruling Karst."

"You mean it's your fault that we've been stranded
here for three months?" Almer said. As with Lieutenant
Angelotti's uniform, Almer's swirlingly loose civilian
garments had been pulled and wrinkled during captivity. Whatever the fabric was, it lost its sheen when
it stretched. "A couple weeks indeed!"

"When *can* we go?" Angelotti asked Adele. Her
hands were pressed together unconsciously, making
Adele wonder whether the lieutenant had a personal
reason to want to be back on Corcyra.

In Angelotti's case and in most cases involving
women of childbearing age, "personal reason" generally
meant a sexual relationship. With men of a similar
age, greed was an equally probable cause.

"As I say, there are details to work out," Adele said.
"It wouldn't hurt for you to get your luggage together
now, because I'm sure that Captain Leary intends to
leave as soon as we've made the arrangements."

She supposed another person would have said that
it would only be a short time. Logically that was true,
but there was no lack of evidence that most people
behaved illogically at least some of the time.

"Luggage!" Almer said. He tugged out the legs of
his pantaloons with a theatrical gesture. "We have
nothing but what was with us in the hostel on Dace!
We weren't allowed to get our baggage from the ship,
meager as even *that* would have been."

Almer turned to Colonel Bourbon. He said, "You
were probably right. The junta would have been more
than willing to put Mursiello in power on Corcyra if
he offered them enough. And from what I've seen

of Mursiello, he'd offer everything anybody else on Corcyra had to get power himself. You and we have had our differences, Bourbon, but as between gentlemen."

Almer is a fop and a petulant little prig, Adele thought. *But he isn't a fool after all.* Her respect for Mistress Tibbs, who had sent the young man as her agent, went up.

"Speaking for myself," Bourbon said, grinning wearily, "I'd just as soon that Mursiello had been cooped up here for the past two months. On the other hand, I would have tried to get him back, and who knows where that might have led?"

"You've been successful in arranging for the missiles, then?" Adele said.

"Oh, yes," Bourbon said. "The price is steep, but we've spread the payments out over twenty-five years, and the junta finally agreed to take the payment in exemption from transport tariffs as soon as Corcyra is at peace again. While the Pantellarians are on the planet, we'll have to pay in copper delivered to Karst at our own expense, but I hope that a year or at most two will end that. After the missiles arrive, of course."

"If I may ask, Lady Mundy?" said Almer with an unpleasant smile. "You said you and Captain Leary were from Cinnabar. What is Cinnabar's involvement on Corcyra?"

Not at all a fool. "The Republic is not involved," Adele said crisply. "My colleague and I came to Corcyra in our private capacities on behalf of the Transformationist community. When we learned of the situation regarding yourselves and the war more generally, we volunteered to negotiate your release ourselves."

Almer pursed his lips. Before the question he was

framing could reach his tongue, Tovera said loudly, "Good afternoon, Elder Paul."

"That's the leader of the gang!" Angelotti said, turning to the door as Adele opened it.

Paul strode in, looking exultant. "Colonel," he said to Bourbon. "I apologize to your and your colleagues. We have wronged you, *I* have wronged you, but I hope that some time in the future we will be able to make it up to you. For now, let me say that you are free to go. Captain Leary's ship waits in the harbor to carry you home."

Colonel Bourbon picked up a small fabric case. He paused in the door long enough to clasp hands with Paul on his way past. Neither Almer nor Angelotti showed that courtesy; but then, the Monfiores weren't really owed it.

Adele and Tovera followed the former prisoners down the track. It would be good to leave Ischia, but Adele didn't feel the urgency that the Corcyrans seemed to.

"If we get off safely," she said to Tovera, "I'll consider this a job well done."

"If we don't," said Tovera, smiling again, "perhaps I'll have a chance to kill a few people. I win either way."

"I'm glad you're showing a positive attitude," said Adele. They were both joking, in their fashions.

CHAPTER 19

Above Corcyra

Though Daniel remained at the command console, he had handed the conn to Vesey on a flat-plate display to make the short hop to Corcyra from their observation point one light-minute out. She would land them in Brotherhood also. Using the relatively poor equipment was good practice.

Vesey had extracted the *Kiesche* 37,000 miles above Corcyra, a lovely piece of work even in so short a hop. She would do equally well bringing the *Kiesche* into harbor... and another time, when Vesey was on her own and perhaps being shot at, she would make a similar landing a trifle more smoothly than she would have done without this practice.

"*Kiesche* to Brotherhood Control," Cory said. "*Come in, Brotherhood Control, over.*"

His eyes were closed, and he was knuckling his forehead fiercely with his left hand. The length of a passage through the Matrix didn't affect the amount of discomfort an individual felt on extraction, and Cory was obviously feeling a great deal.

Daniel rotated the couch of his console to check the Corcyran envoys. He had decided to bunk the three of them in the main cabin, moving crewmen—including Woetjans at her own request—to the overflow bunks in the hold.

Lieutenant Angelotti looked cheery, Colonel Bourbon was sitting on his bunk with the expression of a man trying to hold up a wall which was collapsing on him, and Almer lay flat with his right forearm thrown across his eyes. The gesture looked theatrical, as everything Almer did was theatrical, but it was certainly possible that the fellow was prostrated by the pain of extraction.

Daniel smiled, remembering the time that had happened to him while he was still a cadet on a training cruise. Oddly enough, it made him feel closer to Tibbs' aide; an irritating fellow to be sure, but surprisingly sharp once you learned his manner.

Hogg unstrapped from the bulkhead jumpseat and propelled himself to the command console. His woodcraft served him well in free fall, as it did Daniel. Hogg always knew where his body was and how much weight he was putting on any surface he was in contact with.

Misplacing your weight in the field meant that a snapped twig alerted your prey or even that you slid down a hillside on top of the loose stone you had disturbed. In free fall you caromed wildly around the compartment, which could be even more unpleasant.

"I figure there's plenty of time to get into your Whites, master," Hogg said, "instead of waiting while the ship cools off and we can open her up."

"Hogg," Daniel said, "I told you that the *Kiesche* wasn't a naval vessel, and I'm not here as an RCN officer. The last thing I want to do is convince people that I represent the Republic on Corcyra. I will wear these—"

He tugged the leg of his dark blue utilities.

"—just as I told you in Xenos that I would!"

"Kiesche, *this is Brotherhood Control,*" the console announced. "*You are cleared to land in the same berth as you had previously. I say again, the previous berth. That's the only place you're cleared to land, over.*"

"*Six?*" Cory asked on the command channel.

At this moment, Daniel and the *Kiesche* had effectively unlimited options. When they began their landing approach, their options shrank sharply.

On the other hand, options for completing the mission successfully were much higher if they landed in Brotherhood Harbor as directed. *We didn't come from Cinnabar in order to fail and go home again.*

"Roger, Cory," Daniel said. "Lieutenant Vesey, bring us in. Over."

"*Roger, Brotherhood Control,*" Cory said. "*Kiesche out.*"

"*Ship,*" said Vesey, "*prepare for descent. And stay alert, fellow Sissies, because it may be rough after we've landed. Five out.*"

Daniel smiled as braking thrust pushed him back into his couch. He had thought of taking the conn himself, but he would probably have other claims on his attention shortly. Vesey had again proven herself precisely the sort of alert, intelligent officer whom he would want in charge of the ship when he himself was in the middle of something else.

Probably in the middle of something lethal.

Brotherhood on Corcyra

The *Kiesche* was wrapped in a blanket of plasma as it braked toward the surface of Corcyra. Ionized oxygen and hydrogen atoms radiated across the electro-optical spectrum, smothering all but the most fragmentary bits of communication and data gathering.

If I believed in Hell, Adele thought, *I would say that I am in it.*

The humor of the thought brought a hint of a smile as she tried to strain information from the static. No matter how hard the software attempted to sharpen the hash, it remained *hash*. Their lives and mission might depend on what Adele heard in the next few minutes, or what she failed to hear.

The *Kiesche* bellied into Brotherhood Harbor in a pillow of steam which turned the last few feet of her descent into a greasy stagger. Adele didn't notice that, nor that her apparent weight returned to normal when the thrusters shut off.

What she did notice was that the roar of static sank to a mere nasty crackle. Data streamed in, and she was back in her element.

Adele set her side of the console to convert her words into a text crawl at the bottom of Daniel's display and said, "Garrison headquarters has just directed the Regiment's missile battery to destroy the *Kiesche* if we should lift from our berth again."

"*Command, this is Six,*" Daniel said orally to the ship's officers. "*Signals, can you lock it out, and why didn't the Garrison alert their own missiles, over?*"

"Lieutenant Cory has locked both batteries," Adele said, switching to voice communication. "The Garrison battery has landline communication to its headquarters, which I cannot intercept as yet. I would guess that Mursiello alerted his own troops as soon as we contacted Brotherhood Control, whereas radioing the Regiment battery was more a matter of hope than expectation. Ah, over."

"The Regiment crew wouldn't have taken Garrison orders without agreement from Mistress Tibbs," Daniel said. *"Which they wouldn't have gotten, though she might not have known what was going on, over."*

Spacers opened hatches in all occupied compartments, including two on the bridge. The main hatch would remain closed until the hull and the ship's immediate surroundings had cooled, but there wasn't the risk of binding and warping smaller hatches. Air puffed in, drawing with it steam and the sharp bite of ozone.

"Six, there's rockets aimed at us from the seawall!" Sun said at the workstation on which he'd brought up a gunnery array. *"A whole rocket launcher under a tarp so we didn't see it coming down! Sir, I can't bear on them by twenty-two degrees! Can you swing us around so I can bear, just a little bit?"*

"Negative!" Daniel said. *"Mundy, can you—"*

"No," said Adele, anticipating the rest of the question. "It has manual controls, and the sights are optical. I can jam radio signals to the crew, but I would expect them to launch even without orders if we open fire. And they're only fifty yards away. Over."

The launcher was a three-tier—three/two/three—rack of eight-inch rockets. They were short-range and unguided; the sort of weapon that might be used to bombard a city or to serve a freighter as defensive armament against pirates. The bursting charges might not penetrate the *Kiesche*'s hull, but they would stun and possibly kill everyone aboard.

"I got it," Hogg said, standing at the hatch between the bridge and hold. He wasn't netted in, but shut down as now in harbor, the background noise was the relatively slight chorus of squeaks, clinks, and hisses of the freighter cooling.

Hogg reached into the arms locker beside the hatch and came out with a stocked impeller. "I'll open the airlock and wait on the spine till it's time. Right?"

"Yes," said Daniel, rising from the console. He tugged at his utilities, pulling down the trousers, which must have ridden up.

"And master?" Hogg said. "Nobody else goes outside with a gun, got it? I don't want somebody starting the party before I'm ready."

"Yes," Daniel said again.

"Master Hogg?" said Hale, standing in the hold with a carbine. "You get the mechanism—"

She nodded to the stocked impeller. Adele had seen similar weapons smash through brick walls.

"—and I'll take care of the personnel. On your call."

Hale hefted her carbine. She was probably able to handle a full-sized weapon like Hogg's, but she obviously preferred the virtues of accuracy and rapid recovery from recoil.

"Yeah, all right," Hogg said. "On my call."

Adele nodded approvingly. She touched her own pistol, a light weapon that would have been no more than a dangerous toy in most hands.

The inner airlock door on the bridge was already open. Hogg disappeared into it; a moment later Hale followed him up the ladder.

"*Brotherhood Control to* Kiesche," the radio boomed. "Kiesche, *keep your personnel on board until the envoys have been carried to the Manor. A vehicle is on its way. I repeat, nobody else sets foot outside the vessel! Control out!*"

Cory looked at Daniel again.

Adele got up from the console. "Agree," she said to Daniel. "There's no choice."

Then, "Lieutenant Angelotti, give me your tunic and cap."

As Adele spoke, she opened the press-seal closure of her own beige tunic. Her trousers were beige also instead of the bleached white—rather grubby now—of Angelotti's uniform trousers. Angelotti's bright-red tunic was enough.

"Acknowledge them, Cory," said Daniel, standing up also. His face suddenly became stricken. "They'll recognize Bourbon and they'd recognize me."

Bourbon, who seemed to have understood the situation as quickly as Adele and Daniel had, stood up. He no longer looked as though he were at death's door. *Though in fact now he is facing probable death.*

Adele's tiny grin would have puzzled anyone—anyone but Tovera—who knew the thought behind it.

"I've been shot at before," Bourbon said. "Can somebody find a gun for me?"

"No," said Adele. "You didn't carry a gun when you left for Karst, so you shouldn't have one now."

Adele took the pistol from her pocket, then tossed her tunic onto the bunk. Angelotti held out the red garment. Adele put it on and transferred the pistol. Since she had kept her own trousers, she still had the personal data unit.

The lieutenant was slightly plumper than Adele and had larger breasts, but the exchange—in this direction—would go unremarked. It would probably go unremarked aboard the *Kiesche* also, at least until the present business was over.

"Wait, what is happening?" Almer said. He was standing and had lost his appearance of fashionable delicacy. "*I'm* not a soldier! Problems inside the Garrison are nothing to me!"

"Be quiet," Adele said. "We need all three hostages, or they'll wonder."

"Four," said Tovera. "Lieutenant Angelotti's secretary is coming."

Adele looked at her. Tovera hadn't asked a question, but Adele was in charge of the operation and would make the important decisions.

"Yes, she should go," Daniel said. He met Adele's eyes. "Nobody looks twice at her."

"Yes, all right," Adele said. She put on the billed cap prescribed for Dress/Casual uniforms in the Pantellarian—and now Corcyran—navy. The original badge, a silver double-headed wolf, had been replaced by crossed pickaxes, rather crudely embroidered.

She, Daniel, and Tovera had just carried out a complex negotiation in fewer words than many people required to decide what to have for lunch. Dealing with people wasn't difficult, so long as all parties were smart and decisive.

"Look, you have three now with her!" Almer said, reaching toward Tovera. Possibly he intended to grab her sleeve.

Cazelet, who had entered the bridge from the hold, stepped between them and shoved Almer back. "Give me your hat and tunic, Almer," he said. "Adele, I'm taller, but I'll pass."

"Yes, that's right," Adele said. She wasn't angry about Almer's behavior—that was a problem for Mistress Tibbs to deal with—but someone on or beyond the verge of panic was dangerous to have with you in a situation like the one shaping up.

Daniel had set the main display to a real-time view of the land side of the harbor. An armored personnel carrier lifted from the plaza and skimmed down Central Street toward the water. It was the less spavined one of the pair which had flown the Garrison delegation to Pearl Valley.

Despite being in better condition than its consort, the APC stayed low enough to be in ground effect most of the way. Pedestrians jumped or, less wisely, flattened themselves on the pavement. Adele didn't see anyone actually crushed, but that obviously hadn't been a matter of concern to the Garrison driver.

"Sir, we can open the main hatch whenever you're ready," Vesey said. She had seated herself at the back of the console, the place Adele had given up. Daniel's couch was empty.

"Right," said Daniel. "Give me a moment to sort things with the crew. We don't want anybody shooting from here."

"They'd probably miss us," said Tovera.

Adele smiled; Daniel laughed and clapped Tovera lightly on the shoulder as he strode past. It was the first time Adele remembered Daniel treating her servant as anything but a dangerous pet.

"All right, listen!" Daniel said as the keyed-up spacers backed to make room for him. Adele and Tovera followed, with Cazelet and Bourbon behind them.

"Any of you have guns, put 'em down right now! When the time comes, we'll go out and sort things with the wogs. We don't need bloody guns to do that, do we?"

No/Hell no/We sure bloody don't!

"So we're all going to move back in the hold, out of sight," Daniel said. "I'll tell you when we go for 'em. And can somebody find me a nice length of pipe?"

"Want an open-end wrench, sir?" Beezely said. "Or, hell, you can have the box wrench I was going to use myself."

"Kiesche, *send out the envoys,*" said the console, clearly audible in the hold. "*Send out the envoys immediately! Brotherhood over.*"

"Open up, Cory!" Daniel said. He shouted toward the bridge instead of using his commo helmet, so that he informed the spacers also. They were already moving aft toward where the extra bunks had been fitted. The hold had been nearly empty even before the *Kiesche* unloaded its cargo of weapons.

Adele and Cazelet placed themselves in front of the hatchway, to either side of Colonel Bourbon. Tovera was to Adele's left and a subservient pace behind. The greeting committee from the Garrison might wonder at Tovera's presence; but as Daniel had said, they wouldn't worry. In all likelihood no one would be looking at anything but Bourbon.

The releases clanged, and the hatch began to descend. More steam and ozone curled in. Bourbon began to sneeze violently. Adele's nose wrinkled reflexively, but every landing was the same and she had experienced unguessably many landings by now.

Unguessably, but . . . *I could sort the logs of my voyages for landings, reduce the number by airless*

*worlds and those with unbreathable atmospheres, and
add those from before I joined the RCN and began
formally logging them. . . .*

The hatch thunked into its cradle on the starboard
outrigger. The port crew had already extended the
wooden coupler from the quay to the float's outer edge.

"We'll go now," said Adele. She settled the cap
firmly and stepped onto the ramp. Her companions
moved with her.

Captain Hochner and five other soldiers dismounted
from the vehicle. Hochner now carried a submachine
gun as well as the pistol in his cross-draw holster. The
other men had Pantellarian-issue carbines.

A soldier stood behind the automatic impeller on
a ring mount on the roof of the cab. The weapon
was still locked in its travelling position, forward and
horizontal. Either Hochner hadn't wanted to be too
obviously threatening at this point, or the Garrison
troops were so badly trained that it hadn't occurred
to the gunner that he might actually need his weapon.

"I'll lead!" Cazelet said as they approached the
wooden extension. "Colonel, you wait till last. With us
in the way, they won't be sure of hitting you."

"I don't like—" Bourbon said. He paused and muttered, "Sorry."

That saved Adele the effort of telling him to be
quiet. She wouldn't have minded the effort. "Well
considered, Cazelet," she said as she followed him
closely across the walkway. They stepped onto the quay.

The APC waited thirty feet away with its fans shut
down. Adele put her left hand in her pocket as she
moved up parallel to Cazelet. Bourbon took his place
between them. Tovera was to the left as before.

Cazelet looked *nothing* like Almer, but the hat brim waggled in front of his face and the flowing tunic looked as well on the slender, taller lieutenant as on the chubby aide. Hochner and his nervous gang had eyes only for Bourbon, though. They were within ten feet now, poised to—

The loud squeal from the harbor was the *Kiesche's* bow gun traversing. Adele knew that the plasma cannon couldn't bear on the vehicle, but Hochner's gang didn't.

"What's that?" a soldier cried. He brought his carbine to his shoulder, pointing toward the *Kiesche*. He wasn't looking through the sights.

"How would we know?" Adele said shrilly. When the soldier glanced toward her, she shot him twice in the face. Convulsing from the brain shot, he slammed back into the side of the APC, then bounced forward again. Cazelet grabbed the carbine, but the hands of the corpse had locked on it.

Adele was aware only subconsciously of the rattle of Tovera's little submachine gun. Hochner's arms flailed as he pitched backward; the man next to him was going down also.

Adele looked up at the gunner just as his helmet spun high in the air. *Ticked by a bullet,* she thought. Then she saw the splash of blood and realized that Hale had shot the man through the bridge of the nose. The carbine bullet had hit the *inside* of the helmet after pureeing his brains.

Colonel Bourbon was wrestling with one of the soldiers. Adele couldn't safely shoot, but Cazelet had finally pulled the carbine away from the corpse. He put the muzzle into the soldier's ear—

And must have realized that he wasn't mentally able

to pull the trigger. He punched the weapon stunningly into the soldier's head, knocking him against the APC.

A Garrison soldier tried to escape through the hatch in the side of the vehicle. Adele shot him through the back of the neck. The second round of her double tap disintegrated on the fellow's helmet—her light pellets were glass propelled by an aluminum skirt which vaporized in the flux of the driving coil—but one was enough.

Another of Hochner's gang must have already gotten back into the APC. Bourbon had the carbine he'd been struggling for. He fired one round through the hatchway.

"I give up!" the man inside shrieked. "I give—"

Bourbon threw the carbine's selector to Full Auto. He fired a ten-round burst into the compartment. A slug ricocheted into the cab windshield, starring the bulletproof panel mounted inside the glass.

The bombardment rockets nearby on the quay blew up. The orange fireball was speckled with bits of the launcher and sheets of rocket casing. Hogg must have kept shooting into the rockets until the fuel of one had ignited and set off the other seven in a very fierce blaze. Technically it had been a deflagration rather than an explosion, but the pressure wave knocked Adele down.

The shock had thrown Colonel Bourbon against the APC. He straightened and aimed the carbine at the hatchway again.

Adele lifted the weapon's muzzle. "Come out with your hands up!" she shouted through the hatch. The burst's high-intensity *snaps* beside her had made her voice sound thin and flat in her own ears.

They could use another prisoner, and there didn't seem much risk that the fellow whimpering and blubbering in the vehicle was going to come out shooting.

If he attempted that, Tovera would kill him before he finished squeezing the trigger.

Another roar slapped the harbor. This was more distant than that of the rocket launcher destroying itself, but it was sharper as well. Adele glanced to her left. The Garrison's three antiship missiles rippled in quick succession from their concrete emplacement. They were aimed back toward Brotherhood.

The first missile was already hypersonic when it struck the edge of the plaza and exploded in a bubble of orange—from expended fuel—and black—the powdered basalt. The missiles depended on kinetic energy rather than warheads, but at such short range a layman would not have been able to tell the difference.

The second and third missiles punched through the flame. One struck the ground floor of the Gulkander Palace; the other scattered the upper portions of the building, which were already billowing outward as the sidewall collapsed.

Daniel, Woetjans, and most of the *Kiesche*'s crew sprinted up to the vehicle, wheezing and puffing. Spacers didn't spend a great deal of time running, and the would-be rescue party had winded themselves with a short gallop. Adele didn't doubt that they could have fought if there had been anyone left to fight.

Adele released Bourbon's carbine and shook her right hand. She would have blisters from vents in the barrel shroud. The Medicomp would take care of it; and anyway, it wasn't her usual shooting hand.

The Garrison soldiers—two of them; Adele had forgotten the driver—crawled out of the compartment on hands and knees. The driver was gray-faced, and his right trouser leg was bloody; apparently a ricochet had touched him. The other soldier was untouched despite the number of slugs bouncing around the vehicle's interior, but he couldn't have been more abjectly helpless if he'd been shot in the head.

As so many of his fellows had been.

Colonel Bourbon cradled the carbine in his left elbow. "Thank you, Lady Mundy," he said, though she wasn't sure precisely what he was referring to. "And thank you also, Cazelet. I try to stay fit, but between the voyages and captivity I wasn't as ready for a tussle as I should have been."

"Adele?" Daniel said. "Can you set up a general broadcast to Brotherhood? To all receivers, I mean."

"Yes, easily enough," she said. "We can do it from here if—"

She started to enter the vehicle, then paused to tug at the man she had killed in the hatchway. Barnes grabbed a handful of the soldier's tunic and tossed him over the seawall.

The APC's communicator was in the console between the seats in the cab; personnel in the rear compartment could use it also. The late gunner's boots dangled over it, but they weren't in the way.

Adele switched the unit to the *Kiesche's* external frequency and said, "Cory, this is Mundy. Six wants to broadcast to everyone in Brotherhood. Patch us into the town's emergency alert system. I set up the link when we first arrived."

She realized she was still holding her pistol. She set it on the console and flexed the fingers of her left hand.

"Done," said Cory. "Ma'am? I apologize for the delay in getting the missiles away. They had a directional *lockout that I didn't notice until they didn't launch the first time."*

As Adele opened her mouth to speak, Cory added, *"Ma'am? I angled them so that the basement level was clear. So long as the ceiling held in the collapse, the library ought to be fine. When they dig the rubble off the floor above, I mean."*

"Understood, Cory," Adele said; and she *did* understand. It was war. Worse things had happened in wars than the destruction of an ancient library—but that hadn't happened this time. Cory was a civilized man, and he had been well trained. "Hold for Six."

Daniel and Bourbon had entered the compartment behind her. "Colonel," Daniel said, "I want you to take the handset—"

Adele offered it.

"—and tell everybody that Pantellarian saboteurs have killed Major Mursiello and attempted to destroy the harbor defenses, but that you've taken charge and defeated the threat. You can end with 'Long live Corcyra!' or whatever seems appropriate."

Bourbon squatted before the console. Adele backed away and said to Daniel, "We don't know that Mursiello was killed in the building collapse."

"We know that he'll be found dead," said Tovera from the hatchway. She smiled, in her way. "Trust me."

"And when Bourbon has finished his broadcast," Daniel said, seemingly oblivious of Tovera's words, "he and I will have a discussion. About ending this war."

CHAPTER 20

Brotherhood on Corcyra

Daniel sat with Adele on a loggia built onto the side of the Spike. A curving staircase led down from the garden of one of the mansions facing the plaza. The rock was sheer enough at this point that the roof of the nearest house toward the harbor was still a dozen feet below the stone-railed alcove. It was a private spot, especially with Hogg and Tovera at the head of the stairs.

"I've been thinking about the next stage of the war," Daniel said. He glanced toward Adele, then looked away.

He wondered whether he shouldn't have chosen a different place to talk with Adele. She didn't seem to be concerned that a carved lion crouched on the parapet looked over her shoulder, but the juxtaposition disturbed *him*.

"I didn't realize there was any difficulty," she said, her eyes on the display of the data unit on her lap. "I'm not a military professional, of course, but I understood you to say that you would leapfrog missile batteries until they're close enough to Hablinger to cover another assault. With the missiles in place, the Pantellarian squadron won't be able to respond as they did before."

"That's true," Daniel said, "and it's about as straight-forward as any military operation could be. All we, well, all the Independence Council has to do is wait a month until the deliveries from Karst start arriving. Maybe a little longer, knowing Karst. And then put out a general call to the miners. There won't be as many as there were for the first attack, but there'll be enough."

He shrugged. "When the Pantellarians realize the missiles are in place, they may simply abandon Hablinger if they can arrange safe passage."

Daniel hadn't chosen this spot for the discussion out of concern for security aboard the *Kiesche*. Yes, of course he and Adele would have been overheard, but the only crew members who might have under-stood what they were talking about were the present or former commissioned officers.

It was possible that a rigger might get drunk and blurt something in the wrong ear. It was no more likely that one of Daniel's officers would do so than that Daniel himself would.

The problem was that he was working possibilities over by voicing them to Adele. With her as an audi-ence, things that had seemed acceptable in his own mind might be reflected as embarrassing foolishness. She didn't have to say anything: Daniel would see it himself as soon as he articulated a bad plan.

Adele was a cool, uninvolved wall from which Daniel bounced ideas. No one else whom Daniel knew could as ably fill that role for him.

"Is a month's delay," Adele said, "or somewhat more, unacceptable?"

"The deal with Karst is unacceptable," Daniel said, "if there's any other way of getting the same result."

He was smiling down on the red/orange/tan roofs stretching down the slope to the harbor. From this angle, the houses were smothered in the foliage of the trees which grew in every garden and courtyard.

Previous experience with mining worlds had led Daniel to expect raw earth and ugly piles of tailings. That was probably true upriver where the mines were actually located, but Brotherhood itself reminded him more of the Bantry estate than of an industrial wasteland.

"I had Cazelet and Cory look at the terms of the contract which the envoys agreed to," Adele said. She looked up from her display for the first time. "They felt that while the Karst junta couldn't be described as a charitable institution, the deal was fair and that they themselves would have agreed to it."

Cazelet's family had owned a medium-sized shipping line before they were killed and their property expropriated by the Alliance bureaucracy. Cory's father was the largest paving contractor on Florentine, his homeworld. Daniel himself couldn't have chosen better business advisors than those two, save for his sister, Deirdre.

"Oh, I don't question that it's a fair deal," Daniel said. "I just don't like to see Karst getting the profit after the way they treated a Cinnabar envoy a few years ago."

He let his smile spread as he looked down toward the harbor. Three freighters similar to the *Kiesche* were loading copper. One was anchored at a buoy in midwater; her crew was bringing the ingots aboard from the barge moored alongside. A backbreaking job. . . .

"I recall the incident," Adele said. Her voice was as cool and measured as if she hadn't herself been present on Karst when young Headman Hieronymos insulted a Cinnabar senator and refused to renew Karst's long and friendly association with the Republic. "That said, Hieronymos is dead. The reason the contract is in place is that you rescued the envoys so that the arrangements *could* be finalized."

"One step at a time, Adele," Daniel said. "Now that we've reformed the Independence Council into a body which actually *wants* to win the war, we can refine the means by which we achieve that."

Adele continued to look at him. "There are those in Xenos," she said, "who would be pleased to hear that the strongly pro-Cinnabar government of Pantellaria has recovered Corcyra from the pro-Alliance exiles who had taken power there."

Daniel laughed and met her eyes. "Those are political considerations," he said, "and I leave them for politicians. We're on Corcyra to enable Rikard Cleveland to recover the treasure which he believes is buried here. I continue to think that a Corcyran victory is the best way to create conditions in which that will be possible. I would just like to achieve that—"

His smile remained broad, but he felt the muscles of his face tighten.

"—without bringing economic benefit to Karst."

Adele watched him without replying. Something was going on behind her eyes, but it didn't leave readable signs on her face.

"I know that the Senate is willing to leave Karst be," Daniel said. "Even Senator Forbes is."

"Senator Forbes may be more willing to forgive the insult she received as envoy to Karst," said Adele, "because that was the start of the sequence that led to her becoming Defense Minister. And led to the assassination of Headman Hieronymos, of course, but I believe that the Senator is too much of a politician to care about revenge for its own sake."

"The junta which killed Hieronymos and took power in Karst," said Daniel harshly, "includes the advisors who convinced the boy to break with Cinnabar in the first place. The fact that they're fawning on the Republic now doesn't make me forget the way they insulted us in the past. You see—"

He grinned, restored to good humor by the thought.

"You see better than most, I suspect. You see that they not only insulted a Cinnabar envoy, they tried to humiliate a Leary. The Senate does as it deems politic, but a Leary takes care of his own honor."

"Understood," Adele said with her usual lack of emotion. Daniel read amusement in her blankness, however.

She pursed her lips and said, "Daniel, while we were still on Cinnabar I was given commissions—I won't say assignments—which go beyond our private agreement with the Sand family."

Daniel shrugged. Of course Adele was involved in other matters. She was too valuable to the Republic *not* to be tasked with additional duties.

"Go on," he said aloud.

"It is possible," said Adele, "that at some point our purposes will conflict."

Daniel pressed his fingers against the stone bench; he didn't drum them, just let his conscious mind focus on the moss-cushioned roughness.

"If that should happen," he said carefully, turning to meet Adele's eyes again, "you will inform me that there is a conflict. I will decide on a further course of action then. At this moment, I would expect to trust your judgment and honor, and therefore I would defer to you."

She nodded crisply.

"And now," Daniel said, rising to his feet, "I will meet with Colonel Bourbon in the Manor. Would you care to come along?"

"Lieutenant Cory says the *Kiesche* has received a message which he'd like to show to me," Adele said as she put away her data unit. "I'm going back to the ship. I'll keep you informed as developments require."

Which was something less than "I'll keep you informed of developments," Daniel realized as they started up the stairs. But there were many aspects of Adele's business on which he preferred to remain ignorant.

Adele entered the *Kiesche*'s bridge, expecting to find Cory, the duty officer, sitting at the command console and no one else in the compartment unless a spacer was asleep in a bunk. The crew had performed without a real break since the ship lifted from Xenos, and Daniel believed in granting liberty to as great a degree as he could.

Cory and Cazelet stood beside the console, facing the hatchway. When Adele stepped through, they braced to attention.

"Ma'am!" said Cory. "I asked Master Cazelet for some help with this, but the responsibility is mine."

"Very well, Cory," Adele said. "Please explain the situation."

She sat at one of the jumpseats and accessed the console through her personal data unit. She was certainly interested in what Cory had to say, but she had found that an individual's explanations were mainly valuable in illuminating the hard data which was an approximation of truth.

"The *Kiesche* received a message in an unfamiliar code," Cory said, still standing at attention. "It was addressed to Shipping Representative, Bantry Holdings. I asked Master Cazelet to take a look at it while I checked the source of the communication."

"Because I had been in the shipping business," Cazelet said. They were both very tense. "I recognized it as a standard Pantellarian shipping code, keyed to the date of the first message in the series. Knowing that and the fact it was Pantellarian, it was easy enough to run it back till the contents stopped being garbage."

"Yes," said Adele. An astrogation computer could handle brute-force computations like that in a heartbeat. Even without knowing that the key was in the Pantellarian calendar, the delay in reading would be insignificant. It was, after all, a shipping code meant to conceal arrival and pricing information from trade rivals for a few days.

"Did you read the communication?" Adele asked, her eyes on the decoded message on her display. She spoke mildly.

"Ma'am, we didn't," Cory said. "We just saw enough to know that it was none of our business."

"Umm," said Adele. "You couldn't be faulted if you had read it, it seems to me. But you're probably better off not having done so."

"We weren't sure whether it should go to Six or to you, Adele," Cazelet said. "I said that since you had carried the Bantry Holdings authorization to the negotiations on Ischia, we'd start with you and you'd take it to Captain Leary if he was the correct recipient."

"Ma'am," Cory said, "the origination of the message was Pantellarian HQ in Hablinger. The sender tried to disguise it, but he wasn't very good."

"I think one can take as a given," Adele said, feeling the humor of the situation, "that someone who uses a commercial code that's at least twenty standard years old—"

The inception date of the series.

"—isn't an expert in cyber security."

The code was probably the one that the Arnaud and Leary businesses had used to communicate from the beginning. When Pantellaria had joined—had been joined to—the Alliance of Free Stars, the communication became treason on both sides, but the code hadn't been changed to something more secure.

Arnaud—because the message was from Commissioner Arnaud—had used it here because he assumed that a ship under Captain Leary brought an agent to discuss his demands for help from Cinnabar in reconquering Corcyra. He was right in his assumption, though possibly not in the way he thought he was right.

"I'm the correct person to deal with this," Adele said. She looked up at the two officers—at her protégés, both of them. They deserved more than a brush-off.

"This is a matter that Captain Leary isn't aware

of as yet," she said. "Though obviously it concerns him. You may reasonably think it your duty to take it to him directly. I will...that is, I won't blame you if you do."

Cory looked at her incredulously. "Ma'am!" he said. "We wouldn't do that!"

"Lady Mundy," Cazelet said. He was standing more stiffly, if that was possible, than he had before. "You've said that you're dealing with the matter, whatever it is. All that I, that *either* of us, need to know at this point is if there's any help we can give you. And you'll tell us in that case, I'm sure."

Why are they loyal to me? Adele thought. *They should be concerned that I'm plotting with the enemy and hiding information from Daniel. Which is just what I'm doing!*

Cory and Cazelet accepted that she wasn't Daniel's enemy, even when the data would support the conclusion than she was. "Support" did not mean "compel," and they trusted her. As they had every reason to do.

"Very well," she said. "I have nothing at present, but I will give you such tasks as circumstances require. As I have always done."

"We'll be in the hold, ma'am," Cory said. "Just call if you need us."

"No," said Adele. "Cory, you're on duty. Stay where you would ordinarily be, which I take to be the command console. Rene, I presume you're at liberty, so do as you please. Chatting with Cory appears much more reasonable than twiddling your thumbs alone in the hold, however."

"We won't disturb you?" Cazelet said.

"No," said Adele, who lost herself so thoroughly in

her focus that the world outside ceased to exist. "I will continue to access the console from where I am now."

She had to respond to Arnaud, but she couldn't say anything substantive until she had more information; she composed a neutral placeholder and sent it back along the convoluted track that would take it to Pantellarian headquarters.

The original message demanded that, within three days, Daniel Leary make a public promise of Cinnabar support for the Pantellarian position—that is, for Commissioner Arnaud's invasion. Because of Daniel's public stature, the Independence Council would believe the promise and therefore be willing to compromise on terms that Arnaud would be able to claim was a victory for him.

The alternative was that Arnaud would publish the whole course of his dealings with Bantry Holdings, claiming that he himself had been working against the Alliance oppressors. Speaker Leary would find it harder to justify the fact that he was building warships for the Fleet. The information probably wouldn't do any good to the career of his estranged son, either.

Adele began working. She had sneered at Arnaud's skill at computer security, but try as she might she couldn't find, let alone access, the computer on which he had composed his demand. It apparently wasn't hooked into the network in Hablinger except during the moments that it was actually transferring data.

Adele had to get into Arnaud's files so that she could modify them in the way she had planned. There was one obvious method: physical contact.

That had its own set of problems, but she could consult experts. Daniel and Hogg were as skilled at physical intrusion as Adele was in her field.

CHAPTER 21

Brotherhood on Corcyra

"They're coming out of the Manor," Tovera said. "They've seen us; they're coming over."

Adele reduced her data unit's display—she didn't shut down—and turned. She was sitting on a block of the tumbled railing at the northwest corner of the plaza. The corner to the south had been carved away by the first of the missiles which destroyed the Gulkander Palace; the transmitted shock had been enough to damage the other end of the retaining wall also.

Daniel and Hogg came toward them across the plaza, picking their way over the tilting blocks with the effortless assurance of water finding a level. Adele waved. She didn't have to call attention to herself as she had thought she might need to do—Daniel hadn't been expecting to see her—but it was polite. It was one of the things human beings did to show that they were pleased by the company of other human beings.

Adele glanced at Tovera and said, "You're a good role model." Tovera smiled faintly but said nothing.

Besides the toppled railing there were other reminders of the brief coup—or of the counter-coup, depending on how you wanted to describe the process by which Colonel Mursiello had returned command of the Garrison to Colonel Bourbon. There was enough powdered stone in the air, lifted by breezes, to make the back of Adele's throat feel dry and itchy.

Much worse were the cloying, sickening combustion products of the propellant which had been sprayed over a wide area before it ignited. Antiship missiles used boron fuel to get maximum acceleration. The residues were poisonous, though at the present dilution they wouldn't be an acute problem.

Adele smiled wryly. She didn't expect to die of emphysema.

Daniel put his foot on the base of the fallen stone banister which had once supported part of the railing on which Adele sat; he stared down what was nearly a perpendicular cliff for the first twenty feet and a stiff slope for the next twenty feet also. RCN midshipmen accompanied the riggers as part of their duties, so it wasn't likely that an officer who had risen to the rank of captain would be troubled by vertigo.

Daniel turned and seated himself on the block beside Adele's. Hogg and Tovera were facing outward some six feet away from their principals, watching other people on the plaza.

"I've been talking with Colonel Bourbon," he said, looking toward the main stream of the Cephisis well to the east. "He's doubtful, but he's willing to support my plan for the time being. In return, he'd like my help in getting fair benefits for his personnel."

"Benefits?" Adele said.

"Bourbon is aware that an independent Corcyra will have very little need for a standing army," Daniel said, "even without the general popular dislike of the Garrison. Mursiello may have thought he could rule by force, but Bourbon is smarter than that. The miners are mostly armed by this time."

His laugh had a harsh undertone. "I don't think Bourbon really has the stomach to try that, either," he said, "but that's a separate question. Still, he doesn't want to see his people dumped in the street after the Pantellarians are gone. Dumped or massacred."

"I see," said Adele. That problem was now being considered in the back of her mind. She had a more immediate concern, however.

"Daniel," she said, "I need to enter Hablinger to meet a man. I hope you have some suggestions. The *Kiesche* could do that, but I would like to return to Brotherhood afterward as well. Could you get me into Hablinger without being noticed by the independence forces?"

"Not directly," Daniel said. He didn't ask why she wanted to meet a man in Hablinger. "Now, it's *possible* that we might be able to meet an incoming ship above Corcyra and transfer you to it. The only ships bound for Hablinger are Pantellarian and in convoy, so that would mean intercepting a normal copper trader and bribing her to take you into Hablinger instead; which we could do, though I'm not sure about timing. Or—"

He pursed his lips as he calculated mentally. *I would be staring at my display,* Adele thought.

"—we could lift for Pantellaria and put you on a ship there," Daniel continued. "They wouldn't think anything in Brotherhood about a Pantellarian ship landing in Hablinger, and of course they couldn't track us from the ground. That would work!"

"I need to be in Hablinger within three days," Adele said. "I'm sorry, I should have said that."

"If you get us to the independence side, master," Hogg said, sidling closer, but continuing to face outward, "I can get her through the Pantellarian lines. Unless you're fussy about a sentry or two, mistress?"

"I don't care about that," Adele said curtly. "Daniel, will Colonel Bourbon give us his support? Because we'll need at least neutrality from independence forces at the point we set out from."

"I'm sure Bourbon would," Daniel said, "but I suggest we discuss matters first with Brother Graves. The Transformationist segment of the siege lines is immediately to the west of the Cephisis channel, which I think would be a good location."

"That's the way I think, too," Hogg said, nodding his head enthusiastically. "I been looking at the satellite feeds all the time we been back on Corcyra. I figured there'd be more ways to get into the city than a couple thousand screaming idiots charging across the fields in broad daylight like last time."

"Yes, I think that, too," said Daniel, grinning. "But as to Adele's matter, Brother Graves is alone in Brotherhood. I trust Colonel Bourbon, but I don't trust all the people around him to keep their mouths shut. We can't afford to have the Pantellarians learn about this—"

He paused. Adele saw his face change, though not in any fashion she could have described with certainty.

"Unless," Daniel said, "the Pantellarians are expecting you?"

"They're not," said Adele. "Not even the person I need to see."

She coughed to put an end to the subject. "I've met Graves," she said. "I can talk with him myself, but it might be better if you joined me to explain exactly what is required. I'm out of my depth here."

"No problem," said Daniel. "We can go to his office immediately. Though it'll be roundabout because there's a large hole where Ridge Road used to join the plaza."

"One thing," Hogg said. He looked at Adele. "Tovera's going to have to watch my young master while I'm gone. It's going to be like having a log chained to my leg, dragging you through the lines. I won't guarantee how quick I can do it, so she's got to be responsible here."

All three of them looked at Tovera. Tovera turned with a lopsided smile.

"And you don't want to haul a second log around, hey?" she said. "Well, I can see that. But bring her back, right?"

"Right," said Hogg, meeting Tovera's eyes. "She comes back, or nobody does."

His expression might have been meant for a smile.

"Which is how it was going to be anyway," Hogg added. "Now, let's go find Brother Graves so we can be done with this crap quick."

Daniel stepped aside at the head of the stairs so that Hogg could reach the top, but he let Adele approach the door of Graves' office alone.

"Mistress," said Tovera urgently. "It isn't latched!"

"No," said Adele. She rapped on the door jamb with the knuckles of her right hand.

"Come in!" a male voice called. "It's open."

Daniel felt himself relax and frowned because he had been anything *but* relaxed. The door was closed but not pulled quite to, something everyone did occasionally. Since it wasn't an outside door which the wind might blow open, there was no reason to worry about it.

Unless you were a paranoid sociopath like Tovera. *Was* there another person like Tovera?

Adele pushed the door fully open and entered an ordinary office. Rikard Cleveland and an older man, presumably Graves, were standing on chairs as they replaced the glass in a window casement. Both panes had cracked across diagonally.

Ceiling plaster had fallen in the corner beyond them. Someone had swept it up, but the chunks waited in a wastebasket to be dumped.

"I'm sorry about the mess, Lady Mundy," Graves said, stepping down carefully. "The excitement yesterday made the building flex a little. The disadvantage of building on bedrock is that anything that happens to the bedrock is transmitted at full strength."

He laid his utility knife on the desk and walked around it, holding his hand out to Daniel. "And you would be Captain Leary," Graves said. "It's an honor to meet you, sir. I'm Dallert Graves, as I suppose you know. Ah? Would you care to sit down? I can bring a chair out of the bedroom?"

"Our servants will stand," Daniel said. He supposed that made him sound like the stern master of storybooks—and of no few noble townhouses, though in the country things were more relaxed.

"I thought they might," said Graves with a sort of smile. He pulled the chairs from under the window, sitting in one and gesturing Cleveland into the other.

"Now," Graves continued. "Please explain what you want from me, Captain, and I'll do my best to provide it. The Transformationist community is in your debt for removing Colonel Mursiello. In fact, all Brotherhood is. Despite the occasional cracked window."

Graves had understood that Hogg and Tovera were bodyguards, which Rikard Cleveland didn't appear to have done despite being in close contact with them on the voyage from Cinnabar. It would be wrong to think of Graves as a dreamy religious nut.

"Captain?" said Cleveland. His hands rested on the back of the indicated chair, but he hadn't sat down. "If you'd prefer that I leave, I won't feel offended."

Daniel had been on the fence about asking Cleveland to go. The volunteered offer convinced him that it wasn't necessary.

"Please stay, Master Cleveland," he said, taking the chair facing the desk. Adele was already in the one against wall, immersed in the display of her data unit. "Though of course the operation depends on keeping the discussion among ourselves. The operation and lives depend on secrecy."

Daniel coughed. "Basically, we intend to put an agent into Hablinger," he said. "We'd like to do it through the Transformationist positions in the siege line, because your contingent is relatively small. Also, I believe your people are more trustworthy than those of other elements in the coalition."

He grinned and added, "I suppose that sounds as though I'm buttering you up."

"Yes," said Graves, "it does. But I also believe it's objectively true—as I suspect you do, Captain. Of course I'll help you. Would you like me to accompany you north and speak to our field commander, Brother Heimholz?"

"Do you think that would be necessary?" Daniel said. The possibility hadn't crossed his mind. "I was hoping for a letter of introduction, so to speak."

"I believe our communications—mine, that is," said Graves, "between here and both the field and Pearl Valley are reasonably secure."

"They are," said Adele without looking up from her display. "Secure from any Pantellarian on the planet at present, at least."

"I was more concerned with the other factions in the independence coalition, to be honest," Graves said with a smile. "But I suppose those risks aren't as great with Colonel Bourbon back in charge. And I'm glad to know that the Pantellarians aren't reading our messages, not that they would find much to interest them."

"If you'd just send a note saying that we'll be arriving, probably tomorrow," Daniel said, "I would appreciate it. A general note like that wouldn't be a problem even if it did get out."

"Of course," Graves said. "Brother Heimholz runs a tight ship, or whatever metaphor would be proper. He's a former captain in the Land Forces of the Republic; and he rose from the ranks to a commission during the recent war."

Graves tented his fingers before him and looked at them. "I think Heimholz may have a more difficult task than I do," he said. "The common soldiers of our contingent are rotated back to Pearl Valley every three months, but Brother Heimholz remains where he is; both for continuity of command and because he's

really the only member of our community who has
the expertise. It's very hard for one of us, a brother,
to be responsible for slaughter."

"Brother Heimholz lives with a community," Cleveland said. "You have nothing, no one."

Then, fiercely, he added, "I don't know how you
stand it! I've only been a member for two years, and
even so the separation of returning to Cinnabar was,
was . . ."

He smiled wryly. "It's good that I've stopped drinking," he said, his voice mild again. "I was an unpleasant
drunk, and I would have stayed very drunk."

"I'm doing it for the cause," Graves said with a
lopsided grin to show that he was joking. He wasn't
joking, of course.

"I'm surprised that the Transformationists"—Daniel's
mind had toyed with "you cultists," but there was
no risk that would reach his tongue—"would be so
strongly for Corcyran independence. You don't seem
to be a very political group."

Cleveland looked blank. So did Graves for a moment,
but then the older man chuckled.

"I was unclear, Captain," Graves said, "and I apologize. Yes, we're an apolitical group as a general matter;
our involvement in the independence movement is simply because we fear that the circumstances attending
a return to Pantellarian rule would be nonsurvivable."

He cleared his throat, then said, "The cause to which
I referred is the transformation of men as individual
thinkers to men as aspects of a single social mind."

"That . . ." Daniel said. He didn't know how to go
on, so he stopped.

"I do not expect this to occur within my lifetime,"

said Graves, smiling. "And perhaps it won't occur within the lifetime of the universe. Still, it's the cause for which we strive."

As before, he wasn't joking.

Daniel rose to his feet. "I'm not a religious man, Brother Graves," he said. "But your religion is one I can honor from a distance."

Graves stood also. "I'll tell the field force to expect you, Captain," he said. "And I assure you that craftsmanship at the level you and your companions demonstrate it—"

He nodded not only to Adele, joining Daniel at the door, but to Hogg and Tovera as well.

"—has my full appreciation also. May mankind be better for your efforts."

"Yes," said Daniel as he led the way out of the room. "We can all hope that."

His own goals were shorter term, but that was a worthy sentiment.

CHAPTER 22

Hablinger on Corcyra

The River Cephisis was an expanse of brown glass when Daniel looked over the left side of the APC. The water wasn't very far from the top of the levee, either: maybe the length of his forearm, maybe not that much. He dropped back into the compartment.

"Mundy?" he said, being relatively formal because they were sharing the vehicle with Colonel Bourbon and two of his aides. "When is high water? What part of the year, I mean?"

"The peak here was about two days ago," said the female aide, Lieutenant Zeffelini, before Adele could answer. "On the other side of the river the road washed away yesterday in a couple places. Usually we'd be coming down on the west levee, though we can hop over the water easy."

"I'm not sure about easy," said Bourbon with a smile. "Can you swim, Leary?"

"Well enough," Daniel said. He didn't mention that Adele *couldn't* swim, but he or Hogg would carry her if the situation arose. "But we should be fine."

They were in the vehicle which had carried Hochner and his arrest team two days earlier. The slugs hadn't damaged the lift fans, but Bourbon had decided to make the hundred mile run north to Hablinger in surface effect for safety's sake. The vehicle didn't lose much speed, and a motor failure on the road was an irritation. Failure twenty feet in the air could be a great deal more interesting, as Daniel and his companions had learned in the past.

Daniel stood again so that his head and shoulders were out in the airstream; he lowered the visor of his helmet. The compartment had a lid of pleated titanium battens, but it was rolled back at present.

Gunfire during the attempted coup hadn't seriously damaged the vehicle, but there hadn't been time to fully clean the compartment. Muggy heat turned residues of blood and brains into a stomach-roiling stench. Downwind of the fish-processing plant at Bantry was worse, but Daniel had no reason at the moment not to be out in the breeze.

Hogg was in the cab with the automatic impeller while Tovera rode on the passenger side of the cab, which would ordinarily have been the gunner's seat when the impeller wasn't manned. Tovera had wanted to drive the vehicle, but Colonel Bourbon had refused to permit that, and neither Adele nor Daniel had made any effort to overrule him.

Tovera knew the basic theory of driving. She would never be good, though, and the APC was much heavier than anything she had experience with. At some level Tovera probably understood that she shouldn't be driving, but her need to control all aspects of her mistress' environment had forced her to ask.

To Daniel's surprise, Adele shut down her data unit and stood beside him. She surveyed the paddies to the right. The land across the river was identical, but the Cephisis was too wide to see across at this point.

Turning to Daniel she said, "I've never seen terrain like this. That is, I've seen imagery even before I began preparing to enter Hablinger; but the real thing is different from the images."

She smiled, more or less. "I prefer the imagery," she said.

The rice paddies were forty feet below the road the vehicle was following. They hadn't been planted or flooded for over a year, but the ones Daniel could see were soppy because of leakage from the river. Weeds and self-seeded rice grew raggedly from the black muck.

The dikes separating each field from its neighbors were about four feet high. The tops of the dikes were grass, but shaggy trees grew out from the sides and curved upward; seedpods like lengths of orange tape dangled from some of them.

"I suppose the terrain is the same all the way to the city walls," Adele said. Her smile quirked again. "That's what the imagery showed, though imagery didn't allow me to appreciate quite how muddy it would be."

"The mud deadens sound," Daniel said. He made his voice a trifle more cheerful than the words themselves required, but he was telling the truth. "You won't clink on a stone, which is the sort of thing that wakes up even a Pantellarian guard. And Hogg will get you through, never fear. I won't pretend it'll be a walk in the park, but all you have to worry about is crawling. He'll take care of the rest."

Daniel's voice changed in the middle of the final thought. Adele didn't need anyone to kill for her; Hogg would simply do the business more quietly. And come to that—

Adele was looking at him with her minuscule smile. *She's thinking the same thing.*

"Your little pistol doesn't make a great deal of noise, granted," Daniel said, finishing the thought aloud. "But Hogg is still a better choice."

"Even Tovera agrees about that," Adele said. "Which is high praise for Hogg, and a relief to me not to have to settle the matter myself."

The hill on which Hablinger rose, a steep-sided mound over fifty feet high, was the only interruption of the flat landscape. Daniel could easily make out buildings without using the optical enhancements of his helmet visor.

"They can see us from there," Adele said. "Why don't they shoot?"

"Because we'd shoot back," said Colonel Bourbon. He must have been listening for some time, but only now did he rise from his seat to join them.

"Isn't that the point of the exercise?" said Adele.

There were openings in the inner walls of the dikes they were passing. A few—two, three; in one case six—people, mostly men, were visible near each, sometimes sitting on the dike itself. Generally but not always their weapons were nearby.

"Sniping would force both sides to keep under cover and make the siege more unpleasant," Bourbon said. His aides were now standing also, apparently concerned that they were being left out. "It wouldn't affect the military situation, though."

Daniel nodded. "Everyone would stay under cover," he said, in part showing that he understood but also making sure that Adele did.

"The combatants would stay under cover," Bourbon said, correcting him. "Hablinger can't be concealed. We don't have real artillery, but automatic impellers could level the town. It's stabilized mud, so the walls would shatter."

He shrugged. "The Pantellarians find billets in Hablinger much more comfortable than muddy dugouts would be, and of course the townspeople *are* Corcyrans even if they happen to be under foreign control right now."

"Most of them don't care about independence," said Bourbon's male aide, a lieutenant. Daniel thought his name was Vanna, but Daniel paid more attention to young women than to men, whether or not they were in uniform. "They're happy as long as the Pantellarians pay for what they take!"

"I've noticed," Daniel said, trying not to sound too irritated, "that the tenants at Bantry worry more about how their crops are coming in than they do about who the Speaker of the Senate is. The crops determine how well they and their families are going to eat."

"Quite right," said Bourbon, though from his tone Daniel had the impression that the colonel's main concern was to stop his aide from arguing with the honored guest who had rescued him. "This is where we'll cross the river, so you might want to get down inside again."

He and his aides ducked into the compartment. Daniel nodded to Adele and dropped to his seat just as the vehicle slowed and bumped down onto the Cephisis. Water spewed up on all sides.

Though the river looked like liquid mud from above, its spray had its usual rainbow beauty in the sun. Some of the iridescent fog settled over those in the compartment, but it was better to be damp than to close the cover and drown if a lift fan failed.

The APC lifted twenty inches in the air to clear the edge of the west levee, then slewed to the right along the roadway there so as not to plunge straight over the forty-foot escarpment. Only after the driver had slowed from the headlong pace at which they'd crossed the river did he nose his vehicle down toward the paddies. He angled his lift fans in order to keep the nose more or less level with the stern, though the latter was actually dragging on the slope.

"General good feeling between the sides or not," Daniel said, his lips close to Adele's ear, "I'd expect somebody in Hablinger to take a shot at a high-value target when a single slug could take out the whole vehicle and everybody aboard."

Tovera, who either had very keen ears or was aided by a concealed antenna, said, "Pantellarians don't think that way." There was more contempt in those few words than even Hogg could have managed.

The APC reached ground level in an eruption of gluey black mud, some of which rained through the open roof. Daniel grimaced at the smear on his left sleeve, but he supposed he might as well get used to what would be a part of life so long as he remained here.

The driver turned hard to the left, back in the direction of Brotherhood, then turned left again. They rocked and bumped, dropped significantly; then dropped again and stopped. Daniel stood and looked around. They were in a sunken chamber made by welding structural plastic into a roofless box.

The walls acted as a coffer dam against seepage from the soil. A pump whined as it threw a column of muddy water over the levee and back into the stream of the Cephisis.

Even before the APC's fans shut down, Bourbon's aides had loosed the catches to drop the rear ramp. Daniel waited before he followed the locals out of the vehicle. The box in which they had stopped was built around a smaller box, fifteen feet by fifteen. The inner box was also formed from plastic, but it was roofed and all surfaces were covered with several layers of sandbags.

Well, bags of dirt. Daniel frowned, and Hogg, who must have been thinking the same thing, said, "Get a good storm and those bags'll be sliding all over creation. And over anybody standing in this hole."

"It almost never rains here in the north," said Zeffelini, the female lieutenant.

There was a sneer in her voice; or anyway, Hogg heard one. "And your pump never fails? Because I want to know the manufacturer if that's so. You get these bags wet, and the soil comes through the cloth like soap . . . which gives you a few tons of slipping sandbags."

Bourbon waved Daniel and Adele ahead of him down the ramp. "I was expecting the Pantellarians to use bombardment rockets when we constructed this bunker," he said. "That hasn't happened, and your servant's concern seems valid, Captain Leary."

He wasn't replying directly to Hogg, but he spoke loudly enough for Hogg and Zeffelini both to hear.

Colonel Bourbon struck Daniel as a modest figure as a military man—but a first-rate politician, which was perhaps a better qualification for leadership here on Corcyra.

A steel door opened in the alcove left in the sandbagged wall. "Glad to have you back, Bourbon," said the man in the doorway. He wore blotch-patterned battledress with the odd purple undertone of the Fleet Marines; his major's lapel insignia was Alliance pattern also. "We're all waiting for you inside. Figured it was easier than trusting to electronics since it was all parties."

"I'm glad to be back, Wiren," Bourbon said as he led the others into the bunker. "Frankly, the time I spent negotiating on Karst wasn't much better than being a prisoner on Ischia. Fellows, this is Captain Leary, who rescued me and has some thoughts about ending this business even before the missiles arrive from Karst. Leary, these are—"

The space was crowded with the new arrivals. Bourbon ran down the names. Wiren was commander of the naval contingent, clearly a mercenary whom Tibbs had hired. Major Gillard was the Regiment's field commander, Pantellarian by birth but not necessarily interested in politics. Brother Heimholz, a sad-faced bruiser of fifty, headed the Transformationist contingent; Graves in Brotherhood had described his background. Three miners were present, representatives but probably not leaders of the troops who weren't members of any official faction.

"Well, it's fine that you're outa jail, Bourbon," said a miner. Her hair was a natural mousy brown on one side and faded blue on the other. "What I want to know, though, is when something's going to get settled here so we can go back south where we belong. I don't remember much happening *before* you went off except we got our asses shot off the onct by them ships."

"Now look, you!" said Vanna, waggling his finger in the miner's face. "You watch your tongue or—"

Daniel expected the miner to slap Vanna's hand away. Instead, she punched the lieutenant in the pit of the stomach, doubling him up gasping.

Zeffelini started to unsnap the holster of the pistol she wore as part of her uniform. Daniel reached across her body to grab her gun hand.

"That's enough! Back off, everybody!" he bellowed at the three miners.

A number of people began babbling, including the blue-haired miner. She appeared to be embarrassed at what she'd done. Tempers were bound to fray during months in these filthy conditions.

"Look, I got a question," said Hogg. "Why don't you just blow the river? The bottom of the channel's what, twenty feet above the ground here? It'd drain so quick the wogs wouldn't be able to do squat to stop it."

It was obvious that by "wogs" Hogg meant the Pantellarians. Half the people in this crowded chamber were Pantellarian by birth, however, and it didn't require much imagination to guess that Hogg would've been willing to apply the term to an even wider circle than that. Daniel suspected that in the right context, Hogg might use "wog" to describe anybody who hadn't been born and raised on the Bantry estate.

"Bloody hell!" said Gillard. "Have you seen where our positions are, you farmer? We'd flood ourselves out!"

Hogg smiled. He had just focused all attention—and

all the anger—on himself. He was the harmless rural boob that nobody here had enough history with to hate.

"It'd be wet here, I see that," he said complacently, his hands in the pockets of his baggy jacket. "You'd have to pull back a ways, though that wouldn't be too terrible. And I was thinking that the Pantellarians might have worse problems without water to drink."

"By heaven, he's got something!" said Major Wiren, looking at Hogg in amazement.

"No, unfortunately," said Bourbon quickly; though not quite quickly enough that Daniel hadn't gotten his own hopes up. "There's so much silt in the Cephisis here that Hablinger has always taken its water from a desalination plant fifteen kilometers out at sea. And the plant is on the sea bottom to keep it out of storms, so there isn't a quick way of capturing it, either."

"Ah, well," said Hogg. He yawned, then stretched his arms toward the ceiling. "We farmers think a lot about water, you know."

"Colonel," said Daniel. "Do you have quarters for me and my personnel? I'd like to sort out some matters with my staff"—*with Adele*—"before I broach my proposals to you."

If Daniel hadn't said that or something along those lines, someone—maybe all the locals together—would be asking what his plans were. He was going to know more about the terrain here before he wanted to suggest anything publically.

In addition there was Adele's business, whatever that was. He would learn when it was time for him to know.

"We've readied a dugout for you, Captain," Brother Heimholz said. He smiled, transfiguring his face. "It's small, dark, and has no amenities, so you spacers should feel right at home. I'll take you there now."

Daniel bowed. "I was afraid it was going to be a pavilion with four-poster beds," he said, "since I know how you Land Force types treat yourselves. I appreciate you going to such effort to make poor spacers feel comfortable."

They trailed out behind the Transformationist commander. When they were clear of the inner bunker, Hogg muttered, "I'm going to rack out now. Come dark, I'll go see what I can see."

"Yes," said Daniel. "You and I will go."

Also, I will be thinking about my own next step, unless Adele comes back from Hablinger and hands me the Pantellarian surrender.

Which, Adele being Adele, might just happen.

Adele sat on a straight chair in the dugout, watching the changes her data unit had found in collating views of the terrain around Hablinger recorded by Pantellarian destroyers. Outside in the night a woman sang, *"I wish I was a little bird...."*

Though the destroyers didn't patrol, they lifted in pairs to escort supply ships in. Hablinger Pool was a bowl sculpted into the course of the Cephisis just downstream of the town, so the automatic logs of the ships recorded high-resolution imagery every time. Any variation in the surface, whether caused by weather or by human activity, appeared as a highlight on Adele's display.

"I'd fly up in a tree..." sang the woman.

From what Adele had seen, here and in Pearl Valley, women in the Transformationist community were treated the same as men, or as nearly so as human beings were capable of doing. There were relatively few women in the community, however. She would have to check with Brother Graves or one of the senior people in Pearl Valley, but the reason could be as simple as statistically fewer women than men emigrating to a mining world.

"I'd sit and sing my sad little song...."

The woman sounded quite cheerful, and her voice was pleasant if untrained. Adele would have been interested to learn the internal society of the Transformationists, if—

She smiled in self-mockery.

—somebody else had compiled the data.

Speaking rather than singing, the woman concluded, "But *I* can't stay here by myself!"

"They're back," called Tovera softly through the blanket-covered entrance of the dugout.

Hogg pulled the drape open for Daniel, then followed him in. Fresh mud stank on their utilities.

Though the only light in the dugout was the data unit's holographic display, Daniel must have read the thought behind what Adele believed was a blank expression. "The good thing about the location," he said, "is that there's plenty of water to wash with. It's got just as much mud, I suppose, but there's probably less excrement in the form of fertilizer."

"I'll get you in, mistress," Hogg said. "You'll likely be bathed in this muck"—he grimaced and gestured with both hands—"but I guess it wouldn't look right to the wogs when you was walking around if you didn't."

"What's this, Adele?" Daniel said, bending forward to look at her display. She'd left it omnidirectional instead of cueing the unit to focus on her eyes alone. "Why, this is the plan of the Pantellarian lines! I didn't realize we had anything so good."

Adele stood and rubbed her shoulders. She wasn't sure what time it was, but she'd been working at the data unit since Daniel and Hogg went out an hour after full darkness to scout the enemy positions.

"I put it together after you left," she said, her eyes closed. "I got into the logs of the Pantellarian squadron. I sent most of the information back to the *Kiesche* for Cory and Cazelet to process, but I kept copies of the local imagery for myself."

"Well, that's wonderful!" Daniel said. "I'm surprised that . . . well, I'm pleased that you were able to get into their logs so quickly."

Adele smiled faintly, her eyes still closed. "You're thinking that Pantellarian security must be very bad for me to open up warship data banks with no more than I have with me," she said. She sat down again and stroked the case of her little data unit. "In fact their security was very good, but they had bad luck."

She looked up at Daniel and half-smiled again. She was tired, but her work and that of her companions seemed to be going well; and tomorrow this would be over, one way or another.

"The new Pantellarian Navy Department, the one put in place after independence," Adele said, "suspected that all their codes and coding equipment were known to the Alliance. They were correct in that assumption."

Daniel nodded. Hogg seemed to be focused wholly on the landscape display, but Adele knew that he was hearing and understanding the explanation.

"They asked Cinnabar for help revising their systems

and procedures," Adele said. "My other employer provided them with help of the highest quality, but of course we kept full records of what codes Pantellaria might now be using and how the codes were being generated."

Hogg snorted in amusement. Daniel remained stone-faced for a moment, then smiled broadly.

"You may reasonably think it dishonorable of me to use information gained in this way," Adele said, knowing that she was speaking more to herself than to her audience. "I made the decision without referring to you or to anyone else."

"If you get yourself killed because you were too proud to look at what somebody *handed* you," Hogg said, suddenly glaring at her, "then I'll be sorry, because I like you and we all like you. But if you get *me* killed like that, I'll come out of Hell for you, I swear."

"Fortunately, that situation doesn't arise," Daniel said mildly. "I'm glad to have this imagery, though I don't think it changes anything we saw on the ground. See, Hogg? Here's the strongpoint in front of us, and here's the listening post. There's six of them between strongpoints, it looks like fifty yards apart. Well, fifty meters."

"There are three listening posts to either side of each strongpoint," Adele said. She suddenly felt tired. There was always more to learn, but she had completed the tasks which had an immediate bearing on her entry into Hablinger; her entry tomorrow into Hablinger. "I think they're connected by wire. The strongpoints report to Hablinger headquarters by radio, including anything the listening posts have reported, but I don't pick up signals from the posts directly."

"Probably just two men in the LPs," Hogg said. "With this lot, maybe only one. I'll slip up the last hundred yards and take care of them while the mistress waits, then come get her and we both go through. There's no more manned posts, just wire, and that's no problem."

"Call," Daniel said. "You don't need to come back. That's extra work and extra noise. You can sound like a field-skipper, three times in quick order."

"She won't hear me, master," Hogg said in irritation. "And she'll get bloody lost on the way. I don't care how simple it seems to you!"

Adele hadn't heard the older man use that frustrated tone to Daniel in the past. It was justified: Hogg had put into words the analysis which Adele had made in her head already.

"I'll catch it," said Daniel calmly. "I'll bring her up to the LP and wait there till the two of you come back. And I won't get lost."

Hogg remained completely still for a moment. Then he said, "Right. I don't need more bloody exercise at my age."

Looking away, he muttered, "Sorry, master."

"You need a distraction," Tovera said without turning to face the others. She squatted in the dugout's opening with a corner of the blanket drawn back, her submachine gun in her hand.

"We'll have a distraction," Hogg said. "I'm going to set a flare midway to the post. When we're there and ready to head in the town, I'll trip it with a clacker. Nobody'll be looking toward us even if, well, if the Mistress is having a bit of trouble with the going."

"A clacker won't work," Tovera said. "It won't have enough juice at three hundred meters."

"I'll put it closer, then!" Hogg said. "Just so the wogs are looking to our lines and not out to the side!"

The clacker was a hand-squeezed generator that set off a blasting cap. Adele didn't have any idea how great a charge would remain at the end of a thousand feet of thin wire, but Tovera was probably correct.

"No," Tovera said. She was icy calm through the whole discussion. "I'll be twenty feet from the flare, holding the ends of your wire between my thumb and forefinger. I'll feel the spark, and I'll set off the flare."

She turned to glance at Adele. "Keeping radio silence, mistress," she said.

"Yes, that sounds good," said Daniel. His tone was casual, but Adele and probably the others knew that the discussion was over. "Now, let's get some sleep. Starting an hour after dark tonight, we all have a great deal to do."`

Adele shut down her data unit and hunched—the ceiling was low—to the bedstead she had chosen. The frame was plastic tubing and there was no mattress over the slats, but she had slept on much worse.

"Yes," she said, putting her rolled jacket at the end of the frame for a pillow.

She fell asleep almost at once.

CHAPTER 23

Hablinger on Corcyra

"The militia field commanders have ordered their troops not to shoot without orders," Daniel said, "and Colonel Bourbon has sent the same order to all the unassigned troops. That doesn't mean the miners are going to obey him, but none of them hold positions too close to where we'll be going in."

"I don't trust the Garrison not to shoot, either," Hogg said morosely. He rubbed his nose with the back of his hand. "But hell, you can break your neck stepping off the curb."

Though Daniel wouldn't be leading, he looked over his companions with the eye of a commander. They were outside the entrance to their dugout, hidden from the Pantellarian positions a kilometer away. Hogg wore much the same shapeless clothing as usual, though like the rest of them he had pulled a gray ski-mask over his head and face. It was more to block the thermal signature than from concerns over visible light.

Tovera wore dark gray coveralls of a harder fabric than her usual garments. Her little submachine gun

342

was in a shoulder holster, looking like an awkward pistol. She wore heavy gloves to keep her hands clean for when she needed them.

A mortar thumped from Garrison lines on the other side of the river levees. "That's the signal," Hogg said. "Hide your eyes. When it burns out, we'll get moving."

Adele was the only one who needed the warning. She wore baggy coveralls over a Pantellarian officers' uniform. Even though it was service garb, its shoulder boards stuck out like the arms of a clothes hanger.

Daniel darkened his goggles manually a moment before the *pop!* high in the sky indicated the flare had burst. Fierce radiance bathed the quadrant of the battlefield centered on the Cephisis and its high levees.

"Still time to grab something a little less clumsy than that damned cannon," Hogg said, flicking a finger toward Daniel's stocked impeller.

"I figure that crawling with this—"

Daniel wiggled the weapon in the crook of his left elbow.

"—isn't as awkward as not having it handy if we need it tonight. I'll be bringing up the rear as soon as we drop Tovera off, so my problems won't slow you down."

He'd slipped a condom over the muzzle. An impeller's mechanism was pretty well sealed, but he didn't want to fire one with the barrel plugged. Nobody could swear that he wouldn't drop his weapon while crawling through this liquescent mud.

The hissing in the sky ended. For a moment a faint white afterglow shone above the levees.

"Send her on after I've got to the next dike," Hogg said. His voice sounded as though the night itself were speaking, soft and almost lilting.

He moved sideways and was gone, unrolling a coil of communication wire behind him. The free end of the wire was attached to the belt of Adele's coveralls.

Daniel watched his servant slither across the paddy. Even with his goggles' light enhancement, all he really saw were the ripples. He kept his hand lightly on Adele's shoulder.

Hogg had taught his young charge how to move in the wild. Daniel thought he was probably as good as most Land Forces soldiers with scout training. Hogg was a different order of creature, though, more like a water rat than a human.

Only because he knew it would be there, Daniel saw a brief hump slide over the top of the next dike. A field-skipper clicked three times.

"You see that light in Hablinger?" Daniel said softly. It was probably an unshaded street light reflecting off a polished roof at just the right angle. "Crawl for that. Just keep going till you hit the dike. If there's a problem—"

How in heaven's name could there be? But Adele's view of the physical world was as different from his as their views of mazes of data.

"—just follow the wire. And needs must, Hogg will come back and fetch you."

"Yes," said Adele. She hunched down and began crawling forward. She sounded like a school of redfish spawning in the shallows off Bantry, but the noise only mattered to senses as keyed up as Daniel's own. There was no danger.

"What was the sound Hogg made?" Tovera said.

Daniel twitched, startled by the words in his ear while he was completely focused on what was going on in front of him. He smiled faintly. Was Tovera nervous? *He* certainly had been.

"That was a field-skipper," he said without looking away from the paddy. "We have them on Bantry. There's an animal here, the webbed treemouse, that sounds the same, only it gives single clicks, not three in a row."

He smiled more broadly. "Now, if there's a Pantellarian out there with as much interest in natural history as I have," he said, "we might be in trouble."

"That's why you have the impeller," Tovera said. Her voice was a rasping whisper.

"I never bothered to learn to use one of those," she added after a moment. "I always figured that I'd get close enough to use what I have, or somebody else could deal with the problem. Now...maybe I should've learned."

Daniel debated what—and whether—to speak. At last he said, "We'll have to hope that one slug will do the job. It's been my experience that with these—"

He hefted the impeller slightly.

"—one usually does."

Tovera looked away, then turned to face him again. "Hogg said you're as good as he is with one of those," she said. No one would ever call Tovera's voice gentle, but this time it had less of the usual crisp edge.

"On a good day," Daniel said. He smiled and would have laughed under other circumstances. "Though on a *really* good day, we won't need to learn."

The field-skipper clicked again. "Head out," Daniel said. "Wait for me at the dike. Hogg and I hope Adele will have gone on ahead."

Tovera nodded, then slipped into the mud. She

wasn't graceful, but she crawled on her elbows and knees instead of proceeding on all fours the way Adele had done. Daniel doubted that the Fifth Bureau had trained her to low-crawl, so the technique—like driving an aircar—was something Tovera had learned on her own.

She was also extremely strong. Her pace across the paddy was as steady as a metronome's ticking. Daniel knew well how much strain low-crawling put on muscles which hadn't been habituated to the exercise.

Tovera reached the dike and vanished. Daniel followed her track, cradling the impeller in the crooks of both elbows. Tovera, who wasn't carrying a long-arm, would have been just as well off using her hands and feet; but she'd learned the "right" technique, and she was going to employ it.

The mud was messy, but it was much easier on the person crawling than gravel or even a woodland littered with outcrops and fallen limbs would have been. The rice had seeded itself raggedly, and the paddies hadn't been properly weeded or irrigated in the past year. The irregular growth was ideal for concealing somebody who knew what he was doing and didn't mind staying low.

Daniel slipped over the dike. Tovera waited on the other side like a bog-hunting predator, an unusually large one.

"Mistress has reached the next wall," she said, her voice barely a modulation of the breeze. Like Daniel himself, she wore RCN multifunction goggles. The night was very dark, but light enhancement brought out ripples in the starlight even though the body making them remained a shadow.

"We'll go on together, then," Daniel said. "The strongpoints keep a close watch on our lines but not on the rest of the landscape. Adele set their cameras to loop the same half hour from last night when we started out, but we should be safe the rest of the way without tricks."

He smiled, though his mask hid the expression from Tovera. "Some Pantellarian technicians are quite good," he said. "I told Adele that we were better depending on poor alertness and woodcraft among their line troops."

"I'll lead," said Tovera. She began crawling forward again.

Daniel gave her a ten-yard start and followed. He carefully avoided closing the gap between them so that he didn't prod Tovera to go faster than she was comfortable doing. That was quite fast enough anyway, and she hadn't slowed from the first hundred meters.

At the third dike, he paused to let Adele finish her scramble over the fourth. The field-skipper clicked again; Daniel gestured Tovera forward and again followed.

The night had its own sounds. Even neglected, the paddies provided rich foraging for small animals and the slightly larger animals which preyed on them. There were even webbed treemice, Daniel was pleased to notice.

The crawl was hard work—he couldn't pretend to be in condition for this sort of exercise—and potentially quite dangerous, but Daniel found it unexpectedly relaxing. It took him back to his childhood on Bantry, when Hogg taught him about the world of the estate's nighttime, whose population was wholly different from that of the day.

Daniel had early on begun using night-vision electronics: a pair of RCN goggles from Uncle Stacy with light-enhancement and thermal-imaging capacity. Hogg didn't forbid the hardware, but he was openly contemptuous of it, saying he could do anything goggles could and that *he* wasn't going to break down when he was ten miles deep in a swamp.

That was literally true, but Daniel hadn't had—and would never have—the forty years of experience that the older man did. Hogg was a wonderful mentor and a father figure for Daniel, but he was not a role model for civilized society.

He joined Tovera at the next dike. Because of the slight angle at which they were approaching Hogg's entry point, they had reached one of the longitudinal walls which separated the paddies every five hundred meters or so. A pair of ten-foot trees grew from this side of the long wall. Fuzzy foliage gave the crooked limbs a ghostly appearance by starlight.

Daniel dug the flare's base into the mud between the roots of the nearer tree and set the blasting cap in the fuse pocket. He handed Tovera the clacker with the fuse wire already attached.

"Suit yourself about where you hide," he said, "but they've got automatic impellers in that strongpoint and a mortar besides. The dikes will probably stop an impeller slug, and the mortars won't do much in this mud unless they fuse the shells for air burst, but I won't tell you this is going to be safe."

Tovera was probably smiling. "Then I won't tell you that you're an idiot, Captain Leary," she said.

Daniel chuckled. He gave her the end of his reel of commo wire; the ends were already split and stripped.

Then he started forward again, letting the wire uncoil behind him.

There was a long way yet to crawl. Daniel had lost the rosy swaddling of nostalgia, but the only way you accomplished a job like this was by going on, putting one foot in front of the other.

Well, one elbow in front of the other in the present case.

Daniel crawled over the next dike and paused to check for sound or movement as he always did. Adele was waiting. She slipped her pistol back into its pocket and put her glove back on.

An almost-emptied reel of commo wire sat beside her. Hogg hadn't taken it with him as he made the final approach of the listening post.

"I'm glad to see you, Adele," Daniel said very softly. "Well begun is half done, isn't it?"

A field-skipper clicked ahead of them. Adele turned her head; she must have heard it, or at any rate heard something.

"Time to move," Daniel said. He grinned. "We'll go together this time. Nobody's going to be listening ahead of us."

Adele nodded. "Yes," she said. She didn't return his smile, though.

Adele hadn't given any thought to the physical demands of reaching the enemy lines. All her concern had been for what happened *then*, after she began to do her job.

Thinking about the crawl wouldn't have changed anything—it simply had to be done, and there had been no time available for physical training. Even so, she felt foolish not to have considered a business which had pushed her so near her physical limits. She had failed herself intellectually, whether or not that made any difference in fact.

Daniel put his hand on Adele's left ankle, throwing her into an instant's nightmare in which the darkness had come alive and grabbed her. She snatched for her pistol and only smeared mud from her gloves onto the flap of the coveralls. She had been lost in a world of her own in which nothing mattered but the mechanical process of crawling forward and the intellectual analysis of that process.

She had almost fallen into the listening post. It was a small pit whose floor of plaited reeds was thick enough to keep the mud from oozing to the level of the two men now lying facedown on it and blubbering. There was also a small field telephone and a pair of electromotive shotguns, single-shot hunting weapons. The men wore loose trousers and open shirts; they had no shoes.

"They're local farmers, master," said Hogg, squatting at the back of the pit with his knife out. "I didn't much feel like cutting their throats, though if you think it'd be safer . . . ?"

"I don't believe that will be necessary, Hogg," Daniel said. They spoke in low-pitched voices; Adele could scarcely hear them. "In any case, if safety had been my primary concern, I probably wouldn't have joined the RCN, would I?"

"I have a use for them if they prefer to continue living," Adele said. By leaning over the edge of the shallow pit as Daniel was doing, the depression itself would drink her words. "For one of them, anyway."

One of the local conscripts was weeping as though he were watching his library burn. Adele smiled at her simile. His chicken coop burn, that would be better.

The other man stopped crying and even turned his head to look up at Adele. She gestured toward him and said, "I want you to call your base on the phone and say that you hear noises halfway back to the grubber lines. Can you do that? We'll let you live if you do."

The farmer nodded enthusiastically. His throat worked, but he didn't—more likely couldn't—speak.

"Nobody's going to hurt you," Adele said, letting her gray precision overcome the irritation she was feeling at this fool. Of course if the listening post had been staffed by better troops, they would be dead and she wouldn't have this opportunity to confuse the Pantellarian strongpoint.

Hogg tied the wrists of the crying man behind his back with commo wire. "Should have brought cargo tape," he said, "but I wasn't figuring on prisoners. Anyway, this'll do."

Adele removed her gloves, then began to strip off the baggy coveralls. Mud caked her knee-high officers' boots well up the shaft, but that was now part of her disguise.

"I'll do it, ma'am," the other prisoner said. "Ma'am, I got seven kids. They just marched in and says to all the men in the village, 'You come with us or you'll wish you had.' So we come, what could we do?"

It was a likely enough story, though that didn't make a real difference. Adele had shot people who were just as innocent as these fellows, people who had simply been in her way. Fine distinctions didn't matter in a war; and in the longer term, nothing in life mattered.

"Then you already understand the terms," Adele said, smiling minusculy. Hogg was binding the fellow's ankles; the fact obviously reassured the prisoner, because it meant that his captors really weren't going to slit his throat.

"Right," the farmer said. "I'll report, just like you say!"

He reached for the phone. Adele put her right hand on it. "Wait," she said. "Hogg, are we ready to go on?"

"Yep," he said without looking up. He was checking the load in one of the shotguns.

"All right," said Adele, taking her hand away. "Call now."

The farmer bent close to the phone—it didn't have a separate handset—and pressed the button between the speaker and mouthpiece. It had originally been glossy black, but in the center that was worn down to the original beige of the plastic case.

"Hello?" the fellow said. "Hello? I'm hearing stuff! The grubbers're coming, I hear 'em coming!"

"Hold one," crackled a voice from the speaker. Moments later the voice resumed, *"Post Three, are you drunk? We've got the scopes on their lines and there's nothing happening. Not a bloody thing!"*

Adele gestured to Daniel. He squeezed hard on his clacker. In the present stillness, Adele heard the miniature generator whine.

"They're coming!" the farmer repeated. He probably wasn't a very good actor, but under the circumstances his voice projected very real fear. "I hear 'em, I do!"

Adele and her companions were ducking beneath the lip of the pit so the light of the distant flare didn't silhouette them. It *did* ruin the night vision of anyone who was looking toward the glare unprotected, and it certainly attracted the attention of anyone in the strongpoint.

Tovera's submachine gun ripped out its whole magazine. It was probably the first time Tovera had fired a burst longer than three rounds in a life which had often involved using a submachine gun.

Three automatic impellers and at least a score of personal weapons blasted from the strongpoint. The slugs' aluminum skirts vaporized in the magnetic flux which drove them down the bore, flickering above the gun muzzles. The barrels of the automatic impellers began to glow.

Other Pantellarians opened fire, followed moments later by troops in the Corcyran positions. The shooting was expanding along the siege lines like a growing brushfire.

"Time to go, Mistress," Hogg said. He slipped over the back edge of the pit, and Adele followed.

CHAPTER 24

Hablinger on Corcyra

"Hey!" Hogg said in a hoarse whisper. Then more loudly, "Hey! Is this Point Three?"

"Who's that?" a man cried from the darkness ahead, his voice rising across the two syllables. "Captain! Captain! They're attacking!"

Adele touched Hogg's shoulder with her right arm to quiet him. "Phlegrya, you idiot!" she shouted. "The password is Phlegrya! Don't shoot!"

"Put your gun up, Perone," a firm voice ordered "You out there? Who are you?"

Adele and Hogg were in what had been a communication trench when it was dug. In the year or more since then, the walls of soft earth had slumped so that what was left was a muddy swale through which she had hunched along behind Hogg.

When Hogg gestured Adele down, she thought that the Pantellarians' Strongpoint Four—Hogg had said Three as part of their camouflage—was about fifty yards ahead of them. The guard's panicked response to Hogg's call had come from less than twenty feet away.

"I'm Major Tillingast," Adele said. "The commissioner, Commissioner Arnaud, sent me to see what was happening at Point Three. They said the trouble was at one of their listening posts, and this yokel they gave me for a guide dragged me through the mud instead of finding it. *Is* this Point Three?"

In order to sound frightened, she imagined that she was going to fail and let down the people who were counting on her. She hoped that the Pantellarians would think that she was worried about being killed.

"This is Point Four," the Pantellarian officer said. "Stand up so we can see you, please, Major."

"Phlegrya!" Adele repeated firmly, then rose into a half crouch. She had gone to some lengths to get a proper-fitting Pantellarian staff officer's uniform—Woetjans had tailored the garment to fit Adele's trim body. She was so muddy after this final leg of the journey that only the epaulettes and peaked cap were really identifiable, but perhaps knowing that the uniform was correct made Adele's own performance more convincing.

Besides, Woetjans had been delighted to do the work. Like most senior spacers, the bosun was an expert seamstress. Her own liberty suit, a set of utilities embellished with patches and ribbons, was a work of art.

"You can come forward, Tillingast," the voice said. "I'm Captain Danes. Sorry for the inconvenience, but with all the shooting tonight—well, you can understand that we had to be careful. Here, I'm tossing over a ladder."

Adele straightened and slogged forward. "I'm *filthy*," she said, trying to sound as though she cared. "All because some moronic yokels in a listening post panicked and started shooting at nothing, and an even greater moron dragged me through the muck instead of to the LP!"

She looked over her shoulder and mimed an angry glare. When she was really angry, her face had no expression at all, but she was acting the part of a disgusted staff officer, and she thought a scowl would be more easily believed.

Hogg carried the borrowed shotgun with the barrel in his right hand and the stock resting on his shoulder. He was chewing a rice stem. To look at him, he had no more wit than a cow and no more concern than a dead cow.

There really had been a Major Tillingast on Commissioner Arnaud's staff, but appendicitis had prevented him from accompanying the invasion force. Arnaud had assigned him to logistics duties on Pantellaria instead of bringing him to Corcyra when he recovered. If Captain Danes had happened to know the real man, Adele would have become his sister.

The strongpoint was built of air-hardening nets formed into double walls two meters apart. The doughnut was then pumped full of mud from the interior of the position. The result would stop small-arms' projectiles and was impervious to energy weapons. Real artillery would scatter the dried mud, but the explosion wouldn't fling lethal splinters around the way as it would from a rock sangar.

Trying to climb the meter-high wall would have been a problem for Adele—and for most of the staff officers whom she'd met—so the rope ladder with wooden battens tossed from the inside where it was anchored was welcome. Hogg could doubtless have boosted her over, but he might have thought verisimilitude required that he pitch her some distance beyond.

Adele's minuscule smile was perhaps less grim than it usually was. Hogg, like Daniel and like Adele herself, was a perfectionist.

She slid down the inside onto a firing step; she would have plunged another several feet to the ground if the Pantellarian captain hadn't caught her arm. Hogg mounted the wall behind her, using the butt of the shotgun as a pole to brace himself. He looked clumsy, but Adele noticed that the weapon's muzzle never pointed at his body.

"I swear we'd be better off not to have recruited these rubes!" Adele said to Danes. He was a short man with sad eyes; his name ribbon was unreadable for mud and fading. "We'd be better off never to have come to this filthy place. Let the grubbers have it!"

"You won't get an argument from me," the captain said. "Do you want a guide to Point Three? Though I warn you, you'd be better off going back into Hablinger and taking the axial road out."

"I'm going into Hablinger," Adele snapped. "And if Arnaud wants to send somebody out again, he can wake up Kaspary! *I'm* going to take a shower."

"Perone," the captain said to one of the half-dozen soldiers standing nearby, "guide the major to the gate and make sure she gets through."

To Adele he added, "You won't have any trouble following the road, though there's a couple places where the mud's over the flooring."

"Tell me something I *don't* know," Adele said. "Come along, Hogg. I'm going to see if the commissioner can't find a more suitable task for you. Like becoming a piling!"

She and Hogg followed the slack-jawed Perone across the interior of the strongpoint. Tent ropes and piled equipment encroached on the path.

So far, so good.

Daniel lay near the listening post, beside the line by which Tovera was approaching. He was in a reverie of the sort familiar from his childhood, when he used to lie in the woods of Bantry and become part of the night.

It was a different experience from hunting, though an outsider wouldn't have been able to distinguish the two. When Daniel hunted, his stillness was that of a coiled spring—a preliminary to action. Now he was a pool of water which simply exists and absorbs.

A many-legged lizard scuttled over Daniel's right glove without noticing that he was any different from the matted rice stems and weeds on which he lay. Several of the tiny feet touched his bare index finger, light as so many hairs; the fingertip rested on the trigger of his impeller.

Tovera crawled past, focused on the listening post. In normal human terms she was very quiet. As she reached the lip of the LP, Daniel whispered, "All clear."

Tovera paused, then very slowly turned her head. She was staring down the muzzle of the impeller which until then had been aimed at the back of her skull. After a few heartbeats of consideration, she giggled. The sound was that of a peevish insect.

Daniel twitched his impeller slightly to the side. "You're in my country now," he said.

"Yes," said Tovera. "I appreciate what that means, now."

"The two locals are tied up in the LP," Daniel said. "We can talk quietly out here, if you wish."

He didn't know what Tovera wished, what Tovera thought, what Tovera felt, if she felt anything. The only thing he was sure about Tovera was that he couldn't fathom her mental processes. Well, that and the fact that she would probably hit whatever she shot at.

"I decided to come forward," she said. "We hadn't arranged for that, so I decided to come quietly so that you wouldn't hear a rustle and shoot at the sound."

Daniel smiled, though his mask hid the expression. "I wouldn't have shot because I heard a sound," he said.

"No," said Tovera. "You wouldn't."

She licked her thin lips and said, "Hogg told me you were a decent woodsman. I didn't have a context for what he said. I do now."

"Hogg is better," Daniel said. "Much better. Adele is in good hands."

A webbed treemouse clicked nearby, but only once. It was part of Corcyra's natural world.

"What would you do," Tovera said, "if the mistress was killed in Hablinger?"

Daniel considered the question. He didn't say that he hoped that wouldn't happen, because Tovera knew that. *Everyone* knew that.

"I would gather data," he said. "And then I would respond appropriately."

He wasn't avoiding the question. He was giving the most truthful answer he could. Daniel didn't have enough information to precisely predict his reaction.

Tovera nodded. "I'd go in there," she said, making a tiny gesture toward the Pantellarian camp by crooking her left index finger. "And I'd kill everyone I saw. I would keep killing them until they killed me. There wouldn't be a place for me in the universe without Lady Mundy."

She could have been reading a grocery list for the sign of anything more serious in her voice. The words were all the more terrible for the lack of emotion or emphasis in her tone.

Again, Daniel thought. Then he said, "I'd give you a home if anything happened to Adele. For her sake, of course; but your services to me and to the RCN have earned you that consideration."

Tovera giggled again. "You think I'm a dangerous insect," she said.

Daniel patted his impeller's receiver with the pad of his right index finger. "I think this is dangerous," he said. "But I don't think it's going to randomly kill me or mine, and I don't think you would either."

He didn't address the "insect" comment. He wasn't going to tell Tovera a lie; especially not an obvious lie.

"Thank you," Tovera said. "Lady Mundy has taught me to thank people who offer me help. But all the same, I think I'd try to kill everyone in Hablinger."

Daniel considered the situation. "I think . . ." he said slowly. "I think that after I've gathered data . . . I might very well decide to join you."

Something clicked in the night. It was just a tree-mouse.

"When we go around this corner," Hogg said, swinging his shotgun butt forward to indicate the angle in the communication trench, "there's the gate. And we'll be looking down the muzzle of an automatic impeller."

He spat and added, "Mind, with this lot I'm not saying that anybody'll be manning the gun."

Adele stepped past him and paused, just out of sight of the entrance to the Pantellarian base. "Phlegrya!" she called. "Phlegrya! Major Tillingast returning from reconnaissance!"

"Solfatara," a youthful male voice replied, giving the response after a noticeable delay. "Come forward, Tillingast."

Adele walked briskly around the angle. As satellite imagery had shown, the trench mouth was blocked not by a gate but rather by three baffles welded from braced rectangles of pipe. Barbed wire wrapped the barriers. Anyone entering the camp would have to step around them under the muzzle of an automatic weapon, just as Hogg had said.

The man who had called was in the gunpit with the impeller's crew. He wore goggles which, Pantellarian optics being what they were, were probably as good as RCN issue. An identical pair rested on Adele's forehead, but she hadn't brought them down lest the gunner's finger twitch when a masked figure approached. She scarcely needed light amplification to follow the trench, and the lack of depth perception meant that goggles wouldn't help to judge how deep the potholes were.

Some of the potholes were knee-deep. She had proven that by experience.

"Ah, sir?" the young officer said. "We weren't told to expect any scouts tonight?"

"I'm not a bloody scout," Adele said as she walked—slogged; her boots were caked with mud—toward and past the gunpit. "I'm on Commissioner Arnaud's staff, and this local *moron*"—she glared at Hogg—"has taken me on a tour of every mudhole on this bloody *planet*!"

Hogg stood blank-faced, chewing on his rice stem. He looked as though he could be on the other side of the planet for all the attention he paid the people around him.

Adele breathed hard, and her thighs ached. The trench had risen steadily from the strongpoint to the outer edge of Hablinger. Some of the elevation came by ramps, but steps had been cut at many points in the zigzag course. Ordinarily climbing stairs didn't bother Adele, but at present the layers of mud trebled the weight of her boots.

"Ah, should we report your arrival, Major?" the Pantellarian officer called as Adele and Hogg walked toward the city park where Arnaud's headquarters was supposed to be.

"Do as you please!" Adele said without turning her head. "I'm not going to report until I've gotten a bath and some sleep. There's nothing *to* report. It was just numbskulls shooting at shadows!"

If the fellow did try to call back on the post's landline, the headquarters commo computer would dump the message into a suspense file accessible only by the off-planet Major Tillingast. They might try radio after the landline failed, but at this hour of the night the worst result would be confusion left for an officer to puzzle out in the morning.

When Adele and Hogg were behind the first line of tenements and out of sight of the guard post, Hogg said, "Let me get the big chunks off your boots, mistress."

He snicked open his knife and used the back of

the blade to shave mud from the boots. The false edge was sharpened, but Adele never felt the tug of steel on the leather.

Great chunks fell off. *As though he were skinning me*, Adele thought. The thought made her smile.

"How do you figure to get in to see Arnaud?" Hogg said without looking up from his task. "He'll have guards, and there's a company at least billeted in the park with his trailer. I looked at the satellite stuff."

"The same way we got this far," Adele said. "I'll claim to be an officer whom Arnaud had summoned from Point Three to see what was going on."

"That's a way," Hogg said. Adele realized that he was deliberately avoiding eye contact while he disagreed with her. "Another way would be if something happened to get all the wogs running around while you waltzed into the tailer and nobody noticed you."

If the diversion doesn't work, I can still try to bluff, Adele thought expressionlessly. Aloud she said, "All right, Hogg. What do you want me to do?"

"Just go on like you're planning to do," he said, straightening and wiping the knife before he put it away. He grinned. "I don't figure anybody'll notice us while we walk through the camp. You go up to the squad on guard and start talking to them like it's where you're supposed to be. When something pops, just wait and duck in the door of the trailer."

Adele smiled faintly. *It's none of my business what he plans to do, so I won't waste time by asking him.*

"All right," she repeated. "That's the park in the block ahead, I believe."

The park was covered with tents in good order. The side-ropes interlocked, but there were proper aisles at the front and back of each row. Adele saw a few stumps; the trees had probably been cut down for firewood.

At least a score of men sat outside their tents, talking and smoking a drug of some sort. When they noticed that Adele wore an officer's uniform they generally made a vague effort to cup their short pipes in the hollow of their hands, thus concealing them. Adele ignored the soldiers, as they clearly expected her to do.

The squad on guard in front of Arnaud's small trailer was commanded by a noncom. An air conditioner whirred from the back of the trailer; curtains were drawn over the pair of windows flanking the door.

The guards didn't notice Adele until she was well into the three-meter space left clear around the trailer. Even then their only concern appeared to be that the strange officer would start shouting orders.

"Commissioner Arnaud ordered me to report immediately about the attack on Point Three," Adele said briskly. "He's expecting—"

There was a hollow *boom!* Adele jerked her head around. A roof of structural plastic flapped into the air. Several of the guards threw themselves on the ground, and there was confused babble from them and the camp generally.

The effluvium of half-rotted human excrement reached the trailer, making Adele's eyes water. No one was watching her. She turned the latch and stepped into Arnaud's trailer, closing the door after her. She switched on the lights.

The pajama-clad man stepping out of the bedroom matched the images of Arnaud in general outline, but he had aged a decade since the most recent. That one had been captured within the year. He blinked at her.

"Good evening, Commissioner Arnaud," Adele said. "Are we alone?" She gestured toward the door through which he'd come. She'd had no way to check as to whether he was sharing his bed with a companion—or a harem, for that matter. It didn't matter in the longer term, since any negative consequences of their conversation getting out would be his problem.

"What? Yes, we're alone," Arnaud said, his voice strengthening. "Who are you and what in *hell* is going on?"

This half of the trailer was an office with a fully capable console and a lesser machine in what appeared to be a secretary's alcove. The larger console wasn't netted into the camp's system, but Adele hoped that the data unit in her pocket was linking with it now that they were in close proximity.

"My guess as to your second question," Adele said, "is that my colleague dropped a grenade into the camp latrine. As to your first—I'm the representative of Bantry Holdings. You sent for me."

The chairs were of the standard office variety, as straight and stiff as those of a warship. Adele turned one to face Arnaud and sat in it, then took out her data unit and its control wands.

"I didn't expect..." Arnaud said. He sat in the other chair near the console, then wriggled to face her. "How did you get into the camp? I was expecting a radio message!"

Adele sniffed, her eyes on the data unit's display. "Then you're a fool," she said. "Senator Leary isn't a man who would entrust treasonous communications to a commercial code which any child with basic math could break if he spent the time."

Arnaud frowned. With an edge in his voice he said, "Bantry Holdings used the code in the past."

"The people who used the code no longer work for Bantry Holdings," Adele said, still without looking up. Her wands danced. "Now, stop wasting time and state your proposal."

"All right, that's simple enough," Arnaud said. He was rattled by the situation, and Adele's deliberate contempt kept him from taking charge of his emotions. "Daniel Leary is on Corcyra, Senator Leary's son and quite a figure in his own right. I want him to announce that he's arrived as representative of the Senate and that Cinnabar is supporting our claim, Pantellaria's claim, to control of Corcyra under the Treaty of Amiens. He can say that a Cinnabar task force is on the way."

"Indeed?" Adele said, meeting Arnaud's angry glare. "Bantry Holdings rejects your proposal."

"Do you now?" Arnaud said, leaning forward. "Well, you can just expect full particulars of Leary's dealings with me during the war to be published—on Cinnabar as well as Pantellaria, and on Pleasaunce, too, just to be on the safe side!"

"Yes, that would be one way of proceeding," Adele said. "If you'll bring up your computer, however—"

She nodded toward the console beside her rather than gesturing, because she had a wand in either hand.

"—you'll find my counterproposal. Apart from possible benefits to Bantry Holdings and its shareholders—"

Her smile was as cold and hard as a crack in ice.

"—you'll find it makes you a military hero as well as returning Corcyra to Pantellarian control."

"I don't . . ." Arnaud said, but he let his voice trail

off as he walked around the console and sat on its couch. The unit came up, finally giving Adele the access she needed. The series of files which she had prepared and queued now transferred automatically.

"This will allow you to capture Brotherhood, the only starport in Corcyran hands," Adele said. "That cuts the independence movement off from their source of weapons and money."

She felt enormous relief. No matter what happened next, she had carried out her mission for Deirdre Leary. That removed any possibility that this business would lead to a resumption of war between Cinnabar and the Alliance. There was still Mistress Sand's concern about her son, but—

Adele's smile was again a tiny glint in ice.

—properly that was Daniel's mission, not her own. And in any case, one thing at a time.

"Ships don't need a port to land at," Arnaud said slowly. His primary attention was on the console's display. "They don't even need water."

"Some ships don't," Adele said. "The sort of ships and crews which are willing to make smuggling runs into Corcyra need something better than dry gullies, though. When you take Brotherhood, the rebels are isolated. Furthermore, if you follow up the capture by attacking the siege lines both with your ships and on the ground, you'll end the whole revolt."

Arnaud shrank the holographic display so that he could look directly at Adele. She turned her head to meet his gaze.

"Brotherhood has missile batteries," Arnaud said. Though he was trying to sound dismissive, a note of hope had crept into his voice. "This plan says I'm to hop troops from here to Brotherhood using my ships. They'll be massacred by missiles."

"Captain Leary's vessel is in Brotherhood Harbor," Adele said. "When your ships lift, the two missile batteries will become nonfunctional. Captain Leary won't act until you're actually on the way so that the Corcyrans won't have time to recapture the batteries."

"By heaven," Arnaud said. "By *heaven*."

"Colonel Bourbon is in command of the independence forces again," Adele said. She spoke without emotion; but then, she almost always spoke without emotion. "He plans to capture Hablinger by a nighttime assault before the missiles from Karst arrive. You know about the antiship missiles, I presume?"

"Yes," Arnaud said bitterly. "But from my own sources on Pantellaria. The Council didn't see fit to inform me of the approaches they'd received from Ischia."

Adele nodded. "Bourbon believes that he can save the considerable cost of the missiles by taking you unaware," she said. "He'll shortly bring all the troops from Brotherhood here to the siege lines, which will make it easy for you to capture the harbor. Bourbon's first action will be to withdraw the units at present around Hablinger to refit them, though."

"If what you tell me is true," Arnaud said, "then we've won. *I've* won."

"In about two weeks," Adele said, getting to her feet and putting the data unit away. "Perhaps less. I'm told that it will take you that long to get prepared, so you can't even consider it a delay."

She turned toward the door. "Mistress?" Arnaud said. Adele looked back over her shoulder.

"Mistress," Arnaud said, "who told you how long

it would take us to prepare our attack? This is not
your plan?"

"No," said Adele. "It's the plan of Captain Daniel
Leary. Corder Leary's son, you'll remember. When
you threatened the Leary family, you brought a very
good tactician into a provincial game."

She touched the latch, then looked at Arnaud again.
"I'll contact you within forty-eight hours with more
details," she said. "I'm leaving an icon on your display.
When the message arrives, open the icon and transfer
the file I've sent to the file which you've opened. It
will be decoded there."

Adele closed the door behind her and started back
through the camp. No one in the squad on guard
spoke to her, but she felt their eyes follow her into
the tents.

Hogg joined Adele when she was out of sight of
the trailer and its guards. He didn't speak.

"We'll return by way of Point Three," she said.
"They have orders to pass us through without asking
any questions."

"Arnaud gave us a pass?" Hogg said. "I guess things
worked out okay, then."

He'd been concerned, Adele realized. Though he'd
given no sign of that while the situation was in doubt.

*Of course he'd given no sign of being worried.
He's Daniel's man.*

"Commissioner Arnaud's console gave us a pass,
Hogg," Adele said. "I didn't want to bother him with
something so minor."

Her mind was working on other things, now. There
was a great deal yet to do before she and Daniel
ended the war.

CHAPTER 25

Outside Hablinger on Corcyra

Daniel wished he could have found a quieter alternative for the temporary headquarters than the back of an air-cushioned truck, but there wasn't one if the command group remained near the siege lines. There were arguments for moving the command group much farther back, but there were no arguments that Daniel himself would have accepted even if the other members were willing.

"Look, what are we waiting for?" said Administrator Tibbs, who *certainly* would have been willing to evacuate the command group. She wasn't exactly wringing her hands, but seemed to be trying to strangle her attaché case's handle.

Daniel smiled, though he looked up into the night sky rather than directing his amusement toward Tibbs, the real cause of his amusement. *She can't have understood how dangerous this really is or she'd still be back in Brotherhood.*

"We're waiting for an hour before dawn," Colonel Bourbon said. "The time we set for the operation."

"That's only five minutes!" said Tibbs. "What difference would five minutes make?"

"Quite a lot of difference for the troops out there, since we told them 4:43!" snapped Lieutenant Angelotti. Colonel Bourbon had done a good job of hiding his frustration with the Regiment's civilian head, but the naval lieutenant was younger and probably less politic by nature. "Jumping the gun puts their lives at risk. A lot of them are probably still in their dugouts!"

Tibbs grimaced, but she held her tongue instead of saying "Who cares about those scum?" or words to that effect. Angelotti might have slapped Tibbs if she had.

Daniel's smile hardened. *Indeed, I might have slapped her; but probably not.*

"I don't guess it'd make much difference," said one of the miners morosely. He took a long pull from the liter bottle which he and his companions had been passing among themselves since they arrived. "Us folk don't pay a lot of attention to what townies say, and we *bloody* sure don't take orders from townies."

The miners' representatives this morning weren't the trio which Daniel had met when he arrived at the siege lines five days earlier. These were all males and much of a type: thin-faced, wiry, and shorter than Daniel's own five feet nine inches. They looked similar enough that they might have been grandfather, son, and grandson—they ranged from an apparent twenty to sixty—but from conversation, Daniel doubted they were related.

"They'll be buried if they *don't* listen," said Angelotti. "And anyway, nobody gave them orders. It was just a warning."

Angelotti was keyed up, though it wasn't clear

whether she was goaded by fear—she *did* understand the danger—or by hopeful anticipation. She was able to do her duty either way, Daniel supposed; and besides, she had nothing to do except be present. None of them really had anything to do.

The youngest miner turned and spat over the side of the truck. Spitting outward may have been an afterthought, which Daniel appreciated. Eight people standing in the back of a one-tonne vehicle didn't leave a great deal of open floor.

"This soft dirt?" the miner said. "Why, that's nothing! You ought to see a cave-in back where we come from."

"Anyhow," said the oldest miner, "I guess it's their business."

You couldn't dig any depth into the Delta's rich black soil without having the excavation collapse. The miners had simply adapted the system they used in their own tunnels to the situation: they used screw clamps to roll sheets of structural plastic into tubes—the diameter differed depending on the size of the sheet, but usually two meters—and welded the join. As they advanced the tunnel, they shoved the tube deeper and added segments at the surface end in the fashion of a well casing.

If a rock layer shifted it could flatten the tube, but the plastic was sturdy enough to withstand the more common problem of a flake—which might weigh tons— spalling off the tunnel roof. The sheets and forming equipment were available in quantity because they were in general use throughout the pro-independence territories.

Under most conditions the plastic liners kept the besiegers' dugouts here safe and even dry. Conditions were about to change; but as the miner had said, that was the business of the people who were at risk if they ignored the warning.

Bourbon hugged himself and grimaced. "If the Pantellarians knew that we've moved three quarters of our strength back," he said, "they'd attack."

"They won't attack," Daniel said. He cleared his throat while he decided how to phrase the next comment. "Officer Mundy would have given us plenty of warning—days of warning—if there were any chance of them attacking. We're talking about the Pantellarians here, you'll recall."

"I don't see how she can be sure of that," said Tibbs, "but there's only minutes to go. If the mine goes off, at least. What happens—"

She looked up at the others in the truck bed. Her expression had gone from peevishly nervous to sudden concern.

"—if something goes wrong with that? What do we do then?"

"There shouldn't be any problem with the mine, mistress," Brother Graves said. He sounded so calmly certain that his tone alone banished doubt. "It's quite a straightforward operation, something I've done hundreds of times. Many of the others involved have laid thousands of charges."

"You got that bloody right!" said the young miner. "Look, honey, if I thought you knew your job half as good as we know ours, I wouldn't be near so worried about all this circus."

"I think everybody here is competent," Graves said, again damping a nervous exchange with his powerful calm. "And most important, I think Captain Leary and his staff are competent. You—"

He nodded to the miners.

"—and I had nothing to do but execute the captain's orders. I'm confident that we've done so ably."

Daniel had brought Graves here not as the Transformationist representative—Heimholz remained in charge of the sect's field force—but because he was an engineer. Corcyra's miners worked in hard rock, and few if any had any better notion of how to tunnel in the Delta environment than a boy at the beach would.

Graves had used one of the drainage pumps as an excavator, carving the silt away with high-pressure water. By sloping the entrance tunnel at a slight downward angle, the tailings flowed back and cleaned the work face without additional effort.

The only trick had been reducing the nozzle from fifteen centimeters to two centimeters to keep the stream sufficiently precise. Controlling the hose required six husky miners, and the teams had to be replaced every few minutes. There were plenty of men and several women available.

Besides, it made the miners feel good about their place in the independence movement. Miners had from the first provided most of manpower, but because of their individualism and lack of structure they hadn't been involved in planning. *Couldn't* be involved in planning, but miners tended to think that outsiders from off-planet were keeping them in the dark out of contempt.

Daniel's smile became wry. There was a degree of truth to the miners' belief, of course. People were complicated and generally further from perfect than one sometimes wished.

"Something's funny, Leary?" Colonel Bourbon said.

"I was thinking that I wouldn't have much place in a perfect universe," Daniel said truthfully. "And that if all women were perfect ladies, I would have had a great deal less fun. But now to work, I think."

Smiling broadly, Daniel keyed the portable communications unit clamped to the back of the truck's cab. In speaker mode, he said, "*Kiesche*, this is Six. Report your status, please, over."

The others in the back of the vehicle were staring at him. Lieutenant Angelotti pursed her lips and murmured, "Can the Pantellarians listen to that?"

"No," said Graves without taking his eyes off Daniel.

Adele set this up so that we're actually using the satellite link through Pantellarian headquarters, Daniel thought. The Pantellarians were intercepting and perhaps decoding ordinary independence communications, but they weren't checking their own.

He didn't say that aloud, because the others wouldn't have found it reassuring. Besides, this wasn't the time to discuss communications security with laymen.

Daniel rapped his knuckles on the roof of the cab to get the attention of the driver, a sergeant from the Regiment. It was their truck. Hogg sat beside him.

"Ammings," he said, bending close to the open window into the cab. "Bring us up to full power. Hover if you can. And get ready for one hell of a ride."

The intake flow built to a roar, and a bearing began to sing. *The motor doesn't have to survive long,* Daniel thought at the back of his mind, *but I sure hope it's got another few minutes.* Aloud he said, "Colonel Bourbon, would you push the button, please?"

"Not me, Leary," Bourbon said. "This was your plan. You do the honors."

Daniel thought, then smiled again. The obvious person to set off the charge was Brother Graves, but though the Transformationist was too nice a person to react to an insult, it certainly would be an insult to a man who strove for peace.

Instead, Daniel gestured to the eldest of the miners and said, "Sir, I think that the people who did the work should have any honor there is going. Will you press the button, please?"

I wish I'd heard his name.

The miner handed the bottle to one of his colleagues and took the necessary step forward to the communications unit. He looked suddenly diffident. He reached out, then looked questioningly at Daniel.

"*Kiesche,*" Daniel said. "This is Six. Wait one, over."

He pointed to the miner and dipped his finger. The older man thrust down forcefully on the EXECUTE button.

Daniel couldn't see what happened to the course of the river a mile closer to the Pantellarian positions because the truck was behind an angle of the levee, but he did see the enormous gout of mud and muddy water lift into the sky. An instant later the shockwave arrived through the ground, bouncing the truck like a tennis ball.

Five seconds later the deafening roar swept over them, but by then that was old news.

Brotherhood on Corcyra

Adele had realtime imagery of Hablinger in the center, but most of her display was given over to the commo threads she was following. Events in Hablinger would affect her, but she couldn't affect *them*. She preferred to give her attention to things she could do something about.

"Kiesche, *this is Six*," said the console. It was the signal they were waiting for. "*Report your status please, over.*"

"*Six, this is Five*," said Vesey. "*All is according to plan, over.*"

Adele was at the back of the *Kiesche's* console; Vesey was on the command seat. Adele was aware that Pasternak had lighted the thrusters, but only because the plasma exhaust put a buzz across the radio-frequency spectrum. Her equipment filtered it out, but the buzz was a factor in her conscious universe which the ship's physical vibration was not. Adele's body might have been aware of being shaken, but her mind was where she lived.

"*Lady Mundy*," said Vesey, using a two-way link. "*Is it all right if I talk to you, over?*"

The first response that went through Adele's mind was, "I'm busy, you idiot! I'm busy trying to keep Daniel from being killed!"

Adele heard the words mentally before they reached her tongue, fortunately, and the shock of embarrassment brought her to her senses. It was as unlikely that anything she was doing at the moment would matter to the Hablinger operation as it was that a meteorite would plunge from the sky and destroy the console at which she was working. To imagine otherwise was staggering arrogance, *disgusting* arrogance.

"Yes, of course, Captain," Adele said. "Is there something in particular that I should be looking for? Over."

"*No,*" said Vesey. "*Lady Mundy—*"

"*Officer* Mundy," Adele said, correcting the ship's captain in a fashion that she wouldn't have dared to do if she hadn't been "Lady Mundy" in her mind as well as in Vesey's. She smiled like a sphinx. But whenever possible Adele followed RCN protocol.

Whenever I think of it, I follow protocol. Which wasn't as often as one might wish, but there wasn't a problem so long as she served under Daniel, and Adele could not imagine serving in the RCN under anyone except Daniel.

"*Officer, Adele,*" Vesey said. "*Please, I need to talk to you. To someone who understands and who'll be honest, which is you alone on this planet. I need advice, over.*"

"Go ahead," Adele said. *Perhaps I am Lady Mundy today, after all.*

"*Should I turn over command to Cory?*" Vesey said baldly. "*He's a fighting officer—you know what I mean. Tell me!*"

"No, you should not," Adele said. "Captain Leary put you in command in his absence. I trust his judgment on such matters, and so should you."

Because of the circumstances, Adele's eyes were on the Hablinger siege lines. A tiny ripple crossed the image every few minutes, rather like an extremely slow raster scan. The signals were being sent from tramp freighters whose optics were mediocre by naval standards, even when the signals were sharpened by the *Kiesche*'s top-of-the-line console.

The Independence Council had sequestered three blockade runners and sent them into orbit under Spacer Hale and two lieutenants from the Corcyran navy—officers superfluous to the *Freccia*'s present needs. It wasn't a surprise that the Pantellarian exiles ran heavily to officers rather than common spacers, nor that those officers had been unwilling to give up their ranks the way Cazelet had done.

Corcyra no longer had any imaging satellites. Both sides had made them targets as soon as the Pantellarian expeditionary force arrived, apparently for no better reason than that it was fun to destroy things. This wasn't a war of movement in which orbital reconnaissance might be crucial.

The Pantellarians would probably send up destroyers to deal with the Corcyrans eventually, but the observation ships had lifted off from Brotherhood only an hour before the critical moment. No officer in the Pantellarian squadron was going to get out of bed before dawn simply because three blockade runners were loitering in orbit.

"I'm not Six, mistress!" Vesey said.

"No, you're not," Adele said calmly. *You should be very glad that you're not. The only thing worse might be to be me.* "You're a known quantity to Daniel, however."

She used the given name to emphasize subconsciously that the words were coming from Captain Leary's friend and confidante. This was in many ways identical to interrogation. Adele was listening to what the other party said and tailoring her responses to bring the other party to the state of mind she herself desired.

In this particular case, that was what Vesey probably desired also, but that didn't matter. What mattered was that an officer on whom Daniel was counting would function efficiently. That was Adele's duty.

"If Daniel had thought Cory or Hale or *I* should be in charge, he would have appointed that person," Adele said, her voice as mechanically precise as a metronome. "He knows what sort of actions will be required in the next few minutes, and he knows how you are likely to perform those actions. That's what he wants."

Adele smiled, though she wasn't certain that her version of the expression would look reassuring. Still, Vesey should know her by now.

"In any case," Adele said, "I believe that you'll do just as well as anyone else, Daniel included, if it becomes necessary for the *Kiesche* to fight a Pantellarian destroyer."

Vesey's miniature image looked out from Adele's display. *"Yes,"* she said, nodding. *"I would. I'd ram them."*

Adele hadn't expected an answer to her joke, and she certainly hadn't expected *that* answer. "Then I presume," she said with a broader smile than previously, "that you now understand why Captain Leary put you in charge in his absence."

"Kiesche, this is Six," Daniel said through the console. *"Wait one, over."*

"Ship, this is Five," said Vesey on the general push. *"Action stations."*

The crew was already at action stations, to the degree there was anything of the sort on a tramp freighter. Personnel who had no duties on liftoff were in their bunks gripping sidearms and such other weapons as they fancied.

The hatch was closed. The ship groaned as Pasternak began reeling up the intake hose. It had been drawing water from the harbor to replenish the reaction mass which the idling thrusters converted into plasma while the *Kiesche* waited in her slip.

On a whim, Adele expanded the image of the Hablinger region on her display instead of returning to communications duties. Anything critical would appear as a text crawl at the bottom of her display.

I'm more worried than I realized. Worried about Daniel.

She was using light amplification with enhanced contrast rather than thermal imaging. The River Cephisis was a brown glitter curving back and forth through paddies which were a mixture of black and green. During the day a shadow bordered the levee on the side away from the sun, but now before dawn the high earthen banks blended into the fields below.

The hundred feet of channel nearest the Pantellarian lines swelled like the surface of a swamp when a bubble rises through it. The swelling burst outward. Its center dimpled down into a crater, but ripples continued to spread. The initial wavefront must have been twenty feet high as it coursed across the soft ground. All it left behind was a flat of mud which continued to tremble.

The river drained with the steady swiftness of sunrise, eating away the ends of the severed levees in its tumbling rush. The silt which had built the bottom of the channel a dozen feet above the plain had no mechanical strength to resist the powerful flow. The blast had homogenized all the soil in the path of the shockwave, but the sheet of water spread a luster over it.

"*Is Six all right?*" Vesey said. "*Were they clear? I didn't know what that was going to do!*"

Adele raised her display's magnification. For a

moment she couldn't find the truck which held the command group—

I didn't know what the blast was going to do, either!

—but then she cued the console to highlight movement. There was the truck, still right-side up and racing directly away from the Cephisis. Adele would have had to raise magnification further to be sure that Daniel was still in the vehicle, but for now she could assume he was safe.

The truck had been a mile from the charge and inside one of the channel's slow curves. As it expanded the explosion crater, the shockwave liquefied several miles of levee. A suspension of mud and water slumped onto the plain. Instead of providing shelter, the earthen walls had almost flowed over the truck and buried it.

The miners had used the same explosive that they did to shatter rock: ammonium nitrate doped with fuel oil to sensitize it. They had said that it was perfectly safe, and Daniel had calmly agreed.

In checking, Adele found that the farmers in the Delta used the same material as fertilizer. At some level, she seemed to have assumed that the explosion wouldn't be very impressive.

The detonation of tens of tons of ammonium nitrate was impressive. In this finely divided silt, the devastation looked like the result of a meteor strike.

Strongpoint 3 had vanished. The earth had opened, not in a crack but by losing cohesion. It had sucked in the troops Adele had deluded a few days earlier.

She thought about the peasants Hogg had spared in the listening post. If they had gone back to the same duty, they were dead now; if not, their replacements were dead.

Everyone dies. I will die.

South of the Pantellarian positions, pink tubes of structural plastic rolled to the surface of the mud and rolled back under again—the linings of the dugouts of independence forces. The troops within a mile of the explosion had been withdrawn, but Adele suspected not even the miners themselves had guessed how far the effect of the blast would travel through the rice paddies.

Troops who had climbed out of their dugouts as they'd been warned to do would probably be all right: they might have been flung high in the air, but they would come down on a surface more yielding than an air cushion. Those who had remained under cover would at best have been battered against the inside of the dugouts and would probably have been buried as well.

Everyone dies.

"*Look! Look!*" Vesey said. "*They did it! Captain Leary did it!*"

Rather than try to guess what Vesey was talking about, Adele mirrored the command display on the left half of her own. Vesey was focused on Hablinger Pool, the shallow impoundment north of the town. It was the harbor for the Delta, holding at present four freighters similar to those in Brotherhood as well as the six Pantellarian destroyers.

The water had drained back from the pool, and the ships floating there had dropped into the mud. Into the quicksand, more accurately. They fell so suddenly that the muck flowed into any open hatch that dove into it. Unlike water, the mud clung to surfaces, holding the vessels down and continuing to pour into their hulls.

Even as Adele watched, a destroyer rolled onto its side when its starboard pontoon had filled and continued to sink, dragging the ship with it. The crew must have removed access plates so that they could work on the float's interior.

Another destroyer was stern-down, and none of them looked quite *right* as they rested on the quivering brown surface. Humans were crawling out of hatches, but they had nowhere to go: the boarding bridges had sunk when the earthshock lifted and dropped them.

"Even the ones that aren't sinking will have clogged their thrusters, let alone the throats of their High Drives!" Vesey crowed. Adele didn't remember her ever before sounding so excited. *"And if their pumps were on, they've blown out or burned out from trying to suck mud into their tanks. It'd take the* Sissie *a week to repair damage like that! And these are Pantellarians, not RCN!"*

"Then," said Adele, suddenly relaxed, "it's time for me to act."

She keyed two separate switches, the electronic equivalent of a caged mechanical control. There was no real likelihood that Adele would throw a switch unintentionally, but she was a librarian: she preferred not to take chances, even when they weren't really chances.

"Commissioner Arnaud, this is Lady Mundy," she said. "I am speaking on behalf of Independent Corcyra."

Her words were being reproduced through the Pantellarian emergency net on every audio or text device in Hablinger. Arnaud was not being given the choice of keeping this ultimatum a secret from his personnel, though he probably wouldn't realize that until after Adele was done.

"Independent Corcyra offers you and all personnel of the Pantellarian Expeditionary Force the opportunity to surrender on honorable terms and to be repatriated to Pantellaria," Adele said.

The console speaker relayed her words to everyone aboard the *Kiesche*. Cory was sending an alert to independence forces in Brotherhood, and the *Freccia* was lighting her thrusters. Captain Samona had brought all his personnel aboard during the night, but he had obeyed Daniel's orders not to take visible actions which could warn Arnaud.

"You have twelve hours to accept this offer," Adele said. "After that time, independence forces will resume actions to remove the invaders from Corcyra."

She paused, then said, "I must warn you that the additional mines placed under Pantellarian positions have antitamper devices. If you attempt to remove them, you will cause the loss of life which we in the independence coalition hope to avoid. It would be a pity to kill thousands of people, many of them civilians, on the verge of a peaceful resolution."

Adele broke the signal and leaned back on the couch with her eyes closed. It was a moment before she understood that the crew of the *Kiesche* was cheering.

Cheering her and Daniel.

CHAPTER 26

Outside Hablinger on Corcyra

Adele was familiar with the odor of swamps. She had landed on many swampy locations since she began accompanying Daniel Leary; and indeed, Bantry's marshes—the water flowed there, although slowly—were a very similar environment. The smell of this warm, wet air circulating through the *Kiesche*'s open hatches was unique in her experience, however.

It wasn't uniquely bad, exactly—though when Adele actually thought about the stench, it was pretty bad— but it was certainly unique. She hadn't particularly noticed it when they landed six hours ago, but it had become more insistent now that the sun was down. It probably had to do with the way the explosion had stirred and homogenized the soil.

"They've stabilized the *Borea* by lashing her to the *Nembo* and a freighter, so she isn't going to sink completely after all," said Cory from the command couch. "I wouldn't bet she could be made serviceable again, though, at least not economically."

Cory was watch officer tonight, so he was helping

Adele sort Pantellarian communications. His expertise made him ideal to monitor the destroyer squadron and the Pantellarian naval presence generally. Vesey's enthusiastic certainty that Admiral Stanzi's ships would be out of action for a week or longer appeared to have been correct based on the discussions Cory was reporting.

"The army is dealing with rescue and damage control," Adele said from her usual place at the console's rear position. "I don't see any signs that an attack is planned. And they've evacuated the remaining strongpoints."

"I wouldn't have thought there was much damage that you could repair," Cory said as he sorted. He—and Cazelet when he was present—worked as though they were Adele's separate limbs, doing what she requested with skill and flair. Though not as yet—she smiled minusculy—as much skill and flair as their teacher.

"The blast shook down houses in Hablinger," Adele said. "They're digging people out and lifting walls where they can, where the sheathing kept the walls together. I'm afraid there are many dead. Another blast could level most of Hablinger."

The only discussion of Adele's claim that there were other mines was between high officers, but the garrisons of the remaining strongpoints had begun dribbling back into the city as soon as they learned that Point 3 had vanished. By the time Pantellarian headquarters put out a formal recall, the outlying posts were already abandoned.

"Are there more mines?" Cory said. "Though I don't think they'd be necessary. The navy at least will mutiny if Arnaud doesn't accept the offer."

"No," said Adele as she continued to cascade data

down her display. "I suppose they could be placed easily enough if they were needed. The miners might have to use other techniques as a result of what the first explosion did to the ground, but I presume Brother Graves would be equal to the challenge."

She had access to everything except Commissioner Arnaud's own communications. Unless he had been killed—unlikely, because someone else would have mentioned it—Arnaud was using couriers and handwritten messages. Or he could be sitting in his trailer in a circle of empty bottles, but his subordinates would probably have been discussing that on the communications net.

The hatch between the bridge and the hold was open, but Barnes rapped on the jamb instead of entering. The rigger was in charge of the four guards at the main hatch.

"Ma'am?" he said, frowning. "There's a guy here to see you. He says he's an envoy from the wogs. The ones we're fighting, I mean. He don't have a gun."

Now Adele frowned. There hadn't been anything in official communications about peace emissaries, though quite a number of Pantellarian personnel had been discussing surrender among themselves.

"Send him to Captain Leary," Adele said. Daniel was in the headquarters complex. Brother Graves and his team of miners and Transformationists had quickly created a hamlet of barracks and meeting rooms from the plastic sheeting which the *Kiesche* had brought on her hop from Brotherhood. "No, escort him to the headquarters. Or—"

She wasn't usually indecisive, but this situation was unexpected. There wasn't a hint of this in the communications traffic. Perhaps she—

"Ma'am," Barnes said, "he says it's you he wants, not Six. That's why the perimeter guards brought him here. He's just a sergeant, ma'am."

"I'll see," Tovera said. She held her submachine gun. "If he's planning to kill you, will you want to question him before I finish him off?"

"Yes," said Adele. That was a Pantellarian response she hadn't considered. Though surely an assassin would be even more interested than a peace envoy in seeing Daniel rather than her?

Tovera slipped out. Barnes stood in the hatchway, holding his impeller crossways in front of him like a quarterstaff.

Adele smiled faintly as she rose to her feet. Barnes couldn't have been really worried that a killer would overcome Tovera, but the Sissies didn't take chances with the safety of the Mistress.

A moment later Tovera said, "It's all right, Barnes," and the rigger moved to the side. Tovera entered, still holding the submachine gun but now smiling. Behind her was a middle-aged man in rumpled, muddy Pantellarian utilities. The blouse bore no nametag.

"I didn't expect you, Commissioner Arnaud," Adele said, taking her hand out of her tunic pocket.

"The fox never had a better messenger than himself," Arnaud said with a shrug. It was probably a Pantellarian proverb. "You and I began this discussion, so I would prefer to resume it with you before I meet with Captain Leary."

"With the Independence Council," Adele said.

"Piffle!" Arnaud said. The anger he let out in the word showed what was really going on beneath his calm. "If I had no one to deal with but the Corcyrans,

I wouldn't be here now. I'm here to talk with you and then Leary, and the rest can go hang!"

Adele considered the situation. "I take your point," she said. She gestured to a jumpseat and said, "Sit down, please. I'm glad to have a chance to discuss matters with you before you say something in public which might cause you embarrassment."

"I'll leave," said Cory, rising from the command console.

"Please sit down, Master Cory," Adele said, though she wasn't sure she was making the correct decision. "You're on duty. While I don't have anywhere else suitable to talk with the commissioner, I think you're safe with anything you might hear."

Arnaud shrugged again and sat carefully on the jumpseat. "You're setting the terms," he said. He sounded calm, but Adele thought she heard his voice tremble under the surface.

To get the basic point out of the way immediately, Adele said, "Evidence in your personal console will show that you were a Cinnabar agent while Cinnabar was at war with the Alliance of Free Stars. You communicated with your handlers through Bantry Holdings. Furthermore, it will show that you conspired with Captain Leary to betray your force on Corcyra to Captain Leary. The signal detonating the mine which stranded your squadron was sent from the network computer in your headquarters."

Unexpectedly, Commissioner Arnaud laughed. "I assumed there would be something of the sort when I realized who you were," he said. "Which I didn't do until you made the surrender demand in your own name this morning, unfortunately. And I'll admit that

I didn't expect quite so elaborate a frame-up, though I suppose I should have done."

He shook his head, then showed another flash of anger as he snarled, "You must think I'm a complete fool, milady!"

Cory was back on his couch, focused so rigidly on his display that he might have been shot and stuffed. He seemed embarrassed to be listening, but it really was the only option.

"I told you," Adele said, "that you hadn't realized what you were doing when you brought Captain Leary into your war. Captain Leary travels with a staff."

"I understand, now that it's too late," Arnaud said. His eyes had drifted to a corner of the floor. He looked up and said sharply, "I understand that I was particularly a fool to threaten Captain Leary, wasn't I? Would he have helped me if I'd come to him in a different fashion?"

Daniel didn't even know about the threat, Adele thought. Aloud she said, "Your situation would not have been worse if you'd approached Captain Leary as a friend. I don't know that he would have agreed to help you even then, however."

"My situation *couldn't* be worse," Arnaud snapped. "I came here to ask for asylum on Cinnabar. I'll be hanged if I go back to Pantellaria, regardless of any treason you've invented for me."

He suddenly grinned in a return to good humor. "By the way," he said, "you won't find any evidence on the console in my trailer. Before I started here tonight, I set off a thermite grenade inside it. I didn't know what you had done to it, Lady Mundy, but I realized you'd done something."

"There was evidence elsewhere, of course," Adele said, getting to her feet again. "But you've convinced me that you're not a fool, Commissioner."

She coughed; Arnaud stood up also, looking tensely hopeful. Adele said, "I'll take to you to Captain Leary now. He's been considering the situation following the end of the war. You may learn something to your advantage."

Tovera gestured Arnaud to the hatch. She had holstered her submachine gun again, which was more a comment on her state of mind than on how quickly she could react to danger.

"Six says he's not a politician," Tovera said. "But he's lying."

She laughed, a cackle that might have come from a peevish reptile.

Daniel awakened in his hammock. He didn't know where he was—neither what planet he was on nor what he was doing there. Here.

"Daniel?" said Adele's voice, bringing him fully alert and back to his present in the conference room where he had slung a hammock instead of returning to his cubicle aboard the *Kiesche*.

"Hang on," said Hogg. His feet slapped the floor, which was sheeting like the walls and roof.

Daniel's eyes adapted to the faint light from beneath the eaves of the quickly constructed building. Twenty-centimeter-high poles from the top of the walls supported the peaked roof. The roof overhang covered the gap, but it allowed in air and enough light to be noticeable in the otherwise complete darkness.

Daniel sneezed; his nose was stuffy from residues

of the freshly welded plastic and the stabilizers mixed with the mud pumped into the gap between the sheeting. When the mud hardened, the sandwich would be weatherproof and excellent insulation, but for the moment it was still curing.

Hogg shoved the door open and unhooked one end of his hammock; he had slung it across the doorway from eyebolts set into the walls. Daniel got up also. His hammock was across a back corner of the room, one bolt in either wall. He was still fully dressed, though he'd taken off his boots.

There was a jury-rigged power line from the fusion bottle in the headquarters dugout, but the light switch was near the door. "Get the lights," Daniel said as he bent to slip on his boots. The three glowstrips on the underside of the roof flickered to what was painful brilliance for a moment.

Adele entered ahead of a burly Pantellarian sergeant. *A spy? Does she have agents inside Hablinger?*

"Captain Leary?" she said, reverting to formality now that he was awake. "This is Commissioner Arnaud, who wants to discuss his future with you."

Daniel laughed, then sneezed again. An Ischian freighter had landed just after sundown. Ozone from its thrusters still lingered in the humid air. Most of the ships in Brotherhood Harbor were waiting for at least a formal armistice before they hopped to Hablinger with building materials, but the Ischians had their own reasons for wanting to arrive immediately.

"Have a seat, Commissioner," Daniel said as he pulled out a chair for himself from the table. "When I saw you, I was only mildly surprised to learn that Lady Mundy had an agent within the Pantellarian expeditionary force. I was much more surprised when she announced who you really are."

Like the buildings, the furniture had been manufactured from plastic tubes and sheeting in the past few hours. It was sturdy and serviceable, though it made the steel stampings of a warship look like aesthetic masterpieces by contrast.

Arnaud remained standing, his hands gripped together at waist level. "I've come to accept your terms, Leary," he said.

"I haven't stated any terms," Daniel said. He frowned slightly. "Though if Lady Mundy has, then—"

"She has not," Arnaud said. "When I have a negotiating position, I negotiate. When I do not, as now, I throw myself on the victor's mercy. State your terms, sir, and I will accept them."

He swallowed and added, "I hope the lives of my troops can be spared, as your initial announcement stated."

Daniel pulled out a second chair and turned it to face his, then sat down. "I think we can do better than that, Commissioner," he said, "but please—sit. I don't want to look up at you, and I sure don't want to stand. It's been a long day."

"Yes," said the Pantellarian, "it has."

Arnaud sat. He tried to brace himself on the chair back but collapsed onto the seat when he was halfway down. He had looked worn but alert initially. Now his face had a greenish pallor which was only partially caused by the bioluminescent glow strips.

The door closed behind Hogg; he and Tovera had stepped outside. Adele was in a chair beside the door, her data unit on her lap. Except for the occasional flicker of her wands, she was as unobtrusive as the dull pink surface of the plastic walls.

"First..." Daniel said. He had rehearsed this meeting, but he hadn't expected it to come so suddenly—or here. "I've arranged with Ischia to repatriate your troops. With the Monfiore clan, technically, but this matter is going to require much greater resources than they themselves can provide. That's to everyone's benefit, as the Monfiores become benefactors of all Ischia instead of being wealthy profiteers in the midst of hostile neighbors."

Arnaud pursed his lips. "That will be an expensive proposition," he said. "I can't commit the Council to paying for it. The Pantellarian council, that is."

He shook his head angrily, glaring at the floor. "In fact, I don't think that anything I appeared to support would pass a Council vote. I'm telling you this because I don't want to see my troops sold into slavery to pay the cost of their transportation."

His mouth worked as though he were about to spit, but he swallowed instead. "Not that I'm likely to survive long enough to see the final outcome."

Daniel made a dismissive gesture with his left hand. "One thing at a time," he said. There was a console of reasonable capacity at the other end of the table, but he didn't think he needed it now. "The transportation costs will be covered by trade concessions, but that's in the future. The most immediate question I see—"

He grinned. It was true that the Monfiores gained in the long term by being forced to share their profits with their neighbors. This plan too benefitted all parties, which pleased Daniel for its neatness as well as other virtues.

"—is what you would consider the best conceivable outcome to the present situation? From your viewpoint."

"Asylum for me on Cinnabar," Arnaud said. "The rest of my force returns to Pantellaria with an undertaking by the Council not to retaliate against them, guaranteed by the Cinnabar Senate."

He shrugged. "If you can arrange *that*," he said, "you'd be welcome to my firstborn if I had children. I could manage a nephew or two."

Despite the joking bravado, Daniel could see real hope in the Pantellarian's expression. It was easy to like Arnaud: he had come himself instead of sending an envoy, and his first concern was for his troops.

"You've told me what you consider the best practical outcome," Daniel said, "but that's not what I asked you. What do you consider the best *conceivable* outcome?"

Arnaud's face hardened slightly. "You surrender Corcyra to me," he said after a moment. "Which, to be honest, I don't believe you have the power to do, but you've surprised me in the past."

He nodded toward Adele. "You and Lady Mundy have."

"Wouldn't you rather be ruler of Pantellaria?" Daniel said. He smiled more broadly.

Arnaud pushed his fingertips together hard at chest height. "Explain what you mean," he said.

"Will your troops support you?" Daniel said.

"I . . . think they would support me a long way, yes," Arnaud said. "If I get them out of this mess alive, most of them would support me well beyond common sense. But I couldn't conquer Pantellaria with this force. I couldn't even conquer Corcyra, though . . ."

His eyes narrowed with a thought. "The plan Lady

Mundy tricked me with—that might have worked. I still think it would have worked, and she said it was your plan. Are you offering to support me, Leary?"

Daniel laughed as though the offer was a joke. At the words, though, his mind had begun considering what it would take and what resources he might be able to raise on Cinnabar....

No.

Before he could speak, Adele said, "I can assure you as an official of Cinnabar, Commissioner Arnaud, that the Republic's government would forbid any action by a citizen which would precipitate renewed war with the Alliance. As the armed overthrow of Pantellaria by an RCN officer would certainly do."

I wasn't going to do it anyway! Daniel thought. His momentary irritation melted away. *But that's an aspect of the business that I hadn't considered.*

He grinned at Adele, then said to Arnaud, "No, you couldn't conquer Pantellaria, but according to my sources—"

Adele.

"—the Council of Twenty isn't very popular. Things were all right just after Guarantor Porra's thugs were thrown out, but right now a lot of folks seem to think that the Council is a bunch of rich people screwing every piaster they can get out of everybody else. Not so?"

"Go on, Leary," Arnaud said, his face almost blank. "But keep in mind that I'm not exactly a man of the people myself. I've improved the family fortune considerably, thanks to investment by Bantry Holdings in some measure—"

His sudden smile was half-amused, half mocking.

"—but we Arnauds are still one of the oldest families on Pantellaria."

"You may have more popular support than you believe, Commissioner," Adele said. "Your shipyard is regarded as a good place to work, and you're a great deal more approachable than many of your *nouveau riche* fellows on the Council. Your popularity with the public is one of the reasons the rest of the Council has been trying to arrange the defeat of your expeditionary force as soon as you lifted from Pantellaria."

"It certainly seems like that!" Arnaud said. "You know, I've had to use my own money to pay the troops for the past three months? The Council hasn't transferred money into the expedition's account."

"I can show you internal communications among your fellows," Adele said. "Though referring to the other councillors as 'your fellows' is probably a misnomer. But that doesn't matter now."

"No," said Daniel. Arnaud was seated between him and Adele, so the Commissioner was snapping his head around like a spectator at a tennis match. "Ordinary people don't have to support you, so long as they don't oppose you. As the residents of Corcyra most certainly have been doing."

"I have provided Captain Leary with a breakdown of the private troops in the service of your other councillors," Adele said. "He is convinced that the force available to you would be sufficient to defeat—"

"You'll scare them into taking their badges off and hiding," Daniel said.

"—or simply overawe them," Adele went on, nodding.

"And your forces aren't simply those you brought to Corcyra, Commissioner," Daniel said, leaning forward.

"There are other troops here who would be more than happy to follow you to Pantellaria. To go back, in many cases."

He and Adele were selling Arnaud on their plan. It was a good course for the Pantellarian, but it was the only course which would also accomplish all of Daniel's objectives.

Arnaud blinked and stiffened. "No," he said. "You mean the exiles, don't you? I won't do that."

"The Self-Defense Regiment and the Navy of Free Corcyra," Daniel said, keeping his voice genially calm. "Which in the past have been paid by exiles, I believe, but that needn't continue to be the case. And the Corcyran garrison, whose members will be particularly willing to leave here. Their commander, Colonel Bourbon, is both competent and honest."

"Look, I know the people, the families mostly, who bolted here when the Alliance pulled off of Pantellaria," Arnaud said. "I don't have problems with them, no more than usual, anyway; I was in pretty tight with Porra's last administrator myself, to tell the truth. But I'm not going to have a bloodbath back at home *or* a return to Alliance control. That's what they'll want, some of them."

"What most of them want," said Adele, "is a return of their property on Pantellaria. And revenge against the political enemies who forced them into exile and expropriated that property, of course. But none of them, and not all of them together, can force through that agenda over your opposition."

A computer-synthesized voice would have had more warmth; it would have been programmed to seem human. Adele didn't bother to do so. And at that, her cold, precise delivery gave the words the solid certainty of a stone wall.

"You're buying internal peace for your planet," Daniel said. "That's a very good return for simply giving back the property of fellow citizens. The Council of Twenty had a good opportunity to bring Pantellaria together when the Alliance left. Instead you simply made yourselves richer. *You* did, Commissioner."

Arnaud's immediate response was an angry glare. Then he coughed a laugh and said, "Point taken. The silver lining in this is that because the spoils were divided pretty much among Council members, it'll be relatively easy for us to correct our mistake. Although—"

His eyes went unfocused as his mind leaped to a different thought.

"—not all of my colleagues will see what we did as a mistake. The Alliance administrators had us at each others' throats all the time they were in charge. You can say we should have done better when they left, but what happened to most of the exiles was no more than justice for what they'd done to others."

"All the more reason to stop doing Guarantor Porra's work for him, I would think," snapped Adele.

"And your colleagues don't have five thousand troops with combat experience," Daniel said. "Don't sell your force short, Arnaud. No, they're not a Land Force Commando, but they've trained together, they've been shot at and they've shot back. That puts them in a whole different class from what anybody else on Pantellaria has obeying his orders."

"Look," said Arnaud. He stood up abruptly. "*Look.* I don't want to be dictator of Pantellaria. I don't want to be a penny-ante Porra myself."

"Then don't be," said Adele. She didn't raise her voice, but her words snapped like a whip. "The Council of Twenty was supposed to be a transition to the elected assembly that ruled Pantellaria before you were absorbed into the Alliance. Go back and tell your colleagues that the Council is going to hold elections for a new Assembly in three months time."

"But—" Arnaud said.

"But *nothing*," Daniel said. "You've got five thousand veteran votes for the proposition, and everybody on the planet except maybe a few of your colleagues will support the idea. And if any other councillors really want to make an issue of it, put them in jail for a few days."

"You may find that more of the Council is on your side than you expect," Adele said. "According to my information—"

Pantellaria had been a major Alliance ally during the war. Mistress Sand's array of spies there obviously hadn't been disbanded when the Treaty of Amiens was signed.

"—some of the minor councillors are concerned at the chance of civil war between their more powerful colleagues, and the smarter councillors—"

Adele's smile was the visual equivalent of her clipped tone.

"Not a majority, I fear. The smarter councillors, as I said, are concerned about revolution if things don't change. Both concerns are valid, even if Alliance agents don't work to increase their likelihood. Which is also a valid concern."

"Lady Mundy and I have seen revolutions," Daniel said. *We've seen the next thing to revolution on*

Cinnabar, and it was the blessing of heaven that it wasn't the real thing. "If you go home and knock a few of the harder heads together, you'll be doing everyone on Pantellaria a favor."

"Including the people who'll curse you every day till they die," said Adele. "Because they don't have your good sense."

"They also don't have your army," Daniel said. "So long as you're satisfied with being rich and powerful, my bet is that your rich, powerful colleagues will come to believe that you're offering a better alternative than hanging from a lamppost. Now, are you willing to try?"

Arnaud gave Daniel a lopsided smile and sat down again. "I'd been wondering what I was going to do with myself on Cinnabar," he said. "I guess that on balance I'd rather go back to Pantellaria and straighten things out. I knew something had to be done before I brought the army here, and from what you tell me things haven't gotten better."

He took a deep breath. "All right, Leary. What's the next step?"

"The next step," Daniel said, "is that we tell Hogg and Tovera to let in the Corcyran leaders and Giorgi Monfiore. I'm sure that Lady Mundy summoned them while we've been talking."

Adele nodded agreement and said, "I have." Her smile was almost that of a normal person.

"We've got a great deal of negotiating to do," Daniel said, rising to walk to the door, "but Corcyra and Pantellaria both will gain from it."

And with luck so will Rikard Cleveland, who's the reason I came here in the first place.

CHAPTER 27

Outside Hablinger on Corcyra

Adele worked at her usual station on the *Kiesche*, sifting the data from Arnaud's personal console. She allowed herself a smile, though it didn't reach her lips: she probably had the only complete copy of the contents, now that Arnaud had melted the unit to slag.

I wonder if he would like the data back, now that things have settled down? Probably not, and in any case Adele didn't see any reason to offer it. If Arnaud asked, she would consider the matter again.

The watch officer, Pasternak, was asleep in his cubicle, and the three crewmen on duty were playing some sort of card game with Tovera in the hold. If necessary Pasternak could light the thrusters and even lift the freighter into orbit using the computer's automated systems.

The remaining RCN personnel were in Hablinger or were involved with salvaging the Pantellarian squadron. Pasternak was there on most days also; indeed, he appeared to be overseeing the operation.

He wasn't a young man, however. Daniel had rotated

him back to the *Kiesche* today and for however long
he was willing to rest. Although the chief engineer
was technically a watch-standing officer, no one would
willingly put him in a position in which he needed
to run more than a fusion bottle—which he did as
well as anyone else in the RCN.

Cory and Cazelet were involved with repairs also,
though they were in charge of crews which were
reconfining the Cephisis and constructing the new
harbor. Hablinger Pool was literally high and dry. It
was easier to move the facilities to a new location
than to force the river into its former channel.

The latter might not even be possible with the available equipment: the Cephisis continued to eat away the
previous levees as it tumbled thirty feet to the level of
the rice fields. In the fifteen days since the charge went
off, the gap had expanded at least ten miles back upriver.

A freak of the breeze brought the sound of a power
saw onto the *Kiesche*'s bridge. Just as the Southern
Cephisis region was well-stocked with mining supplies
and equipment, so in the Delta, supplies for working
with water and soft earth were on hand.

The huge earthmovers were on floatation tires, but
they still needed better support than they could get
from soupy mud. As soon as a simple berm confined
the river, the ground behind it would quickly dry to
adequate stability, but that initial berm required track-
ways of structural plastic for the equipment to move on.

The river's new western bank had been roughed
in, so that the *Kiesche* was again on reasonably solid
ground. Now the farther bank was under construction,
and sheets for more trackway were being cut to size.

Ordinarily Adele would not have noticed outside

noises while she was working, but the scanning she was doing at present wasn't really work. There was no rush on the business; in fact there was no real purpose. She had time to think.

She smiled with wistful humor. That was never a good thing for her. Because she had been immersed in a study of recent Pantellarian politics, her thoughts had swerved into particularly unpleasant channels.

Within Adele's lifetime, Cinnabar could have broken up as several different factions fought one another in a civil war that could not have a true winner. The fighting among powerful families would also have set off a class revolution in the slums of Xenos. Several, perhaps most, of the worlds which the Republic ruled in a more or less paternalistic fashion would have declared independence.

And all that would have happened even if Guarantor Porra had not been stoking the fires for his own purposes, which he most certainly would have been. The Three Circles Conspiracy had been funded in part by Alliance money. Adele was able to hope that her father had not known precisely where the funds were coming from, but Lucius Mundy had not been stupid or unobservant. He must have guessed.

Cinnabar hadn't spiraled down into the chaos which now threatened Pantellaria because Speaker Leary had crushed the conspiracy. His tool had been the Proscriptions, directing the death of thousands of his fellow citizens without trial; the *murder* of thousands of Cinnabar citizens, Adele's immediate family among them.

And if I'd been advising Corder Leary, I would have told him to do just what he decided to do on his own.

Daniel wouldn't have ordered Proscriptions. The most he might have done was to look the other way while his advisor, Lady Mundy, saved the Republic. That would have been good enough.

Adele went back to sorting Arnaud's data and correlating it with the information from Mistress Sand's files. She wondered if she should share some of that information with Arnaud. Used wisely, it would greatly ease the job of remaking Pantellaria; Arnaud had regularly showed himself wise, particularly in taking advice when he realized his ignorance.

Mistress Sand's clerks and administrators would oppose giving Arnaud information, since that might compromise the spies and techniques which had gathered it. Mistress Sand might herself agree with her underlings.

But Adele Mundy was the officer on the ground. She was a librarian, not a bureaucrat, and her instinct was always to share information. *Arnaud will see anything which I think may help him. Mistress Sand can dismiss me if she doesn't approve.*

Smiling at the joke no one else had heard and very few would have understood if she had spoken aloud, Adele went back to Arnaud's viewpoint on a conspiracy involving himself and five other councillors to fix the price of fish protein. They had failed, but only because Arnaud had secretly backed a rival bid to do the same thing. Arnaud had come out of that very well, at a cost paid by his former partners and the Pantellarian public generally.

People can change for the better....

Adele didn't really believe that, but she did believe that an intelligent and motivated person could learn to *imitate* a better person. Tovera, as an extreme example, did very well at appearing to be a human being instead the conscienceless killer that she really was.

Conscienceless killers tended to have short lifespans. The people closest to them, the ones who would be described as "friends and colleagues" if the killer had been human, quickly realized how dangerous the killer was to them if they allowed him or her to live.

Tovera had found a niche by killing only people whom Lady Mundy directed her to kill. Not that Adele felt that she herself was really the same species as those with whom she worked. The Sissies accepted her because she was Daniel's friend, and Daniel accepted her for some reason Adele couldn't fathom.

Perhaps because I am his friend.

While the *Kiesche's* junior officers were working on the levees and harbor, Daniel was closeted with Arnaud and the leaders of all the anti-Pantellarian factions on Corcyra. They were trying to merge their forces into an effective weapon to take to Pantellaria.

Well, they were discussing a merger; most of them were more concerned with enhancing their own position than with real coordination. That was normal for human beings, in Adele's experience as well as from what she had learned by reading. Daniel was present as an advisor, but he had quickly become the referee. He was the only neutral at the conference, and he had the respect of all the other parties.

Daniel had told Adele that he would not take an active part in what was at least the next thing to a coup when Arnaud returned to Pantellaria. He hadn't lied to her—Adele didn't imagine that Daniel would ever lie to her—but neither was she convinced that he would avoid being talked into coming along when the convoy of troops lifted. Just as an advisor, at first.

Adele smiled faintly. It didn't matter to her; and it

certainly didn't matter to Tovera, who could reasonably expect to be pointed at further targets.

A corner of the display glowed amber. Adele reduced the data she was mining. The incoming call, though classed as nonemergency, was from Brother Graves, so she answered it immediately.

"Mundy," she said. She was using video despite her long habit not to do so. Her duty now was to gather information as well as to dispense it, and a person's face provided a great deal of information.

Graves' face was worried, though he was obviously trying to sound cheerful when he said, *"Lady Mundy? I was wondering if you know where Brother Rikard is?"*

"I believed he was with you in Brotherhood," Adele said, "though I haven't given him any thought."

She was mildly embarrassed at the truth of the latter statement. Granted, Cleveland was technically Daniel's responsibility—but she had undertaken to help Daniel, and "technically" was a coward's word. She was a Mundy.

"Yes, Rikard has been acting as my aide here," Graves said. *"There's more going on in Brotherhood affecting the community than there is usually, of course, and it really makes it easier to, well, to be away from Pearl Valley if it's two of us together. Instead of just me. Now—well, I'm probably being silly."*

Graves cleared his throat.

I'm not the only one in the conversation who feels embarrassed, Adele thought.

"Rikard went to the Manor yesterday morning to coordinate the return of our contingent from Hablinger," Graves said. *"We've been helping with the reconstruction work, you know, since some members of our community have useful skills from before they joined us. I wasn't*

*really worried when he didn't return immediately,
but this morning I asked the officer whom Rikard had
gone to see."*

Simply because it was what she did, Adele checked
a directory on the left half of her display while she
listened. The deputy adjutant in Brotherhood was a
Lieutenant bes-Shehar, seconded from the navy.

*"She said that Rikard had left her office at about
midday, but that she'd seen him in the lobby a few
minutes later when she went to lunch,"* Graves said.
*"He was with some spacers whom he seemed to know.
So I thought perhaps Captain Leary had sent personnel to take him to Hablinger and he hadn't had time
to inform me. Rikard hasn't had contact with any
spacers that I know of except the crew of your ship."*

"Brother Graves, I'm going to break this call now,"
Adele said. "I'll deal with the matter. Six and I will
deal with the matter. Out."

Daniel wore a commo helmet during the present
discussions because it gave him access to the *Kiesche*'s
database. Adele opened a two-way link to him. As
it connected, she brought up a list of shipping in
Brotherhood Harbor.

Adele was already fairly certain of what she was
going to find. The *Kiesche* wasn't *quite* the only starship
whose complement Cleveland had had dealings with.

Daniel swayed, but he held himself upright when
the converted tank skidded over a dike and slammed
down on the other side. The four other spacers took
the shock with equanimity also: bad as the ride was,
a starship descending through an atmosphere bounced
around worse.

Hogg gripped a stocked impeller with his right hand. His left alone wasn't enough to prevent his hobnailed boots from slipping on the sloping armor. His whole considerable weight hit Daniel in the back like a giant beanbag. Daniel grunted, but he managed not to go down, or worse—to go over the side.

The vehicle was a light air-cushion tank with a superstructure of woven-wire fencing. The six passengers clinging to the fence-stake struts supporting the basket badly overloaded it. Military vehicles were always overloaded in the field anyway, so the extra half ton didn't prevent the makeshift bus from roaring across the paddies. It certainly prevented it from doing so smoothly, however, and the fact that the Pantellarian driver was a hotdog didn't help.

"Can't that stupid bitch slow down?" Hogg growled, using Daniel's shoulder to brace himself upright again.

"Sorry, master. Won't happen again."

"She's not driving any faster than you would be if I'd let you," Daniel said, shouting over the intake rush of the drive fans. "And there's the *Kiesche* right ahead. We're almost there."

This tank was one of twenty which the expeditionary force had brought to Corcyra as cavalry. Their armor was proof against slugs from the carbines carried by most of the fighters—calling the miners' militia "soldiers" would be a stretch—but a burst from an automatic impeller would go through the hulls the long way. The fixed barbette holding a five-centimeter plasma cannon was thicker, but not a great deal thicker.

The Pantellarians had converted half a dozen tanks into light trucks by welding a framework to the superstructure and wrapping fencing around it. The vehicles could still be used for combat as-is in an emergency, though a workman with a cutting bar could remove the framework in a minute or two.

The Delta region had very little civilian ground transport for the invaders to commandeer, so they had had to improvise. The jury-rigged trucks couldn't have been very satisfactory, but they would have greatly eased the problem of resupplying the strongpoints across the mud.

The crust on this side of the Cephisis had dried to a thickness which could almost support the tank's six tons, but when the vehicle leaped over the dike, it splashed liquid mud to all sides. They didn't bog—it was almost impossible to bog an air-cushion vehicle unless it sank in over the fan intakes—but balls of mud spattered the passengers as they bulled their way forward.

"The next time I'll walk," said Vesey. She flicked mud off her visor, though that further smeared what was left. "Or swim."

"We're almost there," Daniel said, smiling toward her. For a long time after Midshipman Dorst's death, Vesey hadn't been able to joke. The presence of Midshipman Cazelet, now passed lieutenant, had been an even greater benefit to Vesey than it was generally to Daniel and the crew of whatever ship he commanded.

The Pantellarian driver had a higher opinion of her skills than Daniel thought justified. She began to swing the vehicle when they were twenty feet from the base of the *Kiesche*'s boarding ramp, planning to raise the leading edge of her skirts to brake them to a stop. She had forgotten to allow for the extra weight of the passengers above the center of gravity.

They didn't actually flip—which might have been survivable in the soft mud or might not—because the passengers, even Hogg, instinctively threw their weight to the high side. The base welds of three struts cracked and the fencing sagged down, but the vehicle came to a halt. Everyone was still safe aboard, albeit in a cursing pile on the back deck.

Evans pushed his way off the bottom of the pile and dropped to the ground, his face red. Daniel had brought both power-room techs back with him, leaving most of the riggers to follow on a later run.

"I'll strangle the whore!" Evans snarled, his voice choked with fury. He was very possibly the strongest person in the crew, squat where Woetjans was rangy, and solid bone and muscle from his toes to the top of his bald head.

Before Daniel could intervene—Evans didn't have the intellect to come up with a threat he didn't mean to carry out—Hogg put a hand on the big technician's shoulder. "C'mon, Curly," he said. "You and me, we got better uses for a woman than that, don't we? Anyway, the Mistress needs us on the ship right now, and *I* sure don't want to disappoint her."

"Oh, that's right," Evans said. "Bloody hell, I shoulda remembered that. Thanks, Hogg."

"Hogg surprised me," Vesey said quietly as she and Daniel followed the others up the boarding ramp. "I thought he was angry also."

"I suspect he was," Daniel said. "But Hogg isn't going to do anything because he's out of control. He knows that killing a Pantellarian driver would cause all sorts of trouble for me, so he made sure that Evans kept his mind on business, too."

"I believe we could have finessed the driver," Vesey said, deadpan.

Daniel was still laughing as he entered the *Kiesche* behind her.

He seated himself at the command console. It was already live with the display which Adele had prepared for him.

The *Madison Merchant*, Captain Sorley commanding, had landed in Brotherhood Harbor two days ago; forty-nine hours now, to be as precise as Adele always was. The ship had lifted off again seven hours later without listing a destination and, indeed, without more than cursory notice to Brotherhood Control that she was lifting.

Which I suspect is true for at least half the ships landing on Corcyra, Daniel thought with a smile. Blockade runners and tramp freighters generally were crewed by people who ignored rules which weren't backed by potential force. Corcyra didn't have guard ships in orbit.

Daniel smiled even more broadly. The controllers on the ground here weren't going to get bent out of shape about such details, either. So long as duties were paid on cargo coming or going—there hadn't been time for the *Madison Merchant* to shift cargo—it was no skin off the nose of Brotherhood Control if ships managed to collide because a couple cowboys had chosen to lift off at the same moment. A part of Daniel preferred that attitude to the care with which he himself entered and left harbor.

A starship's astrogation console automatically dumped its log to the port computer on landing. That default could be circumvented or even faked, but Sorley hadn't had any reason to do so—if he or anybody aboard his rustbucket even had the skills. Daniel wasn't sure he could have reprogrammed the log himself.

Adele had highlighted the data. Dace had been the most recent landfall before the *Madison Merchant* reached Corcyra. The Garden was a typical waystation for ships approaching the Ribbon Stars from the Galactic East, so it would have been on Sorley's course from Cinnabar.

Daniel switched to the command channel. With the pumps running and all the *Kiesche*'s other systems in readiness for liftoff, there was too much noise to trust unaided voice.

"Vesey," he said, "plot a course for Dace. Figure an hour, but I plan to lift as soon as everybody's aboard."

Cory and Cazelet should arrive within minutes with the remainder of the crew which had been on duty at the construction sites. Woetjans with Dasi and Barnes, her two strikers, had gone into Hablinger to pick up the off-duty personnel.

No former Sissie was going to deliberately miss a recall signal, but there was a decent chance that some of them were going to be blind drunk or dead drunk. Spacers who couldn't remember their own name or who weren't hearing anything except the cymbals being clashed by the cherubs in their skulls might not react as quickly as they would wish the next morning when they had sobered up.

Woetjans and the bosun's mates could carry them back unconscious or, if necessary, knock them unconscious and carry them back. An hour was plenty of time to get everybody aboard, though it might be a day before some of them were really up to speed.

Adele highlighted a separate batch of data. The

context wasn't immediately clear to Daniel, so at first glance it meant nothing.

"*I searched all the files in Brotherhood for mentions of the* Madison Merchant *or any of its officers,*" Adele explained on a two-way link. "*As soon as the ship landed, Sorley checked with every chandlery in the port to find a reaction-mass pump.*"

She spoke matter-of-factly, as though anybody could have combed every database in a city five hundred miles away—in less than an hour, since Adele wouldn't have started searching until after she had alerted Daniel. *Of course, I've seen people blink when I tell them that I've shaved days off a plotted course by going out on the hull to keep an eye on conditions in the Matrix.*

"And didn't have any luck, I'd guess," Daniel said. When the ships in Hablinger Pool had dropped into the muck, they'd burned out more pumps than there were replacements on all Corcyra.

"*That's correct,*" Adele said. "*Chowdry Sons offered to adapt a bilge pump taken from a surface barge; which seems odd, but Sorley had arranged to look at it later in the afternoon. The* Madison Merchant *took off before the meeting was to take place.*"

"Adapting a bilge pump is rather a clever notion," Daniel said. *I'll have to drop in on Chowdry Sons when next I'm in Brotherhood.* There wouldn't be any real purpose in seeing the ship chandlers, but meeting clever people was never a waste of time. "If you can seal it properly, which would be difficult."

Probably much more difficult that Captain Sorley realized, but that wasn't the real question, because Sorley hadn't bought the unit. The *Madison Merchant* had lifted with a pump which had been failing when Daniel glanced over the tramp on Cinnabar.

The *Merchant*'s pump in its Cinnabar state wouldn't have been able to load significant amounts of reaction mass from Brotherhood Harbor, and if Sorley had planned to buy a replacement, the situation must have gotten even worse. Rather than head straight for Dace with the kidnapped Rikard Cleveland, Sorley might look for a place where the ship could fill her reaction-mass tanks at leisure and the crew could make what was doubtless yet another attempt at repairing the pump.

Adele might be able to find suitable planets which hadn't been catalogued, but Sorley wouldn't have that option unless he or one of his navigating officers had operated in the Ribbon Cluster previously. Sorley hadn't, according to the biography Adele had prepared in Xenos; it would be just bad luck if one of his officers had local experience.

Daniel brought up *The Sailing Directions for the Ribbon Stars*, then chortled in triumph. He'd found a planet within three days' sail of Corcyra which was listed as suitable for watering in an emergency. The notation had a green star, however.

"Lieutenant Vesey," Daniel said on the command push, "please plot a course for Point HH1509270. Same time frame as before. Break."

Two more makeshift jitneys had arrived outside the *Kiesche*. Spacers tramped up the boarding ramp in puzzled enthusiasm. The liberty group from Hablinger had yet to arrive, but they wouldn't be long.

Switching manually to the two-way link, Daniel continued, "Now, Adele: What can you learn about why HH1509270 is listed as being biologically hazardous?"

CHAPTER 28

The Matrix, between Corcyra and HH1509270

Daniel loved the blazing splendor of the Matrix, and he found discussions with Adele to be informative and generally delightful. A discussion with Adele on the hull while the ship was in the Matrix was private—the only place you could expect privacy on a starship—but brought with it the nagging worry that Adele was somehow going to drift off into a universe which wasn't meant for human beings or even for life.

Adele was tethered to a ringbolt on the hull and by a second safety line to Daniel's rigging suit. Daniel could not imagine how she might become separated from him or the ship, but Adele had done quite a number of things which no one else could imagine. Most of them were good, but she really *had* proven remarkably clumsy on shipboard.

Radios couldn't be used in the Matrix without throwing a starship incalculably off-course. Daniel touched one end of his communications rod to Adele's helmet, then moved his own helmet firmly against the other end.

The rods were of hollow brass and filled with a dense liquid. Artificers on the Bantry estate had made them to Daniel's direction when he realized he needed some better way of holding discussions on the hull than by pressing his helmet against that of the other party.

Daniel hadn't directed Old Fogleman and his assistant to engrave the rods with the Leary arms or to chase them with fine arabesques, but he hadn't been surprised to see the embellishments. The tenants and craftsmen of Bantry took pride in their jobs, knowing that the Squire took pride in *them*.

"What's your guess as to why Sorley took Cleveland?" Daniel asked. The rod provided a medium in which sound vibration could travel between the hard surface of one helmet to the hard surface of another.

The discussion wasn't really secret, but Daniel preferred to keep speculations away from the crew. Uncertainty made spacers nervous. Known dangers, including the risks of going into battle and simply the natures of their jobs, weren't nearly so worrisome.

"Sorley may plan to return to Corcyra when his ship is repaired and to use Cleveland to find the treasure according to the original plan," Adele said. "I consider this less likely than that he will go to Cinnabar and demand a ransom from Mistress Sand and her husband."

The *Kiesche's* antennas rotated thirty degrees. That changed the angle at which the fabric of the electrically charged sails impinged on the Casimir Radiation which was the sole constant throughout every bubble universe in the Cosmos.

Reflexively, Daniel looked up to observe the rig.

The topsails and topgallants were set, but another mechanically transmitted command reefed the latter by a batten each. The starboard topgallant caught, so a rigger climbed quickly to clear the balky sheave.

"I suppose he could hold Cleveland on some world which the Republic doesn't control," Daniel mused aloud. He hadn't let either end of the rod slip out of contact when he turned to watch the course change. "Even Pleasaunce, I suppose. I don't think the truce means that Guarantor Porra would be willing to do a favor for Mistress Sand."

"Captain Sorley would be a marked man no matter where he went afterward," Adele said. "He and all his crew. Mistress Sand has a long memory, and so do I. But I've seen no evidence that Sorley understands the concept of long-term consequences."

There was a tick of sound that didn't quite transfer through the communication rod. It was probably a sniff.

"Or not such long-term," Daniel said. "*I'll* make a priority of looking for Sorley if things go wrong. But that's if we don't find Cleveland when we make planetfall tomorrow. As I hope and expect we will."

The heavens blurred as the *Kiesche* slipped from one universe to another. The pattern reformed, almost identical to what it had been before except that the apparent colors had shifted lower in the spectrum.

Daniel knew he wasn't seeing true colors—universes didn't emit light into the Matrix—but his brain was displaying relative energy levels in a form that his mind was used to reading. Because the *Kiesche* had entered a universe of higher energy than the one she had left, the appearance of the cosmos changed in accordance.

"Adele," he said, "when I'm out here, I really feel that everything in the cosmos is part of a single machine, and I'm one of those pieces. It's not power, it's purpose. *Everything* has purpose."

"I'm not religious myself," Adele said.

For an instant Daniel thought that she had changed the subject; but of course she had not.

"I think it would be a fine thing to have purpose," Adele said. "I'm not sure how I could tell, though. I can't think of any objective data which I would regard as evidence."

Daniel watched the heavens ablaze with all majesty, all existence. "Adele," he said. "What do you see here in the Matrix? Anything?"

"I think there's a pattern," Adele said after a moment. "I don't see it, though, which is very frustrating. I do better with data, I'm afraid."

The communication rod twitched. Adele had shrugged in her air suit, but she brought her helmet back into contact as soon as she realized.

"I don't believe some questions have answers," she said, "so I prefer not to think about them. I'm more useful looking for information about this world where we hope to find Sorley."

"I wish it had a name," Daniel said, frowning. "Calling something HH1509270 is cumbersome at best."

"I suppose we could call it Cleveland's World," said Adele. "Or Sorley's Grave, if things don't work out."

Daniel laughed, though if Tovera had made the statement he wouldn't have been sure it was a joke. He chose to believe that Tovera's mistress had meant a joke, though.

"Daniel?" Adele said. "If we find the *Madison*

Merchant in orbit instead of being on the ground, will you fight him? If we find her at all, that is."

Daniel frowned, letting his soul drift in the cosmos while his conscious mind went over that question again. "We might get away with it," he said. "Our popgun isn't going to penetrate the hull of a three-thousand-ton freighter like the *Madison Merchant*, so we won't risk hitting Cleveland. Even to a tramp that's in bad shape, we're no danger. The problem of course is that the *Merchant* mounts a four-inch cannon herself."

"I haven't found much information on the ship's personnel," Adele said. "I copied the crew list when we were dealing with the situation in Xenos, but I can only cross-reference it against databases on Cinnabar. None of the names I found have a gunner's rating in their background, but there are twenty of the crew on whom I have no information. At least under the names they're using now."

"It's unlikely that the *Merchant* will have a competent gunner," Daniel said, voicing the sequence of thoughts that had been caroming off the sides of his mind for some hours. "They almost certainly won't have a gunner as good as Sun. Those are probabilities. The certainties are on Sorley's side: a four-inch gun against our two-inch, and the *Merchant*'s much sturdier hull and frames."

He looked at the Matrix and the glowing, splendid universes there. *They aren't looking down on me, I'm here* with *them,* Daniel thought. *But this decision is for me, not for the cosmos.*

"I think it'd probably turn out all right," he said aloud. "But I'm not going to gamble the lives of my crew on a chance when I think there'll be better opportunities later. If we find the *Merchant* in orbit,

I'll wait and act according to what Sorley decides to do. If he inserts, we'll follow him in the Matrix. I don't think he'll believe that's possible, so we have a good chance of taking him unaware when he extracts again."

"If you'll give me a list of possible alternative destinations," Adele said, "I'll see what additional information I can find to add to what the *Sailing Directions* say."

The sails were adjusting: the main courses fluttered down silently. They normally remained furled. They had greater surface area than sails higher up the antennas, but they provided less leverage for turning a ship in the Matrix.

"We'll go inside now," Daniel said as he reached the decision. "I'll get you that list."

Instead of walking toward the airlock at once, he paused to look again at the Matrix. He replaced the communications rod firmly against Adele's helmet.

"You know?" Daniel said. "There are only two places where I really feel content: in the Matrix, and on Bantry. And I can't stay either place for very long."

"Life itself is temporary, Daniel," Adele said.

She started for the airlock. Daniel followed, making sure that there was only the right amount of slack in the safety line.

Adele was right, of course.

It doesn't feel temporary here, though, or when I'm relaxing after a celebration with the tenants....

One Light-Minute from Cleveland's World

The box of files had been in storage in the attic of the Manor in Brotherhood. On top of it were piled discarded items—trash—which had been thrown out over centuries if not a millennium.

The lid of the box—it had originally been a case of ammunition—was stencilled MINING RECORDS, but Adele had glanced inside. Many of the chips were of the standard type used for log recordings by Pantellarian and Kostroman ships some centuries in the past.

If Adele had had time, she would have copied the files to her data unit the way she had done similar files in the basement of Navy House. She had located the box the day that Daniel blew the breach in the Cephisis, so she had only had time to ask Cory to carry it aboard before the *Kiesche* shifted to the outskirts of Hablinger.

It nagged Adele that she had absconded with stored documents, though even she could scarcely describe the box as having been "filed." No matter; she had worse things on her conscience.

Adele had sorted the chips immediately and found that most of them were indeed logs of ships from three to five hundred years back. She hadn't had time to go through the chips properly until now, however. Pursuit of the *Madison Merchant* made them a first priority for Adele and the spacers with the correct expertise, a group which now included Able Spacer Hale.

Adele was so lost in her pursuit of knowledge that she didn't hear the announcement that they were about to extract into sidereal space. The transition felt as though hot sand were being rubbed on the inside of her skin.

Her mouth opened in a silent gasp. She blinked, then regretted it because the imaginary sand was under her eyelids also. Discomfort was nothing new, and the effects of extraction went away promptly.

One corner of Adele's display echoed the command screen; it showed a planet in the fuzzy detail of high magnification. An orbiting ship would not have appeared at the present scale, but Adele's quick check of sensor data showed no sign of one. The *Merchant* had either landed on Cleveland's World, or it wasn't here at all.

Adele went back to the logs. The *Kiesche* had extracted a light-minute out from the planet so that Daniel and his officers could observe activity on and around it unseen. They didn't need Adele's skills to accomplish that.

A few of the logs were from ships which had never made voyages to the Ribbon Stars. Adele couldn't imagine why they had been placed in a box in a Brotherhood attic.

Most had more local significance, but they didn't involve HH1509270 or any other world which might be the right one under a different name or no name at all. Occasionally Adele had asked Cory to check recorded course data to see if an unidentified landfall could have been the one the *Kiesche* was looking for. None of them had been.

Until this one.

"Captain," Adele said on the command channel. She sent the file to everyone in the command group in the form of an icon slowly pulsing between red and magenta. "I have something, I believe."

"Roger," said Daniel at last. *"What is it, Mundy?"*

The delay before Daniel responded had been brief but was still longer than Adele unconsciously expected. *He and the others are searching for Sorley's ship,* she realized. Of course it would take them a moment to transfer their attention to a centuries-old logbook.

"It's an entry from the log of the *Khai-red-din*, a Hydriote ship from the sixth century post-Hiatus," Adele said. She couldn't put the date more precisely because the log used a notation specific to Hydra, and her files didn't include a cross-index to that system. When next she lifted from Cinnabar, she *would* have the necessary information.

"The *Khai-red-din* landed where I think was here," Adele continued, "though they refer to it as Number 614 on Antigonas' List. Their reaction-mass tank had frozen and split, so they needed to repair the tank and replenish it with water."

The Hydriotes were excellent spacers, whether they were acting as transport agents—as they mostly did now—or as pirates, which they had been over much of their history. Hydriotes were clannish and secretive in either role. Antigonas' List was obviously a registry of potential landing sites, but this was the first time Adele had seen a reference to it.

Rather than interrupt Adele, Vesey set a text at the bottom of every display on the command channel: *MADISON MERCHANT* LOCATED ON SURFACE AT STANDARD GRID FF4430-8259. Anyone who wanted to switch from Adele's presentation could highlight the icon Vesey posted with the text and go to imagery of the freighter on a small lake.

"The entry reads..." Adele said. Part of her mind thought it was silly to tell people what they could read for themselves, but experience had taught her that she could not make things *too* simple for people asking her help in finding information. "'Refitting required sixty-one hours. Before landing we welded caps over the High Drive outputs, and on the surface we ran the thrusters for ten minutes every two hours. Because the drives were under water we could not check the seal. When we had lifted to orbit, we found that three High Drives had been compromised because the plugs had been partially dislodged in the atmosphere, and there was enough build-up on the thruster nozzles to prevent the leaves from sphinctering properly.'"

Adele cleared her throat, then realized that she needed to say "Over" so that the others would know that she had finished.

"Sir?" said Cory. "If the algae is waterborne, then we don't have a problem, do we? We've got plenty of water, and landing on dry ground is a piece of cake for us, over."

"We're at three-quarters on reaction mass," said Vesey from one of the flat-plate displays. "We were topped off in Brotherhood Harbor, but we weren't able to take on any at Hablinger because the water was so turbid. Well, we could have, but I didn't think we needed to. Over."

"I think our tanks are quite adequate to land and to get us back to Corcyra," Daniel said, "and that's all I propose to do. I'm just as glad not to have to run the evaporators to filter mud out of our internal water, and I'm even happier not to chance running the local algae through our system. So that's not a problem, and thanks to Officer Mundy—"

He nodded, probably toward Adele's image inset on his display rather than toward the person herself on the other side of a double curtain of holographic light.

"—we have a way to release Cleveland without risking an attack with the plasma cannon while the Merchant was on the ground. Which I'm afraid was

*the best plan I had come up with until I learned how
virulent this algae is. I—"*

"Six, I can take out their gun if we just make one
pass at a hundred feet," Sun said, stepping on Daniel's
transmission. "*Even if there's somebody standing in
the open hatch, this pipsqueak gun won't so much as
give them a sunburn when I jam their four-incher's
traversing gear. Which I can do, over.*"

Adele heard a note of desperation in his voice.
The gunner had been expecting to show off his
skill; now it sounded as though he would not get a
chance after all.

"*Sun, if I thought that were necessary,*" Daniel said,
"*I'd order you to do it and have every confidence in
your success. I prefer to negotiate in as nonthreatening a fashion as I can, though, so we'll simply land
nearby and go down to talk to Captain Sorley in a
polite fashion. And—*"

Adele locked the sending units of the others on the
net. Woetjans and all the males were volunteering.
Daniel, of course, was saying that he was the proper
person to negotiate.

"Captain Leary," Adele said in the enforced silence,
"the negotiator has to be nonthreatening. *I* will be
the negotiator. I will take Tovera—"

Because Tovera would follow Adele to the *Madison
Merchant* unless Adele shot her first.

"—in case there should be difficulty. I've met Sorley
and his crew. They're not men who will look beyond
the fact that two small women have come to treat
with them. Over."

She released the others' commo and leaned back.
The babble subsided quickly when the others came to

the paired realizations that Adele was right and that Adele was not going to be moved from her position.

"I'll accompany Lady Mundy and her secretary in my second class uniform," Vesey said unexpectedly. *"There should be a commissioned officer present, and I have a lifetime of experience in not being threatening, over."*

There was a pause. Daniel laughed, breaking it.

Adele smiled, though there was more than humor in the expression. Aloud she said, "Yes, I think Lieutenant Vesey would make a welcome addition to the negotiating team."

"All right," Daniel said after a brief hesitation. Adele realized she had failed to close her transmission again. *"Then the next order of business is to plot our landing. Six out."*

CHAPTER 29

Cleveland's World

A quarter mile from the slope where Daniel stood, steam wreathed the *Madison Merchant* an instant before the sound arrived. It was a snarling roar instead of the usual pillowy thump of a ship lighting her thrusters. The freighter's bow lifted, then slapped back onto the water as the man at the controls closed his throttles in panic.

"They didn't flare their nozzles!" Cazelet said. "They're lucky that they didn't break her back when they came down like that."

"Didn't or couldn't," Daniel said with satisfaction. "They left the thrusters sphinctered after they landed. When the algae coated the petals, they wouldn't open properly."

Daniel had landed on a knoll which was at ninety degrees to his quarry's long axis. For the *Madison Merchant*'s gun to bear, she had to rotate at least forty-five degrees; sixty would be better. After Sorley's abortive attempt to lift his ship and turn, the *Merchant* floated in exactly the same relation to the *Kiesche* as she'd had to begin with.

"Why won't they be able to lift now, though?" Cazelet said. "They'll have burned off the algae. Or do you think they won't dare try because they don't know what the problem is?"

Daniel grinned, though his eyes were following his negotiating team. The thoughts behind his expression weren't quite as cheerful as he tried to project. Adele had paused for a moment when the thrusters lit, but she and her companions resumed their trudge downward when the *Merchant* settled back. Adele held a white flag in her right hand, but nobody imagined that Sorley or his crew would take any notice of it.

"The algae fixes calcium," Daniel said. "Not huge amounts, of course, but too much for the tolerances between the petals of a thruster nozzle. Calcium vaporizes at well over twenty-two hundred degrees. Yes, it will burn off—but not cleanly enough to allow the petals to slide properly, not from a short pulse like that."

The *Merchant*'s attempt to rise had shaken the outcrop on which the *Kiesche* rested. Steam puffed out of a recent crack in the rock, sending a scatter of pebbles down the slope toward where Daniel and Cazelet stood. This side was too gentle to manage a real avalanche; the rattle of stone on stone petered out before anything reached the men.

"I hadn't thought about our thrusters cracking the rock," Daniel said. "It would've been embarrassing if we'd gone sliding down into the lake beside the *Merchant*, wouldn't it? Not the sort of impression I was trying to give Captain Sorley."

"I don't think it happens very often, sir," said Cazelet. "I don't know of another captain who would have willingly landed on a point of rock."

The *Madison Merchant* floated in what was either a lake, a lagoon, or a meandering river, depending on how it was fed. A campsite with sailcloth shelters and a remarkable amount of trash for no more than two days of occupancy stood on the beach at the end of the catwalk from the main hatch. The men whom Daniel had seen onshore while the *Kiesche* was in orbit had vanished back into the ship, and the freighter's hatch was closed.

"I didn't really need to land so high up, I think," Daniel said. "The algae doesn't seem to advance more than twenty feet from the lakeshore even in the wet season. It must be drawn to metal—or maybe electrical charges."

He gestured. Cleveland's World was placid atmospherically and geologically. The lake's barren margin resulted from regular flooding.

The *Madison Merchant* lighted its thrusters again, but only three of them and all toward the stern. They were properly flared, so though the ship rocked as the water around it boiled, there was no risk of it trying to lift off again.

"She's got eight thrusters," Cazelet said, "but only six were functioning when she lifted from Brotherhood Harbor—I checked imagery from the harbormaster's office. And three won't lift her, even if they weren't asymmetric."

"Well observed," Daniel said. The praise was real, though the warmth he put into his voice was a little exaggerated. "They seem to have checked their instruments this time and only lighted the units which opened properly instead of just assuming they were working."

Cazelet was an excellent officer, a man Daniel would be pleased to have serving under him even if Cazelet were not Adele's protégé. He came from a commercial rather than naval background, which was useful for many reasons. For example, Cazelet was more likely than Cory—or Daniel—to check the harbormaster's records to see how well a freighter's plasma thrusters were functioning. RCN officers—or their Fleet equivalents—came to assume that a starship's basic systems were operating properly unless there had been an emergency.

Cazelet was personable, cultured, and intelligent. He was a stabilizing influence in Lieutenant Vesey's life, with none of the exuberant manliness of Midshipman Dorst, her previous lover. Dorst had never been consciously cruel, but he was a young man to whom a few too many drinks or an attractive stranger were not so much a temptation as a way of life.

Daniel smiled. *Much as I myself was. And still am, to a degree.*

Dorst had been thick as two short planks; his sister Miranda appeared to have gotten a double set of the brains of their generation. Cazelet by contrast was extremely clever, though he didn't rub other people's noses in it.

Despite all the reasons to feel otherwise, however, Daniel had *liked* Midshipman Dorst more than he expected ever to like Cazelet. Though he knew that wasn't fair.

The note of the *Merchant*'s thrusters sharpened, then shut off again. Water slopped back and forth against the outriggers, subsiding slowly.

Sorley or whoever was in charge of the present operations had apparently tried to swing the ship with the three functioning thrusters. It would be possible to do that; but it wouldn't be possible for *that* clumsy hand on the throttles to do it, at least not without a serious risk of flipping the ship on her side.

Adele and her two companions hadn't stopped at this bloom of plasma, though they weren't moving very quickly across the rough landscape. The most common species of local plant sprang in knee-high starbursts from a common base. Daniel had examined a clump that grew from a niche in the outcrop near where he stood. The leaves oozed sticky sap if the ends were brushed. The sap wasn't dangerous—there were no browsing animals here for the vegetation to protect itself against—but, like deep mud, it was unpleasant and a thing to avoid.

Besides, the negotiators weren't in a hurry. Letting Sorley stew for a while longer might be useful.

Most of Daniel's crew was still aboard the *Kiesche*, in part to keep them out of the way if something started to happen. Hogg was moving down the slope well to Daniel's left. The stocked impeller he held at the balance didn't look particularly threatening unless you knew Hogg.

Hale was working toward the *Madison Merchant* on Daniel's right with a slung carbine. Woetjans accompanied her. The bosun's baton of high-pressure tube was thrust through her belt, but she didn't carry a projectile weapon.

Woetjans couldn't hit a target with an impeller from much farther away than she could with the tubing, so that was good judgment on her part. Besides, Woetjans had taken three slugs in the chest a few years ago. Though she had survived, she was even less inclined to pick up an impeller than she had been before.

The *Madison Merchant* remained buttoned up. "Sorley's watching them, though," Cazelet said in a harsh tone. "Their optics are pretty decent. Better than any of that can's other equipment, anyway."

He was watching the negotiators—he watched Vesey, at least—with an angry expression. Turning to Daniel, he said, "I ought to be down there with them!"

Daniel didn't smile, though that was his first impulse. Well, his first impulse was to sneer, which wasn't like him and wasn't fair. *I wonder if I'm jealous because he's close to Adele?*

Daniel blinked in horror at the thought. Adele had taken in the orphaned grandson of the woman who had supported Adele when she lost her family in the Three Circles Conspiracy. Resenting the boy was... well, it ought to have been unthinkable!

Aloud he said, "This business will work best if Sorley and his crew don't feel threatened. I suspect that men of their ilk don't even notice people like Tovera."

To the extent there were other people like Tovera. And to the extent that Tovera was a person.

"I suppose," Cazelet muttered. He squeezed the grip of the submachine gun slung across his chest.

The gun was for show, and only because he'd asked for it. Cazelet had proved himself brave and capable in the tussle with the squad waiting to kill Colonel Bourbon in Brotherhood, but he had used his carbine as a pole rather than a gun. That was more than satisfactory, but Daniel suspected that in the crisis Cazelet hadn't been able to pull the trigger.

He wouldn't be able to pull the trigger this time, either; but there wouldn't be any cause to. Hogg wouldn't have to shoot, either; nor Hale, who was working closer than Hogg to get within comfortable range for her less powerful carbine.

The impeller slung over Daniel's shoulder wouldn't be used, either, but...

"Sir?" said Cazelet.

Daniel realized he had been grinning, after a fashion. "If I had to," he said, "I'd aim at the traversing gear of their plasma cannon. The plating there is just for streamlining, and the hydraulic hoses inside won't deflect an osmium slug."

"They can't bring the gun to bear anyway, can they, sir?" Cazelet said. "We've seen that when they tried their thrusters."

"I wouldn't be doing much good, no," Daniel agreed, "but it would be *something* to do."

He shrugged fiercely, trying to shake his mind out of the direction it had been drifting. "There won't be any trouble. If there were, Adele and Tovera would settle it without any need for the rest of us."

That was all true. Daniel spoke forcefully to make the words sound more convincing to Cazelet—and perhaps to the speaker himself.

He kept remembering that Midshipman Dorst had been a crack shot. Not that it would be any more useful to have two impellers rather than one turning the *Merchant*'s gun housing into a colander, but there would have been a degree of companionship that he didn't seem to have with Cazelet.

Which is my fault.

Daniel chuckled as the situation reformed in his head. He unslung his impeller and laid it on the slanting rock behind him. Straightening he said, "I've been thinking about this whole business in the wrong way. Let's watch and be entertained by how Adele and Lieutenant Vesey deal with Sorley and his boneheaded crew."

Daniel heard the squeal of metal rubbing metal before he saw that the freighter's hatch had begun to open.

Worst case, Daniel and Cazelet could watch how Tovera dealt with the kidnappers; but there wasn't any mystery about that.

Adele waved the flag from left to right in front of her, then back again. It was a linen napkin attached by grommets to a length of half-inch plastic pipe. Reed and Walkins, both riggers, had made it for her with as much care as if they had been scrimshawing gifts for people back on Cinnabar.

Possibly they were even more careful than that: they were doing this for the Mistress, for Lady Mundy.

The flag flicked back and forth. Adele felt extremely foolish, but the uniformed Vesey was in titular charge of their detachment and Tovera was staying properly in the background. It was Adele's job to display the truce flag, so she would do so properly.

Besides, Reed and Walkins had been so proud of their handiwork that it would have been churlish not to brandish it proudly. She was Mundy of Chatsworth: *noblesse oblige.*

When they closed the boarding hatch, the Madisons had left their floating extension attached to the shore and to the starboard outrigger. It was a jury-rigged construction, made by bolting boards onto empty lubricant drums. It was over six feet wide, however, which Adele found comforting in comparison with the more technically impressive boarding bridges she was used to from RCN service.

The tight rolls of beryllium alloy with inflatable floatation chambers which Woetjans and her crew extended from the *Sissie*'s ramp—Mon had equipped the *Kiesche* with a similar unit—were compact and impressive. They were only thirty inches wide, however, and Adele found that a little tight when bobbing on the surface of the water.

She was in the lead. When she was thirty feet or so from the shore, the freighter's main hatch shrieked, beginning to open. "Hold up, please," Vesey said in a low voice.

Adele paused. She had been skirting a plant that looked as though it had been made by gluing brown drinking straws together. *I wonder if I can find information for Daniel on these plants?*

But of course she couldn't; not here. She had searched every database on board for information about what was now Cleveland's World, and the scant references had been only to the algae.

"Stop where you are!" called a distorted voice from inside the *Madison Merchant*. The speaker seemed to be using a bullhorn to shout through the opening at the top of the hatchway. "Don't get onto the boarding bridge!"

Adele stopped at the base of the bridge. Vesey came up on her right side; Tovera remained a pace behind on the left. The hatch began to jerk downward with occasional squeals. Adele waved the flag back and forth, just to be doing something.

Mon had fitted external speakers to the *Kiesche* at Daniel's direction, but they weren't normal equipment for a tramp freighter. This alternative made the whole business seem foolish, though, which was a good attitude to have toward it. Captain Sorley was silly, not threatening.

When the hatch had pivoted down enough to expose

the main hatch, Adele saw Rikard Cleveland standing in the middle of the hold. On either side stood a crewman wearing a hardsuit. Cleveland was wearing some sort of harness. Safety lines were clipped to it and to the belts of his attendants.

Tovera giggled. Vesey noticed the sound. Rather than speak to Tovera, she turned to Adele and said, "Why is she laughing?"

Adele had to speak louder than she normally would to be heard over the sound of the hatch lowering, but it was unlikely that anyone on the ship was listening through a parabolic microphone. For that matter, it wouldn't really matter if Sorley overheard her.

"They must think the rigging suits provide protection," she said. "A suit might stop a round from a pocket pistol at this range or from a small submachine gun, but both Tovera and I aim for the head. And those glass-reinforced plastic panels won't even slow slugs from the long-arms which Hogg and Hale are carrying."

Both Madisons held pistols which they aimed in a theatrical fashion at Cleveland's head. It was an absurd show, though if the weapons were loaded there was a real risk that one of them might go off and blow the hostage's brains out accidentally.

The main hatch banged down onto the starboard outrigger. Six more Madisons entered the hold. One was Schmidt, the first officer, whom Adele recognized as the large man who had been guarding Cleveland upstairs in the Dancing Girl. They were armed with a mixture of pistols and long-arms, often supplemented by knives of various sorts.

The only ones who would survive the first two

seconds, Adele thought with clinical detachment, *are those who throw themselves flat on the deck where Tovera and I can't see them from where we stand. We'll have to run up the ramp to finish them.*

Not that it was going to come to that. Adele waved her flag again, figuratively brushing away that sequence of thoughts.

"Captain Sorley!" Vesey called. The visible Madisons were thirty feet away, across the extension and the boarding ramp both, and Sorley must be farther yet. "I'm Lieutenant Vesey of the RCN. We've been sent to procure the release of Rickard Cleveland, a Cinnabar citizen, whom you're holding against his will. Obviously."

"Well, you can just go away again!" came Sorley's magnified voice from the down companionway. The hatch was open, but the captain was standing far enough up the helical staircase that he couldn't be seen. "Master Cleveland made a deal with us back on Xenos, and we're not going to let him welsh on it."

"This planet is listed in the *Sailing Directions* as being suitable only for emergency refuelings," Vesey said. "You've already learned that you can't take off again because of damage to your thrusters. You'd learn if you got to orbit that your High Drives won't work at all. There's a calcium-depositing algae on this planet which is drawn to charged metal, which means any ship which has picked up static while landing through the atmosphere or which has grounded electrical equipment running."

Adele wondered if Sorley had a copy of the *Sailing Directions.* He might have picked the location from a simple chart which didn't have even the *Directions'* brief warning.

"You can test it yourselves," Vesey said. "Look at your outriggers where they're in the water. Scrape the deposit with a knife and see how thick it is."

One of the crewmen turned to Schmidt and said something in a querulous whine. Adele wouldn't have sworn to the words, but it appeared to be something along the lines of, "Is that why the bloody thrusters near flipped us over?"

"Go on," Vesey said, managing to sound contemptuous. "Nobody will shoot you. I promise."

Adele knew the tone was acting. She had never heard Vesey express real contempt for anyone, despite ample justification.

Adele smiled bitterly. Vesey was very different from Signals Officer Mundy, in that respect as in many.

Schmidt snarled a curse. He drew a machete from its canvas sheath and stomped down the boarding ramp. From the corners of his eyes he was watching the marksmen on the slope. His head flinched slightly away as if to increase the distance between him and the gun muzzles.

"When you've released Cleveland," Vesey said, "we'll carry you and your crew back to Brotherhood in safety. If you think your ship can be salvaged, you're welcome to come back and try. Assuming Cleveland remains in good health, of course."

"I'm fine, Lieutenant Vesey," Cleveland called. His voice was steady but perhaps a little higher pitched than it would have been if he hadn't had a pistol socketed in each ear. "I'm very glad to see you."

Schmidt reached the outrigger and swung himself toward the water, holding onto a bitt with his left hand. For a moment his body was almost out of sight from the shore. Adele heard the *skreel!* of steel on steel, then a curse.

Schmidt lurched back onto the top of the outrigger. He glared at Vesey, then turned toward the hatch and bellowed, "It's like she bloody says! It's like a coat of bloody green enamel!"

Sorley stepped out of the companionway, holding a bullhorn. He dropped it as he half-ran, half-hopped to put himself behind the hostage.

"Look, we deserve something!" he called. "We had a deal, me and Master Cleveland, and he tried to walk out on me. The law's on my side."

"There was no deal!" Cleveland shouted. "I had talked to—"

Sorley slapped the back of his head, knocking Cleveland forward. That left Sorley in plain view and the two gunmen pointing their pistols at one another.

"See here!" said Vesey, starting up the ramp. Schmidt stepped in front of her and grabbed her arm. The machete still waggled in his right hand. Vesey kicked him in the crotch with no more hesitation than a spring releasing.

Schmidt bent forward. Vesey gripped the back of his head with both hands and kneed him in the face. She wasn't strong enough to make that as effective as she must have wished, and she almost fell over as the big man slid past her down the ramp.

Adele's hand was in her pocket, but she did not draw her pistol. She didn't look back to see what Tovera was doing, but there were no shots; that probably meant the little submachine gun was still concealed.

Vesey was breathing hard, and her face was white.

She glanced down at Schmidt. Her right knee was bloody, so she had at least broken the fellow's nose.

Adele reminded herself to buy Vesey a set of Grays, then remembered that Vesey was no longer a midshipman without private means but rather the First Officer on ships commanded by Captain Daniel Leary—and therefore staggeringly wealthy in her own right from prize money. Much like Signals Officer Mundy, only more so.

Vesey picked up the dropped machete. Schmidt lay doubled-up at the bottom of the ramp. Adele didn't think he was badly hurt, but he seemed willing to remain out of the action.

She decided to ignore him, since the alternative was to shoot him through an eyesocket. That seemed needlessly harsh to Adele, but it would certainly be Tovera's response if Schmidt threatened to make a problem again.

Adele walked along the floating extension to the outrigger. The Madisons were watching events with expressions ranging from blankness to terror. Occasionally one twitched his gun, but no one actually pointed a weapon at the negotiating team.

Schmidt's cap had fallen off. Vesey picked it up on the point of the machete.

When Vesey bent, Adele had thought she was going to stab the mate through the kidneys. Adele wouldn't have tried to interfere if Vesey had finished the fellow off, but she found it reassuring that the younger woman hadn't changed *quite* that much from the person Adele had thought she knew.

Vesey waved the cap carefully, so that she didn't fling it off the blade. "Captain Sorley!" she said. "I just saved the life of this man here. He may have thought that I was too close to him for my friends on shore to shoot, but—"

The cap billowed and spun as though a gust of wind had caught it. The impeller slug hit the ship's hull with a painful *whang-g-g-g*. The impact was toward the bow, meaning the shot had been Hogg's. There was a neon flash where the osmium projectile bounced from nickel-steel, gouging a divot from the plate.

The cap hung on the machete an instant longer. The second slug hit the blade tip as well as the cloth, flicking the hilt out of Vesey's hand. The machete spun away in a shower of white sparks, landing in the water. The sound of the carbine's projectile hitting the hull sternward had an unexpected bell-like purity.

Vesey lowered her hand, flexing her fingers. Adele hoped the lieutenant had been holding the machete loosely, but even so it would have stung like an electric shock when the slug hit the blade.

"You've heard what the choice is!" Vesey said. "Lay your guns down and surrender or die. Which will you have?"

"Fagh!" Sorley said. "The thrusters are screwed. We have no choice. Throw your guns down, all of you!"

He drew a pistol from a cargo pocket of his utilities and tossed it on the deck. "Let this one go," he said, unclipping one of the safety lines attached to Cleveland's harness; a guard loosed the other one.

The visible crewmen—there were almost thirty others unseen within the ship—began laying down or throwing down their weapons. The jangle of metal on metal was discordant, even without Adele knowing that a gun might go off at any instant.

Sorley walked to the front of the hold, gripping Cleveland's shoulder firmly.

A few of the crewmen raised their hands; the rest did the same, though Vesey hadn't ordered them to do so. Additional crewmen came out of the companionways and entered from side corridors. The hold was filling up.

Adele nodded to Cleveland. "Take your hand off this citizen, Captain Sorley," she said. He jerked his hand away from Cleveland's shoulder; which was good from Sorley's viewpoint because Adele had not forgotten him slapping the boy on the back of the skull. *If I shot him in the wrist, he wouldn't do that again.*

"Thank you very much, Lady Mundy," Cleveland said. Seen at close range, he looked worn and badly needed a bath. "I have my faith, but there were times I felt completely alone."

Adele felt a surge of sympathy. She said, "I know the feeling."

Cleveland's harness wasn't an impediment, but his wrists were bound with a locking tie. Adele was puzzling over how to release it when Hogg stepped past her with his knife open. He severed the tie with a quick pull.

A dozen of the *Kiesche*'s crew and Daniel himself had reached the *Madison Merchant*. They began walking the personnel down to the shore. Adele had supposed the prisoners would be tied or hobbled before they were taken aboard the *Kiesche*, but the Sissies seemed ready to keep control with clubs. The Madisons weren't going to make trouble.

"I know it wouldn't do me any good to sue in Xenos with all his noble friends," Sorley said, "but he owes me a share of the treasure anyhows!"

"I do not owe you anything, Captain Sorley," Cleveland said with a calm determination which reminded Adele that he was a Transformationist—and a civilian, because any of the Sissies present would have replied in a much shorter, harsher fashion. "I don't even know that there is a treasure. In any case, we don't need it now that the war is over."

"*We* don't need it?" Sorley said. "You say that, do you? Well, *I* bloody need it. There's no bloody justice!"

"Some of us," said Tovera, stepping so close to the captain that they were almost chest to chest, "should be glad that there isn't justice. Think about it, Captain Sorley."

Sorley jerked his head back by reflex. Hogg was behind him. His calloused fingers slapped Sorley's skull forward. The blow sounded like a mallet driving a tent stake. Sorley's nose banged against the muzzle of the submachine gun which Tovera had finally taken from her case.

Sorley yelped and threw both hands over his face. Blood dripped down his cheeks.

"Say it, Sorley," Tovera said. "Say you don't want justice. Otherwise I'll *give* you justice."

"Don't!" Captain Sorley said through his fingers. "Don't! I don't want justice!"

"Let's get back to the *Kiesche*, Master Cleveland," Adele said. "We're not needed here."

And I don't want justice, either, Captain Sorley. For I have much more on my conscience than you do on yours.

CHAPTER 30

Brotherhood on Corcyra

Woetjans called, "Hup!" She and the four riggers carrying the extension started down the *Kiesche*'s boarding ramp before it had clanged home on the outrigger. Brother Graves and a squad of troops in naval utilities waited on the quay, but Sissies didn't need an audience to show off their skills.

Daniel stood at the edge of the hatchway with his hands crossed behind his back as though he were on a reviewing stand. He felt a quiet pride. To Adele he said, "The hatch doesn't stick anymore, did you notice? It just needed to be run-in properly. We'll be returning the *Kiesche* in better condition than when I bought her."

"My other employer will probably leave the additional electronics in place," Adele said, looking toward the quay. Daniel wasn't sure that she was actually seeing anything in the present, however. "I'll clear my personal software. Not that it seems likely that the normal crew of a ship like this would be able to use it."

"No, I don't suppose they would," Daniel said mildly.

I doubt the signals section of a battleship would be able to do what you do with it, Adele, he thought, but he didn't say that aloud.

The riggers had clamped the boarding bridge to the end of the ramp and were unrolling it toward the quay. As soon as the far end made contact with the concrete, Hale and Connolly trotted down the bridge to lock it into place. Woetjans turned and bellowed, "All clear, Six!"

"All right, Dasi," Daniel said. "Release the passengers."

The bosun's mate removed the padlock from the cargo cage which held the former crew of the *Madison Merchant*. Barnes, his partner, swung the chain-link partition wide open.

"All right, you filthy scuts!" Dasi said. "Get out and get out fast. If you're still inside when we turn on the steam hoses to clear the muck, that's your lookout!"

Evans, wearing thermal gloves, was indeed holding a charged steam hose. His size and strength made him obvious choice to handle the hose, but Daniel hoped that Evans knew wasn't *really* supposed to open the nozzle until everybody was out of the hold. Worst case, well, there'd be too many burn cases for the *Kiesche*'s Medicomp to handle, but Brotherhood served a mining region and ought to have good medical facilities.

Most of the *Kiesche*'s crew waited on the bridge or in the forward part of the hold. Except for the anchor watch, they would be going ashore shortly in a port with numerous amusements tailored to spacers and hard-rock miners. The groups had similar tastes.

They were all Able Spacers, and their liberty suits ranged from colorful to works of art. The suits were ordinary RCN utilities, but decorated with ribbons along the seams and embroidered patches commemorating ships the spacers had served aboard and landfalls they had made.

The Kiesches were a happy crew. They had money in their pockets and their captain's blessing to spend it on anything that didn't leave them dead or jugged for something he couldn't bail them out of.

"By heaven!" Daniel muttered. "I'm the luckiest captain in the RCN to have a crew like this!"

"Yes," said Adele. "Just as I'm lucky to hit what I shoot at ten times out of ten. Practice has nothing to do with it."

Daniel looked at her and grinned. "Well," he said, "let's just say that we make a good team, the crew and ourselves."

The Madisons shuffled out of the cage, giving Evans as wide a berth as the tight space permitted. Vapor leaked from his hose nozzle, just in case anybody thought the threat was a joke.

The passengers—or prisoners, if you preferred to think of them in that fashion—carried the gear they had brought from the *Madison Merchant*: duffel bags and a variety of makeshift containers. Daniel had allowed anything—except weapons—which they could carry aboard in one trip. The hold had plenty of space. If it was short on other amenities, that was a problem which the Madisons could have avoided by not kidnapping Cleveland.

"Master Cleveland?" Daniel called. Cleveland was in the hold but squeezed into a corner of the forward bulkhead. "Come and join Lady Mundy and myself, please."

The spacers standing in front of Cleveland pushed their neighbors aside to make room. Cleveland passed through with a muttered apology to the spacers and a grateful smile for Daniel.

Spacers took for granted a degree of physical closeness a well-born youth must find uncomfortable. As for the Transformationists—they might believe in the Community of Mankind, but from what Daniel had seen in Pearl Valley, they also believed in a reasonable amount of personal space for each individual despite the barracks-style housing.

"I see Brother Graves waiting for us on the quay," Daniel said, nodding toward the hatchway. "As soon as Cory has released the liberty party, we'll go meet him."

Cleveland nodded. "I'm amazed at all that's happened," he said. "I mean everything—yes, you releasing me so quickly, but being abducted itself. And *everything*—the war being over and Corcyra being at peace again."

The last Madisons were leaving the cage. Sorley had hung back. When he followed Schmidt at the end of the line, he held a case on his right shoulder to conceal his face from Daniel and Adele. Daniel smiled but said nothing.

"If I may ask, Captain?" Cleveland said diffidently. "What will happen to Captain Sorley and his crew?"

"They'll find berths on the ships that begin landing here as soon as word of the peace gets out," Daniel said. "Somebody's always going to need spacers, even spacers like Sorley's lot."

"They will be drafted into the Pantellarian navy," Adele said crisply. She was still looking toward the quay, where the troops were collecting the Madisons as they stepped off the boarding bridge. "Commissioner Arnaud's squadron of the Pantellarian navy, at least."

"Drafted?" said Daniel in surprise. The Madisons weren't from Pantellaria, and some of them—Sorley himself—were Cinnabar citizens.

"Sold, if you prefer," Adele said. "They committed the crime of kidnapping on Corcyra. They were tried in their absence by the Interim Council and sentenced to hard labor—which was commuted to banishment from Corcyra in the custody of a competent authority."

"Tried?" said Cleveland. He was clearly puzzled.

"Justice is quick here," Adele said with her usual composure. "I had a word with Colonel Bourbon and Commissioner Arnaud before we left, and I provided them with an update from orbit while we were waiting for landing permission."

"I see," said Daniel. He did, and he began to smile broadly.

Sorley reached the end of the boarding bridge and realized what was happening to his crew. He turned and shouted, "You dirty *bastard*, Leary! You're going to have us shot, aren't you!"

Woetjans was standing on the quay; she had gone across to check the way Hale and Watkins had trussed the bridge to the bitts. She grabbed Sorley by the shoulder and turned him to face her, then punched him in the stomach.

Sorley doubled up. Woetjans held Sorley's head out over the edge of the bridge so that his mixture of bile and undigested food spewed into the harbor. When Woetjans decided there was no more to come, she tossed the captain to Schmidt's feet and said, "Get him out of here."

As an afterthought, Woetjans kicked Sorley's case into the water also. Dusting her hands together with a grin, she walked back toward the *Kiesche*.

"*All* Kiesche *personnel on liberty are released,*" Cory announced over the PA system. "*Report back in twenty-four hours local time for further orders. Command out.*"

"Hallelujah!" Lorano called, but for the most part the crew filing off the ship was muted though cheerful. The hop to and from Cleveland's World had been short, and it hadn't involved the space battle that most had expected. Some had even been looking forward to a battle.

"*I* bloody well wasn't!" Daniel said. He added to his companions, "Wasn't looking forward to fighting the *Merchant* in space, I mean. Say, Master Cleveland? You may not know that we named the planet after you. When we get back to Xenos I'll register HH1509270 at Navy House as Cleveland's World."

"Really?" said Cleveland. "You can do that?"

"I don't think there'll be a protest," Daniel said. He thought of adding, "It's not really much of an honor." He let the initial statement stand instead.

"Really," Cleveland repeated, this time without the rising inflection. "I... well, thank you. My mother will be pleased, I think. For a long time she didn't get much news of me that pleased her."

The officials waiting on the dock had come up the boarding bridge when the liberty party was past. Brother Graves was following a man and a woman in gray uniforms of different cut.

The man's tunic had a plastic badge on the left breast reading CUSTOMS SERVICE; it didn't quite cover the unfaded strip of fabric where an embroidered patch had been recently removed. The band on the woman's cap said *Harbormaster*.

"We're here to collect customs duties," the man said.

"And docking fees," the woman added. "The procedures were instituted, ah, recently."

From the way you put it, they were instituted this morning, Daniel thought. *At any rate, it couldn't have been longer than four days ago, because they weren't in place when we lifted off.*

Aloud he said, "I believe Lieutenant Cory can deal with docking fees, madam. And we carried only passengers on this arrival, but you're welcome to search the hold. You'll be more comfortable if you wait until the hold has been sterilized, but it's your choice."

He turned and called, "Lieutenant Cory, will you come aft, please?"

"Brother Cleveland, I'm very pleased to see you safe," Graves said, edging to the side so that he could speak to his fellow. "I'm afraid I've got bad news for you on the below-surface scans you asked me to look at, though. If we can go to my office, I can show you there. When the captain is free, that is."

Cory entered from the bridge. He'd volunteered to be duty officer so that Vesey and Cazelet could take the initial liberty.

Hale is on anchor watch, come to think, Daniel realized. Not that he was concerned about a problem until the former classmates were off duty in turn; and then it was none of his business.

"We can use my equipment," Adele said. "Unless Cory needs the console?"

"Cory, you're relieved on the bridge until further

notice," Daniel said. "Come this way please, Master Graves, and I'll show you the hospitality of the ship."

Graves looked doubtful. "Ah—I've scanned Pearl Valley, with much more sophisticated apparatus than what was used on the scans Brother Cleveland found on file. The results take a great deal of specialized capacity."

"I think you'll find that my hardware will be sufficient to the task." Adele said. Daniel noticed that she said "my" rather than "our." "If not, we can adjourn to your office, Brother Cleveland."

Where we will wait for the sun to rise in the west, thought Daniel. *Because that's about as likely as the chance of Graves' software overpowering Adele's equipment.*

He closed the bridge hatch behind them, leaving Cory to deal with the local officials in the hold.

Adele took the data chip from the case which Graves handed her. Setting it in the console's holder, she said, "It will project in the center of the compartment as well as on the two displays, but you'll probably want to manipulate it, Brother Graves. Take the command seat, and I'll sit at the back. As I usually do."

Instead of seating himself immediately, Graves frowned and said, "I realize this is a very powerful unit, Lady Mundy, but the programming necessary to read this format—"

A holographic index of files appeared in the air where Cleveland and Daniel could read it. So could Hogg and Tovera, for that matter, though Adele doubted they had any desire to. She said nothing.

"I apologize," Graves said politely. He sat down and brought up a file with the stylus he had drawn from his pocket. Adele said nothing, but she appreciated the simplicity of Graves' apology.

The image meant nothing to Adele. It might have been a close-up of luncheon spread: an inverted arch of basically pinkish color, with overlayers and inclusions of contrasting colors, generally shades of pastel green. Near the bottom of the U was a black speck; below was a layer of sullen crimson.

"This is a cross-section of Pearl Valley," Graves said. "The pink is mudstone laid down thirty thousand years ago. The underlayer is granite, and there are blocks of harder rock which were engulfed as the mudstone formed when the valley was part of a lake bed."

Cleveland nodded. Daniel didn't react, but Adele assumed he understood as clearly as even she did.

"The item Brother Cleveland noticed is here," Graves said, circling the black dot and then expanding it to fill the image area. "I suspect the original surveyors ignored it because it was too small to be of significance. They were looking for copper ore, after all."

"That isn't a natural occurrence," Daniel said. "It has shape. No crystal could look like that."

"It has shape . . ." Graves said. Adele heard an unexpectedly grim tone in his voice. "And it's hollow, which we can see because one end is open and there are holes in some of the facets."

He switched to another image, this one a schematic of pale blue lines. The image rotated slowly. The shape was irregular, something like a drinking tumbler which had been squeezed in the middle and whose sides were pleated. Besides the open top, holes shaped like twisted teardrops pierced the sides in several places. The bottom, though concave, was solid.

"It isn't a container of jewels," Cleveland said, "but it's something. And somebody, Captain Pearl or *somebody*, buried it there."

"Pearl Valley's mudstone would be very easy to bore through or trench," Graves said, returning to the image of the object in its matrix. He reduced the scale slightly. "It couldn't be disturbed without leaving evidence of the disturbance, however; not when I've examined the site with equipment as sensitive as what I've been using."

He grinned and turned toward Daniel. Adele watched his face, now in profile, as an inset on her display.

"You may be too polite to ask whether I could have made a mistake, Captain," Graves said. "Yes, of course I could, though these images don't require very subtle analysis. I asked two other engineers to look over the scans. They aren't members of our community, but I trust them personally and professionally. They came to the same conclusions that I did."

Graves shrugged. "The mudstone appears to have formed over the object," he said. "If it's an artifact, it isn't a human artifact, and it certainly isn't something that Captain Pearl buried."

Adele had a great deal of experience in sharpening fuzzy images, but these had not been manipulated. She was looking at raw data as it came from the surveying equipment, and they were razor sharp even at the highest magnification.

"Brother Graves?" she said. "What is the object made of? It would appear to be very dense."

"Yes, Lady Mundy," Graves said, turning toward her with a troubled expression. Adele had inset real-time images of the three other principals on his display, but Graves seemed to be trying to look through the holographic screen to see her directly. "It's almost impossibly dense. Granted that our scans have a degree of error and that gravity plotting is suggestive rather than solid proof—"

He shrugged again. "My colleagues and I believe that the artifact is made from a stable transuranic element," Graves said. "Element 126, presumably, though the element's existence is merely a prediction, and it has no name. Well, unbihexium, but that's a placeholder unless and until the element itself is discovered. Which we apparently have just done."

"Then it's valuable after all," Cleveland said. He too looked worried. "Even though it isn't a case of jewels."

"I suppose you could say that the artifact is of incalculable value," Graves agreed. "There isn't a market for such a thing, because it would be unique in human experience, but it's certainly valuable."

"I don't see any sign of an antenna, a wire, or a spike on the end," Daniel said. "I thought it might be a sort of cavity resonator, trapping signals and reemitting them on a different wavelength."

"What sort of signals, ah, Captain?" Adele said. "I didn't make a detailed search of Pearl Valley, but I think my equipment would have noticed anything that didn't fit standard parameters."

"I don't know," Daniel said. He grinned engagingly. "Nothing electronic, then, not if you didn't pick it up."

He looked from Graves to Cleveland, then said as if idly, "You believe Pearl Valley is a good place to live, Master Cleveland. For that matter, I liked the atmosphere myself, though I'm probably not a good example. I generally like places."

"Yes, that's so," Cleveland said, obviously puzzled

at the change of subject. "About the valley, certainly. And I'm glad to hear that you're a happy man, sir."

"Pretty generally, yes," Daniel said, still grinning. "What do you suppose feelings look like? And how would you transmit them?"

"There's no evidence..." Graves said. He let his words trail off, perhaps because he had thought further and had realized that there was no objective evidence on *any* part of the matter. The healthful, welcoming nature of the Transformationist community was wholly subjective.

"Since we don't appear to need weapons anymore, thank goodness," Cleveland said, "then we don't need the money we were going to buy weapons with, do we, Brother Graves?"

"I don't accept the connection between the artifact and our faith," Graves said. "I'm confident that if we drill down and bring the object to the surface, which we could do very easily, it will have no adverse effect on Pearl Valley or the Transformationist community."

He shook his head slowly and continued, "But no, I don't see that the community has a serious need for money. Many of those who join us do so after successful careers in the wider world, and the members who guide our investments are quite skilled."

"Then I suggest—" Cleveland began.

His face changed, and he straightened on his seat. "Captain Leary," he said in a formal tone. "Forgive me for forgetting that you and my mother are each due a third of any treasure which the expedition finds. And it appears that we *have* found a treasure."

"If my sister were here," Daniel said, "she might have an opinion on the matter. But she isn't here, and I'm not in the business of money."

He shrugged and said, "No treasure has been recovered. You owe me absolutely nothing, and I'm confident that Mistress Sand would say the same. Not that it matters, because she isn't here any more than Deirdre is."

Daniel looked at Adele and raised an eyebrow. "Do you have anything to add, Lady Mundy?" he asked. "You had some business of your own to transact on Corcyra, I believe?"

"I've accomplished everything I came to do," Adele said. *In a neater fashion than either Deirdre Leary or Mistress Sand can have imagined that I would. Neater than I imagined myself.*

"Then I think we're done with necessary business," Daniel said nodding. "However—"

He looked around the compartment. His grin was just short of splitting his face. "Although it doesn't matter to anybody and therefore nobody can be disappointed, I *do* have an idea as to where Captain Pearl hid whatever it was he brought from Bay. Anybody else interested in seeing if I'm right?"

He's really a little boy, Adele thought. Then, *May he never change!*

Cleveland stood up, grinning back at Daniel. "I may have found peace and enlightenment," he said, "but I haven't lost my sense of curiosity. I certainly would like to learn!"

"And I," said Graves, rising also.

"Hogg?" said Daniel, getting to his feet. "You usually carry fishing lures, don't you?"

"Aye," said Hogg. "And I've got a shotgun if you'd like to try the local game besides."

"Just the lure," said Daniel. "We're going fishing for treasure."

CHAPTER 31

Brotherhood on Corcyra

The *Kiesche*'s whole crew stood near the pool in front of the Manor, waiting for Daniel to do something. He hadn't made any announcement, but obviously somebody had.

He looked at Vesey. She nodded. The set of the lieutenant's jaw showed that she was uncomfortable, but her voice didn't tremble as she said, "Sir, it seemed to me that this is what we came here to do and that the crew ought to have a chance to watch if they wanted to."

She drew a deep breath and swallowed. She said, "And before you ask, I talked to Captain Samona—"

Arnaud had made the former exile leader second in command of the Pantellarian naval forces on Corcyra.

"—and he offered to send ten spacers under Commander Angelotti to the *Kiesche*, so that I could relieve Lieutenant Cory and the anchor watch to join us."

Daniel thought for a moment, then grinned and said, "Very good, Vesey."

His only hesitation had been his surprise that Vesey,

459

of all people, would make such a decision on her own. It was *good* that she had—but surprising.

Sweeping the gathering crowd with his eyes, he said, "If this is the way you Kiesches want to spend your time, you're welcome to do so, though I'll say that I usually found more interesting things to do on liberty. Before I became a staid and proper commanding officer, that is."

He cleared his throat and said, "And you know, I might decide to get a little improper myself once I've taken care of this little problem."

He grinned at the laughter. "I don't expect this to be very exciting, though."

"Well, we're ready for it if you're wrong," said Barnes. He and Sun had drawn stocked impellers from the arms locker, while Dasi had a submachine gun. Woetjans held a cutting bar instead of her usual length of pipe.

What in heaven's name has Vesey told them? Daniel trusted those four spacers with the weapons they carried, which he wouldn't have said about everyone even in this picked crew. He couldn't imagine how their hardware would be useful in the present situation, though.

"People want to help, Daniel," said Adele quietly from his right side. "They don't like to feel that they're useless, even when they obviously are. None of us like that."

She smiled. Daniel was used to Adele showing nothing in her expression. He had never seen her looking so sad, though.

Hogg squatted on the lip of the pool, working with the controller. The lure dangled in the water, collecting nerve frequencies which the controller sorted and analyzed.

The shallow end of the pool had originally been four feet deep. Several inches of detritus, mostly organic, covered it. Woetjans had used a whipstaff to probe down ten feet before she found hard bottom at the deep end, but the muck over the plasticized base was at least four feet thick. You could no more stand on it than you could stand on the water itself, but things certainly lived in its darkness.

Daniel stripped his tunic off, then cinched his belt tighter to make it more difficult for things to wriggle down inside. He had bloused the cuffs of his trousers under the tops of his spacers' boots, which themselves were tough though flexible. They could be worn within a rigging suit as well as by themselves. While the boots didn't make swimming easier, neither did Daniel expect them to be a great hindrance.

Hogg looked up and said, "You know, master, I've never been the hand at one of these that you are. How about you take the controller and I get in the water? It's hot, and I wouldn't mind the dip anyhow."

"We'll do it my way, Hogg," Daniel said. He didn't try to argue: there was nothing to argue about. One or the other of them was going to take his chances with the sponge, and Daniel Leary would make that decision. *Had* made that decision.

The water in the pool circulated clockwise, driven by slow strokes of the sponge's tentacles, but the surface remained a mirror to the eye. Daniel could see the bottom here in the shallow end, though the water itself was dark and the muck was smooth except where something—a twig or in one case what looked very much like a surgical pin of stainless steel—stuck out of it.

A worm-shaped animal the length of Daniel's thumb writhed into view, then vanished again beneath dead fronds from the plants in pots on the Manor's porch roof. The creature had scores of tiny legs and a pair of mandibles half the length of its stubby body.

Hogg rose, holding the controller in one hand and the lure in the other. The filament that connected them was a ghost in the sunlight. It coiled itself on a reel in the controller when the lure came out of the water.

"Suit yourself," Hogg said with bad grace. "If it was me doing it, though, I'd lob in a grenade first."

"That would divide the sponge into bits," Daniel said, "without killing them. It would make the pool into the equivalent of a bath in acid for any animal life, unless the lure works. If the lure does work, then the grenade wasn't necessary. And it *will* work."

"I said what I said," Hogg muttered, but he wasn't really arguing.

Daniel couldn't imagine why the trick with the lure wouldn't work. Even if things went wrong, the Kiesches would get him out before he was devoured and the Medicomp in the ship would take care of the stings. *It's going to work fine!*

As soon as Daniel and his crew had arrived, loafers on the plaza had begun drifting over to see what was going on. Now more civilians joined the spectators, some of them people who had been crossing the plaza but also guests from the hotel portion of the Manor and staff members from government offices on the ground floor.

Daniel hadn't paid much attention to the audience.

Logically he had nothing—well, almost nothing—to worry about, but millions of years of instinct told his nervous system otherwise. Then Adele called, "Good morning, Captain Monfiore," and Daniel looked away from the surface of the pool.

"Giorgi!" he said. "Say, you must have made good time."

Hogg placed the lure against Daniel's chest and covered it with a length of cargo tape. The tape could be removed easily with alcohol, though it would leave a red patch that itched like a case of hives. That was inconsequential against what might happen if the lure didn't stay in touch with his bare skin, masking Daniel's own electronic signature.

"When we get an offer like yours," the young Ischian said, "we make the best time we can. And I'm here as a representative of the planet, not just the Monfiores. Though other clans will be sending their own negotiators shortly, you can count on that."

Monfiore shook his head with an expression of amazement. "Daniel," he said, "you've saved Ischia. There'll be a statue to you in every clan capital on the planet, I swear it. And any help I can give you myself, well, just let me know."

"You and Ischia generally have already helped a great deal," Daniel said. "And believe me, you're going to earn whatever haulage fees you work out with Commissioner Arnaud. But you'll have to forgive me for the moment, because I have to clean up a little job right now."

Hogg had finished cross-taping the lure. He stepped away, looking at the readout on the controller. His face was stony.

"What are you...?" Monfiore said, looking down into the pool between himself and Daniel. He blurted, "By all heaven, Leary! Is that a firepot? I've never seen one that big! And what's it doing here anyway?"

"That's what I'm going to learn," Daniel said. "I think that a spacer named Captain Pearl brought it from Ischia, and I hope to learn that he brought something else with it."

Cleveland and Graves, the only civilians who knew what Daniel was about, waited patiently. It was a credit to their philosophy that they showed no signs of impatience. *Though surely they must* feel *impatience?*

"Wait!" Monfiore said. "Daniel, you're not thinking of getting in there, are you? Those pants won't be any protection if the firepot grabs you, and one that size, well, I wouldn't doubt if its tentacles could reach the whole length of this pond. You don't know what the stings feel like, but trust me, it's worse than you can possibly imagine."

"I'll be all right, Giorgi," Daniel said. "The sponge, the firepot, will think I'm one of its cleaner lice, that's all. The trousers are for other things that might take a nip out of me. I'll risk losing a finger, but there's parts I won't risk."

Daniel was impatient, however well the Transformationists were handling the delay. He sat on the lip of the pool and looked up at Hogg. "Ready, Hogg?" he said.

"I'm ready," Hogg said. "And you're as pigheaded as any man born. Except that pigs is really pretty smart, and you bloody well aren't!"

"Daniel, please," Monfiore said. "I was stung by a firepot when I was clamming, no bigger than my little finger, so I didn't see it when I reached down to clear the scoop. I was in bed for a month!"

He started to come around the pool, but he had fifteen feet to go and one of the Kiesches would stop him if necessary. They didn't know what Six was doing, but they knew that no civilian was going to keep him from doing it while his spacers were alive.

Daniel slid into the pool. Trickles dribbled down into his boots before the water really penetrated the fabric of his trousers. It was much colder than he had expected. He wondered what the rate of flow of the spring feeding the pool was.

His feet squished onto the bottom, lifting the muck. The current was too slight for Daniel to notice a direction in the way the cloud spread. He didn't move for a moment, waiting to see how the sponge would react.

There was no reaction. Despite Monfiore's warning, Daniel doubted whether the creature's tentacles could reach him here; the handbook on Ischian natural history which Adele had found said that the tentacles rarely were longer than the firepot's body. The specimen here was probably larger—and much older—than the creatures got on their world of origin where they faced predators; but even so.

Daniel moved forward by slow steps. He'd be in over his head shortly, but he preferred to walk for as long as he could, hoping to make less disturbance that way.

The water on his bare torso was startling at first, but as expected Daniel didn't notice it after the first few moments. That was one of the reasons why he hadn't gone straight into the deep end where the sponge was attached, though that would have been the least disturbing way of getting there.

Entering at the deep end would also mean that his first contact with the sponge would be full-body. That seemed an even better reason to move up slowly.

Weed rooted in the bottom trailed across Daniel's skin. The leaves were fan-shaped but so thin that he hadn't noticed them when he looked into the water from above. They were being browsed by inch-long creatures—worms? larvae?—wearing cases glued together from bits of debris. They must be why the weed hadn't completely choked the pool, since the sponge wasn't a browser.

"Hey!" cried an onlooker. "Hey, get that feller outa there! There's a thing in the end that'll eat him alive, and I don't mean maybe!"

"Shut up, ye bloody fool!" Woetjans said. "Six knows what he's doing!"

I wonder if the weed and the insects are native to Corcyra? It was a less disturbing subject to consider than wondering whether tentacles were going to grip his waist and snatch him into excruciating pain. *The Medicomp won't help if I die of anaphylactic shock before they get me to the ship.*

Daniel's next step put his chin into the water. He bobbed up and stroked forward easily with both arms. The trousers were a drag, and he wasn't kicking his booted feet, but his arms would support him well enough for the few yards he had to go.

Something trailed across Daniel's bare belly. It had been a tentacle, six feet long at least. The natural history database had been wrong, or at least it wasn't correct for Ischian firepots transplanted to Corcyra.

The tentacle had brushed him instead of grabbing, and the stingers which covered the sponge's arms as well as all other portions of its exterior skin had not come out. The tentacle had simply been moving the water to bring food toward the creature's maw.

Daniel took a deep breath. Another tentacle danced over his skin, trailing from his right shoulder to his left. It felt like the caress of an insect's wing.

He ducked under water. The sponge was a mass of pink and brown as big around as a washtub. The dark water muted its colors, but that filter blurred everything else to make the sponge stand out sharply.

The creature was attached to the end of the pool. Daniel extended his right hand to feel the wall. The body of the sponge felt like a half-full wine sack against the inside of his arm. His fingertips touched a hard, slick surface, the pool's plasticized end wall. The long side nearest the Manor was natural stone through which ground water percolated.

Daniel pushed hard at the sponge, his mind disconnected from knowledge of the thousands of fiery cilia he was trying to squeeze out of his way. He touched a latch, but that took the last of his breath. He surfaced with a splash and a loud gasp, his eyes shut.

"Six! You all right!" Woetjans bellowed. Other Kiesches were shouting a mélange of similar things.

"It's fine!" Daniel said and almost splashed under again. "I'm fine. I think I've found it."

He took three deep breaths in sequence. He didn't try to answer questions as he trod water. With his lungs full, he ducked under again.

Daniel knew where to go this time and thrust down with both hands. The sponge's body resisted like a roll of rubber matting, flexible but too massive to be easily moved.

Cleaner lice the size of his thumbnail crawled onto his arm. His skin prickled as they nipped off hairs—dead protein.

Daniel gripped the latch lever and tried to pivot it downward. The tentacles touched him, trying to shove him away the way they would have done a floating log. The sponge was a communal entity which had no central nervous system, let alone a brain. Nevertheless, the species' responses had allowed it to survive since the appearance of multicelled life on Ischia.

If the tentacles rip the lure off my chest . . . Daniel thought.

Adrenaline—he wasn't in a panic, but his glands operated on the orders of his lizard brain's hundreds of millions of years of reflexes—flooded his system. His hands twisted convulsively, snapping the corrosion that had bound the latch.

The access plate of what was intended for a filter compartment swung sideways, taking with it the sponge which was attached to the perforated panel. The creature's body was so large that Daniel couldn't open the compartment fully, but he was able to reach in with his right hand and grasp the drawstring bag his fingers found there.

Daniel shoved himself back, popping to the surface well away from the wall of the deep end. He backstroked, kicking furiously this time.

The sponge lashed the water wildly, much as it would have done if a storm tore loose the rock which held it to a shoreline. *If a tentacle grabs me now, it'll try to use me as an anchor, and I might very well drown.*

Daniel laughed at the thought. The spectators probably thought he was laughing in joy at having survived, but the truth was a little stranger than that. He wouldn't try to explain it to anyone, though.

Hands gripped Daniel's upper arms and half-jerked, half-dragged him onto the plaza on his back. Cory had his left and—heavens, Adele!—had his right.

Daniel looked up at her. "You're stronger than I thought," he said through wheezes.

"Hysterical strength, I suppose," Adele said, stepping backward.

Daniel lurched into a sitting position, then rotated to bring his left hand down on the plaza to help him stand. The Kiesches were cheering. Actually, most of the spectators were cheering, even the majority who didn't have any idea what was going on.

Daniel turned to the Transformationists—who were cheering also. Their faith didn't prevent them from defending themselves or from feeling enthusiasm about wholly nonreligious matters, apparently.

"Master Cleveland," Daniel said. "You might see what's in here. I rather hope it's what you were looking for."

He held out the bag. The fabric was an extruded synthetic, but the drawstrings appeared to be purple silk, tied off in a bow.

Cleveland undid the bow, then carefully teased the mouth of the bag open. Instead of pouring the contents into the palm of his hand, he reached in with two fingers and brought out a jewel.

It was a perfect ovoid about the size of a hen's egg. Though the clear stone was smooth, not faceted, it blazed in the sunlight. Around it was a network of hair-fine metal with a purple cast.

"I'm not an expert, Cleveland," Daniel said, "but I

would guess that you have a diamond. And I wouldn't be greatly surprised to learn that the filigree is your unbihexium, Brother Graves, because it certainly doesn't look like any metal that I'm familiar with."

There were more cheers. Daniel cheered too.

"I'll report on the library's installation when it's complete," Brother Graves said as he and Cleveland accompanied Adele down Central Street's final slope to the harbor. "Is the best way to reach you through your townhouse in Xenos, or should I send the information in care of the navy?"

Adele didn't answer immediately, because the roar of the ship landing overwhelmed speech. The vessel's computer tried to hold it in a hover, but its poorly synchronized thrusters started a wobble. It dropped the last ten feet into the water as the best alternative available to the machine intelligence.

Adele's tiny smile was perhaps colder than usual. The computer was correct, of course, but the crew which had just been badly jounced was probably cursing it rather than their own poor maintenance for causing the controlled crash. Saving stupid, lazy people often required hard measures. In Adele's experience, they never thanked you for it.

Brotherhood Harbor was much busier now than it had been when Adele saw it first from orbit. She would never have a real spacer's eye for a ship, but she knew that the vessel was a moderate-sized freighter, an ordinary tramp though larger than most of the ships which called here while fighting was going on.

Daniel—or even Evans—could probably have told her where the ship had been built. Study would accomplish many things, but real skill required a knack as well, a degree of focused interest which Adele would never have for starships.

As the echoes of the splash receded, Adele said, "To Chatsworth Minor, I suppose. But there isn't really any need to report. I'm pleased that you've taken on the task, since it needn't have been any concern of yours. And that you've given refuge to Master Lipschitz as well."

"Master Lipschitz doesn't appear to be any kind of burden, milady," Cleveland said, smiling. "As thin as he is, he won't be straining the commissary to feed him."

That's the first time I've heard him joke, Adele thought. *Perhaps he's been taking lessons from Tovera.*

More seriously, Cleveland had been calmer and more centered since they had landed on Corcyra and he'd come back into contact with fellow Transformationists. That meant mostly contact with Graves, of course, who was looking better also. Adele wasn't sure that a philosophy—or religion, whatever term one wished—that punished people who weren't in the company of other people was a very beneficial one.

Daniel was waiting with Hogg in the plaza where Central met Harborside. There was no longer a platoon of soldiers stationed there, but traders had laid out their wares on blankets—the same sort of food and tawdry whimsies that bumboats hawked to the anchored vessels.

With peace had come buskers. A man was juggling, and a couple—the boy was young and the girl was very young—was singing a dialogue between Lord Randall and his mother. The girl wasn't very convincing in the part of an old woman, but her voice was clear and pleasant.

Adele stepped ahead of the Transformationist; they slowed deliberately to let her reach Daniel alone. Tovera had been following the three of them. The fact that she didn't sprint ahead to put herself between her mistress and the two men showed either that she was mellowing or that she trusted Hogg to prevent Cleveland and Graves from attacking Adele successfully.

That Tovera trusted Hogg seemed more likely.

"Daniel," Adele said, "I regret that I'm late. I wasn't noticing the time or I would have informed you that it was taking longer than I'd thought to remove the last case of books from the rubble."

"We weren't going to leave without you," Daniel said, smiling. "With an ordinary spacer I might have sent out a squad under a bosun's mate to check the bars and jail, but I didn't think that would be of very much use in finding you."

He gestured the Transformationist forward. "Brothers," he called. "I'm glad to see you again before we lift. Or have you decided to return to Cinnabar with us? You at least, Master Cleveland?"

The juggler was using four cubes whose faces flashed changing imagery as they spun. His hat lay on the ground in front of him with a few coins in it, but a young boy was also working the spectators, offering to sell similar cubes.

"Thank you, Captain," Cleveland said. "I'm to go back to Pearl Valley as Brother Graves' aide. Sister Rennie will be replacing him in the office here. She has the skills, and her, well, other skills don't appear to be needed to defend the community at present."

"Will Colonel Rennie be bringing a companion?" Adele said. A few years ago she wouldn't have spoken, and until she joined Daniel and the family of spacers around him, she wouldn't even have understood the reason she was asking the question.

"The workload in Brotherhood should drop back to its previous—pre-invasion—level," Graves said, calmly but with a slight frown. "We need an agent here, but there's no need for a second person to be removed from the community. Someone will replace Rennie in a few months."

Adele shrugged. It was none of her business, and she had never seen any point in arguing in support of the obvious.

Daniel looked at her sharply, then said to the Transformationist, "You feel that separation from your community is a hardship. What Lady Mundy and I have noticed is that both of you seem much better off with the other's companionship than you were while you were separated from *all* your fellows. Speaking as an RCN officer, if the operation were under my command, I would assign at least two personnel to every detached location."

He grinned and added, "Just as I would to a listening post. Eh, Hogg?"

"It'd help if the folks assigned wasn't rubes who couldn't find their asses with both hands," Hogg said. "But yeah, one guy alone is worse 'n useless."

Graves and Cleveland didn't understand the background to the discussion, but they understood there was one—and that they were listening to experts. Adele would have let the Transformationists make their own decision, their own *stupid* decision. Daniel was treating them as ignorant, not stupid; which was kinder and probably more accurate.

Adele smiled faintly. *I will never become Daniel. But that doesn't matter, so long as I have Daniel around.*

Cleveland looked at Graves. "I'll stay with Rennie for, for a time," he said. "You can do a better job of explaining to the community why we think the policy should change."

"No," the older man said. "The rest of the troops from Hablinger will arrive this afternoon on their way back to Pearl Valley. I'll speak with Brother Heimholz. I think he'll agree to stay with Sister Rennie until they both can be replaced."

Graves gave Daniel a sort of smile. "I'll borrow your analogy, Captain," he said. "Rennie and Heimholz will understand it even better than I do."

"Thank you, Daniel," Adele said, using his first name to make clear to the others that she was speaking as a friend rather than as a colleague. "The Transformationists have dug out the library, the books, from the basement of the Gulkander Palace."

"Not just Rikard and me, Captain," Graves said, smiling again. "The first half of our Hablinger contingent arrived yesterday on their way back, and I asked them to help excavate as a small return for what you and Lady Mundy have done for us and for the planet."

Adele didn't remember having seen the agent smile when the *Kiesche* had first arrived on Corcyra. Time spent in the company of Cleveland had improved his mood even more than she thought at the time she remarked on it.

"Considering that the palace was hit by a pair of missiles..." Adele said. She had been horrified when she first saw the ruins of the building. "It's a miracle that the library wasn't crushed by stone blocks. Cory aimed well, the pillars and arches supporting the ground floor had been well constructed, and the collection's librarian had placed the books carefully where they were as protected as they could be under the conditions. Which brings up another matter."

She turned to Graves and made a slight bow. To Daniel she continued, "The librarian is a man named Lipschitz. He went to live with a cousin after Colonel Mursiello moved into the Palace. Brother Graves agreed to allow Master Lipschitz to accompany the books to Pearl Valley, where I think they'll be safer than anywhere else on Corcyra until matters stabilize a little more."

"We have plenty of room in the *Kiesche*'s hold," Daniel said, his tone making the words a question. "If you'd like to bring them with you, I can have Woetjans take a party to wherever you've got them now and pack them aboard safely. It won't take an hour."

Adele realized that though the *Kiesche*'s thrusters were cold, her pumps were running. Their vibration made the water around the ship's outriggers and hull tremble into tiny pointed waves.

They've waited liftoff for me, Adele realized. She should have sent a message, but she had been so involved with the process of disinterring the books that it hadn't crossed her mind. At the back of her mind, she had assumed that if Daniel needed her, he would call *her*. Instead, he and the rest of the crew had waited quietly rather than disturbing whatever she was doing.

"I've been discourteous," Adele said without an explicit context. "My mother would be upset to learn that. She felt that courtesy was the most basic rule which set human beings above the beasts."

"I doubt that your mother and I would have gotten along well," Daniel said. "More to the point, I suspect your mother would have been useless to the RCN, whereas you are valuable beyond anything I could compare you with. Now, shall we bring the library back with us? And Master Lipschitz won't be a problem, either, so long as he doesn't expect the *Kiesche* to have luxurious staterooms."

"No," said Adele. "I think the Gulkander Library is part of Corcyra's cultural heritage, though it may be some while—generations, centuries even—before the planet understands that. Our friends here—"

She nodded to the Transformationists; they smiled briefly in response. They had remained expressionless while Daniel and Adele discussed the situation.

"—will keep the collection together while the process goes on. While Corcyra becomes civilized."

She decided to smile as though the final comment had been a joke. It wasn't.

"Master Lipschitz won't leave the books," Cleveland said. "He was sneaking into the palace basement at night to make sure that they weren't being injured, even though he knew that if Mursiello's thugs caught him they were likely to shoot him right there. I got to talking with him a bit while we were we were moving rubble."

He gestured to the dusty work shirt and coveralls he was wearing. The right-side pocket of Graves' similar outfit was ripped half open where something heavy had snagged the fabric and continued on in whatever direction it had been going in the first place.

"I suggested that we do it by hand," Graves said with a rueful glance down at his own garments. "I was afraid that if we used heavy equipment, we might finish what the missiles had started. That was the right decision, but by the time we were done I was wishing that our other fifty soldiers had come back from Hablinger with the first company."

"Master Lipschitz is really very welcome," Cleveland said. "The community has a number of members who will be as pleased to see the books as you were yourself."

He grinned engagingly and added, "Well, *almost* as pleased."

Daniel shrugged and said, "Who knows? Perhaps Lipschitz will wind up becoming a Transformationist himself."

"I very much doubt that," Adele said, hoping her voice didn't display the horror that she felt at the suggestion. "I believe that Master Lipschitz regards spirituality much the way as I do—as something other people talk about."

"You might find peace with us yourself, Lady Mundy," Graves said quietly. He smiled, but she could see that the expression was an attempt to lighten the sadness of his tone.

"No doubt I'll find peace one day, Brother Graves," she said, nodding crisply. "Thank you for the offer."

I'll find peace, I'm sure. From an impeller slug or perhaps when a missile blasts the ship I'm in to vapor. But Graves meant well; they all meant well, and she kept those thoughts to herself.

"Well, if you gentlemen are satisfied," Daniel said, nodding to Cleveland and Graves, "and you've finished your business, Adele . . . ?"

"I have," Adele said, nodding.

"Then we'll take our leave," Daniel said, straightening. He offered his hand, first to Graves. "I hope things continue to go well for your community. If you happen to be on Cinnabar when I am, I'd be glad to show you Bantry. I find it as peaceful as you say Pearl Valley is. I'm sure I didn't see Pearl Valley under the best circumstances, of course."

Adele straightened also. She wasn't precisely looking forward to Cinnabar, but she would be as glad as not to be off Corcyra. The only people on the planet who cared about the things that were important to her were some of the Transformationists, but she had more in common with farmers and hard-rock miners than she did with a band of cultists.

"Ah, if you please, Captain?" Cleveland said, reaching into his right cargo pocket. "There's one more thing I'd like you to take care of."

He brought out the blue bag and started to open it. Before Cleveland could bring out the huge diamond, Daniel squeezed the mouth of the bag closed.

"I'll take it on faith that the contents of the bag are what they were when we found it," Daniel said. "I'd just as soon not tell everybody on the harborfront what we've got here."

Tovera giggled. Hogg grunted and gave his version of the same thought: "Let somebody try."

"I prefer a quiet life," Daniel said, grinning at Cleveland and Graves. "I realize that not everyone shares my preferences."

"With respect, Captain Leary," Graves said, "I'd be surprised to learn that you won the Cinnabar Star by living a quiet life. It's the highest decoration that the navy awards, is it not?"

"It's not nearly as pretty as the sash and medal that make me a Companion of Novy Sverdlovsk, though," Daniel said. "But if you prefer, let me correct myself by saying that I'm never more content than when I'm standing at the masthead of a ship in the Matrix, except perhaps when I'm fishing on Bantry."

Everything Daniel said was the truth, Adele realized, but it was also a way to blur the real truth into the background. Daniel was brave without thinking about it; he was skilled in his profession beyond most other naval officers; and he was a gentleman who would no more brag about such things—or let others brag for him—than he would cheat at cards.

You might have gotten along better with my mother than you think, Daniel. Daniel was charming to women; though women had to be younger and prettier and *far* less intelligent than Evadne Rolfe Mundy before the charm would have any practical object.

Miranda Dorst was a welcome exception to Daniel's string of stupid bimbos; but then, Miranda was an exceptional person in many respects. *Which Mother was not, unfortunately. Perhaps if she had been, her head and Father's might not have decorated Speaker's Rock after Corder Leary broke their poorly managed conspiracy.*

"I assumed you would dispose of this," Daniel said, hefting the bag in the palm of his left hand. "I'd be happy—and I'm sure your mother would be happy, Cleveland—to accept my share of the proceeds after you've arranged for the sale."

"You're in a better place to deal with an item like this, Captain," Graves said. "There are members of the community who have expertise in jewelry, but this is a unique item. While we trust our off-planet agents, it seemed that a principal should oversee the sale. Rather than one of us—"

Cleveland grinned and interjected, "Or even two of us."

"Yes," said Graves, grinning also. "Rather than members having to leave the community for the purpose, we thought you could handle the matter and remit our share to a community account on Pleasaunce or Xenos. You made the discovery and took the risk, after all."

"Umm..." said Daniel. "I dare say my sister could deal with this. Heaven help anybody who tried to cheat her. But if you don't mind, I think I'd rather put the matter in the hands of Mistress Sand. If you have a starship to command, I'm your man. Business, though, I'd rather not be responsible for, even if I have confidence in my agent."

Cleveland chuckled. "I trust Mother, certainly," he said. His expression became wistful. He added, "It would almost be worthwhile going back with you after all, just to put that—"

He gestured.

"—in Mother's hand and watch her face as she opened it. I've disappointed her many times, but she never gave up on me."

Adele was uncomfortable thinking of Mistress Sand as a person, a mother, instead of being the efficient spymaster for whom Officer Mundy worked. "If I may ask?" she said, changing the subject. Her tone had no question in it. "Do you still intend to buy arms with the proceeds?"

"Thanks to your initial cargo," said Graves, seeming a little surprised by the question, though he didn't hesitate to answer, "we're really quite well armed already. We did consider a battery of antiship missiles and perhaps even armored vehicles, though. After clarification by the experts in our community, we decided that all such equipment would do would be to make us targets for any future group which wanted to launch a coup."

"We'd have made ourselves worth robbing," Cleveland said. "A surprise attack on us would be the first act of the plotters."

Daniel was nodding agreement. Adele saw the logic, but it hadn't been intuitively obvious to her.

Someone could attack me to get the pistol I carry, she thought. Then, *Or to get my belt purse or my jacket or my data unit. They're welcome to try.*

"We'll build more dormitories," Graves said. "There will be more people arriving on Corcyra with the change in circumstances. Most of them will be coming to get rich—"

He smiled.

"—the way I did, for example. But some will visit Pearl Valley, and some of those will stay. As I also did."

"And the rest of the proceeds can go into the community's bank deposits off-planet," Cleveland said. "Which could be used to purchase missile batteries, if necessary, though of course we hope that will not be the case."

"Lady Mundy?" Graves said, looking at her. "If I may ask a question in turn...?"

She nodded.

"How will you be compensated? You're not a partner in the enterprise, but your personal involvement was crucial at several points over the past months."

Daniel looked at her. Adele shook her head minusculy; she didn't need help handling the question.

"I'm not very interested in money," she said, "but in point of fact I've got quite a lot of it. Probably more in terms of ready cash than my father could have put his hands on at the height of his political power."

That was an understatement. Lucius Mundy had mortgaged everything he had or could claim a future interest in. In a manner of speaking, the biggest losers from the collapse of the Three Circles Conspiracy were the moneylenders—although relatively few of them had their heads displayed on Speaker's Rock.

"I'm wealthy," Adele continued, "because I have been a warrant officer on RCN ships which won large sums in prize money, and because my shares have been administered with great skill."

She coughed. "And it's my understanding," she said, "that Captain Leary intends to divide his share of the treasure, the jewel—"

She gestured with her right index finger.

"—among the crew as though it were a prize. A very lucrative prize."

"Lady Mundy is correct," Daniel said. His voice was mild and cheery, apparently unaffected by what could have been read as Graves' suggestion that he would have cheated his crew. "But as she also implied, no one signed aboard the *Kiesche* because of the money they expected from the voyage."

A ship lighted its thrusters two by two near the top—south—end of Brotherhood Harbor. The noise wasn't too loud to talk over, but it didn't encourage an extension of the present conversation.

I might be interested if I were listening to it through a surveillance microphone. Adele smiled at her own thought.

"One thing before we all go off to our duties, Captain," Graves said. "You know that there's a new harbor at Hablinger to replace the previous one. You helped design it, in fact."

"Given that Hablinger Pool was now thirty feet in the air and baking in the sun," Daniel said, "there wasn't much choice about creating a new harbor. And I didn't do much about the design except convince the Independence Council to commit more resources than they might otherwise have done. If Commissioner Arnaud can move his whole force in a single lift, there'll be fewer problems en route and on Pantellaria."

He shrugged and turned his hands palms-up. "It was just common sense that benefitted everyone."

"Indeed," said Graves. His tone was barely neutral, certainly not one of agreement. "Be that as it may, they—the Council, *we*—have named the new installation Leary Harbor."

Hogg turned his head and spat toward the water. The gobbet didn't quite clear the edge of the quay.

"Wonderful!" he said. "Daniel Leary of Bantry is honored for his services to bloody farmers."

"Actually, I *am* honored," Daniel said, raising his voice enough to be heard over the thrusters—all six together now. "And Hogg, you might recall that many of the Bantry tenants are farmers. You and your ancestors among them."

"Well, we were bloody *bad* farmers," Hogg said. "Which is why we had to get so good at poaching."

He grinned broadly. "And I guess there's poachers in the Delta here, too," he added, "so I take back anything I said about Leary Harbor."

Daniel waved to the Transformationists rather than

shaking hands again, then turned on his heel and started down the walkway. Woetjans and a team waited to roll it up as soon as Hogg and Tovera were clear.

Daniel stretched as he and Adele walked up the ramp together. "I'm looking forward to some real fishing," he said. "Instead of groping about in a waste pond, however pretty the toy that I found there."

"I've never understood the attraction of fishing," Adele said. "I'm glad that you do, though. It seems to relax you."

They stepped over the coaming and into the main hold. Daniel looked at Adele and said, "I hope your other employer will be pleased with the way things worked out here."

Adele stopped and looked at him. There were several spacers close by, but that didn't matter.

He thinks my other employer is Mistress Sand rather than Corder Leary.

"She will be very pleased," Adele said. "The outcome which you engineered, a neutral government on Pantellaria, improves relations between the Republic and the Alliance instead of sparking a full-scale war between us."

That was almost a lie, but it wasn't a lie; and it will make my friend happier than he would be if I explained the whole truth.

As she resumed walking she thought, *Even my mother would approve.*

Cory started the hatch rising as Woetjans trotted up it behind the riggers who carried the walkway. The thrusters remained cold. Pasternak was waiting for everyone to board.

Daniel ducked under the bridge hatch, a reflex

action from naval vessels whose internal piercings were tighter than those of civilian vessels, where hull strength wasn't as much of a requirement. He would take a jumpseat, allowing Cory to lift the *Kiesche* to orbit from the command console.

Adele made her way to the back of the console, left open for her. That was merely a courtesy, since she had no present need of the better display. She appreciated courtesy, here and in all circumstances.

She wondered how Deirdre would react when she learned Adele's price for saving the family name: transfer of the Bantry estate to Daniel Leary for his life and the lives of the heirs of his blood. Expensive lawyers had assured Adele that not even Corder Leary could break the estate's entail, but this extended life estate would have the same effect so long as any descendent of Daniel lived.

Adele seated herself at the console. Discussions on the command channel were preparing the *Kiesche* for liftoff. On whim she brought up an image of Bantry, looking from the seafront toward the hamlet and, to the left, the sprawling Manor.

Miranda already liked Bantry. It would be a good place for a wedding, and an even better one to raise the sort of children that Squire Daniel Leary would want. Adele was sure that the Manor would always have a guest room for Lady Mundy, if she chose to visit.

The *Kiesche*'s thrusters thumped to life. Using a two-way link—Daniel wasn't really involved in the ship's business at the moment, after all—Adele said, "Daniel? Do you think you could teach me to fish? With practice, I might come to appreciate it."

The following is an excerpt from:

INTO THE MAELSTROM

DAVID DRAKE & JOHN LAMBSHEAD

Available from Baen Books
March 2015
hardcover

CHAPTER 1

Magnetar

Tap—Tap—Tap went the claw on the window.

Commander Frisco pressed her eyelids together tighter than a virgin's knees in the hope that the damn thing would go away.

Tap—Tap—Tap.

It didn't—go away that is.

She opened her eyes slowly and very reluctantly. The goblin leered at her from the other side of the airtight screen from where it perched on the blunt shovel-nose of her ship. Triangular was a word that summed it up, triangular and blue. Its head was a downwards pointing triangle ending in a long pointed chin. Its mouth V-shaped with triangular teeth, its chest V-shaped, even its bloody ears were triangular.

Stroppy was another good descriptive word. The creature thrust vigorously upwards with two fingers topped with triangular claws. It made the time-honored Brasilian gesture indicating that she should indulge in sex and travel. She tried not to notice what it was doing with its other hand.

Most of the time the Continuum looked like a seething mass of multi-colored energy but every so often ship crews saw and heard illusions. The philosophical postulated that such phantasms were the product of some sort of arcane interaction between the human mind and energy leakage through the ship's field. In truth, no one had a clue why the phenomenon occurred but the illusions were usually specific to each individual.

Such ghosts materialized when one was under stress causing fears to be dredged from deep within the mind. Helena Frisco was hard pressed to explain why her subconscious might harbor blue goblins with triangular body parts and obscene habits. It was probably Finkletop fault: most current problems in Helena's universe originated with feckin' Finkletop.

Satisfaction with her promotion to commander and the captaincy of the Brasilian Research and Exploration Ship *Reggie Kray*, nicknamed the Twin-Arsed Bastard by the other ranks, rapidly eroded when she shared her first cruise with Professor Obadiah Finkletop. The good professor held a Personal Chair in Cosmic Evolution at Blue Horizon University. No doubt his peers considered him a learned savant. Helena considered him a pain in the arse.

Finkletop alone she might have coped with but the old fool was completely under the spell of his research student, a curvaceous young lady who went by the name of 'Flipper' Wallace. What Flipper wanted Flipper got and her desires were entirely capricious when looked at from a naval perspective.

The catamaran hulled *Reggie Kray*, hence its nickname, had all the naval equipment including the engines and field generators in the "A" hull so that various "B" hulls stuffed with different scientific equipment could be added or detached as required by the current mission objective. The mission in this case was to convey Finkletop's research group to a neutron star deep in the Hinterlands. The exercise involved gathering "stuff" to test some scientific hypothesis or other concerning nova chains. Finkletop failed to volunteer details and Helena felt no desire to enquire.

The *Reggie Kray* was about as large a ship as could usefully be navigated within the Hinterlands where the gravity shadows of star systems were tightly packed in the continuum. This stellar proximity channeled chasms, or streams, of boiling energy that made the passage of larger ships too slow and laborious to be viable. Speed equaled range in the Continuum because passage time was capped.

The *Reggie Kray* handled like a pig because of the asymmetric design. On the plus side Helena did not have so socialize too much with the bloody academics. They tended to keep to their own territory in the "B" hull.

A symbol flashed in the area by her command chair reserved for holographic controls. Finkletop desired communication. She sighed and keyed the comm symbol, ignoring a mischievous impulse to activate the B hull emergency detachment bolts instead. The goblin gave a final leer and disappeared. Helena did not recall that the detachment icon was a blue triangle. No doubt that was just as well.

"Ah, Frisco?" said Finkletop's voice by her chair. She had switched out the video. It was bad enough having to listen to the man without looking at a caricature of personal grooming that would cause a Naval Academy drill instructor to self-immolate. She rearranged her features into a neutral expression because he could no doubt see her.

"Professor, what a pleasant surprise to talk to you again and so soon after our last conversation."

"Flipper, Ms. Wallace, needs to be closer to the neutron star. You will move to point gamma-3-alpha-99."

The two ratings on the bridge with Helena froze. They developed a deep fascination with their consoles. It was not normally considered good naval practice to give orders to a ship's captain on her own bridge. Not unless you were an admiral at any rate. Even then an order was usually couched as a suggestion. As research team leader Finkletop had the authority to choose the survey sites but the bloody man could show some deference to her rank.

Helena gritted her teeth and keyed in the necessary course as she couldn't think of a good reason to refuse. She automatically checked storage heat levels as she did so. Ships' fusion engines supplied effectively unlimited fuel but electromagnetic radiation could not pass out through the Continuum field reality bubble to any extent. Waste heat had to be "stored" in heat sinks made of frozen iron cores. Captains worried constantly about heat build-up. When levels got too high there was nothing for it but to find a suitable world with available water to dump heat and refreeze the cores.

Unfortunately the *Reggie Kray* still had an

adequate reserve in the sinks. She hit the command key. Her staff would attend to the details of the course change.

"And could you part phase so we can observe the system."

"Why not?" Helena asked, waving a hand to the appropriate minion to indicate that he should comply. "Anything else we can do for you? Brew up some tea and send it 'round to your hull, perhaps?"

"We are too busy for a tea break. Some of us have work to do," Finkletop replied, killing the link.

The bloody man was impervious to sarcasm.

The pilot slowly part-dephased the ship on approaching the neutron star. With its fields at low power the reality bubble enclosing the *Reggie Kray* was subject to a degree of interaction with electromagnetic energy from realspace. That meant that the crew saw into the real universe, albeit in monochrome. In return, light-speed limitations slowed the ship to a crawl. Not an issue in this case as they had only a short distance to travel.

The neutron star was tiny despite its huge mass. It gave off only a dull glow in the visible spectrum. Helena had to look hard to find it against the background star-field but the body's effects were out of all proportion to its size. It probably weighed about 1,000,000,000,000 kilograms per milliliter. That gave it a gravitational field so strong that escape velocity would be measured in significant fractions of light speed.

A large chaotic debris field rotated at high speed around the star. Helena found it unnerving to watch the lumps of ice, metal and rock tracked on the navigational hologram. No doubt similar junk hurtled through the ship's realspace location at speeds too high to be visible to the naked eye. She could create a holographic representation of the bombardment for the crew's edification but doubted they would enjoy the experience.

Deep space made sailors uneasy. Most voyages started and ended on the surface of habitable worlds, the ships phasing within the world's air envelope. Fields enclosed air within the reality bubble so most commercial vessels and small frames omitted an air-tight hull as an unnecessary expense. The naval architects designed the *Reggie Kray* to sustain human life even with the fields off because of its unusual research function.

Massive tidal effects commonly produced swirling fields of junk around a neutron star but this one was positively frenzied. Helena ran an analysis using the limited electromagnetic radiation that penetrated the ship's field.

The comm link lit up. Helena sighed and keyed it.

"We may've found it," Finkletop's voice shook slightly with excitement.

"Oh good," Helena said, wondering what "it" was.

"You must dephase completely and turn off the shields so we can obtain samples."

"Must I?"

"Yes, it's possible the frame field might interfere with the specimens."

Helena touched the "hold" icon while she recovered her calm.

"Have you looked outside at all, Professor?" Helena eventually asked. "You may have noticed something of a debris storm."

"Never mind the paintwork on your ship. This research is too important to be held up by petty military regulations. I'd explain but you wouldn't understand."

"It may have escaped your notice, professor, but I captain this vessel. As such I am responsible for it and the crew. *If* I decide your request," Helena emphasized the word if, "is too dangerous then it won't happen."

"I shall complain to the Grant Committee!"

"Indeed."

The opinion of an academic grant committee carried about as much weight with Helena as a petition from a delegation of rock apes. She answered to the Navy Board and she doubted they cared a fig what a bunch of academics thought either. On the other hand the Board could be downright unreasonable to captains who smashed up their ships.

"It may also have escaped your notice, professor, but that is not just a neutron star out there but a magnetar, a star with a massive magnetic field..."

"I know what a magnetar is."

Helena continued remorselessly as if he hadn't spoken.

"... which is why the debris field is so energetic and chaotic. Iron debris is subject to different forces to non-magnetic rocks and hence has different trajectories. The resulting collisions cause endless fragmentation. It would be like dephasing into a shotgun blast of hypersonic pellets."

Finkletop said. "Well, if you're frightened..."

"Be careful, Professor," Helena's knuckles clenched until they were white.

An officer of the Brasilian Navy could display many faults from drunkenness to licentiousness and still prosper. Cowardice was the one intolerable weakness.

"We'd also have a major problem with magnetic forces such as diamagnetism which is the..."

Finkletop attempted to interrupt. "I know what diamagnetism is but I don't see..."

"... temporary opposing magnetic force induced in materials by an ultra-magnetic field. Our ceramic hull is a good example, as it is repelled by the star. Other materials are paramagnetic and will be dragged towards it. Furthermore, while naval architects use nonmetallic materials as far as possible in a ship's construction to limit drag and hence heat build-up while moving through the Continuum, sometimes there are no acceptable nonmetallic substitutes. Our large iron heat sinks are a good example."

Finkletop tried again. "Well..."

"So if I dephase at our current location the ship's hull and heat sinks will push in opposite directions while I try to dodge high velocity debris on chaotic trajectories."

Dead silence.

There was a compromise option. She told herself she was all kinds of a fool for even considering it. Unfortunately, Finkletop was stupid enough to insult her honor without seeing that she would have to call him out. That could wreck her career. No one would openly blame her for protecting her reputation. Nonetheless, she would always be remembered as the captain who killed her charge. Actually, she reflected, Finkletop wasn't stupid. A Blue Horizon professor just couldn't be stupid. He was simply incredibly focused and limited in his world view.

"How big a specimen do you need?" she asked.

"What? Just a few micrograms would do."

"Very well, I'll harmonize the field of a small jolly boat to pass through the ship's fields. The boat can phase out for the few seconds necessary to recover your sample without endangering the whole ship. Magnetic tidal effects are limited on such a low mass object. It will also present a smaller target to incoming rocks. I won't risk trying to bring the jolly back in through the ship's field as the harmonization will drift out of phase within minutes. We will rendezvous and recover the boat from a quiet area beyond the debris field. Is that satisfactory?"

"I suppose so, seems a lot of stuff and nonsense to me, usual bureaucratic ineptitude, typical of the military..."

She cut the link while Finkletop was still blathering and gave the necessary orders.

❖   ❖   ❖

The *Reggie Kray's* field shimmered metallic green when the jolly boat pass through. The phase harmonization with the boat's field was less than perfect. That observation caused Helena little surprise. No human procedure in the history of the universe had ever achieved perfection. She saw no reason to assume that this was about to change any time soon for her benefit.

Finkletop insisted on supervising the sampling personally. Helena had been equally insistent that a naval rating coxswain the small craft, not one of the academics. She watched the boat's progress on a holographic screen. Once clear the boat adjusted its heading and moved to match speeds with a debris pile. It stopped while the coxswain waited for a signal from the ship indicating he could dephase safely. Well, not safely perhaps but at least without facing instant destruction. Safety is one of those irregular nouns.

Communication was impossible over any distance through the continuum. Anything not protected by a field rapidly decayed or was ejected into realspace. At short range lasers could exchange narrow bandwidth data. Small open frame crews often resorted to hand gestures and flashing lights.

The ship's information analyzers tracked and predicted the immediate debris field. An icon indicated a break in the debris bombardment. It was now or never. She sent confirmation to the jolly boat.

The boat's field flicked off and it drifted towards the debris. Steering thrusters fired to brake the craft alongside a stream of gravel and match velocities. A mechanical arm extended and took a sample. Sparkles ran along the arm where microscopic dust moving at a high relative speed struck the ceramic surface.

The arm had almost withdrawn when the jolly boat shuddered. Its hull flexed under the impact of particles larger than microscopic dust. A ceramic plate peeled off and span away. Jets of escaping air distilled into arches of silver crystals that fanned out in the magnetar's strong tidal gravitational and magnetic fields like a celestial peacock's tail.

Helena swore.

The jolly boat should have been safe enough in realspace for that short period of time. The ship's autos predicted a ninety-five per cent chance of success. She should have anticipated that the unlikeliest disaster would happen at the first opportunity. The gods of probability delighted in shitting on mankind's collective head from a great height.

She crossed metaphorical fingers and waited for the jolly boat's field to reform. Survival suits would protect the crew for a while. She counted slowly to three but it never happened. The boat's field generator must be knocked out. The gods were piling improbability upon improbability today. They probably didn't like Finkletop any more than she did but why stick the boot in on her watch?

The boat's crew were in the deepest possible fertilizer. It was only a matter of time before a bigger impact smeared them like raspberry jam across a slice of toast.

"Close and try to enclose the jolly boat in our Continuum field," Helena ordered. "Finkletop you feckin' lunatic," she added under her breath.

The *Reggie Kray*'s pilot swung the ship around as if it was a one-man frame and accelerated smoothly. They reached the boat just as its field unexpectedly flicked back on. The two energy bubbles interacted dynamically in a sharp release of violet lightning. The boat couldn't penetrate the ship's field because its field had drifted out of phase during the off-on transition. The debris strike probably hadn't helped either.

The ship pushed the smaller vessel with its field like a ball on the edge of an avalanche.

"All halt," Helena said, trying to keep her voice calm.

Then something happened, something unfathomable, something she had never witnessed before in all her years in the navy.

The boat imploded soundlessly leaving nothing but a black stain. Helena had the impression of spreading darkness. A dark spear thrust into the *Reggie Kray*, collapsing its field like a pin going into a balloon. The ship rang like a bell struck by a hammer. That's not possible, Helena thought, we're only semi-phased. Nothing that powerful can penetrate our field. A deep chill froze her bones and the lights went out.

—end excerpt—

from *Into the Maelstrom*
available in hardcover
March 2015, from Baen Books